ANNA'S COUNTRY

ANNA'S

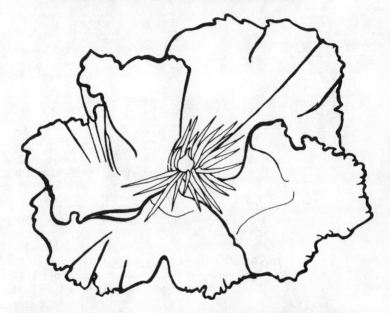

COUNTRY

ELIZABETH LANG

THE NAIAD PRESS INC.

1981

Cover design by Tee Corinne

Typesetting, editing, layout and design
by duck type, Minneapolis

Elizabeth Lang teaches in the City University of New York
and lives in the Bronx.

To

B. E. E.

CHAPTER ONE

TIPPED on its side with green plastic surrounding that brown ball of dirt and a red cord holding it all together—a blue spruce. She crouched to read the directions. Could take her all day. The ground was solid. She found the perfect spot, under the maple where there was a small dug-up section. The builder probably thought new owners would like a flower bed there. So anyway she'd have to dig less there.

She tugged the spruce along the ground, got a shovel, and one half hour later it looked pretty good. She put the spruce's roots in the shallow hole and began to cover them with soil.

"No water?"

She looked around for the voice.

"It'll need water—peat moss." Casually a woman swung a long leg over the post-and-rail fence separating their lands and stepped across to hold the spruce upright by its topmost vertical growth.

She brought her arm up to her forehead keeping the sweat from running into her eyes to look at this cool woman with the clean jeans.

"I'm just following the directions the nursery gives out."

"Did they say to plant a blue spruce under a maple tree?"

Sitting on the ground, putting her hands on her knees, she looked up and wiped the hair out of her eyes. "I suppose you're my neighbor."

The blond woman nodded briefly, gestured her back from the tree and lifted it out of the carefully dug trough. "Rest a second. This is a fine little tree. In five years it will be crowding the maple, growing up right under its arms. Soon the two trees will be fighting for their lives to get the available water. Right?"

Anna nodded. Her luck to have a busy next door neighbor.

"First place: Think about the way you want your place to look ten years from now. Where would it be best to have a beautiful evergreen?"

"In the livingroom at Christmas."

Her neighbor looked at her quickly but began to stroll around her grounds. Just when Anna was thinking about getting up she heard the clear voice again somewhere around the back. "Look. This is a good spot. You have a large open space here, lots of room for it to grow. The landscaper set up a good stone bench. No . . . maybe not. You might want a shade for sitting under." And she was off again.

1

In a few moments she was back with a pitch fork. "Come on . . . See if you approve this spot," and she extended her gloved hand to Anna to pull her up from her earth mound.

"Gloves?"

"Your ground's hard, really hard . . . Pitch fork's the only way." She pointed to an open place in the front at the corner where her privet hedge met Anna's new post-and-rail fence.

"How do you know about all this?"

"Ought to. Run a nursery. Threshold. How do you like that spot?"

"Threshold? That's where I got the tree."

She nodded. "Saw the tag. How do you like that spot?"

"Fine. Oh, a lot."

The neighbor put her foot on the pitch fork then and pushed the fork into the turf only about an inch. "This will take a while. Only right since I stopped you from your work. You can sit."

But Anna could not sit. She started for the garage, turned back, then stood wondering if she should get something.

"Do you have a hose connected? Bring it here then. Any peat moss? Never mind, I've got plenty." As she worked she commented on why a wide hole was needed, why deep and not shallow, why peat moss, what 'puddle it in' meant and why it was a good way to plant trees, although it wasn't on the tag.

"For a person who wants trees in the living room your—" Her neighbor stopped suddenly and looked at her. "—questions aren't bad. I'll get the peat moss."

While she was gone Anna went into the house to get some iced tea. At least that she could do. Excellent tea. When she walked down the brick steps into the front yard carrying the tray she found her neighbor waiting in the sun, her cotton shirt sticking now to her back in dark patches.

"Now you should see this so you can do it later for yourself. See, its roots aren't crowded and the peat moss I brought over in that bucket is already wet. I leave it outside in a tub, catching the rain. Good to mix it with the soil if you can, though." And with what seemed very fast motions she slopped the peat moss into the hole, pushed in the heaped up soil, mixing them at the same time, and holding the spruce upright began to tamp down the sides around the base of the trunk.

Anna stood holding the tray and wondered what kind of shade tree her neighbor would suggest. "Let me offer you some iced tea at least. My name is . . . " but her neighbor was walking away saying something about mint water. Baffled, Anna continued to walk toward the table in the back yard, heard the hose going, and saw her neighbor re-emerge from around some shrubbery holding newly washed sprigs which she shook free of water drops and let fall into the tea pitcher.

"If you like it, I'll give you some. It grows anywhere. You have to watch mint or it will take over your garden. Thank you for the tea." The ice clinked as Anna wondered what to say to this woman. "Tell me . . . Why is it called Threshold?"

"I really don't know . . . but I like it."

"Most nurseries are called Rosehill or Green World, like cemeteries."

"It's a name for the new gardener, just starting out . . . Threshold. . . . Good tea. Well, I. . . ." She was starting to put down her glass.

"It was very generous of you to help me sweat over my little tree this morning. You were shocked at what I was doing? Carl . . . He's some kind of city-romantic. Expects his city wife to grow corn and put up tomatoes on the old plantation."

The woman settled back. "He was transferred here?"

"No. New job. His big dream . . . House and land on the Hudson and the kiddies in quiet schools away from zip guns."

"Zip guns?"

"In the city you can't give your child too much money for lunch because he may be robbed on the way to school. I tell them to hand it over, not to fight. Carl teaches them to put their thumbs in the other guy's eye." Laughing, Anna looked up and found the serious face observing her. Her eyes were not that wonderful blue-violet color. They were more like light blue denim. The kids should be home from school soon.

When the tanned arm reached toward the cookie dish, Anna asked, "What is a woman with Camay looks doing in this dull town?" That she blushed suddenly surprised Anna.

"I was transferred!"

"Not free choice?"

"Definitely free choice. You'll feel differently after a while. It's an old town. After ten years here I'm still considered a 'new person'."

After that slow start they chatted more easily, but Carl was odd later about Hope's helping her. As if she shouldn't have accepted help or something.

"What's a woman want to work in a nursery for?" He'd get a man over to help her if she needed help. The screen door slammed and sneakers came pounding down the hall.

"See what Timmie made?" and a wet clay mound was shoved into her hand.

"Well, Timmie, look at this! Marvelous." She was turning the gray mass with admiration.

"A bear," Tim said, with that gauzed-over look children have knowing and not knowing that his reality wasn't quite visible to her.

"A wonderful bear. Where'd you make it?"

As Tim answered and she saw Jamie hovering on the edges wanting to get her word in, Anna wondered whether a woman could enjoy working in a nursery.

"Good shot!" A hard driving cross-court caught Dorothy unprepared. As they changed sides she stopped to towel her racquet's handle and said to Hope, "What's happened to you?"

"A good day for tennis," Hope answered from the other side of the net. Non-committal, as usual.

Hope loved good tennis, and Dorothy, from childhood tournament days, could supply that. But that was all. She had tried, years ago, but Hope was always evasive. She found herself, sometimes, just loving to watch the way Hope moved on the court, slow it seemed and graceful, but Hope was always there in balance at the shot. Her own bouncy peppiness seemed so boring as she watched that long balanced stroke.

"Damn it. Again. OK, Hope, my girl, you've had it!" She advanced to the net and put it away. Sop to the ego, she thought as she picked up two balls for her serve.

"So, what is this then? You getting interested in a straight lady?"

"I was *telling* you about all the trees we were selling and the new people who are having to landscape their places."

"Right. But I was *hearing* a lot about someone called Anna—her husband Carl and their two children Timothy and Jamie." Dorothy's smile was superior.

"You never quit, do you, Dot?"

Dorothy tried to make up and asked Hope to come with her and Holly to dinner and on to Belinda's to dance. In the early days Holly used to pick up people at Belinda's, but she knew that wasn't Hope's style.

Hope shook her head saying she had Horticultural Society letters to write. Of course, no one dared criticize Hope for the hours she spent on that, but most of them thought it was a waste. What did those straights know or care about her? She watched Hope pulling on her white sweater and wondered how long it had been since Anna and company had moved in.

"We thank you for your continued interest in the Stevensville Horticultural Society. Sincerely yours, Hope Charity Alford, Secretary-Treasurer." She put the letter aside and started on the next, planning to sign them all later. She thought of the letters she used to get at college from her father dictated to his secretary and signed with the business letters, "Sincerely yours, Arthur R. Alford" or "ARA." He had come to her graduation though, with camera, had spoken to strangers, telling them his daughter was graduating with honors.

She got up from the typewriter and began to prowl about, walking into her little greenhouse to look at the seedlings in their plastic tents—checking on the moisture in the camellias. Evening was no time for this. Plants shouldn't be watered at night. She was crazy. Stalking. Well, what was the trouble? Have children, then, to indulge these attacks of nurturing.

She went into the kitchen for a cup of something hot. That mixture of rebelliousness and helplessness, sitting there in the dirt, dark locks sticking to her forehead looking with exasperation at the sturdy spruce. "Why am I here? What do I have to do with this thing that I didn't want and don't understand?" her expression had said. Hope had wanted to say, "Let me take care of it." She swore she didn't mean, "Let me take care of you."

Beth-Ellen appeared at the door sill, all white face and chest, seated comfortably looking up at her. "You want something to eat?" She took some cod out of the refrigerator, flaked it into Beth-Ellen's blue dish, and put it on her special strip of white linoleum.

"My nocturnal habits have ruined you."

She did not want to comfort and shelter a waif. She had wanted only to help out a baffled woman who was going to kill a good tree by ignorance. She settled in a favorite chair and swallowed the hot sweetened tea. In the first place she was not looking for anyone: man, woman, child, or beast. She had finally regained composure and was going to hang on to it. In eight years and with good treatment a waif who looked out of hollowed eyes had turned into a fattened bird of prey. Gratitude had turned to condescension and finally the waif had gone off with a younger waif. And what had little Hopie been doing all this time? Loyally squashing growing desire for a younger waif. Disgusting. Now who was Eleanor with? Someone new, someone Hope hadn't met, but the ex-waif was a union organizer in Detroit.

"The only way to avoid being someone's dinner is to avoid dining." When Hope had said that, Dorothy had said, "Better watch your imagery, dear—all that devouring and eating."

With Dorothy one couldn't make a slip. She would be in there using her insights like a club, if Holly did not interrupt. Holly would laugh, raise a thumb like a hitch-hiker and gesture towards Dorothy with a shrug, "What can you do? The wind-mill keeps grinding."

"All of us into bits," Hope wanted to answer, but liked Holly too much. With Holly there, Dorothy was bearable. Otherwise she might push on, to corner the prey. She would go up with her tea and do some more letters. She wondered why Holly and Dorothy didn't live together.

They had been inseparable, at least on week-ends, for close to four years.
Was it family? or Dorothy's struggle for tenure? or perhaps they just
needed air. She walked slowly up the chilly stairs.

Mrs. Carl Johnson senior looked at the kitchen clock and turned the
oven to 350. Carl liked turkey, so it should be turkey, but she was never
satisfied that it was moist enough. Even the trick with the tin foil didn't
satisfy her. The zucchini he liked, fixed as she did it with garlic and tomatoes and onions. Anna was happy with anything she fixed. She should
be fatter. The children should arrive in about an hour. She'd set the table
on the porch and pretend it was really spring. A heated porch with potted
plants was a pleasure. Her husband never would have let her put heat out
there. "Why heat the backyard?" but one of her first big decisions after
he died was for sliding doors and heat to the porch. She had been proud
of her decisiveness. With three months of deliberation, conversations with
all her friends, four calls to carpenters and heating men, she wasn't sure
it could be called decisive. But still, she had done it. She stood back from
the table—flowers, deep blue table cloth, white linen napkins. She always
used the silver napkin rings because Timothy and Louisa liked them,
Jamie, that is.

In the clatter of the welcomings—the embraces, Carl's prickly new
beard which she couldn't get used to, the children's moist cheeks, "Mother,
how lovely everything looks. Look, Carl, she has the photograph you took
of father on the mantle"—she remembered to check the popovers. Dump-
lings were good, but she could cook popovers if Carl liked them. They
were popping nicely and sent a bready fragrance through the house.

"Gramma, what smells? Whyn't you make it, Mom?"

Anna looking guiltily toward her mother-in-law. "Cold cucumber
soup. Delicious, isn't it, Carl?" Anna was smiling, dabbing her lips with the
linen napkin and avoiding her lipstick. "Mother, I'll never be a cook, but
I would appreciate . . . "

"I have already prepared the recipe for you on a little index card.
Have I shown you how I keep recipes? I learned from *Ladies Circle*,
a lovely magazine. Every week something. Carl, more soup?" and she
carefully ladled a new bowl for everyone, cheeks pink under her newly
'done' white hair.

"Mother, you'd like my boss's wife, Miriam. They're older people
and like you she likes plants and cooks up a storm. Their kids are all
over the world now. One's in India. A girl, if you can believe it, is studying
in Norway."

"I didn't know that. What, Carl?" Anna asked.

"Ceramic or weaving or tapestries—something. Another son's building
bridges in Turkey."

"Maybe they don't like home so good," said Anna. But, catching her husband's look (grammatical irreverence was not approved), she said, "Of course, the family is quite international, Mother. Mrs. Green teaches something in one of the city colleges."

"Political Science."

"So? and cooks too! How does a woman my age get to have so much energy?"

"She's not quite your age, Mom."

Mother Johnson got up and went into the kitchen saying over her shoulder, "Women nowadays . . . They are trying to do so much. Like super-ladies. My day, we did less. They make babies. They make novels. They nurse sick children. They get Ph. and D's. Where are they?" She emerged triumphant with the gloriously popped popovers. "I tell you. They are suffering. That's what." She set the white china serving dish before Carl saying. "Hollow. Burnt out. And starving. Have a popover."

"Jamie, look at these. Popovers! Your favorite." Jamie was sitting carefully in the starched dress she wore to visit her grandmother. She smiled correctly but her eyes glistened as she waited for the butter.

"Timmie, don't reach," Anna said quickly and passed the serving dish toward Timothy on her left. On the whole Anna felt the children were behaving rather well, and, to leave well enough alone, suggested that they go into the yard after dinner.

While she and Carl's mother were cleaning up Anna said, "Mother, about the soup recipe . . . "

"Yes, dear, I have it right here."

"Mother, if you give it to me, I'll have to try to make it . . . and I just know it won't be like yours. Then the kids and Carl will . . . " She was looking at the begonias on the sill and Mrs. Johnson's solid frame standing there at the sink washing dishes and hardly knew what she wanted to say.

Mother Johnson turned and nodded conspiratorially, "Honey, I'll give you this index card. You'll keep it in a little box like mine, see that. But when you go I'll give you the left-over zucchini, but also," her smile was gleeful, "I'll give a quart of the cucumber soup. You freeze it. Then later in the week, you put out your recipe card on your kitchen counter and heat up the soup. They'll think it's yours. They'll never know." She hugged Anna, "All right?" As those warm arms hugged her and she felt the formidable bosom against her, Anna was shocked at the sudden gulp of hysteria she felt rising.

"From time to time when you come for dinner, I'll pass on some soup. Different kinds. Who cares? Baby, baby . . . it's not important . . . not important."

Carl was cornering the Buick deftly and shooting down back roads at 80. Until he got to know the state troopers he'd better not do this too often. Bob Green should see that he'd be a good man. His job was safe for a year anyway, but commissions counted a lot. With gas going up, expenses for long vacations out of sight, more people'd be staying home, a good argument for selling pools. Green liked it. Really liked it. Said, "Make us a slogan with that." So easy. What did he know about advertising slogans? Green should get the word-boys for slogans. He pushed the pedal to the floor and felt the power surge. "Why go away? Drown at home!" At first he'd thought he knew where he was with Green: a Jew, city man, liked good food, cigars, knew baseball scores back to forever, but now this crap, "You've got a good idea? Well, do it. Don't talk about it." He'd thought they were friends, that he'd have some advantages. He was new to this place, at least you'd think Green . . .

In the weird dream, the Scott Joplin music pool side, the blondes smirking down at him as the water rose, shut up in some kind of glass bubble that said, "Get a Green Pool." He beat against the slippery sides as the air ran out. The blondes passed the canapes and toasted each other with frosted mint julep glasses. He swung his head around, twisting his muscled torso against the cement hiking boots as the tall blonde leaned on a janitor's brush and smiled down at him.

He swung up his driveway and ground to a stop. The front door was open, so Anna was home. He imagined catching that smirking blonde by the ankles and pulling her down deep into the water. He was about to shout for Anna when he heard what sounded like low laughter. The kids had lunch at school. Whispers, almost conspiratorial, sounded as if they came from the back bedroom. He raced up the stairs three at a time, four strides down the hall, and pushed the bedroom door open.

Two figures were crouched in a corner. Anna was making a grey smear along the wall chuckling like a kid. The tall broad from next door was sitting back on her heels praising her. Anna was almost gurgling. "Look at that. Hey, look at that! Not bad . . . right?" Then she saw him. "Isn't that pretty good, Carl?"

"Not bad. Any chance for lunch? Anyway, if it doesn't look great, we can always get somebody in to do it over." He nodded at Hope Alford and went to the porch where he'd left his morning paper.

"So, how come she was here again?" he asked later.

"Called to ask her about beauty parlors in town. We got to chatting."

"You ask her to help you or what?"

"I told her about that messy corner in the bedroom, said I had to get the contractor back, complained about men tramping through the house again. She said it sounded like a simple spackling job and that's the way it went."

"Doesn't she work?" he said turning to the financial columns.

"On her lunch break. Carl, your lunch is on the table," Anna called from the kitchen. "Why don't you like her?"

"I like her." He shrugged, putting his feet on the foot-stool and shaking out his paper. "I like her fine." Then getting up and dropping his paper back in his chair. "I just don't like women who know all the answers, never have."

Anna was remembering that when Carl came into the room to look at the corner, Hope had stood up, still holding the wall compound in one hand and the metal mixer in the other. She had smiled pleasantly down at Carl. "Smooth job, isn't it?" Carl had looked up at her, nodded briefly and left the room.

"She has to save where she can. It'll never be as smooth as you pay for, I guess, but if we save something, wouldn't that be good?"

"Good salad. Meeting in forty-five minutes. Sure, a penny saved, et cetera. And we can always get a professional if it cracks up or looks terrible."

Carrying a dish of potato chips and her salad plate Anna went to join her husband. Spackling was much simpler than she had thought. Hope said that all you had to do was follow directions on the package, that anyone who could read could do it. Once you got that trick of the slant of the metal trowel-thing and you made smooth even gestures and got the stuff in the patches and smoothed it over evenly, it was done. She'd let it dry, as Hope said, and then sand it.

Carl hated smart women. He always said so. Still, Anna couldn't help admiring people who could really do things, but of course Hope hadn't married. Too tall probably. She mustn't forget that she could do things too. She had brought up the kids nicely. She kept a pretty clean house and cooked . . . but it was probably only a question of reading the directions.

CHAPTER TWO

A FTER standing in the hall a few minutes after class chatting and listening to some students' comments, Dorothy went to her office to leave her books and go down to lunch. She'd meet Miriam down in the cafeteria.

"Committee going all right?"

In the crowded elevator she looked up. Harrison was smiling down at her, his handsome face and long jaw in an odd perspective over her right shoulder. He was a smoker of strong cigars. The smell was deep in his herring bone tweed jacket, but she liked him.

"Having lunch? I'll join you."

He never felt he had to ask politely and really he was right. He and Scott had been canoeing last summer with her and Holly. Although they never spoke of it, there had been quiet acceptance and enjoyment of one another, and mysteriously, since she and Harrison had become friends many men who had ignored her before at college were being pleasant. The ways of the male network were impressive.

Holly was out of this whole thing. She had quit her Ph.D. studies and as far as Dorothy knew she never regretted it. She boasted about Dorothy's Ph.D. but seemed content teaching reading at a Community College. It left her free to read what she pleased, to pick up and put down hobbies, free to "become informed" she would say, making a pompous face. In fact, she *was* well informed, but she was damned if she would submit to the publishing pressure.

She and Holly had "been together" for over five years, always working intensely during the weeks so that they could go off together on week-ends to her place on the island. Their life was filled with subterfuge, of course, vague remarks to family and straight friends like "going off for a few days," "visiting friends." Their lives were over-strained and over-packed—with work at one time and play at the other. Still, who could achieve Margaret Anderson's harmony with the fabulous Georgette? And pure fable she probably was. With malice Holly had called her cat Georgette, "to celebrate our contentment," she had said.

Dorothy supposed that she couldn't live with Holly because she needed, after all, to keep herself intact. Holly had a way of puncturing balloons. And who could deny fear of boredom? As she stood in the

11

back of the elevator she saw the profile of Livia O'Malley, delicate features composed, always inscrutable, beautifully shaped head poised slightly back. As she leaned forward to ask Livia a question she could hear Holly saying, "Sexist!" laughing.

When the elevator doors slid back at the basement level, the steamy mixture of too sweet smells, warmed air, and the throbbing electronic guitar washed over them all. She walked through the immense room where the students gathered eating paper bag lunches, drinking coffee, chatting, and studying. Table after table was littered with cups, books, ice cream, Butterfingers and Mars Bars in messy confusion. Cooking smells mixed with the over-sweet smell of burning incense, voices rasping over radios, and the interminable piped-in music from the students' radio station. Two lovers kissed as if they were alone on a beach. Faculty usually got their food quickly and withdrew to the faculty dining room.

When Miriam Green came over with her tray, they muttered to one another. Miriam, who had endured the clamorous demands of anxious students and agonized faculty for twenty-five years, said, "God knows I don't regret the passing of the days of maids and tablecloths. Eight years ago we wore white gloves to Majors' Teas—had candles at long tables, wives pouring tea—the works. Now, plastic forks."

When Harrison and Bill joined them they were talking about the unending city budget crisis and fears of losing good teachers. Harrison repeated his views on tenure and its uselessness.

"Harrison, the temptation to fire teachers just before they retired would be overwhelming. Think of the money saved on the pensions!"

Harrison pushed at the fruit salad with his yellow fork. "Well, we can't carry out foolish expenditures *and* put in new programs."

"Like what?" Dorothy asked quickly.

"Yes, like what," said Miriam looking sharply from Harrison to Bill. "You want to freeze the curriculum at some happy date—like 1640?" Miriam looked annoyed at the noisy table on their left, which had just burst out in laughter. Just then a heavy explosion made the floor shudder. The pause was momentary as people checked and reassured themselves— just the usual building detonations.

"God, this place is insufferable," Harrison said, wiping his face. The students have been let in here and they take over as they always do. Dean McNamara, tell me," he said to the stunning woman who was setting down her tray.

"Sorry, can't hear you, Harrison," she said, leaning over, smiling.

Harrison's neck was turning red as he shouted, "Noisy here! Can't we get the students out?"

"That's all the noise you're noticing?" She looked around the table. "Have I come at the wrong time?"

"No, Agnes, sit down. Harrison is growling and the lunch room seems noisier than ever." Miriam pushed her own plate over to the left and made more room for the Dean of Humanities. As Dean McNamara sat down she gestured to a woman standing behind her. "Beulah Demarest, our guest from the Ford Foundation, is visiting the college today."

"You might as well hear the grousing that goes on here. They tell me it's healthy."

"Dorothy, I'm sorry," said Harrison, "but frankly it's the Women's Studies thing that's sticking in my craw. Just why should that new program be proposed when we can't float what we've got?"

"For one thing, it's needed," Dorothy stirred her coffee. That Harrison felt this way she knew. She realized that gays thought they understood women better than women did. Why should women want to throw away ruffles, alluring make-up, all those attractive frivolities like spike heels and lacy slips that made up femininity in their opinion? No wonder gay men thought women crude. She knew that Harrison, despite his size and bulk, felt that he made a more splendid looking woman than most models, partly because he felt he understood femininity better than they did. Yet what he most valued was what feminists wanted to pitch overboard.

"For one, Dorothy, will you tell me why it's needed?"

"Now, exactly, Dorothy," said Dean McNamara. "While we speak here informally, just why is Women's Studies needed? We don't have Men's Studies, do we?"

"Of course we do," Miriam laughed. "Agnes, dear, what do you think we've had all these years? The Freshwomen are like young Anthropologists searching for a trace of woman in text books called *Man's Search for Self, The Development of the Hero, The Growth of Man's Cities.*"

At this point, with the brilliant scarlet smile of an old Coca-Cola ad, Beulah Demarest intervened. "But tell me why really; I know I'm just a visitor here, but why are women so interesting to some women? I just can't understand why women would *want* to study themselves and other women with such fascination, do you?" She looked at Dorothy, guileless as the snake in Eden, batting her lashes and smiling, showing beautiful, even teeth.

"But surely, no more than men. Ask Melville why he put so many women in *Moby Dick, Billy Budd,* and *Beneto Cereno,*" Dorothy said, hating Demarest's eye make-up.

"Oh, but now," said Harrison. "Let me tell you what happened to me today. . . ." In the story that followed Harrison displayed just that flicker of swishiness that he suppressed so well usually. Here it beautifully expressed his competitive envy. Dorothy watched him knowing that what was coming would be funny but disasterous for her. The Women's

Studies group was to present its program to the Faculty and Student
Senate in a matter of weeks, and this kind of discussion among the faculty
could hardly help them. . . .

Harrison was imitating the student, " 'Then,' she said, 'Well, women
are more interesting than men anyway. Why should I spend my time
being bored?' and flounced out of my office, if you *can* flounce in ex-
cessively tight jeans." He tossed his head.

"Sorry to leave such a harmonious group," Miriam said, tidying her
tray. She smiled at Dorothy, "Tomorrow at two?"

Dean McNamara glowed at Bill, "Aren't you unusually silent?"

"I saw us skidding off the rails too early to get interested. And it's
too noisy here," he said, catching the eye of a slim, curly-haired student
who was standing at the door to the lunch room. Dorothy saw the snap
in his eyes as he got up to walk over and chat in the doorway, a dapper,
rotund man wearing a neat red vest with his grey suit. The student seemed
shy and hesitant, then very pleased at something Bill said. Bill returned to
the table, smiling, stroking his vest, and then abruptly his face smoothed
over again, casual and composed. Dorothy knew that student from one of
her classes. He'd needed an extension on a term paper. Looking downcast
he had told her that he and his fiancée had broken up. He just hadn't
been able to keep his mind on his studies.

She had probably just witnessed his reconciliation with his fiancée.
The male faculty "made out" with the female students; why shouldn't
they with the males as well? Dorothy knew she was square, still belonged
to the "teachers are priests and doctors" school of thought.

The noise and confusion were suddenly too unpleasant to bear and
Dorothy made her apologies briefly, saying that she and Harrison would
live to fight another day. She knew they would all think that the battle
over Women's Studies had made her leave, and she hated to suggest any
weakness that might invite later tangles. But she loathed Bill's jaunty
step as he returned to the table.

She knew she had to stop being so sentimental-minded. The students
were often the predators, using every advantage of youthful sexuality and
flattery to seduce their aging teachers and nab an 'A'. Some people argued
for the validity of "love," whatever that was, the primacy of educating the
spirit over professorial decorum, but for Dorothy all that was nonsense.
She considered herself an old-time believer in productive sublimation.

"So, of couse I muttered something about men's view of women and
women's view of themselves, but it sounded pretty vague, I'm sure,"
Dorothy said, sipping her wine later at Holly's place. She put her slippered
feet on the coffee table and groaned. It was such a comfort to rest her
head back against the cushions and let the clamor and the suppressed

quarrels of the day slip from her mind, like sharp glass fragments tipping
out of a bowl.

Holly jumped up from the couch, "I'll get a *Pix*. Let's have a quick
dinner and go to a jolly movie." She was down the hall in a second and
calling out from the clutter of her room, "You haven't classes tomorrow.
I bet your meeting isn't until four. Any conferences? See—*Alice Doesn't
Live Here Anymore* at the Jewel." Triumphant, she appeared at the door
waving the magazine which she tossed to Dorothy. "Look it up and read
how good it is to me while I fix the fish."

"Do it with onions and butter," Dorothy called.

"Right. Read."

Dorothy began to flip the pages back and forth. "I never can cope
with the organization of this damn magazine."

"Movie reviews—back pages . . . honestly!" Holly banged her spatula.

"I've got it . . . I've got it! 'Young widow . . . um um . . . new life . . .
tries for singing career . . . poignant, sensitive performance, humor . . .
pathos . . .' Sounds OK."

"Good, that's settled," Holly said over her shoulder as she buttered
the fish pan. "Great idea to go to the movies. Haven't seen a flick since
Lady in the Dark."

"This lady is in it," grumbled Dorothy starting to set the table. When
she reached up for the plates Holly gave her a nudge with her hip and
laughed. "Sour ball."

They trudged silently out of the movie house over to Dorothy's
car.

"You drive."

"I don't feel like it. You have energy."

Holly put her key in the ignition. "So what's the summary sentence?"

Dorothy seemed to be dreaming out the window. "I liked it a lot in
places."

"Me, too."

Holly drove along smoothly. The car was silent for the drive back.

"Did you die when she repeated what the tough waitress had said,
'Jerk off in a bag?' That was really funny."

Holly was opening the door to her apartment. "Her expression!"
Holly imitated the actress's bafflement, disbelief, horror. 'Jack off?
Jerk off? In a bag?' She couldn't believe it. . . . But they became friends."

"Of course . . . the whole thing was a cop-out."

"Right . . . a real pity."

"When she said to her friend in the beginning, 'Want to come with
me?' And her friend really did want to . . . That's what she should have
done. In my movie the two women would have set out for Albuquerque

or Dubuque, wherever it was—together. Right? 'Drive along with me Dearieeeee,' " Holly was dancing around Dorothy with her hand on the top of Dorothy's head, 'And you'll never be drearieeee.' "

Holly caught her shoulders and made a dreadful grimace of pain— drawn eyes of anguish; voice quavering, she said, "Poor widow woman, bereft . . . poor lonely creature." Arm flung over her eyes, "Like Judy Garland in *A Star is Born* she searches and she searches." Waving her left arm in front of her Holly walked along the top of the couch, "over the hills . . . through the woods," entered a closet, closed the door, opened the door, and backed out of it, "to find . . . to find . . . herself and what she needs. . . ."

Holly began to stalk through the living room with bent knees and Dorothy followed through the kitchen hands shielding their foreheads from the desert sun, arms parting the jungle grass, machetes at the ready . . . "And what she needs . . . isn't a new self, or an old self, or a job, or new career."

"Never, lo and indeed never," said Dorothy peering through the vines. "Ahaaa . . . Eureka and Allah be praised. . . . What she needs is . . . a GOOD MAN! NEW IDEA!"

"So he can jack off in his own bag," Holly rolled with laughter on the bed.

Dorothy gave her a push, "Take her to a movie and she gets vulgar! In a bag, indeed." Dorothy slid down beside her.

"Right . . . the old male fantasy." Holly was holding one foot in the air, examining it critically. " 'Sensitive, fine performance . . . humor, pathos,' and Christ here we are again." She sat upright and shouted, "All she needed was a fine young man . . . !"

"With a house and farm, don't forget." Dorothy pulled her down beside her again.

"Ah—but willing to give it up for her—that's something."

"And not likely to beat her up like the other guy almost did. . . . That's another small plus."

"One small step for womankind."

"Still the two waitresses when they were sitting in the sun together. That was nice," Dorothy said, curling around Holly's back.

"The whole thing was a movie that pointed to the real loving relationships . . . " Dorothy murmured.

" . . . but wrote toward the approved ones," Holly finished.

"Right." Dorothy hugged her closer. "I liked the blue-eyed guy with the beard, though."

"Sure." Holly was up and walking down the hall. "I'll feed Georgette, now, but you feed her at two a.m. if she prowls. Ok? . . . In hock to a cat," Holly muttered, going into the living room for the watering pot.

"Was that a personal remark?"

"Eleven p.m. is a good time to water plants. They appreciate it," Holly said.

CHAPTER THREE

IT WAS later in the week when Dorothy and Hope went to a play with Harrison and Scott. Holly had refused to go, saying she was "finished with trying to pass"; so Dorothy asked Hope. Holly's absolutism, her sudden stands on principles, ruling one thing out and another in, sometimes exasperated Dorothy. How they could have gone canoeing together, to who knows how many plays, and then suddenly have Holly act as if all that was part of some pretence, "trying to pass," Dorothy could not fathom. It pushed Dorothy to a pitch of irritation she rarely felt with Holly. It did not occur to her than that other things were bothering Holly. Dorothy's way was to be utterly rational until she flew apart and then had to face her own chaos. When opposed with a rational argument she answered precisely to that issue, never casting the net wider, or letting herself suppose that there were reasons, many perhaps unguessed, for someone to select any argument. So when Holly objected to "passing" Dorothy simply rejected the argument as irrelevant and invited Hope.

Harrison and Scott arrived in Scott's battered Ford, carefully vacuumed out for the occasion. Scott chatted about the play, its producer, its cast, the foibles of the director—all of which he knew in great detail. Although he taught history, his obsession was the theater. Dorothy knew that his amusing chatter usually took place in moments of strain when no one else could manage to be to be entertaining—part of his code.

After picking up Dorothy they drove through the darkening streets to Hope's home. Stevensville's irregular streets, laid out it seemed by leisurely cows in the days of Major Andre, wandered along vertical cliff sides and descended suddenly into the Hudson valley, giving a car's passengers spectacular views, but the driver had to concentrate fiercely on the road's angles. Streets bearing the old Dutch names still twisted up in the old tracks with tall houses perching top-heavy at the road's edge from the days before snow plows when it was not desirable for houses to be set back from the roads. Part of Stevensville had the feel of a Dutch colonial town, but part owed its prosperity to the General Motors plant at the foot of its hills, resting at the water's edge and spawning low buildings and factory outlets there. On the outskirts of Stevensville were the new developments.

Hope's land fortunately met at its edge a reservoir and she could still enjoy the wooded paths that circled the lake. In winter from her greenhouse

17

she could see the children skating, their red skirts and bright knitted caps flashes of color. In summer she heard their shrill cries from the pool and tennis courts near the picnic tables. But a developer had begun construction about four blocks away, the orange bulldozer heaving up rocks and overturning old trees that lay flat with angular roots exposed. Everyone knew that the numbers of young families and their needs for space, play areas, parking, schools, sewerage, electricity, and shopping "plazas" would transform the old Stevensville. Ten years' residence had made Hope feel that she owned the woodlands and their narrow paths, but now as she looked out her wide window and walked about waiting for Scott and Harrison, she was merely glad that she didn't have to see the daily digging, the leveling, the building that was going on just out of her sight. The state reservoir permitted her to imagine that the woodsy paths were still there, just on the other side.

As she watched for them she saw the newly washed Ford and was amused to think of Scott's doing his best to bring their transportation up to the occasion. Harrison had already told her at least twice that his Jaguar would be "still in the shop." Hope had tried to look festive to make them glad she had been included, knowing that she could hardly have been their first choice. But she had substituted before when Dorothy had given a paper somewhere and Martha Graham's dancers were on tour. At times she found the men completely considerate and entertaining. Harrison's vanities she could forgive after she learned about his brilliant success as a young poet. In his youth he promised to be "a new Elliot, greater than Stevens or Pound," the critics had said. Now he was given occasional books to review. To Hope his posturing seemed forgivable, although it must be hard for Scott to live with. Still, Scott revealed nothing. At home with guests, Scott sashayed around, joked about wearing ribbons in his hair, and made Harrison's heavy jaw relax into laughter.

Although Hope discounted such things, she was pleased by Scott's enthusiastic reaction to his first sight of her that night.

"How beautiful she is, Harrison. Don't you love her in white? She looks quite Greeky, doesn't she? Why, Harrison, you look positively envious!"

She had done her hair up in a French twist mainly because she couldn't think how else to do it after a wash in the time she had. She was always unsettled by people's reactions to her looks, partly because she had been so gawky for so long. It wasn't that she would rather be in the garden quietly digging and weeding. She was quite glad to be well-dressed, going out into the spring evening with pleasant people. She wondered what it was she was trying not to think of. She had no worries, no reason to have anything but a lovely evening.

They went to a favorite pre-theatre spot that specialized in good salad and hamburgers and far-out sandwiches. The only reason to go there, Scott said, was to see the show people who dropped in for a quick sandwich before show time, and Scott loved to point them out. They set out

for the theater through a sudden rainstorm. Horns blared and yellow
taxis rushed by splashing pedestrians at the corners. With triumph Scott
opened up an enormous umbrella and gave Harrison another, having won
his bet. Harrison held out his arm for Hope, raised the umbrella high, and
they walked briskly along the wet sidewalks, Harrison very conscious of
what a striking couple they made. Scott followed with Dorothy, both
content to jump over puddles that longer legs stepped over. They arrived
at the theater flushed and laughing, stamping rain from their shoes as
Scott shook the umbrella free of water drops and folded their coats. The
lights were flickering as they sat down and they could enjoy the swift
dimming of the houselights in that delicious moment of tension before
the curtain rose.

In a strong first act the doctor was revealing to the painter the nature
of his wife's illness when a door at the back of the theatre burst open.

"Don't care about your fucking sign. Stupid shits. Paid my ticket . . ."
A large, dark shape half fell at the top of the aisle near the door.

"Shh, shh."

"Pipe down, in back."

Four people stumbled down the left aisle in darkness as the ushers waved
their lights. "Please sir, please sir, wait until . . . "

One man led, apparently pulling a slight woman behind him. Two
other people hung back at a distance. "Come on, come on. Seats up
front," the heavy voice said.

"For God's sake—shut up, will you!"

"Throw those people out!"

The woman could be heard whispering, "Excuse me, excuse me.
I'm sorry, so sorry," as she was dragged along the row tripping over people's
ankles.

At the intermission Scott and Harrison went out to smoke, but Hope
and Dorothy sat quietly not attempting to make conversation. After a
few moments Hope looked over to Dorothy to ask if she had a play-bill.
Dorothy was staring at a broad-shouldered man who was getting up and
moving along the fifth row, apparently shouting at a man in a tuxedo.

"Hope, on the left of those men arguing, isn't that Miriam and Bob
Green?" Hope looked down and saw Carl Johnson's red face menacing
the man in the tuxedo, two empty seats next to Miriam and Bob Green.
She looked for Anna. She saw a slight woman walking up the aisle, carrying her raincoat, her face white, her hair in an upsweep that had come
loose and was falling forward as she looked at the ground and walked
quickly up the ramp to the door.

After clapping heartily for four curtain calls Miriam and Bob Green
waited, knowing that exit from the fifth row could be sluggish. The play
had been disturbing, of course; she hadn't expected to be calmed, but
it was satisfying, too. After some plays she and Bob had had some of

their worst fights, but other plays left them contented. They would enjoy walking close together letting the rain pour in streams off the edges of his umbrella and sluice in rivers down the streets. Bob was starting to move out into the aisle and held out his hand to her. His hand was still chilly from the emotion of the play.

They drove in silence for a while. Bob said finally, "Good play." They began to ask each other questions about it. They worried over the play, pushing at little bits here and there, motivations for actions and feelings. The rain driving hard against the windshield forced Bob to go more slowly than usual. He kept his eyes turned from the cutting lights of approaching cars. The water was gathering fast in the low spots of the parkway, making thumping sounds against the fenders as the car splashed through. They had been silent for some time when Miriam said, "I'm glad that at least Carl and Anna left when they did, so that we could enjoy the rest."

"Damn right."

"He wouldn't have gone if you hadn't told him to clear out."

"I didn't tell him to clear out!"

"You said that if he wasn't going to be civilized he might as well leave."

"I said that?"

"Right." Bob didn't like her to hold his arm while he drove, so she had her hand on his chunky thigh muscle.

"Fool, can't hold his liquor."

"How many drinks did he have before dinner?"

"Miriam, I counted four martinis. Too much. What did he say to that man in black tie?"

"Bob, I swear I think I heard him say, 'Stand back, you phony mother-fucker, I'm getting my shit out of here." Honest. I wanted to laugh."

"Never would have hired him if he hadn't been a good salesman. Friends or not. Could be pressures—but, so what?"

"He wants very much to be successful here."

"Miriam, if he can't shape up, I won't keep him on the payroll. I can get plenty of salesmen who won't get drunk, insult their wives and miscellaneous onlookers in restaurants. One more act like that and he's out. I'll speak to him in the morning." Now he could settle back and think about his driving. Bad night. He didn't care if Carl had been going through a rough time. Ralph Giletti said something about his drinking more than he used to do and maybe getting bounced from his last job for it. They had an AA chapter in Stevensville. Friendship went just so far. He had given him this chance . . . . "Hey, on a night like this, that's not funny. We might skid."

"Just wanted your attention. Now that we have some time I want to bring you up to date."

"Then I'll have a cigar." Miriam quickly opened the car vents. If a man wanted to smoke, she supposed he must, but she didn't have to say she liked it. She would tell Bob about her plan to have that nice young couple over for dinner and invite Anna and Carl. They should meet some other young people in the community.

"A week from Saturday? OK," Bob said, turning slowly into their driveway. "I'll cook my fancy shishkabob in the outdoor fireplace." He pushed the button on his car, the garage door slid up, and he drove the Buick in. "So, high and dry, honey." He put his arm around her as they walked under his big umbrella toward the darkened house with the porch light burning.

Anna had said nothing since they left the restaurant when he had called her that. She was determined to say nothing that he could twist against her. She kept remembering the expression on the waiter's ascetic face when she had been reaching for her handbag to go and Carl had said, "Ready, slut?" The waiter's elegant nostril had fairly curled with distaste. "I'm the Mohammed Ali of swimming pools. Ring a rhyme a rosy . . . " People had turned and laughed at first when he raised his glass saying, "Fornication . . . ve go to the Kitskills." He slammed his glass on the table. "Bobby-baby, slogans are shit. Not man's work." As if to sing a chorus of Abie's Irish Rose he tipped his head to one side and chanted, "I'll do my stunt in my wife's—." She shivered in the corner of the front seat. Bob had gotten up at that, shouted to the waiter for coffee and told Miriam to take her off to the ladies' room away from the diners, who had gone silent around them.

Miriam sat quietly saying nothing in the dressing room while Anna combed her hair and tried to think of ways to take a long time with her make-up. When they had come out of the ladies' room the clattering voices and cups seemed to leap out at her and send her head-first into the mirrors and the smoke, but she found her way quickly to the door and waited for the others to come out. She had needed to breathe, not to think. She didn't know what the men had said to one another or how people had acted when she didn't come back.

Now they were shooting down the wet streets in a black glaze of reflected lights, careening around corners. She drifted into a fantasy—they would go squarely into a cement abutment and she would never have to decide anything again. The car's wheels locked on a turn and skidded sharply to the left, swinging the front end around to the right. Carl wrenched the steering wheel to the left and the car almost turned over. Down West End, rushing the bright turning of the lights, speeding away too soon, just missing another car coming to a stop at the cross-section, and finally he turned down under the bridge and they moved out onto the slick darkness of the parkway.

If Bob wanted him to do his jack-ass work making up fucking slogans he would give him more than he bargained for. He was a damn good salesman, had proved it at John Deere. They knew it. Stevensville was peanuts. Boondocks. The boonies—no matter how fancy the boobies' houses were. Miriam had nice ones for her age. Had to be fifty if she was a day. Drive in rhythm, swing to the left, swing to the right. Good fast pace down the old black ribbon. That pansy with the tux asking him please to wait a moment—while his broad-assed wife heaved herself out of her chair and he replaced his fucking monocle. Anna saying, "I'm sorry," as if she did anything. Never did do anything. He had to do everything. Work, pay, drive, fuck while she lay there. Dear, dear Anna, nothing from nebbishland. The most obvious one yet—"Bring your tool and fuck in our pool!" The greatest. They weren't going to make an ass of him. Who was Green—a little Jew boy from Brooklyn who'd made good in the suboibs.

He pulled up with a sudden stop, brakes grabbing. Anna got out of the car and raised the garage door, barely getting clear before he drove the car in. She pulled her coat around her and hurried to the house, standing shivering under the gable of the front door while he found his key and opened the door.

He threw his coat on a chair and pushed her up the stairs.

"Carl, I want to hang up my coat."

"So? I want something else."

"Carl, it's late. Don't be silly." The slap stung her right cheek.

"No one calls me silly, silly." His left hand came hard across her eyes. "She calls her husband a fool. Now, we're in this fancy house—let's try the fancy bedroom." She was thrown against the roses of their bedroom wall as he stood before her. "Don't run from me. You're my wife. Come here. I said, come here and take it."

She cowered against the wall, her arm up to protect her head, face smarting, looking at his strange face, puffed, with blood-shot eyes and white spittle on his lips. His hand stroked his pants open as he came towards her. "You've had it before, Nebbish-lady." He slapped her again across the mouth, knocking her head against the wall. As she cried out he ripped down her pantyhose and drove into her before she could slump to the ground, banging his pelvis against hers and her body against the wall. In pushing against him she shoved herself against the wall and he rammed into her again. As she struggled he muttered, "turn on the hook." Holding her up he pushed her so that they fell together onto the floor, Anna locked beneath him. The wind knocked from her lungs by the fall, she sucked air into her throat with wheezing gasps. She tried to be limp but her muscles had gone tight. She could only wait until the hot mallet stopped pounding. She lay still under his weight stuffed with wads of hot clay.

When she tried to move he roused instantly. "Want more? Want more?" He heaved up, raising his massive chest and grinding his hips down upon her.

"Please, Carl." She saw a line of peach that cracked her eyes and bounced her head like a dented melon on the floor.

"No, please Carl . . . no please, Carl . . . please, please, no . . . nuh . . . nuh," he grunted in his agony of pleasure, until, slipping in sweat and sperm he rolled off her and lay still.

It was about one o'clock when Hope let herself into her house with her own key. The lights were streaming from the house next door, although surely they had reached home about ten. She couldn't tell if they were still up but doubted if they would leave the lights on if they weren't. Even if Carl drank more or went to bed stoned, Anna would go about turning off the lights, she supposed. If they were better friends or if Hope knew their habits better, she would go over to ask if everything was all right. What could be wrong? Carl could be throwing up—quite beneficial, considering. This was all unbalanced. Husband and wife are one flesh. She turned the thermostat up to 73. She just couldn't seem to get warm.

After a hot shower she put on her warmest bathrobe and went to the kitchen to heat some milk. She would read; that would help. She brought the hot milk to her bedside and settled among the pillows to read a book she had been looking forward to. At two o'clock it seemed luxuriously self-indulgent to open the book, nestle her shoulders into the high pillows, take a hot sip of milk, and turn the first page. The room became silent except for the scratching turn of the page caught by the sheet. Beth-Ellen slept with her white paws crossed over her eyes. Hope had read the same paragraph for ten minutes when she swung her feet out of bed, pulled on her bathrobe again, and went down to her greenhouse to see how the plants were doing.

CHAPTER FOUR

IN THE week that followed Anna did not look forward to Miriam's party. She could guess that his boss's wife would be wanting to make Carl and his family comfortable, and when she heard that Miriam wanted to introduce them to "another new couple" she became even more uneasy. Anything that underlined Carl's newness to Stevensville made him more edgy and her more fearful. When she was first playing house hadn't times been different? He had called her "doll" and "baby." The new house was becoming settled now. More impressive than any they had lived in. She would have to call Hope, though, and ask her again what she had said about wood stain. She would try to stain the bookcase left unpainted by the men. She wondered why she had never tried to do any of this herself before. Money had been even shorter when they had lived in the city.

She was moving around the living room picking up papers, going into the kitchen sponging off the surfaces, moving from room to room slightly bent over, eyes on table tops, the floor, window sills, never looking up or out, only down and inward. She didn't notice the bent-legged padding she adopted as she moved in this restless fashion picking up, gathering together, like a small animal rustling leaves together making its lair. She hadn't expected bowers of roses as the wedding pictures promised. She stopped, a dust rag in her hand, and looked out, her eyes striking the opaque surface of the closed blinds. She remembered her mother leaning over her father's shoulder as he read his paper. Her arm would circle his back, her hand running along his side, and she would say something that would make him grin or put down his paper and pull her next to him. "Look what Reston says here," he would say.

She ran the rag over the books, now carefully arranged in the living room bookcases. If anyone ever looked at her books they would see—*European Drama, Art History of the World, The Stoic and Epicurean Philosophers* and most of them, except for some Rollo May and Konrad Lorenz, or the Simone de Beauvoir that she hadn't read, her college text books. She wondered where that life had gone. She had been in those days, eleven years ago, boiling with energy, studying like a fiend, playing field hockey, tennis, squash, fencing, packing studying in during the week so she could go off on week-ends. She had discovered Art History when

she was a junior in college, almost too late to major in it, but she had
chucked all her other ideas, let the credits fall where they would and had
taken all the Art History courses she could in one delighted gulp. She
dusted the Phaidon Donatello carefully, pushing away from the back-
binding. At one time she had even done some sketching.

Now, most of the time, she was too tired to finish an article in the
Reader's Digest. In her group on campus were the editor of the literary
magazine, the head of *Dramatis Personae*, people everyone knew were
going to make it in theatre or journalism. She didn't know where most
of them were. Anyway, they were all married and busy raising children.
She was sure of that. Only five of her classmates hadn't married. One was
in a sanatorium, two were dead, killed together in a motorcycle crash,
one had leukemia, and the fifth always had been odd. The college alumnae
quarterly kept writing about Boops Reilly who was skiing with her husband and five children in Austria, and Anna Maria Marengo who was
now head of three volunteer groups and her PTA and running for director
of a settlement house. She would watch "Not for Women Only" while
she got a cup of coffee. Or maybe she could call Hope at work and ask
her about the stain.

Carl strode along the slate steps that led out to the grill where Bob's
brilliantly colored back bent over some skewers.

"God, man, how'd she get you into that get-up?" When Carl pounded
him on the back, Bob turned, just catching a teetering tomato.

"Hold it. . . . You don't like my apron? My grandchildren gave it
to me." He turned so "Daddy's the Chef" in large red letters could be fully
admired. "Now that you've seen it, I can take it off."

As Carl was looking about, saying how much he liked their place and
its lay-out, Bob had to point out the impressive outdoor fireplace. It
stood five feet high and included hefty stone wings set low enough to
rest mustard, salt and pepper, tongs, fire mits and such in its rustic niches.
Soon they were all standing around the fireplace. Glasses in hand they
chatted and Bob told them all how he and his sons had built it, how they
had mixed the cement and set in stones carried from the stream down
below.

While Bob told his favorite story, Miriam got Anna to help her keep
an eye on drinks as she brought out hot hors d'oeuvres.

On the edge of the low stone wall near the picnic table "the new
couple" were perched. Alan's dark head was bent to hear Sally, and when
he spoke, he seemed a gentle-voiced bear hovering over a yellow spot of
color.

"I don't even know your favorite dishes. Do you like shishkabob?"
she whispered as if she murmured ambrosial delights.

"Anything you cook . . . but brussel sprouts and liver."

"I'll avoid them. Still, liver can be. . . " Sally looked into those trusting eyes. "But we'll forget liver, brussel sprouts, finnan haddie, and turnips."

When he said, "Finnan haddie!" in shock, she curled her fist inside his large hand and chuckled.

When Bob brought the skewers from the grill they all sat down, adjusting napkins. "I learned how to cook this from the Turks, when I visited Len at his digs in Anatolia. They don't mix up all the vegetables like in pictures in *Cosmopolitan*. That dries it out."

"Anatolia?"

"Len has been there two years," Bob said, sliding the meat pieces down the skewer onto Sally's plate.

"When men do women's work they really do it." Carl nodded with approval.

"Iced tea, Carl?" Leaning near Anna, Miriam said, "You all right? You look pale-ish."

"Fine, oh, I'm fine. Shouldn't wear black—makes me look morbid." She accepted some tea. "What does Alan do?"

"Teaches handicapped children—physical education, dramatics, some math, that sort of thing. Right, Sally?"

Sally nodded vigorously, caught chewing a piece of gristle.

"You do?" Suddenly animated, Anna turned to Alan. "How old are the children you work with? The nine-year-olds at Jamie's school did the *Trojan Women*. I couldn't believe it. In what way handicapped?"

Alan turned and looked at Anna for the first time. Anna and Alan began to babble to one another, running over one another's sentences, catching each other's half-done phrases to complete, describing plays seen, parts acted. For Anna the party jolted into color. The food was delicious. Alan had acted in summer stock; he knew all sorts of gossip about actors. He told her how effective he thought children could be on the stage, how true their imaginative intuitions were. He spoke a great deal of loving, compassionate, sophomoric nonsense, Anna supposed, but she loved to hear him. And Sally, swimming about in the warm puddle of passionate puppy love, cooed about how she loved being on Alan's pedestal and how she would do her best to stay there, even including avoiding finnan haddie and brussel sprouts.

Unfortunately there was a moment when Sally foolishly asked something about Jewishness and Anna heard Carl say, "Oh, don't you worry about that. Everybody in this town'll love you two. It's their kids' friends they worry about, not their teachers, right, Bob?" He laughed, knowing he had said something clever. "They expect the Jews to be the smart ones, right, Bob?"

"More rice, Carl?"

For Anna the next few minutes slide away in a chill as she looked from face to face, watching their expressions, but unable to take in what was said. When she could hear again, Miriam and Sally were talking about TV commercials.

"Like the one showing the pregnant women in the exercise class and when one woman gets a chance to talk to the other she asks about diapers."

"Not me. I'll ask the basics. Like how much will it hurt."

"A woman never wrote it." Miriam had sharpness in her voice.

"Here is Thomas Jefferson preparing the Constitution for the morning's meeting and dear wife, really a Thurber cartoon, keeps turning off the light so he can't work, so the dear boy can get some sleep."

Sally laughed. "I think that one's cute. Why don't you dig it? It only advertises somebody's lamps."

Miriam glanced at Anna. "Sally, if you think it's cute, I can't explain it to you."

"You really are women's lib, aren't you," Sally said, smiling sweetly.

Red-faced, Miriam said, "I keep forgetting how timid young women are."

By then Sally was blushing and starting to say something about it being time to go. When Anna looked for Carl he was in a quiet conversation with Bob, who seemed to be telling him something important.

Before they left Miriam whispered to Anna how embarrassed she was at her treatment of Sally, but she was tired of the young, suddenly. Anna smiled, but looked sharply into Miriam's face and asked her, "How do you keep it all so clear, Miriam?" Anna shook her head and turned away abruptly to look for her sweater. As Carl walked toward his car, Anna asked Miriam if she could drop by in a week or two just to chat and to ask her advice about something. Miriam watched the thin hands pulling the black sweater tight across her shoulders and answered her warmly, lightly touching her arm, saying of course she should come any time the spirit moved her. It was such fun to see them both and she hoped to see them both again soon and Anna said what a lovely dinner it was and what good hosts they both were and how glad she was and surely she would . . . and ducked her head down and walked rapidly toward Carl when he called her.

"So, what did you think of them?" Carl said as he got out of the car slamming the door. "You talked with both of them long enough."

They were walking toward their own front door, the gravel crunching beneath their feet. Anna could see the lights from Hope's house shining steadily beyond the old rhododendrons at the edge of Hope's property.

"Oh who?"

"Alan and Sally, but it's Sally and Alan there. . . . She'll wear the pants," Carl said, stepping heavily on the front step.

After such a confusing evening how could he be so sure of what he saw? "How do you figure that?"

"He's got to be some kind of fag to be working with handicapped children. And in theatrical stuff? It's classic."

Anna went ahead and turned on the lights. He was clearly out to get her for some reason. She tried to think of what had been said that evening. She was glad the children were with Mother Johnson overnight.

"Well?" Carl caught up with her and put his hand over hers as she touched the wall fixture at the foot of the stairs, "Don't you agree?"

"Agree about what?" She turned away.

He caught her right hand upraised still near the wall fixture. Anna looked down. "You know I don't, Carl."

"Why don't you? You had a good talk with him, didn't you? Did you find him your garden variety male?"

"I don't know what that is." Anna's voice was low, almost sullen. They had had this fight before; Carl, whose stern father thought it effeminate to wear a wrist watch, was always on the look out for "fags."

"What did you like about him? Tell me!" Carl unbuttoned his collar button and yanked at his tie.

"He was sweet . . . "

"Sweet! Adorable! How'd you like his soft rose-colored shirt?"

"I mean he was interested in his job, kind about kids, and understanding about these kids . . . handicapped, after all. He must be a gentle person."

"I'll bet he's gentle."

She delayed putting her foot on the first step. "I had a really fine teacher once." She smiled, working at it, "I guess he reminded me some. I guess I just liked him, Carl."

"You would." He pulled her hand down and pinned it to her side. "That's the kind of man you want, I'll bet." When he turned toward her his eyes glinted. She felt his excitement and stared. All of this had been a set-up, to permit his fury. She put one foot behind her and felt for the first stair. As he reached for her shoulder she pushed hard and slipped away to the side, tipped over a chair into his path and ran down the hall. The small sound in her ears was roaring, filling all sound. She couldn't hear the table turning over, the vase shattering as she dashed through the living room, pushing things over to fall in his way. Gasping as the blood thudded into her chest she rushed for the side door, snatching to find the knob in time. As she reached the door all the lights went out, but she caught the Segal lock, flipped it to the right, and sent the door slamming after her.

Instead of trying to sprint down toward the front walk she ran around the side of the house staying in darkness and then dashed for her neighbor's clumps of bushes. When Carl opened the side door and stepped out, there was no sound. A shrub brushed by her arm moved softly on Hope Alford's property, but her husband couldn't see it fifty yards away. Her lungs strained to breathe, but she clenched her lips as her heart pounded, sending blood so hard to her head she thought it would gush from her ears. Still she stayed rigid, crouching, a frightened nocturnal creature in the bushes. She heard her husband's shoes step quickly, clicking down the front walk, crouching on the brick as she turned, walk more slowly up the steps. She heard the door close loudly and the metal bolt click into the lock position. Then she let the air pour into her throat.

Water was running down her back as she dug her fingers into the ground and began to rock forward and back silently, her teeth beginning to chatter. She wound her arms around her legs and rocked, crouching, a grieving creature in the shadow of the old rhododendron. She heard breath sucked into lungs in short rasping hiccups and then groans like some animal grieving over a terrible loss, some piece of the body cut away, some child wrenched from arms and killed before its mother. What grief could this be to make a creature groan and sob so? Then as the lights of the house went out on the way upstairs and the yard remained silent the groans began to lessen. Chilled and shaking, Anna slipped away from the sheltering arms of the ancient rhododendron and in a crouching run, finger tips almost touching the ground, head looking down and out from hunched shoulders, she padded softly along the rims of shadows into the darkness surrounding Hope Alford's house. The porch light was on as was the custom in that community when the owner was at home, but Anna avoided the front steps. The green door was formal with its burnished brass knocker in the shape of a wreath. Old civilities of welcomed guests, amenities of families greeting, and their courtesies shadowed in the wreath, only menaced Anna now. With their black suits and sober gravity they would imprison her, shake their heads against her wildness and give her pills to make her sleep. She rushed on, forgetting to dodge as low hemlock boughs whipped her face and tangled in her hair; she was running with her head down again, arms crossed, holding her belly.

The single notes slowly chimed their gentle dance signifying fifteen minutes after eleven as Hope finished the fifth letter for the evening. Beth-Ellen was curled in a deep cushion within a circle of light. As the notes followed their final pattern, Hope was signing her name to the letter to the neighboring Horticultural Society President asking her to join the Stevensville group at their annual meeting. She folded her letter in three parts and slid her hand across the surface to crease the folds, and heard a pattering sound. Her chair squeaked on the wide flooring as she rose, feeling a little stiff after sitting for hours. She started toward the window to close it against the rain when she saw a shape at the window. She quickly reached over and turned out the light in her study. The dark shape had seemed low to the ground and massively hairy like some dog off a leash, a runaway, perhaps. She went to the hall and flicked on the powerful overhead beams that instantly poured over the lawn, even penetrating the old lilacs and rhododendrons, and stepped out onto her stone steps beneath the projecting roof. She stood in the silence a moment and then, just as she turned back, she heard a kind of whimper and a rustle of leaves and sudden footsteps when a black shape fell at the side of the porch. Hair wild, tangled with hemlock, her black dress torn and dirty as if she had been rolling in dirt and leaves, Anna's face was almost hidden as she clutched the side of the stone porch groaning her name.

Hope bent down putting her hand on the shaking shoulder. "Come around to the steps. Come in, everything is all right. Everything is all right."

Anna looked up at her. Her expression was vague, as if she could not quite translate the words Hope was saying. She shook her head violently and clutched Hope's foot, put her head down on it, held it with both hands as her body shook. Her fingers and their nails were blackened as if she had clawed up pieces of sod. Hope put her hands beneath Anna's arms and almost carried her into the house. She closed the front door, double-locked it, flicked off the overhead lights and took her into her small study. Gently she lowered Anna onto the couch and uncurled her fingers from their grip on her arm so she could go to the closet to pull out a warm quilt to tuck around her.

Anna sat huddled and shuddering under the blanket while Hope went to get some brandy. Her dirt-caked hands accepted the glass, but she sat gazing into the room as if she had forgotten she was supposed to drink the brandy. Her violent shaking sloshed the caramel liquid into a tiny tempest in her glass. She crouched forward, shivering.

"I won't go back there." Her voice was hoarse.

Hope was surprised that Anna could speak. "Hush now. Curl up and get warm. You don't have to speak about it, or think about it, now." Hope sat beside her on the couch.

"But I won't, you know. You won't make me, will you?" Her intonation startled Hope, who reassured her that she didn't have to do anything she didn't want to do.

Anna pulled at her, "Stay with me. Lock the window and stay with me. I'm so afraid."

"What could happen?" Hope was watching the dark enlarged pupils, eyes darting to the side.

"Can't you see? Afraid he'll come, break in." She looked over her shoulder toward the door.

"There are still laws around here," Hope said, thinking of the heavy, iron fire tongs by the fireplace in the living room.

The woman was still shaking, her lips pale and trembling like a chilled child's after swimming beyond its strength. She could stay in this room overnight, but there was the possibility of someone's stepping through the French doors that opened onto the garden. She would lock those doors carefully and take her upstairs to the guest room beyond her own, so that if anyone did come in the house she would hear him pass her door. That was foolish. Carl Johnson didn't know the plan of her house and, of course, that would be "breaking and entering." She never had bought a gun and regretted that now. But she had that heavy piece of pipe under her bed, ghoulish as she had always felt it was to keep it after the plumbers abandoned it. She would use it on Carl with pleasure.

Anna's grimy hand caught her arm, "Don't go away."

Hope looked down at the white face with its mask-like streaks of black. The burnished chestnut hair had bits of hemlock tangled in it. Hope lifted a thick mass of hair that had fallen forward and smoothed the wet-cold forehead. "I won't go. Drink. You don't like brandy? All right, then, sip just a little. You need to get warm. I'll take you upstairs to the extra room. It has a strong lock on the door. You'll feel safe there." Consciously she made her voice as soft and calming as she could, wondering at the ways of heterosexuals. Was this S and M stuff part of Anna's game? Would she smile in the morning and trot happily back to her master?

Anna nudged her head against Hope's shoulder. "Hold me. Hold me. I'm cold, cold." After sitting for a moment in full view of the French doors trying to will the heat out of her own body into Anna's, Hope stood up. "Come, dear. Skip the brandy. Let's get you upstairs into a warm bed."

Clumsily they made their way upstairs. Anna clutched Hope around the waist, and Hope tried to hold up Anna and parts of the blanket as they moved slowly along, bumping against the wall on one side and the bannister on the other. They stumbled on up the stairs, stepping onto the quilt and pushing one another off balance. They managed the short walk down the hall past Hope's room in the front of the house to the middle room, Hope flicking on the lights as they went. She sat Anna on the edge of the large double bed and walked immediately to the windows and pulled down the shade. The lights in the Johnson house seemed to be on in the back room. She wondered if that was their bedroom. The houses were half an acre apart but too close.

When she tried to loosen Anna's high-heeled sandals Hope began to realize the extent of Anna's terror. The fragile kid straps were mud-caked and one was almost torn off. Her stockings were ripped and spattered. She must have come from some party that ended in this terrifying chase or flight. Spring mud on her shoes, a black dress. Her teeth were chattering again. Hope clicked the electric blanket to high, and, putting her hand under Anna's knees, lifted them onto the bed as she parted the bed clothes for Anna and her quilt to slide into their warmth. In a few minutes the trembling stopped.

"Don't leave me." The eyes had opened again. "He can't get in, can he?"

"No, dear, he cannot. I'll leave this light on across the room so that if you waken you will remember where you are. I'll be just down the hall. If you want anything I'll hear you. Sleep now." Hope left the door ajar and walked to her own room thinking about the red marks on the younger woman's face. Some were clearly marks from branches, but there were others that looked like bruises.

Still, it was not her business. Anna was a married woman, mother of two children. She must have lived with this boor for nearly ten years. It was to her taste, apparently, to be reduced to a frightened hiding creature every so often. A brilliantly colored picture slid across her vision like a still movie frame in a darkened room. She had been fourteen and out hunting. By "luck" she had been "in at the kill" and had seen the fox, a vivid brown-red flash before, now caught at a corner in a grey stone wall, unable to move, the rusty curve of body turned back, facing the hounds as they came down upon him. She remembered the warm entrails that she felt sliding along her face when minutes later she was "blooded" by the Master with the others at their first kill. Standing proudly on the ground beneath her, the Master of Fox Hounds had held up the warm red mass and told her to lean down from her horse. She had shifted her body forward in the saddle and leaned her cheek down toward him as he gently touched her face and had run the warm bloodied mass along her cheek. Her vision was filled with his scarlet coat, a color brighter than the fox's rust. People beside her murmured congratulations at being in at the kill as she looked up, her cheek still feeling warm, and watched the hounds thrashing and biting at each other in a small clump by the wall where the Whip and another horseman in scarlet were trying to draw the hounds back.

It was much later when Hope began to be able to let her muscles and limbs relax in her own warm bed. Just when she heard the birds begin to feed and the song sparrow begin those liquid notes like water sounding clear in a stream was she comforted and able to sleep.

CHAPTER FIVE

HOPE was moving quietly in her kitchen, boiling an egg, preparing her tea, setting out dishes and flatware, listening to a bluejay's harsh cry when she heard a timid "Can I help?" Anna was standing shivering in the doorway, her black cotton dress and sandals looking even worse than the night before.

"You must be freezing, Anna. Go upstairs to my room and see if the things I've laid out on the bed will do, at least for warmth. Do you like eggs?" She called after Anna who was walking obediently up the stairs again. Hope went after her; she had been too off-hand. She stood in the doorway as Anna looked down at her bed, at the blue wool skirt, soft grey blouse, and warm sweater. She was standing still as if she didn't know what to do. Tears stood in her dark eyes.

"Shoes? What will we do for shoes? I don't know when I last saw goose bumps on a human ankle!" Hope disappeared into her closet to rummage in the winter section. "You will look pretty funny but ski socks are the answer." She emerged with bright red and yellow wool socks with soles sewn on. "Pretty lurid for winter evenings . . . fine for a rainy June Sunday," Hope said.

Anna was slipping her dress off over her shoulders. Hope busied herself in the closet before she closed the door. The skirt was very long, but that would keep her warm. The ballooning blouse was quite satisfactory. The sweater made her look like a tiny full-back.

"Excellent. Now, come downstairs and we'll feed you."

Anna looked up at her as if she was about to say something, but she turned away to put on the socks. Hope went on down the stairs trying to decide whether to turn up the thermostat or to light a fire.

"Da-daa!" Anna stood in the doorway, right hand behind her head, left at her hip. "Here I am, Miss America!" With the wool socks up to her knees and the skirt down to her ankles she looked like a soft bundle of warm wool. Her cheeks were pinker. "Now, I will skate over to the stove and help you." With arms swinging and long sliding, skating steps she pushed her crazy foot gear across the floor to stand beside Hope, looking up at her again.

Hope said, "Eggs? How do you like them?"

"Boiled."

35

"Good."

"Bacon? or sausage? or neither?"

"Neither."

"Never? It's Sunday and you need your strength."

"Bacon would be lovely. . . . Are you ever going to let me thank you?" She was standing turned away from Hope, her voice very low.

"Let us get breakfast together and then sit down and talk. First, Beth-Ellen." The white and grey cat was seated looking up at the refrigerator door, waiting patiently.

"That means she wants to eat?"

Hope nodded and set down the milk and cod. Beth-Ellen turned away from her vigil at the white door and walked sedately to her milk. The time before they sat down to breakfast was spent conversing about Beth-Ellen, her advanced age, how Hope got her and when, how neurotic the rest of her feline family was, her operation for encysted ovaries, its beneficial results; until, by the time they sat down, both of them had coated over the anxieties of the hours of darkness.

After they sat down and the business of opening the eggs had been accomplished, Anna said, "I guess you think I'm crazy."

"That's the last thing I think. Anyone who runs from a beating is quite sane."

"How did you know that?" Her voice suddenly went out of control, and she stopped, put her napkin to her mouth and reached for the glass of juice.

"Anna, why should you appear at my steps? Why would you be afraid that he would break through a locked door? Don't let's go on with this. You don't have to tell me anything. This is your life and your privacy."

Anna apologized, saying that she didn't mean anything, just that she couldn't remember too well what she had said and done. The click-chink sounds of forks on plates, of cups replaced on saucers, and the rain drumming on the porch roof set them apart on a time island.

"This tea is delicious. People say tea can be good, but I never believed it."

"You're a coffee drinker! I forgot. Forgive me." Hope was up and reaching for a pot.

"Hope, stop. I mean it! This is good. Cinnamon? What else? Cloves? Some orange?" Her hand was out to Hope. "Please, don't fuss. I really love it and, please, you have been so generous."

Hope came back to the table. Coffee drinkers needed to start the day with coffee, not tea. She would hate to be forced by some diligent hostess to start the day with coffee. Her habits of living alone always came out and revealed her self-absorption.

"I must be going soon. I can't impose on you much longer."

"Where will you go?"

"Don't know. . . . But I have to . . . do . . . something. The stupid thing is that the most obvious place to go is to his mother's. Imagine? She would . . . if not understand . . . at least. . . . Miriam Green too, but the wife of his boss? Crazy!"

"Your own family?"

"Impossible. Divorces . . . even separations do not happen in well-regulated families. My failure, of course."

"Thinking that far? Divorce or separation?"

"I'm a coward. I hate pain. It simply isn't worth it. Watching to see . . . keep a marriage going . . . for what? What has it been anyway? I mean—really? Who was I?" She couldn't speak.

"If I were a good wife, I would want to help him. I would figure he must be under some terrible strain. He's drinking more. Maybe . . . if I were a good wife. He never . . . struck me before. But really—he has contempt. . . . The other night after the play . . . " The black drive swerving over the glazed streets, the blows of his hands against her ears, his heavy body used against her, images, hot and tactile, were not to be expressed.

"If I were a good wife, I would go back. . . . But I never will." She looked up directly at Hope. Although her lips were shaking and tears were running down her nose, she said each word as if she tapped it precisely out on copper. "I never will." Her small fist was curled in a tight knot. She jumped up. "I never will. No one can make me." She walked from one side of the room to the other, shouting, "I can run away. I never will take that again. I will kill myself first . . . or him."

Shouting, her fists shaking, eyes closing, her mouth in a child's down-curving "u," tears rolling down her cheeks, suddenly she crouched over, holding her knees with her arms, rocking back and forth, "Never, never, never, never. I'll get a knife. I'll put it under the bed. . . . " Her harsh voice rose to a shriek; she gasped for breath, sobbing, trying to shout, gulping air.

"Hush, hush. You don't have to go back. You don't have to go back." Hope knelt near her and put her long arms around her and rocked back and forth with her. "Anna, Anna, listen to me. Honey, listen, come now." She led her into the living room, almost tripping over the moccasin socks. She set her down on the couch, a rotund twelve year old in blue wool. "If you are determined to get away, if you mean it, you should do it and you can. This hasn't happened before, has it?"

Anna sniffed and rubbed her eyes, "What?"

"Your deciding to leave him."

"I wish it had. I should have seen this coming. I've been such a . . . nothing." With her arms out like a child's doll, she turned to Hope and embraced her so tightly that both of their bodies shook with her heavy sobs. What had the years and births been about? She held tightly onto Hope and wept.

The only thing to do was to let this happen, let all this be wept out and then, in quiet, try to sort out what was to be done. But she had to have some time to think, a feat she couldn't perform easily with this sweet innocent clinging to her, her warm breath and wet mouth brushing her cheek. It did look as if Anna should get out of Carl's reach.

Gently Hope extricated herself, "Can you hear me?" Anna nodded. "Now I want you to rest here on the couch or up in your room. If music helps or the Sunday paper, some coffee—whatever. However, you can rest."

"Are you going away?"

"No, Anna, no. I'll be right here—in my greenhouse fussing with my friends there. After a morning of quiet you'll feel better and I may come up with an idea."

"I'll stay here where I can see you." Anna tucked her red and yellow legs up under the voluminous skirt and curled into a soft doll in the corner of the couch. She accepted the warm afghan with a sleepy smile, and when Hope touched the phonograph needle to the rim of the turning record she snuggled lower into the couch murmuring something.

Part of the reason Hope had turned on the music was that she could not bear the sense of someone looking at her while she tried to be alone. Evidently Anna had no need to be alone, ever? Or was it just for the time being—considering the threat from next door. As Hope thought, she carefully took seedlings out of their pan where they grew too thickly, like a congested urban environment, and set them out in flats leaving much more space between plants. She checked some other seedlings growing under up-ended juice glasses and turned to a job long delayed. The African Violet was growing in two crowns and had to be separated for the plant's health, too packed now within the pot. As she rapped the bottom of the pot smartly with a trowel and then slid the trowel close to the sides of the pot, circling the plant, she thought of how difficult it was going to be for Anna to leave her family. If she was right that she could not bear to live with Carl—still, how was she going to live apart from them, Carl and the children? She would remove both plants from the pot and carefully separate the mother and daughter plants, repotting both of them. The trick was not to injure either in the process but to leave each free to grow and spread out. There, she did have to cut those heavy links between them. No, she could never take responsibility for this. If Anna wished to leave Carl that was her affair, but she could never even advise her.

Still, she knew this unwillingness for anyone to intrude on a family forced many women back to the men who abused them. There were places Anna could go, even in Westover, near-by. There were half-way houses where women could stay, be cared for while they were counseled and tried to decide what to do. As she settled the smaller plant in its new pot with fresh dark potting soil and a touch of peat moss and vermiculite, it seemed a sensible thing to do. She would be cared for, counseled; but again, as she took down a larger pot for the mother plant, it seemed wrong. Such houses were for people who had no friends, nowhere to go. Anna was her neighbor. She was known to her. There was no need for Anna to be cast into the arms of some impersonal charity run by the state or some agency, as if she were destitute of friends and resources. She could see it, if all her friends were her husband's friends, or if she were . . . and as Hope poured water into the soft pit she had made ready to receive the lusty green plant, she rejected the idea of the half-way house.

Apparently Anna wasn't troubled about the children because Carl's mother would take care of them. Would she move in or . . . Heifetz had finished a brilliant passage and a new record had clicked into place. Anna's eyelids were down and her face looked relaxed. Hope turned to deal with some aphids that had appeared on Emily's camelias. With a cotton swab dipped in alcohol she touched the white spots on the underside of the plant Emily had given her to treat. Emily's garden group had asked Hope to talk to them Monday night on mulching roses. She should gather some notes for her talk, remember to have some useful books to suggest for their reference libraries, give herself some time to anticipate the sorts of questions they would ask. She needed to select the slides she would use to demonstrate planting displays.

Her mind drifted off to think of her mother's beautiful garden, done by platoons of gardeners: gorgeous arches of yellow roses, gravelled paths, spokes out from the central rose display—all very old-fashioned but splendid. An old world gone with Tara's halls—beautiful and dangerous. Her mother had planned Hope's wedding in the rose garden with brides-maids and small flower girls. She had been baffled as the years passed and her daughter remained engaged but never married. The engagement was the satisfactory arrangement of two old friends both needing a good, working disguise. When her mother died Hope had been released and played the game only when Ron flew in from San Francisco and needed a cover.

Anna dozed through some Bach cantatas while Hope worked on her notes for the next day's talk to the garden group. Her mind kept circling around Anna's problem until the obvious solution trumpeted in her ear with a horn concerto. As she prepared the soup for lunch she kept check-ing her plans, possibilities against realities. Finally after their lunch, laid out on the low table by Anna's couch, Hope said to her, "I think you should not stay here. No, Anna, sit back. I don't mean that you have to leave this minute. I mean—am I right that you are afraid that he may try to find you and come after you?"

Anna nodded vigorously, looking as if she wanted to nestle against Hope again, but Hope got up and went into the kitchen. When she came back with a coffee pot and a trivet, Anna was sitting erect, feet together on the floor. "What were you going to say?"

"It is now June 6th," Hope said, slipping into the arm chair across from Anna. "I was planning to take off for Ontario June 21st—to go camping for ten days. I think with some maneuvering I could get away the ninth, this Wednesday. That would get you out of here and out of reach while you sorted things out. Not a good time for the nursery, but possible."

Anna slowly studied Hope, the serious face with its beautiful planes. She did not dare to ask the obvious question. Instead she said, "You don't . . . mind the extra person . . . and the . . . ballast?"

"I don't know. We'll see, but it gives you the time. You will understand if I go off into the woods or go fishing or something. Actually—I don't fish."

"Of course, I would understand."

"Fine then. That's settled. Most of my gear is in the attic. I'm not a real camper; just a modified tourist."

"I've never camped at all. Do you have to be very rugged—Hemingway and all?"

Hope added coffee to Anna's cup and tea to her own. "That depends. I suppose back-packers are the real thing, and suffer, but I like nature in her benign aspect. I hate to get cold or wet and love quiet spots away from mobile homes and children. That is . . . "

"It's all right. Mine can't hear you. I guess Mother Johnson will step into the breach . . . as she always has." Anna sighed and got up to walk back and forth around the room. She went to the window and touched a terra cotta pot. "I've never seen such an intense blue." She peered down at the African Violet. Had she ever seen such a rich, almost passionate color? She turned back. "I am irresponsible. What kind of a mother? Walking out. . . . Still, Mother Johnson's more of a mother that I'll ever be."

Hope wanted to ask if Carl were proof of that, but said, "I may have some old jeans we can cut down for you. My little sister's sweatshirt and even some shorts, I think, are up in the attic somewhere. Today we can heap together some clothes for different weathers for you. Tomorrow...." Hope paused and looked away from Anna across to the French doors. "Tomorrow, you will have to think about arranging matters, telling Carl or not telling him where you are and where you will be."

"I should tell him before that—he may have the police out now." Anna stopped and stood looking down at her feet. She stood there for seconds, hands at her sides, like a small child at attention. Beth-Ellen appeared at the door, looked at one and then the other, walked over to Hope, hopped up on her lap, walked out to the end of Hope's knees, and settled herself carefully with her back toward Hope, looking out toward the middle of the room.

"I will call Mother Johnson and tell her where I am, that I am going away for . . . ten days? . . . and that . . . and that I think I'm leaving Carl for good." She put her head down, cupping her hands on her forehead.

"If I could hold to it—what an idea! How'll I live? I don't know how to do anything anyone wants. How can I hold to this? What an idea! How can Anna Carroll Johnson have such an idea?"

"Take it slower. We've decided about the next thirteen days."

"Right."

"This is a fine morning for the attic detail. We need the tent, sleeping bags, camping stove . . . all the gear."

"Sleeping bags? Then you are a real camper."

"You're a stickler for definitions. Wait till you hear about Shakespeare. On to the attic."

"Shakespeare?" They got up, and Hope led Anna up to the attic floor where, in the fashion of some old houses, there were several small rooms.

They seemed to Anna to be filled with materials from different lives. Some things looked like photographic equipment for a dark room, shallow trays, containers of developing fluids, large black sheets with pictures pasted on listing shutter speeds and apertures. One pile in a corner looked like the equipment for book binding, the press, small tools and hammers, pieces of leather. A sewing machine might have been used recently because the standing lamp was placed near the sewing table and the portable machine was open with a piece still held by the lowered needle. Hope watched her and nodded. "A lot of toys for a grown up. Come to the seasonal department." Hope led her to a back room that held Christmas ornaments, the green Christmas tree stand, boxes of old Christmas cards, sheafs of Christmas music for the piano and recorder, two large golden paper mache Christmas trees, and, in another section, tennis rackets, large and small duffle bags, a green camping stove, and a large gas lamp.

"I get it. Winter and summer!" Anna was thinking of the mess her old attic used to be with its small trap door and lowered-down ladder, the heaps and boxes, old screens, ropes and children's toys.

"Problem is," Hope said, "would I have stored Laurie's clothes in Summer or in Old Clothes? Let's look in Summer."

While Hope was bending over boxes trying to read labels in the semi-darkness, Anna went about touching the rough khaki duffle bag, testing the weight of an orange nylon bag that clanked with metallic bars in it. Her own life had been so filled with Carl and his needs and the chldren and theirs that she had never thought of hobbies. Think of having the time to learn book binding. Not to mention why. She supposed that Hope's family must be wealthy for her to afford all this and guessed the water color of an old house against the wall had something to do with it. Her family's past. The wealth thing didn't make her uneasy really, but it did explain a lot—how she could own Threshold and how she could avoid being married. Though why should she avoid it? She was so lovely that any man would turn to water looking at her. If men did that. Of course, she was tall. She wondered if Hope ever painted.

"That's our tent."

"What?"

"What you are lifting there."

Anna looked down at her hands. "The metal things do what?"

"They're the skeleton—the scaffolding for the tent. We can put it up outside if you like. Really we should, to check out the seams. If you put epoxy on the seams it doesn't rain in."

"We're keeping dry this trip."

"That's the idea." Hope gave Anna a large box with LAURIE'S THINGS written in red. "Why don't you take these down to your room and try them on. Select what you like and we'll confer later. I want to look over the camping gear here. I'll call you later to help me down with anything I decide on." Anna realized that she had been dismissed and walked slowly down the stairs as Hope turned back to look over the camping stove.

CHAPTER SIX

IN THE days that followed Hope watched to see if Anna would try to reach Carl, but she did not. She did not leave the house. When Hope closed her front door at seven thirty each morning, she heard the dead bolt at the bottom of the door slipped into place. Anna seemed to cower far within rooms, refusing to sit near the window. But she did call Mother Johnson promptly and talked for almost an hour. Hope did not inquire about what was said.

Worried about Anna alone all day with nothing to do, Hope came home for lunch in those days before they left. The first day she came home she found Anna sitting on the floor in the guest room staring into space. She had gotten up. smiled, asked what Hope wanted for lunch and had gone down to the kitchen as if it was her job to get Hope's meal for her. Hope had let her set the table but grilled their cheese sandwiches herself, rapidly, with no frills. That evening, when Hope had to talk to Emily's garden group she asked Anna to go with her. Anna sat in the back of the room with her coat on throughout the lecture. During the coffee afterwards she sat off by herself holding her white polystyrene cup in both hands, her eyes never leaving Hope.

The second day Hope took Anna on a quick shopping trip to Westover to get her a pair of sneakers. She acted like a docile child in a day-dream. Anna tried to make conversation over dinner in the evenings but often stopped, apparently having forgotten what she was going to say. She would look away, return, apologize and quietly resume eating. When she learned that Hope had tasks to do in the evening to prepare for her ten-day absence from Threshold and the Horticultural Society, she said good night like a polite little girl and walked upstairs to her room. She showed no interest in books or TV. Hope supposed she sat in a chair and went over and over what had happened.

Hope felt inept, unable to say the simple words of comfort. There was so much that she could have said, but it would mean one thing to her and another to Anna. Tenderness and loving compassion would be volatile for her. They led so swiftly and so naturally into the warmly enveloping arms and then to desire . . . that she could only avoid it. She didn't know why it all was so difficult for her . . . this approaching. Although, of course they were not. . . . It seemed a dislocation almost, a resetting of her center, when she turned in love to someone. She couldn't understand how people found it so easy to pick up people, the way Holly used to do, though Dorothy couldn't either. As for seducing the young or wooing a married woman, the thought almost made her laugh. She was a square gay—a paradoxical point that—but many, perhaps most gays, were. She was so wound up in her own intricacies, her withdrawals and sensitivities, that unless the Angel Gabriel, or better, Athena, came down and said, "Here, dear, take this one; she'd love you to," she would go on taking up new hobbies.

So, lacking things to say to Anna, she tried to find things for her to do. She set her to shaking out the sleeping bags, putting epoxy on the tent's seams, and then they planned the trip together over the map. Anna seemed to enjoy that. Her small finger followed the route carefully. "Saratoga! That's not too far off. Can we go try the spring water?" So the they had agreed to do that on the return trip, although Hope supposed the spring water would taste of hell-fire or rancid oils. They agreed on a trip up through Binghamton, upstate into Canada, then along the coast to Manitoulin island, then east to one of the remote spots, and home with a crossing at Cornwall and down Route 87 by Saratoga Springs and Albany. Hope's earlier plan before including Anna on the trip had included a few days at Stratford, to see a few plays, and then to find a peaceful spot to pitch her tent for a day or so before moving on to a new camp site. She had tickets in hand for late June, but these would have to be returned.

She said to Anna, "Now, about Shakespeare."

"Shakespeare?"

"You know, Shakespeare at Stratford."

"Can we go?"

"*We* are planning this trip. Of course we *can*. In fact, I'm planning to. Would you like to?"

"Yes, yes, yes. I haven't seen a play since—oh God, I mean a Shakespeare play. Will this keep happening to me?" Her hands had gone to her head. "Will I never . . . never . . . " She pushed away her chair and left the room. Hope stood a moment listening to the quick steps running up the stairs. She left the map where it was and went to the phone to arrange to leave Beth-Ellen at the vet's, to get Richie from Threshold to come over daily to water the plants in the house and greenhouse, and to arrange for reservations at Stratford.

The packing had gone easily, although Hope had to tell Anna every move to make. Anna kept stopping and listening or looking toward the house next door. Just before they slammed the car trunk she heard a child's screech and went rigid. She turned as if to go next door, but the shrill scream slid into high laughter. "It's Jamie," she said, her eyes dilated. "Hope, let's go. Quickly."

They did. Hope slapped on her sun-glasses, slammed and locked back doors, told Anna to sit in the car as it idled and she locked up the house, checked gas, turned off the oil burner, and emerged ten minutes later, smiling, carrying two hats, one bright lime green, the other a sunny yellow.

"Now we are tourists. This is your tourist hat." She presented Anna with the yellow one. "My hat, somewhat older, is necessary, even in the car. To remind me that I am a tourist." Every word was said with heavy emphasis. "You are now *not* mother, or wife, but Tourist Anna on a trip to the wilds. OK?"

Anna nodded, unable to speak. She looked across at Hope as she backed her car smoothly out of the driveway, the silly green hat balanced on her hair above that lovely face. She seemed quite unconscious of her looks. Anna had noticed that there were few mirrors in Hope's house. Her own house and her mother's had mirrors everywhere: in halls, on the landings of stairways, over the mantlepieces, over bureaus, long ones on doors, near closets. One day she realized that she had gone around her house cleaning, watching herself from room to room, seeing herself holding the dust cloth, running it along the edge of the bureau. She had done this for years and suddenly wondered why. She wasn't admiring herself. Trying to catch herself off guard, somehow. One day she thought her eyes looked frantic, like the eyes of a zealot. You with the crazy eyes, she had thought into the mirror, what are you looking for? They looked beady, intense, quite mad, but she was only vacuuming the rugs. What was there to get intense about in that? She wondered if other women looked in mirrors the way she did.

She awoke choking.

"You all right? Thought I'd stop here, under some trees for a break. Want some iced tea?" Hope was reaching back for the fat thermos jug. The sudden darkness of the trees helped. The picnic spot had many tables, a few water spigots, one family with children.

"Do you drive?"

"Doesn't every mother who lives in the suburbs?"

"Oh, right. Look, forgive me. Motherhood is so . . . far from my experience."

"Forget it. You are very . . . capable and I need to remind myself sometimes."

"Of what?"

"Of things I can do. Good iced tea!" Anna raised her plastic cup. "Where'd you go to college?"

"Up near where we're going, Cornell, but I thought we might spend the night at Watkins Glen, old New York town, instead of Ithaca. Watkins Glen is just at the southern tip of Seneca Lake."

"Do you always deflect?"

"Deflect?"

"Turn the conversation away from yourself."

"Did I? I didn't notice. Want some cheese?"

"Thank you, no. But I will drive, if that's all right with you. I guess that's plumbing over there, that discreet red brick building." With that Anna was gone, stepping quickly along the path, her new rubber soled shoes feeling soft and light as she moved. How dare she intrude on so reticent a woman, practically bully her into talking about herself, but Anna was aware of some thwarting that she did not understand. People were usually more direct about themselves in her experience. Why wouldn't she say where she had gone to college, and what she had studied, and how she had felt about it?

The place was clean. She was surprised. As she walked back she chose a path through a piney section and watched her sneakers pressing down on the brown pine needles. When had she last noticed her own feet? The children's feet were tiny and needed new shoes every time she turned around. Probably for summer they'd need sandals and sneakers. Carl didn't approve of sneakers for them, said they'd ruin their feet. She meant to ask the doctor about that. Flickering light along the path, hot stones under the sun. A small greenish creature with . . . a salamander? Red spots. "Hope, Hope, look!" She bent down to peer at the tiny creature which did not seem to notice her particularly. Hope was there beside her leaning down. "Sure looks like a salamander, a newt, I think." A delicate head, slim body, and a whip-tail. As they walked back to the car Anna cried out, "Lots of them! Look, Hope . . . three . . . five, another, but they're brownish. I thought they took on the color of their surroundings. They don't seem to."

Anna's curiosity and zest seemed to arrive with the salamanders. Maybe it would go with a rain storm, Hope didn't know, but she was glad for the lift it gave their conversation. Hope hadn't known that she could discourse for five minutes on the private life of the salamander, but Anna seemed to enjoy it. It was pleasant finally to sit back and let Anna take over the car. She approved her careful checking out of the dashboard first and her judicious trying out of the brakes as she moved out to the highway. Her hands were relaxed on the wheel, but she did not, as many women did, turn her eyes from the road if she talked.

"I go on up 81 to Binghamton, then, just following signs, now, really, and then west on 17 toward Corning?"

"Right."

"Good car. It must be all new under the hood. It's a 71?"

"I don't drive it much, only 40,000 miles on it." A car came up very fast on the left and then drove beside them for a few minutes, the men in it looking them over. Anna's face didn't move a muscle. She held her pace. The car sped off at 75. Hope settled back and tipped her green hat over her eyes. The woman drove like a man, no, like a good driver. She didn't talk all the time either.

Hope felt herself blushing as she thought of Dot's reaction when she learned that she and Anna were driving off for a camping trip together. Who would tell her? Probably Miriam Green who'd know it from Bob, unless Carl tried to keep the whole thing quiet. But commencement was over, wasn't it, so Dorothy wouldn't run into Miriam so easily. That was some relief. Dot would get it all wrong, of course, would suppose there had been some kind of seduction scene and that she was carrying Anna off for some privacy in the woods. Hope opened her butterfly window. Dot would be cynical. The matter was simple: the woman needed to get away from Spider Johnson and her son, Stanley Kowalski.

She felt herself smiling as she remembered Holly talking about Daisy Calloran, the much married matron who flirted with all the lesbians at Holly's community center. "Women like that ought to be locked up," Holly had said, banging her spoon on the kitchen table. "Just trouble, nothing but trouble," Holly had grumbled and passed the relish. "There's poor Stevie, fresh from, pardon the expression, 'normal school' and there Daisy daughter-fucker is making Stevie's poor heart go pit-a-pat. Would Daisy like her to help her hang drapes or perhaps carry the piano upstairs at a trot? Certainly, let Stevie do it, even if it gives her a hernia."

"Hernia? Women don't get hernias," Dot said, accepting the relish.

"Some do. Never mind. Women like that should be locked up!"

"Poor Stevie. Does she still wear men's underwear?"

"Shirts anyway. How would I know about the rest?"

"How would you know about the shirts?"

"Shows through, dummy."

Why Dorothy didn't break down and live with Holly, Hope really didn't know. Neither of them really gave a minute of extra time to anyone ᵉᶦˢᵉ.

Dorothy had told them somewhat apologetically that she was still in the closet and felt she had to remain there, that her students would never believe anything she said about morality or society if she didn't. Holly had whooped, "Christ, haven't we gone beyond 'Come out, come out, wherever you are' yet? People who come out can't go back. It gives me a thrill—frees me to be rid of IT, the Big Secret. You'd suffer. So stop fussing. Keep your job, baby—so you can keep me in wine and yachts." She gave one of her flips with her hand on hip and swiveled into the kitchen to get more cheese.

And Dorothy had gone on about Bill's picking up a student and how she knew men picked up women students but she couldn't accept men picking up men students. "I suppose I should relax and say 'why not?'

If the heteros can do it, so can the gays, and if it helps both people get through their lives, why not? It doesn't matter in the universal scheme of things—like preferring cake to pie."

Holly had appeared at the doorway. "I thought you were a believer in productive sublimation! Dorothy, why don't you relax and let your common sense guide you? You know damn well that a person who is sleeping with you can't be treated like a student. Or if they, he, she is, there is resentment, hostility—in short, they, he, or she can't learn from you. The other students get the clue, feel jealous or angry, or unfairly treated, even if they don't really know what's going on. Finally, my friends, the key reason not to shack up with one's classes is that it wrecks them. Now, is there anything else I can help you on?"

After a short pause Dorothy has said, "I really can't figure out how she learned all that. As far as I know, she has been a model of propriety, if not virtue, all her teaching career."

"That's seven years and don't you forget it, baby. But," she signed, "one recalls one's passionate youth. Much could be told," she nodded wisely.

Hope sighed. As a couple she enjoyed them both; singly she didn't think she could take much of Dorothy, although she played excellent tennis. Holly she guessed she loved.

"Do you know Dorothy Roberts?" Hope asked Anna, and they spent the time before lunch trying to discover if they had any friends in common, other than Miriam and Bob Green. Miriam evidently had impressed Anna as a remarkable and somewhat frightening woman with an unbelievably kind husband who was willing to give a lot of *his* time to helping her do *her* housework. Hope changed the subject.

When Hope pulled in to the Watkins Glen State Park, the heat had been pounding the windshield for hours. She lined up with the husbands to receive the map and get instructions as three vans with what looked like thirty-six youngsters ground up, pebbles springing from their tires.

"We've got to keep away from that crowd," Hope said, slamming the door and passing Anna the map.

"What's this? How cute! A child's map! Seneca Village, Oneida Village, Mohawk Village."

"Named after Native Americans, not meant to be cute." Hope rushed the car into reverse hoping to beat a family of five to Onondaga.

"Children must love to play indians here. How do we know where to go? There must be six settlements with . . . must be . . . " Anna began to count the numbers of sites listed in each "village." Meanwhile, cars kept driving up with hot-faced men and women, and children hanging out of windows.

"Want to go to Onondaga, near the rim, see up there, the gorge trail." Hope pointed on the map. If she didn't get out of this car into some air. . . . She knew camping must seem stupid to someone who had never done it—perpetual adolescence with everyone playing leatherstocking tales while surrounded by stereos and "wash and wipes." They were driving ten miles an hour, as required, rolling up and down small lanes looking for empty campsites.

"Good lord, this is crowded! I thought people went camping to get away!" Anna's voice was high as if she had snapped out of her doze. Since Hope had taken over the wheel Anna had been silent. Now, when Hope could use some peace, she was chattering on about everything.

"There's one, Hope. There's one!" Anna shrieked, pointed and twisted in her seat as the site rolled by. "Why didn't you stop?"

"It's right at the end of the road. We'd get car lights in our eyes all night."

"Oh."

Mercifully Anna said nothing more until Hope asked her if she liked camp site 189 or 190 or 191.

"Why ask me? I don't know anything about this."

Hope quickly explained advantages and disadvantages. One spot was close to water without a good place for the car, another lacked sheltering trees, another stood too near the showers. "What looks perfect at 8 p.m. may be invaded by singers and shouters at 1:30 a.m." Hope backed the car into 190, setting it at an angle to protect them from observation.

"Just tell me what to do, so that I can help." Anna stood staring at the crowded trunk with its duffle bags, green metal boxes, white polystyrene containers. Anna tried to conceal her stupidity about how a small alpine tent might be constructed. Hope had hold of three pieces that made a sort of curve and was waiting for her to set two legs made up of three pieces each into two circular slots set within the curved piece. In triumph Anna got the two rods into the curved piece and looked up to smile at Hope as the bottom pieces fell out, banging against the rocks.

"Take it easy. You may have to start at the other end."

Anna started at the other end, fumbling, wishing to fit everything expertly into place. She couldn't believe there were so many segments that fitted into one another, hooks that attached just so, all to be held in tension on the metal frame.

Finally, to Anna's relief, Hope went off to report to the office their choice of 190. Anna supposed they'd be checked off on some list. Some camping. She had thought they'd be roughing it, but here they were with bathrooms down the road, spigots fifty yards away, picnic tables, arrows pointing to chopped wood for campers to bring back at fifty cents an armload.

A car rolled slowly by, its occupants staring at their equipment. "Are you and your husband just coming or going?"

"We've just arrived," Anna said, "that is. . . . " But the Chevrolet was already down the road. They looked as if they might pull into 191, but fortunately they didn't. There must be comething she could do now that the tent was up.

Carrying a duffle bag and a canvas sack she crouched down to unzip the tent flap. It was orange inside as the light came through, soft under her knees with the sleeping mats down under the sleeping bags. She understood why children loved this small enclosed space that made everyone in it so important. Any men and women traveling as campers had to be lovers, she decided. You could hardly avoid it in such a small place. It took pretty impressive gymnastics to change her clothes, but soon she emerged backwards out of the tent and breathed the cooler air. A cicada throbbed in the woods. That fresh-bitter pine smell again. When Hope returned Anna was sent on several missions. Soon she smelled chili cooking. Six o'clock and she was ravenous.

"How did this happen? The chili?"

Hope was setting out light chairs. "How about a bourbon? It's all I brought, except wine, that is."

"Bourbon on the rocks—possible?"

"To a restful vacation." She raised her yellow cup.

"Camping surprises me," Anna said. "Delicious."

"Don't tell me about it," Hope said quickly. "Hold your thoughts for a while; one can reject it too fast. Camp sites are different. Besides. . . . " She took a cool sip of bourbon. "It's all a little crazy. We use the plastic products of the technological revolution to let us rough it." She shrugged.

"I wasn't going to reject it," Anna said, looking hurt. "I had expected Hemingway stuff, and it's congested even, hard to find a place to be private. Not that we, I mean. . . . "

Hope was almost amused at her confusion but she was not going to try to convert an urbanite. "There is more privacy than you think." She sat back. She had to set her limits. This was supposed to be her vacation, after all, and she wasn't going to spend it defending herself. She crossed her ankles and stretched back against that stiffness that driving always gave her. "Later we can get some kindling for a campfire—just for warmth and ornament."

"I love a campfire," Anna said, closing her eyes and wondering how she was going to manage ten days. She kept running into thorns unexpectedly like a bare-legged child. "Were you a family of campers?" she asked.

Hope pushed at the pine needles with her foot. "We were not great on togetherness. Not spontaneously anyway." Soon they were talking about their families and beginning to talk about their own early lives. Hope's father, a metallurgist who travelled between New York and South America, had left her mother to follow her own interests. Her mother rode horses and showed hunters and encouraged her sons to sail and her daughter to ride with her. Anna's father knew all the train schedules from Maine to California but worked in a bank and never went anywhere. She thought of her mother and sister and their drudge contests.

"Who wins?"

"The one who never sits down."

"Is your sister younger than you?"

"Yes, but she learned it quicker."

"A natural drudge?"

Anna's laugh tapered into a sigh. "It would be funny if it weren't so bitter. . . . Anyhow, I really love to cook. It's just that the guilty-guilty bit gets tiring."

"You could always sweep the pine needles, I guess. Ready for a guilty bourbon?" As Hope reached across for her glass and looked at her directly, Anna, caught in that blue gaze, nodded 'yes,' glad not to speak. Something seemed to speed up as if her whole system had been jarred awake. Who was this woman? She would ask her other questions. She got up and went to stir the chili herself. That she knew something about.

She asked about the Coleman stove, saying it was "her field, after all." Briefly Hope showed her how to work it, how to pump it up for pressure and how to balance the flow of fuel to cook on both rings. She was alone at the stove while Hope was away getting kindling when the two cars drove up. The first car looked like Carl's station wagon at first, but, with much calling to one another and what seemed like alcoholic hilarity, the car with six tanned blond adults spilled out and led the six or seven tanned blond adolescents to the nearest camp site. By the time Hope had returned the adults had finished setting up the tent and were driving off, leaving their children.

"Can they really be leaving those kids?"

"Looks like it, Anna. Forget it. Let's have our own fire and be on vacation. It's their problem." Hope bunched up paper, setting light pieces of kindling criss-cross on top.

Anna was interested to see how their camping was going, so she wasn't surprised when the young man who had been trying to start their fire finally turned up at Hope's campfire to ask for matches. He stared at the two of them sitting before their camp fire, and after the well-expressed apologies and courtesies of the "well-bred," he made his request. With many thankings he turned and ran back to his campfire crowing and waving his matches. Soon, after laughter and elbowings and settlings against legs and cushions, they were sitting by the fire passing around a joint, but Anna didn't mention this to Hope, who might be shocked.

Hope had set up the gas light and was studying a map laid out on the table. When Hope looked up she saw that Anna had left her coffee cup at the fire and was casually taking off her shirt. She was bent slightly so that the gang of young people wouldn't see her behind the tent, but apparently she saw no reason to be concerned if Hope looked up or did not. She had lovely shoulders and full breasts now disappearing into a tee shirt for sleeping. Hope realized she was blushing, feeling like the voyeur that she was, and got up to take her shower.

She enjoyed the walk back in the darkness. Most of the camp fires were out or burning low. The tents were yellow glowing spots that outlined the dark heads and shoulders of the family groups within. She avoided using her own light and listened to her feet crunching on the path. But the damn kids were still up, sitting around talking and laughing. Someone shouted, "Quiet over there!" After a sudden pause and some giggling they shushed one another.

The young people had begun some soft singing as she zipped open the tent flap and slipped into the tent. After putting her sneakers at the door and her jeans rolled up on top of them, she slid into her sleeping bag and, with a sigh of relief, zipped it up. She was surprised at her own sigh. Was it such a strain with Anna after all? So many things that couldn't be said.

But it was always this way with straights. They simply presumed their assumptions were your assumptions. One smiled and went through the paces, acting by their rules, unable to admit or speak about basic world facts that were different. Like those arrogant heteros who drove up in their two cars and felt because they owned the world they could strew their progeny on it and booze it up down the road. She knew there were people who would say she was lucky to be let alive at all. In China and Cuba they killed homosexuals who refused to "reform." What kind of reform would that be?

The wild clanging, like garbage pails struck by banging metal, and a long scream raking her ears, jolted her awake. She struggled out of the tent and found Anna standing outside, her flashlight pointing toward the nearest camp site. Someone off to the west shouted, "For Christ sake over there. Shut up!"

Anna said quietly to Hope, "It's all right now." Her light picked up two figures, one rocking back and forward moaning, the other holding him. She clicked off her light.

"Damn well better be!"

"Don't go, Hope. They're all right now."

"How do you know?"

"I was up. A bad trip the kid had, I think. Knocked over the camp garbage pail and screamed at the sound. The others are helping him. See?"

"Drugs? Out here?"

"Where better?"

"Why are you up?"

"Coffee. I'll swear off it for the trip," Anna said, reaching for the tent flap.

"The comforts of the wholesome life," Hope grumbled.

Anna eased down in her sleeping bag and closed her eyes, apparently going to sleep on the instant. Hope lay listening to the moans of the youngster and the murmuring of his friend.

CHAPTER SEVEN

A S SOON as Hope stirred in the morning Anna sat up, gathered her
soap, washcloth, shower cap, towel, and clothes for the day and
with her knees up to her chin she slipped out of the sleeping bag.
It wasn't so easy to slither down to the front of the tent with all that gear
without jabbing Hope in some vital part, but she managed, unzipping
the tent flap and emerging without standing up too soon or she would
have lifted the whole tent off the ground. Lilliputians must have invented
alpine tents, but Hope seemed to manage smoothly, even gracefully.
Outside the bright orange tent she stood motionless. There was no sound,
then a faint crackle, a swift stirring in the bushes, then silence. She looked
up, her eyes following the line of evergreen. The air seemed even blue.
Had she ever looked at air before? Somebody painted while looking at a
mirror, not his subject. The difference between the mirror's reflection and
the scene looked at directly was said to be startling. This air was blueish,
unmistakably, and early light filtering greyish blue caught the light motes
of forest stuff floating on it to fall slowly down and settle on the forest
floor. When tears stung here eyes she realized she must be tired and began
to walk briskly to the shower place where a warm shower might pull
her together. In the middle of her shower she thought that Jamie would
probably be up by then and eating her raisin bran.

While Anna took her shower, Hope washed in the water bucket.
Sausages were cooking in the pan, oranges were out, water was just about
to boil when Anna appeared down the road looking like a kid in her jeans
with her bathing things wrapped up in her towel. Hope knew she had to
remember that Anna was a city person. How quickly she understood about
those kids and their drugs the night before. She hadn't even seemed
surprised.

Hope nodded her good morning to Anna and poured out the eggs
onto the hissing pan as she approached. With a few smooth passes of her
wooden spoon the eggs were scrambled and set onto the tin plates beside
the hot sausages. "Now, the first rule of this camp is comfort," Hope said,
as she gestured Anna to her place all set at the table. "You may not be
strong on The Nature so feel free to reject some of the Camp Director's
plans."

Anna reached eagerly to hold out her tin plate. "Gorgeous eggs! And sausages!"

Hope told Anna about a walk along the gorge that she liked to take, assuring Anna that she didn't have to walk the whole way. "But there is a pretty waterfall to see that I think you might like. Anyway, I have stacks of mystery stories stowed in the back for whenever you get bored."

Anna was still, looking down at her plate. She said without looking up, "I don't expect to be bored." She remained sitting, looking down with her hands in her lap until Hope reminded her to eat. She picked up her fork and began to eat slowly.

"Don't you like it?"

"Oh, your cooking is very good. The sausages especially. The eggs are very light, too. . . . Perhaps I should stay here and keep an eye on things while you go for your walk."

"Only if you want to. The walk is really quite beautiful. You don't have to worry about your things out camping. People really leave each other alone. Come on, get your fancy new sneakers on and let's go . . . after tea. Tea, OK?"

It was ten o'clock before they were walking steadily along the forest path. They stopped to look at the dark brown painted shelter set up for hikers along the route. Soon they were walking down the stone steps leading to the rim. They would walk along on one side toward the headwaters, cross over and then walk down the other side before they crossed over in their return. Hope wondered if Anna would manage the walk all right. They were caught for a few minutes behind an over-dressed couple as the wife tottered across stones in her spike heels. Anna stopped to look at the water falling down, cutting curling sweeps out of the rocks. She seemed oblivious to the other tourists.

They walked along a broad stone pathway that ran parallel to the rim. The rushing water soon made conversation impossible, but Anna stopped often, touching Hope's arm to show her something. As they walked upward, the erosive action of the water became quite visible and they reached a flattened area where the separate rock planes received small water falls. Soon they were ducking down and walking into a darkened tunnel. Anna was walking behind Hope, her fingertips touching the wet walls as she moved cautiously forward with Hope now around the corner out of her sight. She gulped in fear that she might get claustrophobic. It was quite dark now and the water sound had grown so that she was sure no one could hear her cry out. The water must be pounding somewhere ahead of here. As she turned the corner she saw light and sheaves of water sailing past her eyes and down to a pool below. The path she was on led behind the waterfall and there she saw Hope leaning against the wall and looking outward through the falling water. Then Hope looked back at her, waved, and walked on to the other side. There was no way to the other side unless she wanted to walk back the way she had come. People were screaming as they darted through the waterfall and scampered to the other side. A serious young Chinese couple carefully covered their cameras and proceeded steadily.

Holding to the iron railing Anna stepped cautiously along the path feeling the spray on her face as she was engulfed by the sound. Someone ran by her dashing to the other side and she stopped. This was no moment to dash through. At the center of the fall she stood back against the wall and, well under the rock roof, she looked outward through the water. Acres, pounds, tons of water were running above her head and sluicing down before her eyes, roaring over the rocks to churn beneath. As she stared through the water she could see the opposite side as if through gauze, but then, with her ears filled by the sound, she pulled her vision inward to watch the water itself, and she saw first silver and then lines of white lights flashing by her eyes. The roar of it, the rich fecundity passed by her eyes in flashing white lights, lines of white lights from the heart of life. Tears sprang to her eyes and were running down her cheeks already wet from the spray when Hope appeared at her side and put her arm around her and led her out by the hand.

They sat on a stone bench on the other side for a while, watching people running quickly through the falls as if it were a scary game in the fun house. They walked farther on to a spot where they could see the great arch of water caught by the lens of the eye, frozen to white stone in stillness, then moving again in an arching fall, and again it stood still, a pillar of roaring ice before it rushed downward again with the heartbeat.

They sat in silence watching tons of water falling into the pool below, transformed by the eye to a white ice pillar standing on its point, supporting the rock roof and those layers of rock above. Anna leaned over to put her lips close to Hope's ear. "The generosity . . . " but she was shaking her head. Hope nodded and they began to walk away from the sound.

Anna said, "When I was a child, although we were Catholic, or my mother was, she always spoke of Mother Nature. That's odd, isn't it? With a vocabulary full of Christ, God, and the Holy Ghost?" She shook her head "Here it felt right." They walked a bit farther and stopped to look back a moment. "Hope." She paused and tilted her head as she looked at Hope. "That was some 'pretty waterfall' you took me to. I almost liked it." Anna laughed, pushed Hope's shoulder and began to run down the pathway to the next overlook.

As Anna drove the next day Hope pored over the camping guide, studying its maps and reading descriptions of camping sites. They agreed that the State Parks were the best and that the more stars a privately owned camp had the worse it was for them. When their preferred state

park was filled up they went to a privately owned camp with only one
star. It seemed pleasantly remote until they parked and set up tent, and
a mammoth, many-tonned truck barreled by above their heads. They had
pitched tent just out of sight of an important state highway, a fact Hope
felt she should have seen, but Anna appeared unruffled. Apparently it
never occurred to her to blame Hope.

They pushed on next day to reach Stratford. Hope hadn't been able to
get tickets for Saturday night, but she had single tickets at the box office
for Sunday and Monday. There were touristy things they could do, of
course. Hope wanted to visit the Royal Botanical Garden and they should
"see" Stratford.

By the time they reached Stratford it was late, about five, and a drizzle
had begun. *Woodall's* led them to Homey Haven—a place that followed
the universal Pasture Principle: open up a pasture and dump mobile homes
in it. Hope drove through it hating the exposure every site imposed.
Finally, with a sigh, she pulled up at the outer-most edge of the camp
ground where woods formed one side and there was only one fully set-up
family nearby; the others seemed reserved for families who had decided
against camping this rainy week-end. Meanwhile the drizzle was getting
heavier.

"The joys of camping," Hope muttered, pulling on a yellow slicker.
"Put on Laurie's slicker, now, and try to keep dry, whatever you do."
Anna trotted around the car ready to do her usual fetch and carrying tasks.

"No, little camper, this time we have to figure this out more carefully.
Where is the wind coming from? Cooking will be miserable without a
tarp. As we drove by I figured we could use these trees to hang the tarp.
Anna, can you root out the yellow nylon cord?"

"Now we see the brilliant purpose for the clothes line; I was wondering." Anna handed the clothes line to her as Hope took out a large piece
of rubberized canvas with holes on four corners. She watched Hope
standing in the rain turning the clothes line around a branch, stringing the
tarpaulin to form a wind breaker, and got an idea. Anna walked into the
woods and was lost to Hope for minutes as the rain got heavier and Hope
was left to hang the tarpaulin herself. "Hopie?" Anna was holding up a
giant forked branch. She trudged out of the woods dragging two of them.
"What if this fork was put under this line, couldn't we stretch the tarpaulin
over here?"

"And then you could pull the rope across there . . . "

"But if you had another forked stick . . . " and Anna was gone, pushing
back into the woods.

After about half an hour of repeated conferences, Anna stood back
from their Rube Goldberg structure, a grey-green tarpaulin rigged with
yellow nylon cord and a gothic network of forked branches. "Gorgeous.
Hopie, you're brilliant."

"It might work. If the wind doesn't change. . . . "

"If it changes, we'll do another. Now I can do my cooking."

"Your cooking?"

"I feel like being useful, for a change."

"Lord knows you were, Anna; if you hadn't thought of that. . . . " Watching Anna's face Hope saw that she was drinking in praise, as if it mattered that their crazy edifice had been done by both of them, but Hope could feel the pull of their egos, each wanting to seem intelligent to herself and each other. Hope had to admit to herself that she liked to set up the tarp alone, and hadn't genuinely welcomed the first gnarled stick a drenched Anna had shoved into her hand.

Anna awoke to what sounded like the cheep, cheep of a bird. She lay still, listening. The rain must have stopped. Her shoulders felt a little stiff. She pulled on her sweatshirt. On her way to the small red outhouses she passed a child pushing herself on a swing. She was tipping her head back so her black hair almost touched the ground as she pumped herself forward. Anna remembered the day she first dared to stand on a swing. As she passed, metal rubbed against metal, grating "cheep, cheep." She wondered how Jamie was doing with her back dive. It would be wonderful if Carl really was to be transferred to New Jersey. Then she could stay in Stevensville, but that town seemed part of someone else's life.

The wild tarpaulin structure looked even more fantastic now that the sun was shining, but they enjoyed the privacy it gave them when the neighbors came out to look at the day and glanced over to see two women traveling together. Hope knew it would be preseumed they were freaks . . . lesbians, that is, unless they felt sorry for the poor, spinster schoolteachers pouring out their lonely tea together. She could hear Alix Dobkin singing with glee, "Any woman *can* be a Les . . . bi . . . *an*." She chuckled and passed Anna the milk for her tea. "So, do you have any plans for today?"

"I'm going to study the brochures and things you got when we arrived last night. Where's my knitting?"

"Knitting? I didn't know you brought any. Knitting? Out camping?"

"Why not? It's better than cards!"

"Probably is."

Soon Anna called out, "Ever been on a safari?"

"A safari? Never."

"This shows one of those habitat places where they keep the animals *au naturel*, not in cages, free—they romp on the veldt or something."

"You must be feeling better. Last night I thought sure you'd get a cold." If Anna was this enthusiastic, of course they would go.

So they went. Anna drove, singing "Born Free" while Hope navigated. Anna chattered on about how she'd like some day to go to a real safari and stay at one of the hotels in the tree . . .

"Like Treetop?"

" . . . and see the animals coming down to the waterholes in the morning to drink. I saw it once in a film. Have you ever gone to an Audubon film? I guess that's the closest I've ever been to a waterfall, for instance. Does that seem incredible to you? It's your field, for heaven's sake. Nature, I mean."

"Well—that's pretty broad, Anna. Turn right up ahead. 'Bardenhagan's Australian Safari.' Oh lord, it's probably pure kitsch. I don't think I want to see this."

Anna began to slow down and looked hesitantly over to Hope. "Nonsense, Anna, of course we'll go. We've come this far." Why did she always have to be so docile? "Don't *you* want to go, Anna?"

"Well, yes . . . I do."

"Come on, then. I'm just being difficult. Ignore it. Let me complain a little, for Christ's sake."

Anna smiled and breathed deeply. "Sure, you can complain."

Anna drove for about a mile down a dusty road before they reached fences and guards, cars parked in lines, signs directing visitors to the pet farm, to the safari, to the restaurant, to the ice cream, to the bathrooms, to the air conditioned cars for rent. A microphone commanded motorists to close their car windows and keep them closed. Air conditioned cars could be rented. Animals were not to be fed. Cars were to move slowly in lines. Hope pulled out her camera and hastily loaded it as they passed through the first fenced in area. Baboons leapt all over the car. Curious creatures, they hoisted themselves up the front window and stared in with large bulging eyes and clown mouths before they pranced onto the car hood crouching on their skinny haunches, their long arms resting on the hood.

"I want to see the lions," Anna said, watching a fat black bear amble in front of the car. Just when Hope got the movie camera going they approached two lionesses resting in the sun. A large male strolled toward the females. One of them got up and began to walk away, obviously unwilling. He followed. Their quick copulation left two children in a neighboring car staring solemnly through their windows while their father had a good laugh.

The giraffes were beautiful with long necks floating out from their slender bodies, four of them sitting serenely in a field apparently looking at the rhinoceroses. Well they might, Anna thought, remembering bestiaries. They had to be imagined by a grotesque or whimsical god, unbelievably malproportioned creatures with great lumpy horns, immense jowls, set on chunky bodies. How could they bear to live in the giraffe's world? When she saw the ostrich she cried out. Moving like a queen, her long head balancing on an extended neck, she came close to the car. Her powerful legs looked as if they should be attached to a llama. One ostrich came closer to the car in front. The car's front window was open as the driver put out his hand with peanuts. When the ostrich put its head toward the food, the window was rolled up, nearly catching the bird's head. The driver and his family were vastly amused.

Hope snorted, "Genesis!" To Anna's inquiring look she answered, "Be fruitful and multiply and replenish the earth and subdue it—have dominion, etc. That's what 'subduing' comes down to here."

"But at least there's an attempt to duplicate the animal's natural habitat, here. Still, most of the trees are dead and the shrubs are all over-browsed. Should be rotating the areas faster—keep them fresh. In nature animals can move to new pastures when they overgraze. Instead of giving them new space, I see their advertisement shows they plan to open up new lands—to display more animals—of Asia. Today Australia, tomorrow the world."

Anna could see that the Pet Farm taught children that animals were for their pleasure. When people stayed in cars it remained the animals' domain, but when the humans were let out to pat, tug, mawl as they chose, the animals were helpless. For that, only mild animals were chosen. Three peacocks, their tailfeathers almost gone, had fled to a coop top, but the mother with her pea chick stayed on the ground, and the tiny creature hopped behind its mother's stately walk. Children crowded around a cage filled with too many ducks. They pushed corn through the fence at a sleeping burro.

"This is pretty pointless," said Anna. "Let's get out of this stench."

They ate their lunch at a picnic table overlooking a man-made lake where an occasional seal glistened on a dive and swans moved, necks extended, toward a bit of bread a child tossed out. The wind was beginning to rise and their wine tasted good.

"More rain," Hope said, catching at a fluttering napkin.

"We don't care," Anna said, pouring more red wine into Hope's cup.

"We may spend a lot of time just trying to keep mud out of the tent."

"Actually we'll be inside at the theatre tonight and maybe tomorrow afternoon and evening, so let it rain on Homey Haven."

"You turned out to be a good camper, you know that?"

Anna looked pleased. "Since I discovered that camping is only steady housekeeping under adverse circumstances, and I know I can do that, I don't have any worries."

"It's not always just that," Hope said quickly.

"Why don't you stop worrying whether or not I can hack it. Just enjoy yourself. This is supposed to be your vacation."

Hope sighed and put her feet up, "Right. All the comforts. OK, little lady." She looked at Anna, who only smiled.

It turned out to be true. It did rain some of every day they were at Stratford, and they did spend much of their time trying to keep mud out of the tent. At one point Anna asked, "Do you think camping is a perverse taste? Why should I enjoy this? While I can *do* it, I don't like steady housekeeping at home. Let's face it, I resent it."

Hope laughed and almost hugged her, but quickly picked up a towel on the table behind Anna. "When I went on my first canoe trip I was amazed at how much time the experienced campers spent in washing their clothes and pinning them up on little clothes lines. One woman, a big Byzantine scholar from the Sierra Club, seemed to spend all her time taking things out of big bags and putting them into small ones.

Tobermory turned out to be the most beautiful provincial park they had visited, with widely separated woodland sites. They discussed staying longer but Hope said she was anxious to get back to her job. Anna said she was growing fond of their little tent. She couldn't believe the lack of recriminations, the lack of criticism. She wondered if most married people lived without criticism and defense, harsh words of contempt that one remembered and flushed at. But of course she didn't speak of this.

Hope had been upset about the safari place, but that was an important subject to her, Anna realized. Hope was so resourceful, always taking upon herself the full weight of responsibility. Anyway they were doing pretty well for two strangers, Anna thought. Anna had always liked to share her thoughts and feelings fully with her friends, had done so since she was a child. Although she hadn't been one of those who told her girl friends everything, she always had had one favorite girl friend even after she began to go steady with Paul. "Have you any really close friend, Hope? Woman friend, I mean."

Hope appeared startled to Anna. "No, not really, now."

"Did you used to? I always had a close friend before we moved to Stevensville, even though Carl didn't like her. A close friend is a comfort."

"Can be. I've taken to having modular friends."

"Models?"

"No—modular friends—word out of architecture—not one friend for all seasons—one for tennis, one for the theatre, that way."

"Efficient."

"Has its drawbacks. We better not forget that we have to get up at four a.m. to make that ferry."

"And everything takes longer, I know," said Anna. "OK, Director, but this place is special. I vote we come back next summer."

They reached Manitoulin Island about 8:30. Anna had to guess because she kept forgetting to wind her watch. The date, even the day of the week, she had lost. She just knew she was happy to be in the car driving with Hope and she didn't care when they got where. They had everything they wanted with them, didn't they? She enjoyed their long conferences about the places they would stay, and loved Hope's extended comments whenever she got talking, except when she got fierce. Often she seemed exasperated and Anna hoped she was glad to talk about things. From the description in the camping guide Happy Dales seemed ideal except for the two stars. They found the "natural site" was a dusty road through a rutted field crowded with laundry lines and cars, motorboats on saw horses, bicycles, shopping carts, trailer after trailer, some with little fenced walks, a sign, two gnomes, a stray elf and a deer in front, and the Virgin in blue poised before an upended bath-tub. Many families were sitting at the breakfast table and their children were running around the wheels of cars as Anna kept driving up and down the lanes as if she was looking for an empty site, but actually because she had lost her way.

"Go left, honey." The word was out before Hope knew it. Anna didn't seem to have noticed, she was so absorbed in looking at people's private lives.

"I guess that's going to be the way it is on this island. Do you think, Hope? Bad luck!?"

Once they were out on the main road again, Hope said, "See that plain sign—Camp Lakewood? Follow that. About ten miles. *Woodall's* says good things about it."

"Read 'em to me."

"Do you have any vacant campsites?" Hope asked the young woman behind the counter.

"Most of 'em is taken—around the lake."

"It's pretty crowded. Do you have any other spots?"

"How many of you?"

"One car, two people," Hope said as the woman tipped her head to see by Hope and glimpse the child reaching for the potato chips.

"There's the woodland loop, but it's far to go for water."

"Where's that?" And as the woman pointed, Hope decided that she liked the place. This woman didn't seem to care whether Hope was traveling with a woman or an orangutang. They had ice and charcoal to sell. The kids ran in and out, but the woman saw everything, accepted change as she spoke to Hope, said, "No more, now," under her breath to the child, and smiled at Hope. "Most people like the lake, but the woodland loop is very new and I like it."

The woodland loop offered the first genuine privacy they had had since they started the trip. Hope conferred with Anna on the merits of each site with much walking about and weighing of facts and possibilities: sun against level tent site, possible neighbors against proximity to a road. Finally, with the satisfaction of partners agreeing on property, they settled on one large camp site with places for the dining room, their sitting room, tent and laundry line, with a gorgeous spot to hang the tarpaulin without forked sticks. After setting up camp they had a brunch superior to anything at Le Coq d'Or and retreated to their orange home for a sound sleep.

When Anna's eyes blinked open the tent was suffused with orange light. She was steaming inside her sleeping bag. Sleepily she reached for Laurie's swim suit, put it on, scribbled "gone swimming" on a bit of paper and stepped out of the tent. Hope's hair had looked moist, flattened against her forehead, but she was as relaxed as a child.

Anna soon felt the shock of the cold water sliding over her shoulders and back, tingling against her scalp and ears. She gasped against the chill, thrashed about, felt mud slipping beneath her feet and then dived into a long swim about the bottom of the lake, opening her eyes beneath the water to see light shafts behind black eel grass waving in the grey-green water. She shot up to the surface blowing water from her mouth and gulping air. She turned over on her back to rest, went limp and watched the clouds.

She remembered swimming out on some lake with a rubber ring around her—her mother on one side and her father on the other. One time her mother was treading water, her white arms floating toward Anna as she backed away, coaxing Anna to swim toward her. All she wanted was to reach those arms that pulled away as she moved forward. She must have been about two then.

She took a few long back strokes and then rested. Her own children adored the water. She felt her legs relax and settle lower and lower in the water until she was almost floating standing up. With a smooth turn onto her stomach she floated, then jack-knifed down and swam along the lake-floor again. Playing.

Beautiful long strokes beside her, the high elbow, lines of water running down the tanned shoulder, glistening, blond hair looking brown, soaked flat, wet eyebrows darkened. Hope's stroke was almost professional. She dived and Anna felt her ankle pulled by a beautiful fish. She gulped air and went searching down in the grey-green world for a mer-foot, but Hope was gone in strong strokes toward the shore. Anna could never catch her, so she turned over on her back and floated, feeling the lovely limpness floating along her bones.

Playing. Floating. Slow turns onto her back and the cool dive down. Then resting limp like a piece of drifting grass. She heard something like a sizzling along the water surface, raised her head to see a yellow prow moving too near her head.

"Look what I have. Pile in."

She tried to pull herself up the side and almost dumped Hope in the water. "For Christ's sake, honey, don't grab the gunwales near you. Grab the far ones. That's it." Hope was spread-eagled in the canoe, legs braced against opposite sides, holding both gunwales, giving instructions.

With a giant heave Anna scissor kicked, half-throwing herself across the canoe, to collapse gasping and laughing on the floor of the canoe as it rocked madly.

"Very tippy," Hope said mildly, stretching a hand out to Anna, then a paddle.

Hope's instructions were brief but adequate, for soon they were moving in a straight line toward an island. As they paddled Hope said, "Do you realize that we are in a lake that is in an island within a larger lake? I want to get us to that tiny island. Then I can say I have stood on an island in a lake in an island in a lake."

"I am too busy to follow that. Am I holding it right?"

"You're doing fine. Amazing, an island in an island in a lake."

"The house that Jack, oops, almost—my balance."

"Take it smooth, with long strokes. You don't have to lean that far forward. You warm enough?"

Anna soon realized that Hope was compensating in some way for her strokes, but didn't dare shift her weight to look, the Fiberglass canoe seemed so responsive to any weight shift. She had heard canoeing was fun, but that it was so smooth, so sexy over the glassy water, no one had ever told her. They were getting closer to the rock outcropping that Hope was calling an island.

"Now when we get close to this island don't you do a thing. Just sit there quietly, rest your paddle on the gunwales, if you want, and I'll hop out." In a second it was done; Hope stepped lightly out holding the canoe so that it wouldn't dance. She moved to the bow and took the painter out, held it and looked at Anna. Laurie's suit just barely did the job. Anna's wet hair was standing up in peaks. She looked glad to get out of the canoe and to stretch out on a warm rock, which she did promptly, leaving Hope holding the rope.

"Come on, camper, let's beach the canoe more securely." Anna turned from her inviting spot and together they pulled the canoe up farther onto the rocks. Then, while Hope sat on the rock's high point looking out over the water, Anna lay flat on her back on the hot rock and baked. She seemed to drift off softly into sleep. Hope kept wanting to look at her, to let her eyes move along her arm, across the delicate skin below her breasts, pulled snug in an inverted V just below her ribs.

Hope looked across at the camp. A few trailers were visible, some wood smoke, some people swimming, all in plain view, and that wasn't the only reason she had to stay away. She lay with her back against a rock to let Anna sleep a while. Then she touched the warmed skin of Anna's arm. Anna's eyes flew open and she sat up suddenly, almost bumping their heads. "Mmf, I've been asleep."

"We have serious business to attend to."

"What's that?" Anna said, leaning over the water to splash her face.

"We have some wild rice to see, some water lilies and arrowhead lilies to visit, and maybe some Indian water pipes to find.

"Indian water pipe is usually in the woods, I hear, but the wild rice you can see plainly. See those reedy-looking grasses over there?"

The next hour ranked among Anna's favorite times to remember during the difficulties of the next winter. They paddled softly among the grasses, reached down to pluck the spikelets with their tightly-wrapped green husks. They opened them and held the feathery styles, the pale beige fluff and tiny rice grains in the palm of their hands. Their canoe slipped among the grasses where the bullhead water lilies grew. Anna had thought the fat green leaves and yellow blossoms would be torn by the canoe, but they slid beneath it to bounce up nodding on the other side. Gathering rice must involve hours for a mere handful. "No wonder wild rice is expensive."

Hope smiled. "Maybe we can buy some wild rice while we're here. The Manitoulin Indians probably gathered it once."

Later that evening they were sitting under the trees, their small cups resting on the arms of their chairs. The breeze was coming off the lake and Anna was remembering the soft paddle sounds, the occasional thump of her paddle against the bow, when she caught a whiff of the fresh water smell. Hope was smiling with her head tipped back and her eyes half-closed.

"What is in that fresh water smell, I wonder." Anna's voice was dreamy. A pinch of dark eel grass, a bit of salt, dashes of cool water running, sliding over sleek scales. They must flash silver, deep down. Not water on still fish, like the wall-eyed things on ice, staring in fish markets. It had to be water as the fish dart.

A trembling, wobbling sound. Not an owl. Anna looked her question.

"Called a loon. The Common Loon."

"Eerie . . . wonderful." Cicadas were throbbing nearby and that light, trembling sound again.

Hope had thought about the existential loneliness of humans on the earth, unable to communicate with another species, wistfully hoping for humanoids elsewhere, thinking of their own deaths, envying the sheep or cat that has no such awareness. Still, to her, human loneliness was greatly diminished by hearing other creatures—by knowing the loon was seeking its food nearby, that the male cicada was making his song in the heat. That he did it by vibrating abdominal membranes only made his life more real to her.

A sputtering roar, bouncing wheel and dust exploded by her ear as a small Honda shot down the cart track toward the north.

Hope jumped up angrily, sputtering. "It's just those boys," Anna said, pulling her knitting out of an embroidered bag.

"What boys? They shouldn't let them run that thing," Hope shouted as the small engine stopped, turned, and came back, two boys clinging like monkeys to its back.

"They must be a group, five or six, living down the way. I saw them before." They had looked at her with interest as she walked by to get water. She supposed they helped out around the place.

"Boys? They must be seventeen to twenty-four." It hadn't occurred to Hope that it might not be safe on the Woodland Loop. When they walked later after dinner to get their showers, Hope went with Anna. As they came back through the darkening woods, a young man was seated casually on the motorcycle under a tree, rolling a cigarette on his knee, "Have a good swim?"

"Yes, thanks," said Anna without stopping.

"Saw you laying on the rock out there," he said, pulling deeply on his cigarette.

"It was very pleasant," Anna said, hoping she sounded every year of her thirty. Hope could think of nothing to say and frowned. He walked along beside them, seated on his motorcycle, pushing it along with his foot," You're not Canadians. I see from your plates." They continued to walk in silence.

"Well, see you around," he called as he roared off, his back wheel-light bouncing up and down over the rough car track.

When they reached their tent, Anna went ahead as usual to undress for the night. Hope walked around outside. The orange tent glowed in the darkness. Anna had left on the big flashlight as she found her night things.

Hope whispered to her to turn off the light. As the light went out Hope saw a brief flicker off to the north down the cart track. Rapidly she walked toward it. She heard laughter, perhaps five or six young men. Six husky men could converge on their tent as they slept. All anyone had to do was slash through the plastic with a sharp knife. She picked up a couple of heavy rocks and brought them into the tent with her. Anna was sitting up. "What's wrong?"

Hope spoke to the dark shape, "I won't put on the light. It's nothing."

"Must be something."

"Those guys have been watching us."

"So? Let them. What's that to us?" Anna was settling down in her sleeping bag.

Hope decided not to undress as she slipped off shoes and left them near her ankles. She lined up the rocks and her flashlight just within reach of her fingers. She lay still. Anna's breathing became regular, then deep and slow until she could not hear it at all.

She heard the murmur of voices first, then a twig snap. The voices became quite clear. She flipped herself out of the sleeping bag and crouched listening, one hand seeking the flashlight and the other a rock. The voices retreated, some laughter, more murmuring, silence. She lay on her elbow listening as the loon's voice trembled from far beyond the island in the lake of their island.

CHAPTER EIGHT

A S THEY drove into Algonquin Provincial Park, Anna knew that
she was being unreasonable. The next day was the 19th, home on
21st, and Hope had been wonderful. She had been generous and
tolerant of a greenhorn. She had taught her whatever she wanted to learn
about putting up a tent, canoeing, bird lore, flowers, rocks. They went
everywhere with Peterson's bird guide and somebody else's guide to the
flowers. They had gone to good plays at Stratford, had seen what tourists
see and more than most. The whole thing had been very pleasant. Now
they were heading toward a park that had nature films at night, guided
hikes with little brochures, and it was all wonderfully informative. Too
informative.

When she had remarked that Hope had an incredible appetite for
facts, Hope had answered, with an abrupt laugh, "Just carrots." Anna
had wondered, but one couldn't intrude on Hope. Anna couldn't understand why even Hope's gentle ways were irritating her. Too much time
with the same person, she supposed. She imagined Carl coming toward
her, his tight tee shirt riding up over his belly. "Coming home to Poppa?"
and she felt faint with anxiety. She didn't think it was too much time with
Hope. Often she was completely contented just to be sitting with her
somewhere in a car or after dinner.

Anna remembered their visit to the Rock Shop to see the minerals
of the area. While Hope was bending over some jewelry at the other end of
the shop, a small white-haired woman had taken Anna's arm and told
her about the Association of Senior Citizens that ran the shop. From her
she learned that all older people in Canada were given a pension even if
they were married women who had never worked outside the home. She
had to think. Women had the money to leave their husbands if they
wanted to. The lined and ravaged face with the film-covered eyes cracked
into peals of laughter. Those old people with their thriving business,
white-haired people singing on a bus, taking their trips with their profits.
Their freedom with their age. Anna thought, conjugal duties for shelter.
Meals and service for shelter. The world went by money, but Anna went
by barter, like most wives. In kind, that was not kind. Her brain began
its tiring round of considerations: jobs she could do that had no future or
interest, or jobs of interest that required training she could not afford.
And the children. Her mother had called them "hostages to fortune,"

a prissy phrase that terrified her now. She, with them, might be held hostage, without work, without money; she might as well be bound to Carl's bed. Her fortune as his hostage.

Anna settled back as she drove. She had done most of the driving between Manitoulin and Algonquin. For one who knew Central Park as "natural" they had driven, she thought, through astonishing terrain. They had gone through lush corn country, north through lake country, and then through the country of the Canadian rock shield where pines grew out of rocks. A mountain top at the timber line. Somebody at a gas station said the astronauts had trained there for rock recognition before their moon trip. Suppose the moon minerals had been different? Hope had appeared amused. "Because your friend, Mother Nature, has, as far as anyone knows, the same laws on the moon that she follows anywhere in the universe—here or fifty galaxies out." Then Hope seemed to think of something else and became detached, unreachable.

It seemed to Anna that they were driving directly toward a grey massing of clouds. Hope had said that in rain forests or heavy storms it was wise to dig a trench around the tent if one wasn't on high ground.

Holding the map of Algonquin Provincial Park, Hope directed them toward camp sites set around a lake. Anna drove slowly observing the ways people coped with the problems everyone shared: sun, rain, privacy, warmth, wind, spatial arrangements, laundry lines and so on and on. All the details of living were transplanted repeatedly into new plots of ground. The yellow hat and the green hat conversed about the familiar list of negatives and positives.

"Stop here, Anna," and Hope was out of the car as soon as Anna's foot went down on the emergency brake. After they had set the tent up, a matter of ten minutes work now, Hope went around from task to task like a wound-up toy. Suddenly she stopped. "What are you doing?"

"Digging small trenches around the tent as I was taught."

Hope stood still, looked up and around her, "You're right." She nodded emphatically, "You're damn well right. Let me do it." She came to Anna with her hand out for the shovel. Anna looked up with sweat breaking out on her temples. "Nope, I'm doing this. Why don't you fix us some lunch; I'm getting hungry." Hope turned and went immediately to the red ice box.

As she carried things to the table and passed Anna, Hope said, "Want to go canoeing? Some beautiful inlets and places to explore on the map? Or swimming?"

Anna just grunted as she turned the corner and began the last trench. She wanted to be sure that if the storm was as big as it looked it would be, the water would run off the hillside and off the tent into those generous channels.

When she was finished she walked toward Hope, taking off her gloves. "Think I'll just loll in that hammock you got. You said you brought along some mysteries?" How could she wish to escape from the escape she was on? Hope would feel this was a reproach, but how could it be? Hope had done everything she could.

Hope returned with a small stack of mysteries, left them by the hammock after she set it up and went off with the car. She wished she could read a brisk mystery, but she couldn't sit still. She ended up washing the car down by a brook. Of all the stupid, unproductive things to do, this one marked the bottom. On her tombstone, let it be writ: "Out in the Canadian woods, she washed her car." Tomorrow she would go birding, at least. Why hadn't she thought of it? She sat by the brook and watched for the shadows of fish. When she returned with the car hours later, Anna was in a fresh, yellow flowered shirt looking scrubbed, her hair still wet. She was sauteing onions in butter. "That smells marvelous." Hope set out the flatware. "What are you planning?"

"Just thought up a new recipe. You wait." Anna chuckled. "Plenty marvelous, I bet." She had been resting in the hammock reading one of those mysteries when she thought of the cold, barbecued chicken Hope had bought. It would be dry. Before her eyes in technicolor like a *Ladies' Circle* advertisement she saw sauteed onions, whole tomatoes cooked down, then the chicken simmering. Excellent.

As she busied herself about the stove, Anna said, "Tell me about Joseph Hansen."

"Who?"

"Author of two of those mysteries you took out of the library."

"Don't know much. Just one of his other books."

"All his mysteries have the same hero?"

"Haven't noticed."

"Homosexual, isn't he?"

"How should I know? Doesn't the bookflap show his picture with his wife?"

"So?" Anna appeared to concentrate intently on the rice just starting to simmer.

"Well, he writes a good mystery. I don't care about his private life." This was going to be an incredible conversation, playing with alphabet soup. She should have brought a small TV for Anna instead of books. Then she could watch the Waltons. Hope was bone tired. Why had she thought she could stand this?

"Actually I was impressed," Anna said, turning down the gas to hold the simmer.

"At what? That a gay writer—if he is gay—could write a good story?" This was becoming intolerable.

"Well, no—that a straight writer would describe his gay hero so . . . so appreciatively. What's his name, Barnstormer, no—the insurance claims investigator—Brandsetter. Never seen a homosexual described as anything but a sickie." She banged her fork on the edge of the pot and firmly

covered the rice. "Want a drink? Love a bourbon. Never could afford
Scotch to get used to it."

Hope began to talk rapidly about a really good scotch that Anna
might like, her mind spinning to a new fix. Obviously her first reading was
off.

"You know, Hope, I always thought the Chinese I knew were very
quiet people. They had no juvenile delinquency and no crime. But I just
read in a book by an Asian American that they shout at each other, really
yell—all the time in their families—and they don't report crime to the
whites. We think they are quiet and crimeless. Do you think that's the
way we are about homosexual people?"

"That they have more crime than we thought?"

"No, Hopie, don't be dense. That we don't know anything about
them—that straight people report them to us. Hansen was unusual, I mean,
in his reporting. I guess I've never met one. How would you ever, I wonder. Have you ever met one?"

"Yes . . . one. Say, when should we figure on dinner? It smells hea-
venly."

"Have a little sweetener. We have to give the rice time." Anna poured
a little more bourbon in Hope's cup. "These are wee cups anyhow. But
what was he like?"

"Who?"

"The homosexual you knew."

"Nice guy. In publishing. Said an interesting thing." Hope propped
her sneakers against a tree trunk as she considered ways to derail the
current subject. "We'd been talking about Women's Lot and he said,
'You girls kill me. I would love to stay home and have someone take care
of me. You don't know when you're well off.' "

"That one. What did you say?"

"I said, 'You would choose to stay home. Most women are put there.
Period. And the house is nailed shut.' "

"What'd he say?"

"He ordered another drink."

"That's it. I don't get it. So and so is a 'man's man'—now what's that
mean? Carl's a man's man, but he'd kill anyone who meant that the
wrong way. And he sure isn't a woman's man, really. Let's get off this
topic."

"Good idea," Hope thought fervently.

"What I mean is," Anna said, pouring herself a touch more bourbon,
"if that's really a man's man . . . the only way to enjoy living with a man
like that, I mean like Carl, is to become Mrs. Hemingway or a masochist.
I know plenty of women have made it to both. But it's like two different
cultures—you're trained all your life to be Little Miss Muffet; then you're
yoked to Tarzan, or someone trying to be Tarzan, and supposed to enjoy
it. Plenty of women do. It's just me. I'm inflexible." She swallowed

heavily. "And having answered it, I ask, why didn't you ever marry, Hope? I guess you didn't ever."

"Never found a good reason to. Shelter, warmth, sex, interest—I can have all that without being bound to a boss. I can 'lif dat bale and tote dat barge' without being told to. I know most women think they're partners with their husbands—but why are they washing dishes while their husbands are reading the newspapers?" Give or take a few crucial elements that was the truth, but she couldn't be expected to say the whole truth talking to a straight.

And, sure enough, Anna did ask about children, and there they were in the Canadian woods talking about why Hope wasn't interested in spending ten years around the house listening for her children's baby witticisms. But Anna was suddenly orating, pointing toward Hope with her spoon, about to drop a reddened onion on the ground.

"If women can't get organized to cope with the care of their children, they'll never be able to get out of the house to live out whatever the hell their other talents are." She returned the spoon to the pot and stirred vigorously. "Look, I'm thirty. Like millions of women I've lopped off a critical ten years—I've got to start with the twenty-year-olds in any work I try for. Now what *we* know, nobody wants. And it's eighty times worse for fifty-year-old women who are suddenly without husbands. We've learned plenty, but who wants it? The economy uses us but just counts us out." She stopped, looked at a squirrel holding his paws up to his muzzle as his long tail shuddered. He dashed up into a branch that bobbed and swung with his weight. "Hope, I really brought my luggage to the Canadian Woods, didn't I?"

Hope shook her head. "Independence is the big thing. Well, what would you like to do?" As Anna told Hope about her early life, Hope felt it began to explain that uneven quality she often felt with her—one minute child, one minute mother. The early years of bookishness and athletics had simply been shelved as she lived out her mother's pattern without building her own vocabulary of life possibilities. It was as if Anna's language hadn't grown with her as she matured. She was like an adult Asian-American who found that her vocabulary in her mother-tongue was that of a child.

She could not speak, in her childish language, what she knew, as an adult, as Anna had no way of living out what her experience should permit. She had to go back to square one, without funds or even possibilities at the moment.

"Anyway, I can be a chef in a Campside restaurant, I'll bet."

Hope was sitting at the camp table, her fork clenched in her fist like a famished child out of Oliver Twist. Anna doled out the rice and chicken, "OK, Olive, *bon appetit*."

Hope's fork danced at the edges of the rice, pushing a rice grain and nudging the chicken. "This looks marvelous."

"Told ya. See! Now taste it." Anna sat back, her arms folded, a big smile beginning.

Hope tasted, rolled her eyes to the top of the tarp. "Heaven! Can I keep you?"

"After a meal like that—coffee?" Hope asked.

"Good, I'll get it."

"My treat. And somewhere in the larder we have real coffee, too, not instant." She began to rummage in the trunk of the car.

After a week of tea the coffee tasted like a rich dessert. Very lightly Hope lifted a few strands of Anna's hair away from her face. "Your hair looks fluffy." Anna smiled and turned her face toward Hope's hand, but Hope got up quickly, her hand dropping to her side.

"Did I burn you?" Anna expected a laugh, but the face that looked down at her was not amused.

Hope poured out the heated water into one plastic bucket and then went for the cold rinse water. Her back was to Anna when she felt a hand on her shoulder. "We haven't much longer, have we? Will you be glad to get back?"

"Yes, very glad." The hand was withdrawn. Hope kept her back to Anna, and as Anna handed the plates to her Hope washed them extra thoroughly. After she had set the buckets to one side to dump later on the fire, she turned to Anna, whose head was bent over the table as she put things together under the plastic cover. She stood beside her a moment and then gently touched her chin, tipping it up so she could see her face. "I have loved our trip, Anna. It's just . . . that I have things . . . worrying me. I need to get back to attend to them, that's all."

Anna looked directly at her for a second and then tipped her head aside, looking up. "Hope, I know you are the weather-lady, but according to my city bones we are going to have one terrific storm, or hadn't you noticed?"

Hope looked about her. The leaves were showing their backs as a wind carried them upward. The air was going chill. "Damn right. Where have I been?" No need to ask. She knew where she'd been.

They scurried about putting away the stove, folding chairs.

"I feel a drop," Anna called from the car where she was stashing the dried provisions. "A fat one. Look at the lake." The surface of the water was ruffling and white tips gleamed on rising waves.

Hope was checking out the tent stakes when Anna shouted, "All campers into their tents," and with a quick duck she dived through the tent flap. Hope followed quickly and just as they zipped up the tent the rain began to fall steadily.

"Listen to that!" Anna was opening the window-flap to peer out. "It is one gigantic downpour. Listen!" Rain thumped on the plastic fly that rested on top of the tent. Hope pushed against the side. "We'd better put those bags up where the wind is coming from, to give the tent more weight at these corners."

Then they lay flat in their warm sleeping bags staring up at the darkened tent roof two feet above their eyes, listening to the wind and the slashing down rain. They could hear it pattering on the trees as it streamed down the trunks, poured into the channels around the tent and began to run off in rivulets toward the lake.

"Ha! and we're dry, Hopie. We're real campers! And I dug those channels. Ha!" Her 'ha!' was triumphant over all those who had told her she was cute and sweet and all those who wanted to protect this dear little bundle. She shrugged out of her jeans. "Jesus, what a storm," Anna said with satisfaction, and snuggled down into her sleeping bag.

Hope listened to the boughs creaking and bending, whipping branches as the tapping and the snuffling of the wind like small animals pulled and nibbled at the tent, scrabbled across its surface like anxious squirrels, whined at the cords that held the tarp and snapped at it when the wind caught it in an updraft. A metal pail from somewhere clattered against stone as it fell. Thumps, creaks, swishing branches and the frantic animal sounds of the wind.

"Christ, Hope, it's marvelous. . . . Are you lying there worrying?" Anna was on her elbow looking down at Hope, "Are you?"

And suddenly Hope felt Anna's soft mouth firmly on her lips, then kissing her cheek. Hope struggled up on her side, one hand touching Anna's waist, when in the first crack of lightning Hope saw Anna's face, pale with glittering eyes. "I can't bear it, Hope." Her head, pounding with her own resistance and whatever Anna's words were . . . her head splitting, hardly hearing the spinning soft words as another rifle cracked overhead and the water thudded on the tent . . . pulled down to the only place on earth she wished to be, Hope sank down to kiss that warm mouth and hold, hold, hold that firm body arching up to her. The wind circled and snapped at the tent. Breathless, Anna heard Hope's long sigh, and the rain poured down. Anna's hands touched Hope's face, her eyelids, her cheek bones, feeling where the shadow was beneath the bone, touching her ears, her mouth, pulling her closer to touch that gentle mouth she had wanted—but, for almost the space of a lightning flash, desperate, baffled.

But "Anna! Anna!" Hope's whispers were in her neck, soft breath was in her ears as she struggled free of Anna's arms, bending above her, scooping her up for an instant as she bent her head down, running kisses along Anna's throat and then slipping Anna's shirt free so that it fell to either side as her hands cradled her breasts and freed them. For a second Anna saw herself locked within the darkened tent as the heavens cracked fire, herself plunging toward darkness. But Hope murmured her name over and over as her hand slid down her sensitive inner thighs and her tongue lightly touched her breasts. They were painfully hard as that burning tongue touched her nipples, circled them, and she felt Hope's sucking mouth full down upon her breast, pulling gently upon it. Her inner body felt like a harp-string plucked, vibrating to the harpist's muscular hand, just before the warm strokes slid between her thighs. A flaming torch was set to the soles of her feet, lapping the backs of her legs, scorching her spine in a gasping fiery sweetness as her streaming body sought an ever more rigid arch of delight.

Hope touched that hardened secret tongue with her own delicate one, and in cascades of warmth Anna felt Hope's strong tongue diving within her as her own body gave way and gave way, wanting to swallow up and include and contain all of her lover that could be given. Then, caught and clenching, struggling close to pain in her avidity, she knew the high flute-note of pleasure increasing and increasing until it filled her brain and body together with exquisite feeling, and all other sounds were lost within her own long cry of anquished delight. Hope held her as she sobbed and the rain pounded down above their heads. In the storm their small tent floated out peaceably on the warm rivers of darkness. It was all so simple. Anna sighed. Whatever that trouble had been . . . and she almost smiled. She kissed Hope's cheek and mouth with her wet face.

"No, Anna, I'm all right."

"I know better." Anna lightly touched the tightened nipple with a soft hand. The tip of her tongue touched Hope's breast and, as she leaned down, brushed Hope's eyelashes and licked the corners of her eye-lids. Her hands loved to be palms, flat and moving over the softness and the bones of Hope's body, so surprisingly smooth. She had expected strangeness but this was her own loved country. She wished to see as the blind must see. The hollow at the hip, the smoothness of the inner thigh. She wanted to memorize the body and, putting trust in her hands loving what they touched, she followed Hope's turning, rising body, her own hands sliding and generous.

Hope led her down another journey and, just when she was lost, a new stage opened before her and that glowing body led her on. She felt that she followed an illuminated torch down warmed serpentine corridors until her own body tensed with the tightened stretch of the mighty cavern walls. With a quick breath in-drawn the powerful muscles clenched and the strong body moved against her in a long embrace, a long arching bridge extending onward and onward to the new land. As they held one another Anna felt Hope's eyelashes wet on her cheek. The world was no longer rolling countryside, a timberline, a rock shield, not even a nation. It pulsed beneath her palm within the circle of her arms, against her cheeks. And when Hope's hand moved slowly along her thighs and up to touch her breast, Anna felt that sudden tightening in her nostril as she gasped. Again her dry mouth was gulping and famished, heat pouring down her back, feeling Hope's muscular back and strong arms, the smoothness of their skin, moving against one another the length of their bodies. That leap to her throat seemed only to need Hope's lightest touch and she was straining, craving, like a child whimpering for more. And her arms circled the world that mattered, rocking, smoothing, holding—lovers' country.

Finally, Anna slipped into a dream of floating on a long stream past the land of Huckleberry Finn, where people lazed in the sun naked, their long hair floating on the river, and small dogs and children rolled in the long grass on the edge of the water. She knew it must be late when she woke up because the tent glowed orange from the sun on its roof, the storm long past. She wondered if Hope was shocked at her. She put off getting up. Hope must be outside somewhere. She heard her moving and the aluminum pans clanking on the stove. She lay there listening to the sput and sizzle as strips of bacon were started. Hope must know she was awake or she wouldn't have started cooking. Some bird began an intense song phrase. To her it sounded like, "Gimme, Gimme, Gimme." She rolled over on her face with hot cheeks.

"So? In there." Hope's head was in the tent.

Anna looked up, "Hello. I'm getting up."

Hope was beside her. "Good," and kissed her lightly. She felt that softness at Hope's mouth, touched her breast and her breath quickened. Her mouth was open, greedily sucking at Hope's lips before she stopped herself. "I'm sorry. I don't know . . . " She was almost sobbing. "What is this? I'm acting crazy. Hope, stop me."

Hope laughed and just held her, kissing her face and her throat. "Don't worry. It's wonderful. But we have to eat—food. Or at this pace we can't survive. Come on, woman. Out of the lair before we get started again."

"Hope, I am started. Come here."

But Hope pulled her out of the tent half-dressed and gestured toward the bucket of cold water at the tent entrance. "Cool water for you." But Hope had to turn away herself when she saw Anna's slim back and tousled chestnut hair leaning over the blue bucket. At this rate they would have to spend the day in the tent before they could act like civilized humans or return to civilization. Return. The thought made her stomach drop. She had planned the trip so well, aiming to get through it in cool chastity. She felt Anna's arms around her from behind her and Anna's lips sucking her ear. "God damn it, woman, I'm cooking!" Hope jumped up.

"Yes, indeed." Anna nodded wisely and handed her the plates to fill with bacon and eggs.

CHAPTER NINE

THEY sat side by side looking out over the lake as they ate their breakfast. The blue clarity of the air after the storm felt like clear water rinsing Anna's mind. Small birds on the opposite shore were picking at food near a rock. Tufts of blue smoke rose above the woods in the hills above the shore. Someone's cabin had a beige window frame. She felt as she had when she went to her first play and, after the curtains parted, she saw a scrim hanging before the stage set. And when the scrim rose, a film had been washed from her eyes, and she saw details of the back set, its balcony, a battered table with a bottle on it, the street in the foreground, someone leaning on a door-frame pinning a small carnation to his button hole.

Details that had been blurred in her mind jumped forward as significant. She could see possibilities, details, questions that had not seemed questions before. She had thought she knew her world and its edges, but in the storm she had been blown across the scalloped edges of her world to some point on a hillside where countries and lakes rolled vast and green below her. The drop from that cliff across was sheer. She could stare down at people like beetles crawling among the rocks as the water boiled below, but she saw no fences, no roads, no borders. Shivering slightly in the morning chill she put her hand around her hot cup of tea. "What kind is this?" She just wanted to hear Hope's voice.

"Morning Thunder."

"You made that up."

"No, on the grave of my brother's turtle, I did not. I found it last night when I dived for the coffee and set it aside for this morning. You chilly?" Hope tucked a warm wool shirt around her. "Gives me a chance to hold you without scaring the Indians."

Anna leaned toward her as Hope's arm circled her. "Hope, I feel like an addict. You're my addiction. . . . Have you felt like this often? No, don't answer that."

But over cups of steaming tea the ancient lovers' questions had to be asked and answered. What did you think of me when we first met? When did you first know how you felt? Did you know that I wanted you when I turned away that time? What did you think when I asked you . . . ? Did you know that I meant . . . ? Then as the Indian family hung their

79

sleeping bags out to air, mother and daughters fixed breakfast, and father went off with two buckets for water, they still sat in the sun asking and answering, reciting, though they hardly knew it, the litany of urgent questions to which the answers are always different and always the same.

Anna suddenly ducked her head and whispered "I want to be closer." Hope nodded, and when the Indian family disappeared into their large tent for breakfast Hope took Anna's hand and they slid into their own bright home.

"It's like living inside an orange," Anna murmured, "like being cradled inside an orange section."

"Hmmm, only no pits."

"But Hope, when did you first know that you liked women . . . um . . . better than men."

"Always," and she circled around Anna's back cupping her in warmth as they spoke softly, and their differences and similarities were gently limned in water colors for one another, not in hard edges which might suggest what one was the other could never understand or tolerate, but in gentle colors that could blur into one another or suggest all the colors in one shimmering passage. Anna had had a dear friend whom she had loved, but now that the scrim was up, she supposed she would have loved her more happily and longer had they ever considered that they could have held one another. Suddenly starving she turned toward Hope and held her in a long kiss that ignored a guitar tuning up somewhere. The guitarist had gone through his entire repertoire before Anna whispered, her lips close to Hope's ear, "Thank you."

"Don't thank me, ever."

"Don't be stern." Anna stroked a lock on Hope's forehead. "Surely your lovers have thanked you before."

"Were you grateful to Carl?"

"Are you crazy?" Anna sat up. "What for? The children—but not what brought them." She shook Hope by the shoulder, "OK, no thank you's. But . . . you think . . . you don't realize . . . forget it."

Anna lay down again and was silent. Then she was up again, pushing against Hope. "I can't explain. . . . You've let me out of prison—really." She gave Hope a quick nip on the ear and slipped down again beside her. Then, "I know why you're grouchy." Burrowing her head into Hope's shoulder she tussled and tickled Hope until they were holding one another fiercely, and Anna, with a possessiveness she did not know in herself, joyfully reclaimed her newfound land. Later, almost triumphantly, she looked down on that slim naked body for the moment exhausted, some lovely creature washed up on a cool shore, resting. She felt the joy and triumph of delighting this splendid woman to her serene exhaustion. Hope's eyelids fluttered. A smile began on her lips. "You. Come here, you." The surprising strength of Hope's arms pulled Anna down to her mouth before her breast and soon Anna was lost herself in the curling fall of the surf.

"Are you hungry?"

"We have to eat sometime."

Anna wondered why she wasn't horrified at herself, lying in a steaming tent, her body slippery with perspiration in an over-hot sleeping bag—a hotbed indeed. "Hotbed of sin" had a grimly funny meaning now.

"Doesn't she look sweet," Mrs. Parker had said as she picked Anna up the day of her confirmation as an Episcopalian. She was wearing her favorite yellow dress with the bow in the back as she stood with the other fourteen-year-olds before they walked in file downstairs into the sacristy for the laying on of hands, the take, eat, this is my body and blood which I shed for thee. Their line faced a large mirror with gilded leaves curling about its frame. Her bright yellow dress and the boys' blue suits. Her hair was shining, curled for the occasion. Her cheeks were exceedingly pink. "How cute she looks." The creaking of the cushions in the smoke-filled car, her blouse down off one shoulder and her right breast out. The propriety of Jim's meeting with her father and mother and speaking correctly, showing the courtesies of the well-brought up. Later, their lying on the floor of her father's study, her parents lying in their bedroom above them. "Fair are the mea-e-dows, fairer still the woo-ud-lands" their sweet voices rose. Her mouth was still bruised and swollen. Unless Jim shaved just before he picked her up at school, a few hours with him made her cheeks irritated—pink and "cute." She wanted to leave the musty smelling vestry. Her mouth tasted soiled. The boys looked so angelic, but she knew she did too. The ritual she had prepared for, against both parents' wishes, by weekly lessons after school for two months. As she walked up the stairs and prepared to kneel at the altar rail, she resolved not to let it be a fraud. Her mouth still tasted of Jim's mouth and his cigarettes when the pale wafer was placed on her tongue.

Did Hope feel sinful about anything . . . about being a lesbian, for instance? She didn't think so. "I could never figure how, if love of one's own gender was so terrible, it wasn't eliminated in the process of evolution. If evolution worked so the species could survive, why hadn't homosexuality been eliminated root and branch? I figured it must have its place in nature."

Anna was silent, snuggling as close as possible. "But honey, maybe it does, but by that argument murder has its place, too. It hasn't been eliminated since Adam either."

"God damn. You're right. And all these years I thought I had the final justification. Madam, you are brilliant. How about some cheese, bread, a tomato, maybe some wine. I am starved."

"Agreed, but let me dress you." Although the process was inefficient, it had pleasures efficiency could never claim, and the questions and answering continued.

Yes, Hope had "tried" men and the sex worked as anatomy will, but the emotional zing wasn't there, so she gave it up as pointless. How did she happen to be so able to give up or take on this or that, like choosing the color of her wool to knit a new sweater? She did not know. Because she was tall, people supposed she couldn't "get a man" so she could act on her own choices, she guessed. But she had learned early that her mother's concern was really for herself and as long as Hope didn't scare the horses or disgrace her publicly, and as long as mother was left to do as she wished, heading up fund drives to open the new opera house and such, Hope could do as she liked. Father was so self-absorbed and such a hypochondriac that a burp sent him to Palm Springs for a rest cure.

"Was your first affair with a woman in college?"

"No, earlier. I was a husky twelve-year old seduced by my pious Aunt. Seriously. Such a good woman. She was a real sicky, Aunt Dicky, but everyone loved her, so soft-spoken, so genuinely devout. Dear Aunt Dicky. I loved to curl up with her in bed. She didn't really do much, but would ask me if she was wet. I would find out for her. She seemed so smarmy about it that I decided to avoid having an ice cream with her after Sunday School class. Then she spread it around that I was a peculiar child. She later married a shoe salesman."

Anna listened to this laconic recital with her jaw dropped. Gradually Anna drew from Hope her story, the many affections, the few love-affairs, the final disastrous one of eight years leaving her solitary, if not celibate, five years before. She admitted to occasional two-week sex binges when she left Stevensville to "visit friends" in those recent five years, but to companionship she would not admit.

"But you must meet Dorothy and Holly. You'll like them." Neither spoke. Hope had reminded them both that tomorrow they must leave. They had talked and loved almost the day away, and people were already building fires for the evening's dinner. She gestured to the small heap of pamphlets that traveled step by step through eight different walking tours. "We may never see the Spruce Bog."

Anna tried to smile but looked as if she felt she was cracking in two.

"Before we go you *have* to see something special!" Hope got up quickly. "Don't worry. I'll be back. There must be one somewhere. I may be twenty minutes." She pulled on her warm jacket as she started walking towards the woods. Anna started to go with her and then did not, somehow could not. She shrugged and began to collect her things for a shower. Tenty minutes was a long time.

Anna was walking slowly back to the campsite somewhat refreshed but trying not to think how pointless and hopeless everything was.

"Come on, clean one. Put those goodies down; take my hand, let's run." Holding hands, they ran like children into the woods. In an instant they were standing within the low slanting light of thick-growing trees. Hope led her quickly along a clearly marked path and suddenly she veered off down toward a small pond. Before she reached the water she stopped, crouched down. "Anna, look. You have to see something special. Indian Horn Pipes."

As Hope's gentle, strong hands parted the leaves to reveal the delicate translucent flower, water coursed into Anna's mouth. What had happened to her? In the parting of leaves by her lover's hands, in the fragile curving of the flower's white blossom, sensuality and the ethereal pulled at her at once. Had the beautiful always been so mixed with the erotic? She caught Hope's hand and held it against her lips and then against her cheek. They sat a minute and looked at the beautiful little organism that cared not for man or woman, or for beauty either.

In the silence a leaf settled. "Hope, I don't think I can bear our leaving tomorrow. It feels as it something will crack, be dislocated or something, if we have to go."

Hope shook her head as if she was looking on an event she could not understand. "I know. I've decided to call them at Threshold, tell them I'm having car trouble, my carburetor needs replacing or something, and they don't have the part here. Give us two more days." Anna would have hugged her, but they both heard voices approaching.

And suddenly they were both giddy, babbling about spruce bog walks, the movie called "Singing Toads and Frogs," Indian Horn Pipes—all the things to do and see. But they did none of them. When the time for the movie came they were on Anna's childhood, her sister and her mother. Soon the frogs began to gulp in the darkness and they sat bundled together in a blanket, protected by the drape of their tarp, and talked more about their parents, their families, their experiences and those of others they knew, filling in the portrait they saw.

Anna had many questions to ask about gayness: who was and who wasn't—actors, movie stars, writers, politicians. She was intrigued by tales of doctors—psychiatrists who lived impeccable lives in the city and set up whole communes in the country where the wives could live with each other and the children and the husbands had their own barracks. She asked about football stars, tennis champions, until Hope felt a little like Othello telling Desdemona about the anthropophagi whose heads grow beneath their shoulders. Inexorably the two days passed. The pamphlets were tossed beneath the car window as the hours passed in endless fascinating talk, treasures of each other's lives opened like a golden box with hours of reveling spent like famished survivors of a mighty wreck surprised by a feast on the shore.

On the day they were to leave Anna awoke much too early, her head filled with dream wisps. She would steal the children from Mother Johnson and take them off to Algonquin Provincial Park where they could live like the children with Wendy. But it would get cold and berries would be in short supply. Stalking the holy gooseberry. She got up quickly and slipped out of the tent. If she disappeared now she could hitchhike to Vancouver maybe and like the character in *Sea Change* turn into a man. But she didn't want to be a man, and where would Hope be? Where could she go to live? And what would she live on? What kind of a job could she get? How would she get the children? She picked up one question after another, looked about, and put it down as it led her on to the next question, not to any answers. She was holding a long skein that did not lead her out of the labyrinth. It kept dissolving in her hand.

She found a spot on a rock with a place for her back. She had to be near Hope. That was one answer. Stevensville then or some nearby town. What work did she know? She began to list her "accomplishments." She had "had" piano from Mrs. Grinnell until she reached beginning Bach. She could ice-skate some, play tennis rather well, speak French a little, knit, needle-point, sew, and play good bridge. All of her accomplishments were frivolous. Except cooking. She could type, true, had typed Carl's reports for him when he was getting his MBA.

She had heard of half-way houses that women could go to if they were running away. There they were fed, housed, counseled. She had heard of one place in California, wasn't it, or was it Washington state? Hope might know.

Suppose she stayed with Hope a while. She imagined Carl striding into Hope's breakfast room and simply dragging her by one arm down the steps and over to their, his, house. Hope had told her about the police certificate of protection. She could apply for it because he had beaten her, not on account of the rape. Then he couldn't kidnap her like a mongrel bitch.

Living next door, seeing his lights, hearing the children. How could she think that would be possible? Would the children sneak over to see her? Would she dare go to see them and possibly be trapped by Carl slamming the door and locking it behind him? She had been pursued in her dreams running through woods, clutched at by branches that elongated and stretched into thorny fingers. When she cried out she made no sound, but Hope had held her and wakened her. "You're safe, baby, you're safe."

Hope had held her until she slept again, but when the birds began to feed she awoke.

In panic Hope had flung herself out of the tent and called out for Anna. She had felt for her but touched only her soft sleeping shirt. It was only about five. She waited a few minutes, then cast about wondering where Anna might go. In a few hours they would have to leave. Everybody clutching, recriminations from all sides awaited her. And there was always Carl—wasn't marital rape still legal in New York State? But the children, the children. "We can't forget the children"—everyone would be singing. Spider Johnson would think, who's to care for the dear ones? Never mind that my dear boy rapes her at will.

Far below her on the hillside, seated on a rock, staring off across the wooded hillside, Anna sat, holding her knees, a small figure in a vast landscape. Hope stood and let the sounds fill her mind, the drift of a leaf, the bird scratching and fluttering in the thicket, bird chit-chat and water talk. The rapid, erratic twitter of birds feeding made the very air vibrate. She had to let Anna be. She slipped down to one knee. If she looked she would find an earwig or an ant lugging a tiny white morsel, or a spider letting itself down a silver line. Crackles in the underbrush meant squirrels or woodchucks, raccoons, a deer. Anna had seen bear claw marks on a tree during a walk the day before. Meanwhile salmon were swimming home to spawn, trout gleamed in the dark pools. All creatures in skins, scales and furs, red caps and wing bars were about their business trying to live as they could. These two human creatures were merely one kind on a planet teeming with creatures spawning, coveting, scrabbling, stroking, dragging, eating, singing, clutching, sobbing, coupling, sighing, grieving, dying, screaming, and giving birth.

If she was very still, something would be revealed. Something cracked a branch far to the right. She walked quietly down toward Anna who turned at the sound of her step. She came to stand beside her, letting her eyes focus slowly on the shadowed forms about her. Another twig snapped far to the right. What had seemed to be tree trunks and brown branches came into focus in a different pattern of dappling: a doe with her baby beside her. The white puff at its tail showed up at this distance. The baby managed on stiff legs, too long for its slim body. The mother's long face turned in their direction. She stood, watching the still creatures by the rock. The moment seemed long as the beings observed one another out of full but different consciousnesses. Then the deer threw her head up, turned and loped in long strides down the hillside while her young one followed at a brisk, stiff-legged bounce.

They remained unmoving until Hope hugged Anna, helped her off the rock, and they walked slowly back to the campsite for breakfast.

"Is it too early for breakfast?" Anna asked, holding Hope's arm as they walked.

"Not if you feel like it."

"I need to talk and don't want to be distracted," she said, running her hand up Hope's arm and pulling the arm over her shoulder. "Guess I'll carry you off to my tent." She ducked under Hope's arm and started a fireman's hold.

"Shush. You'll wake up the Indians." Hope unscrambled herself and began to set up the stove for breakfast.

"That's my job," said Anna, pushing her aside with her hip.

"Who says? We don't play roles in this camp."

"Sorry. I am very proud of my chef-dom and plan to retain it. Nobody usurps."

"OK, then, I'll get you sausages, applesauce, and bread for toasting. No eggs. We're out."

"Good planning."

"It is good. No point in carrying extra gear."

"But you will have to eat when you get home. Oh, dear." Anna sank on a bench staring at her shoes. "Home."

"Don't say it."

"And three days ago you said you wanted to go home as soon as possible."

"Don't remind me."

"Such honor. Oh, Hope, I admire it . . . but our time has been so short."

"So?"

"What do you mean, so?" Anna had turned pale and was standing rigidly staring at Hope.

"I mean, darling, we don't have to separate. We can stay together."

"How can we? We're lesbians. At least, I guess we are."

"Many lesbians live together."

"Well, I don't know any. At least I didn't."

"You crazy coot, I told you about enough. Jane and Edna who run the Cooking Pot in the village, Marie and Louise who sell jewelry, or those two women in Westover who run the pottery shop, and Dorothy and Holly, but they don't live together exactly."

"Jane and Edna are sisters."

"Sisters-in-law."

"How do you know they're queer?"

"They are not queer. They're great people. Edna was in the WAC's . . . "

"So every woman who was in the WAC's was lesbian? Great. My cousin . . ."

"No, listen. When she was stationed in Washington and Jane was running the shop she used to come home every week end and that was a six-hour drive. She did that for four years. Does that sound like mere sisters-in-law?"

"Well, no. But how do I know about all these women? So now the world's gay."

"Wait till we go to Belinda's."

"But I can't let Carl know. Picture that. And my God, my own mother . . . Jamie and Timmie."

"Were you thinking of a one-night stand then?"

"Hope. I wasn't thinking at all. I just wanted you."

"Past tense?"

"Christ, Hope. Stop this! . . . Hold me." She looked quickly toward the Indians,' "No—help me make the damn breakfast."

"I haven't thought of this at all, Hope. I have no idea about the gay life—or me in it. It's you I want to be with . . . period."

"Unfortunately, I come in a package . . . in a house in a village in a world with people's ideas about what I am. . . . Look, you have to live somewhere. Why not live with me?"

"What about Timmie and Jamie?"

"What about them?"

"Hope, I want to live with my own children. I can't lop off my own hand or arm. . . . And I don't want his mother bringing them up like her. She's a lovely woman, but . . . "

"Or worse, like him."

"You're right, you're right. She can't be such a great mother to have produced a bully and a rapist, can she?"

"They say the psychological profile of your average village rapist is as normal as apple pie."

"Normality begins to sound sick to me. Let's have this wild looking breakfast."

"Leave it at this, then—you will come back to stay with me for a bit until you get yourself sorted out. You may want to see if you can find a job in Stevensville or Westover. Do you think he'll let you keep the children?"

Anna briefly touched Hope's hand. "I want to stay with you as long as I dare. Mother Johnson would be horrified if she understood. But I think he would let me have custody of the children, if he didn't . . . you know . . . understand. He's never had much time for them."

"If he knows we're living together?"

"Why should he guess we're lovers?"

"Anna, now you're swinging around the other way! Many people do think of it, especially rebuffed husbands. But we'll be careful and probably you'll find a job and a place in a few weeks." Hope wondered at herself rushing into this. An eight-year stint had warned her off marriage for good, she had thought. Now she was starting up again. And with children. She didn't know them, really. They might be hyperkinetic monsters running, shouting, whining, begging. Cynthia's tyrannical six-year-old gobbled up her and her time whole, and swallowed with a bland and smiling face. Dorothy said that Cynthia's career in Victorian scholarship moved at inch-worm pace as tiny Tom hacked off time-slices that Cynthia couldn't use unless she paid for a baby sitter. Often three hours at the library didn't bring tangible returns; sometimes one sentence in a footnote was a treasure. From the ocean of hours he demanded, she selected work-hours like pearls.

"I don't even know how old they are."

"Jamie is six and Timmie is four. Jamie was to start diving lessons this summer." Anna looked away. "Timmie was jealous. Mother Johnson will help out for a few more weeks. . . . Poor woman. I abuse her . . . by inflicting the children on her. . . . Then I blame her for her effect on them." They were standing in the living room. Nana says it's all right if I have another praline, Jamie had said, her dark eyes cunning. Me too, said Timmie. But dear, they have finished their lunches and are going to take their naps. It's not a reward, Mother Johnson. Pralines are pure sugar. Of course, whatever you say, dear. I only thought . . . Jamie's reproachful look, walking stiff-legged over to her book corner to sit on her small chair. Timmie standing looking up, swinging his arms back and forward rocking on his toes.

"Well, at least that's settled. . . . You're staying with me for a bit. Now, about Saratoga. . . . "

Anna's voice was suddenly shrill. "Don't make us go. Maybe we'll never be able to be together again. He may stop us. The police may . . . "

"Baby, we'll be together tonight, I promise. You are staying with me. No one will know . . . or would care if they did. Anyway, the police couldn't care less. It's not against the law for women anyway."

As they dismantled the orange tent Anna tried to memorize where it had stood, jaunty on its sand plot with neat channels around it. Would she be able to find that spot again? She would wish to remember it, even if Carl got her again.

She had learned that amazing things were possible—days of pleasure, gentleness, and quiet talking. Even if she had to give them up for now she would never think she had ended looking until she found them again. She pushed the metal frames into the tentbag and went about her tasks. When the car was packed after their breakfast she let herself look around again. Suddenly, she went over to their fire site, now flattened by the dousing they had given it the night before. She bent down and picked out a small smooth stone that was partly blackened from the coals of their fires. She slipped it into her jacket pocket, turned from the cold hearth, put her back to the empty tent site and walked quickly to the car.

CHAPTER TEN

ALTHOUGH they made good time coming down 87 into Saratoga from the north, Hope could hardly care. Anna had sat silent and pale for a full three hours.

"Anna, this is a real, old New York town. Look at those large porches and great trees."

Anna nodded or said, "Yes, it certainly is." Polite, docile, courteous.

They did not stop at the grandiose spas in the southern section of Saratoga, but drove to the free-flowing spring that was available for all people in the middle of town. The simple wooden roof covered a stone basin with two arching spigots like two small candy canes from which the spring water flowed continuously in gentle gushes. A counter nearby sold empty bottles for the spring water, cheap postcards, small knives that said Saratoga Springs, and hats with indian feathers. The counter attendant was chatting with an ancient man who was telling him how he had drunk this water, man and boy, for sixty years. The counter attendant looked as if he had heard it every day of those years.

Hope gave Anna their plastic cups to fill and a thermos bottle.

"Come on out of the car, Hope; let's toast!"

They raised their bright blue and yellow cups, clicked them, and paused. The sulphurous smell that reached Hope made her eyes smart. Anna's nose was wrinkling as she sniffed. Then Hope boldly took a big swallow and regretted it. The sulphur and carbonation made an evil combination. Anna was coughing and sputtering. She ran behind the car and spat out the noxious stuff. Hope followed her, saying "Are you all right?" but a merrry face looked up, water running out of her eyes. "Didn't want the old guy to be offended," she gasped, before she began to hiccup, cough, and finally to laugh.

"Well, we tried it."

"Ghastly," said Hope, walking away to fill the thermos bottle.

"What are you taking it for, for heaven sake?"

"Don't want to deprive my friends of an experience."

After what she called her trial by Vichy water Anna returned to good spirits. They began to talk about the Stevensville Bicentennial celebration.

"Anyone within reach of New York would be foolish not to go in for Operation Sail, I guess," Hope said, noting the sign indicating 100 miles to the city's outskirts, and she began to tell Anna what was planned. When Anna showed some interest Hope went into detail about the Windjammers. She even told Anna about her childhood dreams of sailing around the world by herself. She told about Chris Christofson and the Ariel and how he had tied himself to the mast to keep from being swept overboard when he was sick in a storm. Anna thought of Odysseus tying himself to the mast and wondered about women growing up among myths that always made them Penelope or Helen, not heroes venturing forth. She could see a young Hope balanced on her boat's flaring stern, holding her tiller with one hand and the mainsail with the other, looking keen and intense as her boat heeled far to starboard and smoothly took the walloping waves. So much was in the intention—in freeing the expectations. She knew even her own mind was becoming freer to use what she knew, as if a wicker cage had been lifted off her brain.

"You certainly know plenty about the Tall Ships, Hope."

"Sounds good, doesn't it? Got ninety-five percent of it from a chart put out by Beefeater's Gin."

They talked about the possibility of sailing at Dorothy's place on Long Island and Hope decided to begin to introduce Anna to the idea of the gay community. There was no point in their remaining isolated needlessly. Dorothy never went to the bars as far as she knew, but she supposed Holly did. Holly knew everyone. Sometimes Hope wondered if she had slept with everyone, too, but she doubted it, although probably everyone wished Holly had. Hope considered herself a closet gay and wasn't proud of it. It wouldn't do her life or her business any good if she admitted she was gay, yet wouldn't it be a relief to be honest? Dorcas had merely shrugged when she had said she was still in the closet, "Honey, let's face it, living either way, open or closet, has its problems. You just choose the one you can stand."

"Hope, isn't it queer . . . odd . . . to be in a room full of women and know they are interested in other women? I mean, don't you feel that people could be grabbing for one another?"

Hope chuckled and reached for Anna's hand, not quite catching it because her eyes were on the road. "Anna Carroll Johnson, what's it like in the subway with all those grabby heteros? Supposed, that is."

"Supposed?"

"Putative."

Then the questioning veered off again on another swing.

"What do lesbians look like?"

"What?"

"You know, in a group."

"Well, each gay woman has a black birth mark on her left earlobe, the mark of Sappho; usually she covers it with a single pearl. Actually you will find the South Shore fascinating—like Manhattan cocktail parties translated to the beach. Very intimidating. Beautifully groomed women in blazers, gold earrings, and silken tans. The North Shore, I have heard, is much more sedate. They have no bars, no night life, fewer restaurants, much less obvious wealth, fewer magnificent homes. Holly calls them the North Shore basketball team because they always dress in jeans and sweatshirts, looking like janitors from City College. That's Holly. She sounds snobbish, but she dresses like a mechanic herself. Holly says that there are more gay women on the North Shore than on the South Shore, but I have no idea."

"It would be fun to visit Dorothy some time."

"Why not?" And Hope began to plan a dinner party for them. "Dorothy's a classicist, hard-working, trying to get tenure at Stuart College." They were just passing the Stevensville water tower and Anna fell silent. The streets were hot and empty as they pulled up slowly at the traffic light on Central Avenue. Anna had pulled her hat down over her sun glasses and was looking intently at the cars parked before the Dari-Freez, but it was six o'clock on a Wednesday night and not too likely that her children would be out with Carl. They turned up Waverly road and there was no sign of the children in the yard. The garage was closed. Hope couldn't see the car through the garage window as she drove by. As soon as the tires crunched to a stop on the greystone, Anna was out of the car loading up her arms to start carrying in the camping gear. When she spoke she whispered.

As they walked into the house they looked around like visitors. Everything seemed so orderly and quiet, so beautifully clean, quaint. Hope enjoyed walking from room to room just reminding herself of her life and her things: the way the dining table looked, the flower bowl on the mantle, her chair under the light. Luxury. After the unpacking Anna cried, "Hot water! A bath, a bath!" and she disappeared down the hall to the guest room from which she did not reappear for an hour.

"I have to call Mother Johnson," Anna said after a long silence. They had finished their dinner, drawn from the frozen provisions that settled living provided. Anna was drawing small lines on the table cloth with a spoon. "I must call her, Hope."

She refused to put the call through in Hope's bedroom upstairs but called from the study. "Hello, Mother Johnson? Yes, we're . . . I'm back. How are you and the children? Good, good. She did? He was? But they're both eating well? Tell them, tell them . . . that you think I'll see them soon. No, Mother Johnson, I will . . . I cannot. I will see him whenever . . . Where is he now? In Jersey? What for? For how long? What will you do while he is gone? Fine, then, could I . . . tomorrow?" Hope began to clear off the dishes thinking that the wife part was not crucial to Anna, but the mother part was and the "part" was not as in "role" but as in "segment."

Before Dorothy and Holly came for dinner Hope had fussed in a way Anna had not thought possible. Anna began to tease her about Cascade commercials and dangerous spots on her glasses. But unperturbed Hope had proceeded to iron the tablecloth and contrasting napkins and to take down red glass dessert plates and crystal water goblets. She planned the seating, arranged flowers, chilled the wine, prepared hor d'oeuvres and veal cooked in wine. She began to seem a confusing mixture to Anna.

As she rounded the corner heading for the linen closet Hope stopped a moment, smoothing her hand softly over Anna's breast. "What do you think—you're the only femme in the place?"

Anna grinned with a wrinkled brow. The butch and femme thing was confusing. She wanted to meet Dorcas, the dentist, and her lover, the fussy little carpenter, who were said to act the butch and femme thing, but Hope said it was more appearance than reality. Anna was reminded of her old friend Shirley who used to build her husband up into such an ogre that when he drove into the garage to get the car fixed the mechanics jumped. A mild man, he delighted in the respect, and she got the car fixed. She would wail to the mechanics, "Oh, my husband will be furious if the car stalls four times as he tries to start in the morning as it did yesterday. He was fit to be tied! Patients waiting, an operation scheduled. You just can't do that to a doctor." Shirley had such pretty red hair and looked so anxious about her bear of a husband that Jake agreed to take her car first thing in the morning.

Just before they arrived, Hope sailed by Anna in a brilliant blue caftan that glittered with gold thread. Her hair was up and as she moved the chiffon floated out behind her. Anna ducked back into her room to consider what she was wearing. Fortunately she had been able to go over to the house and take out virtually anything she might want to wear during the summer, but granted that her clothes were all so . . . so like Mother Johnson. They were neat summer dresses, or pants and flowered blouses, shorts and shirts. No dress she had was appropriate for tonight. Actually the most appropriate thing she had, she was wearing. With a twinge she realized that in her pants and blouse she was dressed more butch than Hope, who looked splendid as a queen.

She knew she was hung up about what she wore. There were days when she used to lay out three different combinations before she decided what to wear. When she lived with Carl. Did this make her look too fat or too tailored, too flat or too plain? Sometimes she put on different dresses while the clock ticked. True, she was just going to the market, but after that, if she had time, she might go to the Motor Vehicles bureau and she didn't want to look. . . . She didn't know if other women had that trouble. She wondered if she deduced too much from what people wore. She would have to think about that. Maybe people were like traveling anthropologists trying to figure other people out by the advertising. She would settle the whole thing—like Holly—by wearing ugly outfits for all occasions. After putting some cologne behind her ears and on her arms she stepped out of her room, trying to avoid a last look in her mirror.

When Dorothy and Holly arrived and were exclaiming over Hope, Anna stayed in the background partly out of timidity and partly because in her fascination with their appearances she had not caught who was who. But then she began to be able to deduce that. One was conservatively dressed in black slacks and a bright paisley blouse; the other must be Holly wearing snug white jeans, some sort of poncho-like blouse in orange, rust and yellow, and sandals with bare feet. Her mother had never approved of bare feet. Usually sandalled feet were not too clean, she always thought, and weren't feet the least attractive parts of the body? Perhaps elbows were, but she loved arms. Holly's husky arms showed beneath that poncho-thing. When she raised her arm one could see all the way to her breast. Dorothy should tell her. And no bra either. Wouldn't that material be rough?

Yes, they had a lovely trip, Hope was saying, wonderful weather except for one magnificent storm, yes, well, how about some drinks? Hope disappeared.

The three women were now seated in a triangle with each woman sitting neatly at a point as if speared by it. "Yes, well," said Anna. "Canada certainly is beautiful. Not all of it. Of course, we didn't visit all of it, or even try to. That is, we did see a lot though. Are you people campers?"

"Dorothy is, but I'd rather cope with city roaches than country ticks."

"Hardly, Holly. I haven't camped since childhood."

"Didn't you do that counselor thing that you loved at camp Hochematoli?"

"Wapemahsocke. And I was all of 18."

"An old crock. Ah, Hope, you returned in time. Dorothy was about to crown me with an oar."

"Paddle, Holly."

"See, she admitted it."

Anna began to wonder if she could find a way to go into the kitchen to prepare the asparagus, when Holly asked her what she thought about the Bicentennial.

She almost asked what there was to think about it. It was a fact of nature or of time—two hundred years and wasn't it to be expected that people would want to explode firecrackers?

Dorothy said, "Holly's upset about the Bicentennial. She says it's racist and . . . "

"Well, it is racist, Dot."

Anna watched the pink cheeks turning to Dorothy, turning back to Anna, raising an arm in a flash of orange. "We act as if there were no blacks here building our agrarian economy with us. We act as if only men lived here—but of course 'we the people' *did* only mean men and only gave votes to men. But how did they eat, who grew the food, who cooked it? We act as if there weren't any Polish, Greek, Italian, Irish, Germans over these two centuries—everybody was WASP, pardon me, Hope, and everybody here was white male. Stupid. As for Op-Sail . . . "

"You have a real point, Holly," Hope said, passing the large plate of celery and carrot sticks with the curry dip. Anna wanted to offer to do some passing but wasn't quite sure if she should act as a guest or part of the hostess' family. Which—child or sister? How did Holly and Dorothy act when they gave a party?

"But you don't agree, right?"

"No, Holly, I do agree up to a point. But . . . " Hope settled next to Anna on the sofa. "I am, will be, part of the Stevensville celebrations and I'm not apologizing for it."

"What'll you be doing, Hope?" Anna asked, wanting to reach over and touch that blue glittery stuff she was wearing. Was that thread interwoven or little flecks of gold?

"Holly, the villages should celebrate, if anyone should."

"And one could argue about that," Holly said.

"But the racist thing . . . that is only partly true. Now wait, Hol. In a town like Stevensville that was founded around 1644 where there weren't any plantations southern style, there really weren't any blacks. I agree that there should be more now, that its suspicious that there aren't, and that most people don't think of the black cowboys, soldiers, or farmers and teachers.

"But it doesn't apply to Stevensville," Dorothy said.

"Because racism was built-in from the beginning," Holly said.

"Right," Hope said, leaning over to pass the chips, but Anna did it for her. "Anna, did you know I'll be preparing the float on the buttonwood tree? I'll be doing some research, too—to see what other types of trees were grown in Stevensville two hundred years ago. Threshold has a float, as do about ten other businesses. There'll be nearly seven floats by churches, including at least three by fundamentalist sects, Holly."

Dorothy took a sip of her gin and tonic, not one inch more relaxed than when she had first sat on the triangle's apex. Anna found herself wondering who was interested in this polite cover conversation. Was this the way gay people really talked? Hope, looking like Hera in blue, was seated among them talking about craft fairs and canoe races, pageants and leather-working. By now in Carl's groups the sexual innuendoes would be flying. There would be sniggering and many jokes about drinking and about the last time somebody was hung over and what he did then to somebody's wife. She had another swallow of gin and tonic, glad she didn't have to count Carl's drinks. Apparently he wasn't back yet from the trip to Jersey. They sent him on to Washington to confer with someone, but he should be home for the fourth.

"Is that someone running his power motor now?" Everyone looked over at Anna as if she has said something peculiar. But it was almost 7:30; who would be mowing his lawn at night? Hope got up and went to the window. She nodded her head to Anna. Did she mean that it was Carl or just someone mowing a lawn? She put off getting up to go over and look. She could do that when they went to the dining room for dinner. She took another swallow of her gin and tonic. The voices continued. Soon she got up and took out the plate to replenish.

She was making a careful design of cauliflowers on the plate when she felt Hope's arms around her and her fresh scent drifted around her.

"You all right? You disappeared. You'll like them when you . . . You don't look well."

"I'm OK, Hopie. You look beautiful," she said, putting her head on Hope's shoulder, her eyes filling.

"You need some food." Hope turned to the stove and set the gas a little higher. "Have a piece of cheese on this wafer." Hope had not expected the turn the evening was taking. When Holly got going on racism she thought the conversation was off and running, but Dorothy was more tense than she had ever seen her, Anna was drinking too much, Holly had stopped being provocative, and suddenly Hope was worrying about the veal. Had it used up the wine it was simmering in? Carl would be running his damn loud mower back and forth, back and forth, for another half-hour yet.

"After all, she's a straight. . . . " Dorothy stopped talking when Hope walked into the room with the glasses.

"A light refill. We'll be eating soon," she said, watching Anna walk over to the window and look out. Anna's face was blank as she turned from the window and took up the raw vegetables. "Raw vegetables are a good idea, Hope, with the dip. Less calories." Anna said, laughing airily, "I'm thinking about becoming a vegetarian."

"Well, Hope, what do you think of Carter?" Holly asked, crunching a carrot with determination.

"He really looks good to me. . . . "

Dorothy leaned forward to Anna and lowered her voice. "Are you a Democrat, Anna, or an Independent?"

Anna looked over at Dorothy. She was speaking softly as if Anna were a small child new to a company of adults. "I'm not very political,

actually. I haven't really though about these things much since college."
Would Dorothy see what she meant? Dorothy looked as if she would
understand how it was not to have time to read the papers, although Anna
had made it a point to read at least one copy of *Time* every two weeks.
Her voice was louder than she expected it would be and crossed the other
voices as she said, "My family has always been Republican and so is . . .
my husband, but I don't know what I think . . . really." Her voice trailed
off as she saw Holly's expression—frozen with her glass in the air.

A timer in the kitchen gave a sharp buzz and Hope smiled. "Come,
darling, help with the rice." She ran her hand down Anna's arm to her
fingers and led her off to the kitchen.

Holly followed waving a celery stalk. "Except for his evangelism, he
seems sane enough, and if he would admit women into that benighted
men's club, and if he would support Bella. . . . "

"How are her chances these days?" Hope asked, trying to think of
butter on the rice and hollandaise sauce on the asparagus. She hated people to talk to her when she was working in the kitchen. Anna had the
sensible idea to fill the water goblets. Was the wine bottle opened?

"Oh God, Hope, she is some woman. I will be on the street corner
of the upper west side passing out leaflets for her this fall and I know
what'll happen. What always does. People of all sizes will vote for Bella,
but the greatest is when iron-faced old ladies come up and tell you they
passed out leaflets thirty years ago—they're too old to now, but Bella is
the one who understands them and the city and what it needs. And we
young people shouldn't give up on the city."

"Oh, Hope, how beautiful!" Holly stopped at the door of the dining
room and smiled broadly at the lighted candles. She hugged Dorothy.
"Hopie knows how to do things right. Why are we such clucks? Look at
this, Dottie!"

Hope gestured each person to the place she had planned. "I love a
celebration," Hope said. "The visit of my friend here has given me the
chance." Anna felt herself drowning in that dazzling smile. Hope began
to serve each plate, her long sleeves making a soft arch of blue as she
moved. For a while they were silent, enjoying the gentle civilities. Anna
watched the reflection of the light on the glasses, hearing the mutter of
the power motor now at a distance. Holly's chatter had resumed and even
Dorothy was sitting back smiling when Holly said, "So I'm carting this
one off to a secret apartment in Hoboken. For Op-Sail of course. So we
can watch everything and count the drownings," she said, impaling a piece
of veal. "Delicious."

At first the small clicking sounds of forks and murmurs and ice clink-
ing in glasses prevailed over the background hum of the power motor, and
Dorothy began to tell of her surprising conversation with Miriam Green.
Anna tried to listen closely. Bob apparently had been furious when Miriam

told him that someone wouldn't come to one of their parties because Miriam's chairperson would be there. When Miriam explained that their friend didn't want his boss to see him with his gay friend, Bob became wilder. The invitation had said to come with friend or spouse and that's what it meant. He didn't care if the chairperson came or God came; at his party people were to know they would be surrounded by loving friends. What the hell was wrong with a Political Head if his faculty felt that way about him and so forth, all of which Miriam had told Dorothy in great detail and with considerable pride.

"But you haven't told Miriam yourself, have you, Dot?" Holly asked.

The heavy knocking sounds on the door and the ringing of the doorbell startled them. Anna half-pushed her chair away and looked at Hope. The power motor sounded as if it was in Hope's front garden.

"I haven't, though I suppose. . . . " Dorothy watched Hope going to the door and continued her response to Holly's questions as Anna tried to hear the background conversation: "My wife here? . . . party . . . see . . . thought . . . speak to her."

Hope stood at the door way, "Why don't you see him in the study, Anna, all right? You going to be all right?"

The power motor thudded in her ears as she pushed away her chair and caught her balance, one hand at the table's edge. She wasn't ready to . . . she wanted some coffee . . . but she nodded at Hope and went into the hall. He stood feet apart in military stance at ease, the white sweat band at his temples, the muscular suburban man doing home duty on his lawn. His tee shirt, given him by Timmy for Christmas, said "Ask my Pop!" and showed a Madison Avenue Indian in red feathers. Anna barely glanced at him, avoiding his eyes, but she could smell the beer. She gestured toward the study.

"Why not talk here? I have nothing to say those . . . women can't hear."

He talked as if he had been storing up invective that had to pour out. "I want to talk to you about Hope Charity Alford." He laughed harshly and ran his arm across his forehead. "See you're havin' a little party. Any men here?" He walked to the door, looked into the dining room. "A pretty fancy party with no men. Candles! Chris' sake!"

"Carl," Anna shouted, "Turn off that damn mower!"

"Why? Does it bother you, Anna baby? I'm not going to stay long here, because you're coming home with me."

"No, Hope, I will do this. Carl, for God's sake come into the study and shout your lungs out there." Anna walked past him and led the way to the study. In her mind she saw them: Hope standing tensed and pale, facing Carl, who was sweating through his tee shirt, his wet mouth sneering. Carl would love to rip that frail blue, glittery stuff.

"Close the door . . . now shout."

"Where do you come off acting like this with me? I'm your husband. Still. I have rights."

"I'm glad you acted like this. Reminded me of the boor you are."

Carl dropped his voice, "Now Anna, naturally I was surprised to learn you were still here. You came here first, Mother told me. But why would you stay? Because of our spat? The kids want you back. They miss you, Anna. They can't understand why their mother isn't at home." His voice was silky, injured. But she knew that old turkey gizzard was rising, yearning to bang at her.

"Carl, I miss them. I have told them I do."

"When did you see them? I wasn't told that!"

"No secret about it. I went over to the house, got my things, had a good afternoon and evening with them when you were in New Jersey or on your way to Washington."

"You got your things? What is this? If you think you're leaving me with the children on my hands . . . you're my wife still. I'll say you abandoned me and the children. I can prove it."

"I have a witness who will say I was beaten. That's not the same as abandoning, Carl, and you know it. Stay away from me, Carl. Stay back . . . "

He reached quickly and snatched at her arm but caught her hand only as she stepped back. He pulled her up to him so that her vision was filled by his teeth, the spittle on his mouth, the black hairs jutting out of his nostrils. "If you don't come back to me now, I will tell any judge that you are living with a degenerate woman known in the town for taking men's wives. I will say that I came in here and found four of you eating by candlelight with cushions all around."

"What cushions? Many wives do that. Are you crazy or just liquored up?"

"No judge in America will let you have our children back. Christ knows I'll say I don't want them to come under your influence and any judge in America would stand with me."

"You couldn't do that. . . . If you think that of me why would you want me back?" she cried out, wrenching herself back, staring at him, at the sweat dropping from his nose.

"And I'll win the children. You'll never see them again the length of your fuckin' life." His arm was shaking as he held himself from striking her. He took his hand off her arm and pushed her, easily, as if casually, across the room so that she slammed her hip against the table edge. "You better get your sweet ass back to my house and quick."

The door opened and Hope stood in the door way holding a long poker. Anna suddenly wanted to laugh. In some crazy way she looked like a furious queen holding her blackened sceptre. As she raised her

other arm telling Carl to get out and Dorothy appeared behind her with
a heavy pipe, Anna began to panic. If it ever did come to actual fighting,
could they survive that fist as big as a pie plate, his powerful knees pounding into their stomachs? He could break them up and scatter them like
evergreen needles. Through her racing fears the power motor roared the
strength he could turn to, to crush them down and plow them under.
Every judge, policeman, law court, and prison, every man on the street
would support him.

He was stepping back. He was walking into the hall. Anna heard the
voices clearly again. Dorothy was saying, "Mr. Johnson, legally you have
no right to march in here and threaten the property owner's guest. Any
judge would find you delinquent at least. It would prejudice any case you
wish to raise if you so much as touched your wife. There are three wit-
nesses to your barbarism and anyone of us will be glad to speak out about
your behavior. If I were you, I would leave rapidly before I did something
I would truly regret." Dorothy had drawn herself up to her full height and
was speaking as if she was wearing her mortar board, not as if she held
a piece of lead pipe in her hand.

He stared at the two women and saw Holly trotting in from the kitchen with a heavy butcher knife held at the ready. "I'm leaving. You are
all," he dropped his voice and muttered, "fucking crazy bitches . . .
Anna." He turned to her and raised his bulging right arm that shook as
he pointed to her, "If you don't come back with me now . . . or soon . . .
I'll fix it so that . . . so that . . . you won't be able to get those kids a-
gain . . . and they'll never *want* to see you again. I'll tell them all about
women who. . . . " He looked around. "They'll learn plenty about their
mother." He looked as if he was going to spit on the floor."

"Carl, get out. You're making a fool of yourself," Hope said.

"You'd better leave now, Mr. Johnson," Dorothy said, opening the
door.

Carl wheeled and strode through the door and spat on the pavement.
He grasped the pulsing handle of his power motor and shouted over its
roar, "You're keeping my wife from . . . from her family . . . her children. . . . Oh, Anna, Anna," he said, shaking his head. He kept shaking
his head as he pushed his mower away toward his post-and-rail fence,
leaving behind him a neat path of cut grass.

Anna turned in to Hope's arms and just held on. Holly said to
Dorothy, "You were marvelous."

Dorothy shook her head. "Put away that murdurous thing, Holly,
you scare me," and shakily she began to laugh. "When I saw you heading
in from the kitchen. . . . "

"Listen, gladly would I slit him from his guggle to his zatch," said
Holly, crouching over the lethal butcher knife and fingering its edge.

Hope locked the front door and the four women returned to the dining room and stood trembling, holding onto one another. They looked at the guttering candles and the partly-eaten food.

"How about some veal sandwiches?" Holly said, pushing at a piece of asparagus with her long knife. "Nothing like congealed hollandaise sauce."

"Hope, I'm terribly sorry. He just blasted everything."

"Not your fault. Let's see what I can heat up," Hope said, as she gathered up plates. Anna started to help her, but Holly took her by the shoulders and said, "Honey, you've had it. Just sit here for a bit. Let Dot and me help Hope now. You gave a wonderful party but now, after this, we're in a different ball game. Just sit and rest. Close your eyes if you can. We have plenty of time to talk." Holly took a coat from the hallway closet and put it around her. Anna began to feel warm again and she actually felt herself drifting into a sleep as the voices from the kitchen went over details of who said what and what did he say and how had they looked when Hope came into the study . . . looking like a queen she was . . . an outraged Hippolyta in swirling clouds of blue. . . . "

"She's actually asleep."

"No, she isn't. I think . . . she is finally awake," Anna said, pushing the coat off and smiling at her three friends as she sat up.

CHAPTER ELEVEN

WHEN Hope and Anna finally reached Dorothy's place on the South Shore they were grimy and tired. The air conditioner in Hope's car wasn't working, and in the long drive from Stevensville they had barely spoken. The hot road extended flat before them, heat waves rising, and a line of car roofs shining light into their eyes. There was no point in stopping to cool off. That would be hard on Beth-Ellen and make starting up even worse, so they drove on speaking only in monosyllables.

The weeks of the Bicentennial had been very crowded for Hope. She had gone every day to work and to the society for a few hours. She had taught children to plant seeds as part of the town's tree replacement program, had set Anna to supervising them when she could, had been a part of the town parade as Anna took pictures. Anna seemed to be occupied but Hope would find her sitting limp, staring into space. When caught, Anna would get up and offer to do something. One day Hope found her drawing an Indian Horn Pipe.

"But that's good, Anna!"

"Yes," Anna said, and put away her pad and pencil.

She seemed absorbed following the progress of Op-Sail, the gathering of the ships at Newport, their rendezvous in Sandy Hook and Gravesend Bay, and on July fourth Anna ran between Stevensville activities in which Hope took part and television's Parade of Ships.

Hope walked in on her crouching in front of the set. "I hope the children are seeing this! What a moment to remember when you grow up!" Hope had nodded, watched for a moment, her knees against Anna's back and her hand gently touching her hair.

People were always so sentimental about children, imagining that when they were older they would "appreciate" this or that. She had been sent or taken to many notable moments, mainly to serve her mother's sense of self-importance. She had been tired, or hungry, or bored. Her mother stood slim and erect before a Delacroix painting—going on about its "rushing motion" and all she had wanted to do was sit down. Op-Sail was a great moment maybe; the ships were splendid, but it was all so hokey and so forced, so much puffery to conceal the country's sickness and fear. After Nixon. Still Holly and Dorothy enjoyed it.

For Hope there had been moments in the Bicentennial celebrations when she had felt finally a part of Stevensville's long life, and she thought perhaps Anna could understand her affection for the town. They had watched the annual town pageant, written by two women from the oldest families, women who had been lovers discreetly for years. No one in the town had anything but respect for Mrs. Willcox and Miss Stevens. Their scripts always honored family life, gave bits of town gossip dredged from the historical society archives, and ended each episode with a still that often included descendants of the colonials described in the script. Grandma Baskins was shown bathing Terry Baskins in a wooden tub, one of his feet in the air, and the audience chuckled. Three generations of the Robinsons were shown helping pursue Major Andre with the plans of West Point in his boot. As the town watched its members represent their ancestors in homely and touching scenes, Hope had known it was sentimental, a sweet idealizing of a difficult time, and weren't all times difficult? Still she was moved, but Anna must have felt excluded.

It was a relief that Holly and Dorothy were out sailing now and she and Anna could rest before they came back.

"What a place! You didn't say it was so modern. And look at the view!" Anna was calling to her from the long porch that ran around three sides of the house. "And look." She had stepped through the porch door and was staring up at the glass bubbles in the roof. "Floor—through, and what a fire place. Hope—all in white, black and grey. How dramatic! I didn't remember Dorothy as theatrical."

Hope was aiming for the refrigerator. "Some lunch? . . . Dorothy rents this house from her aunt, a painter, who takes off for the mountains in the summer. Here, Dorothy has left us some tuna fish salad all made up, umm, with parsley, and onions, aren't you hungry?"

Anna was walking along the balcony looking into the bedrooms and calling down into the living room from what seemed a great height. "Who else is here, Hope? Looks like two rooms are in use." She appeared suddenly above Hope. "They do share a room, don't they?"

Hope laughed, "You look so stricken. Come on down, Anna-parsley, and join me for lunch. With luck we can have a nap before they come back."

"Oh, in that case," Anna said and appeared almost instantly beside her. "What did you say about the other people?"

Putting out the lettuce that Dorothy had left in a moist towel in the refrigerator, Hope said, "Biracial."

"*And* gay? Good grief," Anna said, putting her hand to her mouth in suppressed giggles before she put it to her head. "Oh, lord."

"What do you mean, 'Oh lord,' " Hope said, frowning, putting out the plates.

"Hopie, I mean, life is so hard, so hard anyway. Being gay is hard enough in addition, that is . . . but then—oh lord, tell me about them. What do they do?"

"Joyce, the white woman, is a sociologist Dorothy met at Stuart where she works, and Brenda works in a brokerage house."

"Oh, a secretary."

Hope looked over at Anna. "Brenda is a broker. Electronics are her speciality." Hope helped herself to some more tuna fish.

Anna sat staring at her plate. When she tried to catch Hope's glance, Hope was looking out the window. "Want some wheat berry bread? I saw some in the refrig," Anna said, getting up.

"No, thanks. In a minute I think I'll go have a nap. You'd better, too. It'll be a long night. Want some more iced tea?"

When Hope gestured toward her with her iced tea glass, Anna smiled. It was as if her feet kept stepping along a familiar roadway that suddenly gave beneath her or twisted sharply, leaving her facing a smooth wall. The road was not familiar and she deceived herself if she thought it was.

When she slid naked under the cool sheet next to Hope's body, she longed, despite her fatigue, to move her legs and arms to let their skins smooth against each other.

"Let's sleep," mumbled Hope.

This large bed, drenched in light reflected from the water, her legs floating limp, resting, her arms holding that cool back . . .

Hours later they were lying again but under the sun and listening to the water sound when the others arrived.

"Hmmm, the life horizontal," Holly said. "They're here," she called back to the other heads just appearing over a sand dune. "I could make some improvements on the Schwepp's commercials, using you ladies for that guy with the patch."

The embarrassments of introductions passed quickly with Holly's zest, and Anna had a moment to look at Brenda and Joyce. Joyce was very blond and looked like a million plain graduate school types to Anna. Her mother had always asked why academic women let themselves be so plain. "Why on earth does Miss Blackstone have to wear such ugly shoes and imagine such thick stockings?" She should have gone to graduate school herself as soon as she left college. But she could not stop looking at Brenda—her beautifully modeled head poised on a long slim neck like a nubian Nefertite. Some stock broker. But Nefertite *was* black, wasn't she? How could her clients pay attention to what she said? When Brenda smiled Joyce basked, Holly glowed, and even Dorothy grinned.

"So Evelyn Heath has another?" Dorothy was saying. "Holly, I forget—give the background."

"Hope has told you that we're going to a dance place, Belinda's, right? Well, Evelyn Heath supports the place—Vassar '51, they tell me. She and about five other women from Vassar, they call themselves 'The Group,' Provided the capital for Sue to start Belinda's. If we're lucky she'll turn up tonight with her entourage. Evelyn's style is to pick up someone who appeals, court her beautifully, woo her passionately and then after a year or two of idyllic devotion, she leaves the dear creature . . . but always with substantial alimony."

"Alimony?"

"Anna, voluntary alimony may not be one's expectation in the world at large, but Evelyn has left behind her a trail of abandoned heroines all educated beautifully. Presumably in every sense. One is now a graduate student in history, another she educated through med school, another she saw through art school and two one-woman showings. Her score is smashing—only one drop-out and one alcoholic writer."

"What does she do herself?"

"Evelyn, my dear, is a resource person. She values brains and beauty, I guess, and why should she do more?"

"Holly, who's the new one?"

"A cute Australian hockey player—left wing, I hear. Evelyn used to play on the Vassar hockey team in her youth—center forward, if you care to know, before she realized—as they say."

"That's what I want to know! When did you 'realize,' Holly? I mean, when did everybody here find out about themselves," Anna asked, then looked quickly at Hope.

Holly turned to Hope. "Is Anna doing a little research project, Hope?" Holly held up her hands as if she were writing busily on a clipboard. "Pardon me, I'm a representative of the CIA collecting some information for Carter's transition team. . . . Madam," Holly said, turning back to Anna, " 'I was taught' as Queen Elizabeth said, 'At my mother's knee, or some such low joint.' "

"Speaking of joints," Joyce was saying, "How about . . . "

"Like when I first knew ah was a black cha-ald," said Brenda and laughed.

Anna was blushing furiously as Dorothy pushed herself away from the porch railing, saying, "I think it's time for showers and dinner thoughts, Ladies of Capri."

As Dorothy began to run down plans for the evening Anna reached for Hope's hand beside her and curled it around her own.

"But, Hope, I love you, why can't it be simple?"

"It isn't simple, honey. It just isn't. You're tense—just take it easy. These people are like anyone else. They'll like you. How could they not?

Shussssh now." Hope was holding her and rocking with her on the bed until Anna tipped her head back and Hope kissed her lips and throat.

"Hope has her hands full this time." Holly rolled her eyes to the ceiling as she joined Dorothy in their room.

Dorothy was sliding one hangar after another down her closet rail trying to find her favorite dancing shirt. "That woman's a fool. Hope really mystifies me."

"She's not so bad, just naive."

"Hope? You're crazy. She's more experienced than either of us—well, maybe not you."

"Not Hope—Anna—forget it," Holly said and walked naked toward the shower.

"I am not going to ride in the same car with the momo," Joyce was saying, roughly towelling herself dry. "I will say that I'm a nut about liking to leave when I please, so we can take our car."

"She's just young," Brenda said, sliding her arm into her sleeve.

"Married with two children? She can't be that young! Maybe she's just stupid. Hope knows enough to avoid straight women."

"Why, honey?" Brenda said with a big smile.

"What do you mean, why? The trouble of it. Who wants all that shit?"

Joyce put her index finger gently on the curve of Brenda's throat where the jade green shirt fell open and smiled. "But ours is worth it."

Feeling herself and an old friend of Hope's, Dorothy tried. She took them on the long tour past Water Mill, "Louise Fitzhugh's old town, remember *Harriet the Spy*, Hope?"

"Do I? My cat is named after Harriet's friend. The other book was kinder to her."

"And there's that other bitchy woman who wrote about that other town and all about the swinging and dope—who's that, Holly?"

"Mabel Frowbin. You know, *The Visitor* tells all about sex in the garden club and ends by almost revealing who's gay in town. Nearly wrecked nine marriages."

"What a score!"

"There was an uproar, I guess," Anna said.

"Not a good idea to wear a sign, is it?" Dorothy turned the corner and pointed out Len Farragut's old place, where she used to raise hunters.

"Now she has settled in Florida. Says training jumping horses in sand gives them terrific spring."

Hope asked, "What happened to Stella Axelrod?" She said in a low voice to Anna, "She used to write mysteries, children's stories, gothics, sex manuals—all under different names—like Lance Overshoot, Rip Master-weather, Sybil Delight."

"We'll probably see her tonight. She's supposed to join us with Dorcas and Gloria for dinner."

"Who's she with now?"

"Been with Sheryl for five years anyway. Was that when you were last out here, Hope?"

"At least."

Holly gave Dorothy a swift dig in the ribs just in time. Dorothy vaguely remembered Stella and Sheryl had played a part in some grim drunken scene just before Eleanor left Hope. Stella would say anything drunk. Stella's whole trouble, Dorothy thought, reducing an unmanageable problem to a simplicity in what Holly called "her" style, Stella's whole trouble was that she hated lesbians. Gay men she could stand, but homosexual women were queer. Dorothy muttered to Holly, "Why the hell did I invite Stella to join us?"

"Simple, you forgot." Holly shook her head. Then she raised her voice as they came to a traffic light. "Dorcas and Gloria will be an education for Anna."

"Oh, right," Hope said. "Haven't seen them in years. Anna, Dorcas is a dentist, a tiny woman and very macho. Her lover for nigh onto eight years is Gloria, a dainty woman who is a stunning carpenter when she isn't playing Scarlett to her Rhett."

"They like to travel on riverboats."

"Dorothy, not exactly," Holly said, turning around in the front seat to tell Anna. "But they do go to golf clubs, Health Spas, Grossinger's, anywhere, Dorcas in a ravishing tuxedo and Gloria in silver lamé, and they sweep down staircases and knock the blooming bejesus out of the staring bourgeoises."

"Stare-cases, indeed," said Anna.

"I'm surprised at you, " Holly said.

"She's full of surprises," Hope said, then, "What is it, Anna?"

"Wouldn't it be a pleasure to have a dentist with small hands," Anna said in a wistful voice. Even Dorothy laughed.

"So how has Belinda's fared, Holly?"

"It has survived, at least, which is pretty impressive."

"Most gay places open and shut in a summer or turn straight by the next summer," Dorothy added for Anna.

"It still isn't Mafia run?"

"Nope. The Group has held out."

"It's different, too, in that the food is good," Holly said with emphasis.

Dorothy watched Anna in the rear view mirror as she said, "Usually the food at gay places is bad or the service is rotten because they figure gay people are so glad to be together away from the straights they'll eat anything."

"Served, anyway."

"True."

Anna wanted to say she hadn't known that but kept silent and just nodded. She wondered if there were bouncers and if all the women wore tuxedoes and watch chains.

"Does Sue employ a man bouncer?" Hope asked.

"Never! She has an ex-olympic lady shot-putter, a Russian who defected. The woman doesn't know much English, but she watches Sue, knows shit, fuck, slut, twat and ass and that seems to suffice. She never heaves out the wrong customer." Suddenly Anna laughed, a crowing delighted ripple that grew and infected them all. As they drove up to Belinda's their car was filled with laughter.

"How did you beat us?" Holly said to Joyce standing in the doorway.

"Brenda drove," Joyce said proudly.

"Sexist." Holly put her arms around Brenda and Joyce and led them to Sue to introduce them.

Anna was surprised at the numbers of cars in the parking lot and the place was on the main road, too. She had expected it to be like an old prohibition spot. The cars were mainly new, not old jeeps, either; she even saw Cadillacs and two Lincoln Continentals. The women probably drove their fathers' or even their husbands' cars. Joyce and Brenda were waiting for them at the doorway when Holly met them, Brenda looking like a movie star in a pale green blouse and slim pants. She could wear a gunny sack and look smart.

"Hello-o-o-o there, Hope. Long time no see." Hope was nodding, smiling at a velvet-eyed blonde as she leaned toward her to introduce Anna.

"Muriel Bowman," Dorothy whispered in Anna's ear. "And she never misses." Anna felt herself propelled toward the roar by Hope on one side and Dorothy on the other, She pulled down her shirt, wishing she had snugger-looking pants. In Mother Johnson's style polyesters she looked like the 1950's. She wondered if she were up to this.

They walked past the bar to a room elevated two steps above the dance floor. Women were lined up at the bar talking in groups of twos and threes. A husky woman set out drinks on the counter. She smiled at them as they came in, showing plenty of silver dental work. Must be the Russian shot-putter Anna thought, and giggled.

What appeared to be a college freshman showed them to a table, her waiter's pad stuck in the tight back pocket of her jeans. After taking their order she pushed her glasses back on her nose, smiled and disappeared through a white swinging door. As it opened, the kitchen clatter floated back to Anna. How could it be so spectacularly ordinary?

"Order for me, Hope," Anna whispered.

"Why? I don't know what you might like, honey!"

"I'll order something dumb, like a pink lady. You order."

"Two Bloody Marys here," said Holly.

"Oh, that's good," Anna said.

"Same, then," said Hope, reaching for the menus. "Dorothy, do you remember the time   Dorcas and Gloria took us dancing at The Roadside, and they were running a porno for the men, and Gloria and I stayed out at the bar and you and Dorcas went in to edify yourselves?"

"Dorcas was very funny, as usual," Dorothy said to Anna. She came out after watching the damn thing for five minutes, muttering . . . . "

"Gloria and I," said Hope, "looked through the blinds watching Dorothy and Dorcas watching it . . . . Dorcas sashayed out . . . . "

"And said, Dorcas said, 'No style. Just two unattractive people being unattractive beside a neighbor's pool,' and she led Gloria off to dance. But Hope and Gloria looked ready to be sick."

"Gloria couldn't and had to carry it off, but, well, I had a quick ginger ale to settle the stomach." Dorothy grimaced.

"It's amazing, isn't it," Anna said, speaking in a daze. "Wives have to put up with that—and so much of it. At least I don't know of any who have the guts to say no."

"Well, yes, I suppose so," Dorothy said, passing celery.

"I mean, maybe some like it, but mainly I hear of people who get cystitis and the gags—anyway they don't consider it a pleasure—doing what they do in porno films and under a kind of force, too."

"OK, Anna, OK, honey. We got your point," Hope said, and put her hand firmly over Anna's. "Now have a good, spicy Bloody Mary, or I hope it's spicy."

Anna took a big swallow of the Bloody Mary, and said, "You could call it a reel turn-off! Top that, Holly!"

Dorothy began to say that Dorcas and Gloria would arrive after dinner when things began to get going. They had a longer drive to make than the others did. "And besides," Dorothy said, "They probably prefer to dine together and arrive gorgeous when the rest of us are rumpled and have grease on our lips from frogs' legs provencal—which, by the way, I intend to have."

Dorothy and Hope conferred about the wine list as Holly chatted with Anna, telling her about the people at the bar, reassuring her that no one she knew would be there, and if they were, why would they be there but for the same reason she was? For Anna, Holly's very solidity of frame was comforting. She radiated a kind of staunch loyalty that made Anna want to hug her. They had been so great when Carl came over.

Brenda and Joyce had been chatting softly by themselves until Joyce called across to Dorothy. "You said this place was segregated, but I thought you meant sexually—not racially."

Dorothy looked aghast and glanced quickly across to the bar and around at the tables. "That's right, I said—Brenda, I didn't think."

Brenda nodded and smiled gently. "I understand."

Holly said, "Brenda, I guess a lot of black women don't know Belinda's yet. But I saw a couple of men when I came in."

"So did, I, honey. Never mind, next time I'll bring my own rock band," Brenda said, and let the red iced liquid slide down the glass toward her mouth.

Anna hadn't noticed many men, but as the music became a little louder people began to come out onto the floor. She felt herself drift out of the conversation entirely and become absorbed by the variety about her. She watched a white-haired woman in a black chiffon caftan, a heavy woman, float about with her arms raised over her head, lowering them gently as she moved slowly around her partner, a tough looking sailor type with a blue visored cap and what looked like a blue undershirt, tight jeans, and boots. The two watched each other, absorbed, until they were joined by another man and danced in a circle together. Two young girls, looking like high school seniors, bounced and shook by, knocking hips and shaking their arms laughing and stamping. Two glamourous women modeled from Rita Hayworth's best days danced by holding each other tightly, dancing slowly with their eyes closed. A woman in a white suit and vest was passing by from table to table, stopping for a moment to speak in passing to each.

"That must be Belinda," Anna said, turning to Hope, who was talking to Dorothy.

"That's Sue, dear," Hope said. "Belinda doesn't exist." To Dorothy she said, "You're wrong. Kindness counts for someting," and turned back to Anna. "Belinda doesn't exist. Sue runs the place. The place was named by Evelyn from something in a poem."

When Sue came to their table Anna couldn't figure out her advertising. The white suit and vest said "fashion," but the heavy body and long brown hair said "matron," while the simple round face devoid of make-up said "friend." She was smiling at Anna. "Alexander Pope, they tell me. 'Belinda smiles and all the world is gay.' Perfect for us, we thought."

"Rape of the Lock," said Brenda.

"Not exactly what he had in mind," said Holly.

"Gay is slang. He couldn't have meant that," Joyce said.

"It meant 'loose liver' in the seventeenth century anyway," Dorothy said.

"Not liver—as in gall bladder?"

"No—as in immoral, idiot."

"Who said the liver was in the gall bladder?"

"Forget it! Forget it!"

"I must leave you academics. Enjoy yourselves and treat the kids right." She passed on to the next table wondering if that group was going to enjoy itself.

"Belinda smiled and all the world was gay." What a lovely idea, Anna was thinking. The whole world seemed to be here too, as the music boomed and feet crunched the floor and the bodies moved close together. She turned to Hope wondering if she dared go out on that floor with her, to get away together a bit, and be close to Hope again. She noticed a striking couple, a tiny red-head in jeans and a shirt and a curvy woman with what must be prematurely grey hair. Their dancing was perfect. The red-head was leading as they swung about the floor, slipping between other dancers, separating, coming together again with practiced grace, and suddenly they stood before them and were putting their arms around Hope and Holly. "Dorcas and Gloria" had become real and Anna loved their ease. This was their world and they possessed it.

But this was the mood of the place. The stamping shoes and the heavy drums, the growing, echoing chords as electric guitars hummed and someone sang "My life, she gave me my life" made Anna restless. She wanted to stand on that same floor and feel that energy pound through her own feet, and she pulled Hope up. Looking reluctant Hope agreed and led her away from the table far back on the dance floor behind a column. Conversation was impossible, but all Anna wanted was to hold Hope and feel her arms around her. But Hope began to dance. Anna knew she should have expected that lithe smooth-wired connectedness, but it was there as if Hope had danced all her life in wild bistros like this one. The music was building as that electric guitar pulsed and the voice wailed, "My life, my life—she gave me my life," and Anna saw arched backs, arms set on hips, smiles, lips, damp hair on foreheads, our world, our world, this is our time. Hope was smiling at her and Anna began to loosen tensed arms and shoulders and to move in a way she never had. Celebration it was. This is our time. "My life . . . " and the stamping shook the building as the sounds boomed and those handsome heads were tipped back asserting vitality and energy that sprang from arms, eyes, lips, and shoulders, from powerful thighs and slender hips, from the heavy-armed woman in her black caftan and the dreaming glamourous Rita Hayworths dancing together forever in the Blue Ballroom.

As Anna and Hope turned away from one another in their dancing, Anna saw a tiny man leap into the air with torsion that made her think of the Bolshoi. She pulled Hope over and together they stood with others watching. The bigger man moved slowly, smiling sleepily as his tight-muscled partner danced like a coiled spring, arms out to one side, then down to the ground in a crouch and a spring and turn, landing, knees bent, then one leg out before him like a cossack. His teeth flashed white as his silver medallion glittered on a leap and fell to his dark brown chest. His partner just turned arms over head letting his hips move slowly. Then the black man leapt at his chest, caught his shoulders and swung both legs up to the left, up to the level of their heads, bounced his feet down to the ground and swung them up to the right and the big man came to life, caught the other around the chest and bent over with him until, as they dipped to the ground, the black man jacknifed his legs above his partner's back.

When the music stopped everyone stamped, clapped and shouted "Bravo!" With much talk, thudding on steps, scraping of chairs people returned to their tables and the bar-people turned back to their drinks and conversation.

"Reminds me of Billy Jacobs, when he was with Stan."

"He's a dancer with Zack Scott, Jane said."

"Did you see that?" Anna asked the table at large.

"What?" said Dorothy and turned back to Dorcas. "You'll see what I mean."

"So you're enjoying yourselves, I see," Dorcas said to Anna and Hope. "Haven't seen Hope dance like that in years. Yes, Hope, I saw you, despite the column." Hope was mumbling something, no one could hear. "Will you dance with me later, Hope?" Dorcas smiled mischievously. "God knows who'll lead, but we'll settle that later." Hope agreed, shaking her head. Gloria turned immediately to Hope and began to engage her in a long story about herself and Dorcas and their car breaking down on the way over to Belinda's when they were passed by Stella driving like a mad thing. Stella, it seemed, had fixed their car with her jump cables and would arrive soon after pulling someone else out. When they met someone else in trouble trying to leave Belinda's as they arrived, Stella had to go over and try to help.

Gloria winked at Anna. "Between books Stella took an auto mechanic's course and now has to be gay auto mechanic for the world." In the general laughter Anna looked closely at Gloria, an impeccably groomed woman made up as Anna's mother would approve—with eye shadow, eye liner, blusher, all the jewelry, cosmetics, and grey wig of someone sitting in a box at the Madison Square Garden Horseshow. Gloria leaned toward Dorcas and murmured in her ear and Dorcas whispered back, like pretty creatures from a Watteau or Fragonard, bending and nodding. Then the music began and Dorcas stood erect, all five feet of her, and led the blooming Gloria down to the dance floor.

"I'll go see if Stella needs help," Hope said to Anna. "You OK? Be back soon." She stepped quickly off their dais and was down among the dancers and moving towards the door. Anna sat back to enjoy watching Dorcas and Gloria dancing like beautifully trained professionals. They seemed to know fifteen versions of the hustle, and she had tried to teach Carl two. Brenda and Joyce did a more sinuous dance, not taking the perfect step in perfect time, rather, pulled on elastic lines of desire slipping apart and drawn together again.

Anna remembered a large chilly community hall . . . the boys in their blue suits and girls in organza and taffeta. Mrs. Clyde Vetch stood fierce and upright at one end saying, "Boys, choose your partners for the samba." Anna picked at her white gloves as Ralph MacCurdy asked her to dance. He always asked her because he danced badly and sweated profusely, and Anna always said what a good dancer he was. He would blush and ask her if she would like to try circling to the left and she would agree. He was less good to the left, he said. Anna tried not to notice how he smelled; she knew it was nervousness and he couldn't help it. Mrs. Clyde Vetch would have been proud of Dorcas and Gloria.

If this was Stella, she had helped sick automobiles when she was half-stoned. Her eyes were bloodshot as she gave Anna a moist handshake. Sheryl stood back and smiled at a distance, looking anxiously at Hope. Did Stella actually say, "So this is your new one?" As far as Anna knew Hope had been quite alone for five years, but with this number of acquaintances Anna began to wonder how that was possible, and why, if it was so, Hope had ever asked her along with her camping. The list of people who would have liked to lope along with Hope began to seem pretty long, starting with the target shooter they had met at the door and maybe including Stella and the rest of Bucknell or whatever college was supporting this place through enthusiastic alumnae.

Stella sat down right by Anna in the chair Hope had left vacant as she went down with Dorcas to the dance floor, and Gloria smiled engagingly at Sheryl who gladly stepped into her arms. Anna dreaded the bloodshot look in Stella's eyes as Stella ordered a double scotch and turned to her. "So tell me all about yourself."

"What kind of thing do you mean?" Anna pushed her plate away, saying she wished the waitress would take their things. "It was a good dinner. Sorry you couldn't be here. You're quite a mechanic, Gloria says."

"Yes, indeed, quite the mechanic. Women should learn more about cars. Have you moved in with Hope?"

"I'm just visiting for a while."

"Oh, I see. Can't make up your mind, it it? Shall I be straight or curved? Young woman, you don't seem to know what you have in Hope."

"Oh, I know she's a wonderful—"

"She's a mighty fine woman. There is no one like her." Stella sat back and lit a thin brown cigar and gestured with her hand as the pungent smoke bit Anna's nostrils. "You don't seem to realize how strong and loyal and reliable and, anyway, she's beautiful and nothing else matters anyway, thanks," and she took a solid gulp of the Scotch just placed on the table. "Sheryl used to know—in the biblical sense—Eleanor, Hope's old flame."

Anna put her hand on Stella's arm. "I guess I don't want to hear this, Stella, please."

"Please what? What kind of kid are you? You better . . . "

"I'll hear what Hope tells. . . . "

"Learn all you can to cope at all."

"If she wants to tell me."

"Hope, dearie," Stella was saying as Hope returned smiling to the table, her arm around Dorcas, "you have chose yoahself a creehah-toor out of the old south, or ahnohther century."

"So Stella, how are ye doing?" Brenda leaned over Stella.

"My God, Brenda, Joyce, you lucky racist." Stella was weaving on her feet, pounding Joyce on the back and beaming at Brenda.

"Stella's out," Brenda said quickly to Hope. "Get her off Anna," and she turned back seductively to Stella.

Hope pulled up another chair at Anna's side, took her hand, "Want your after-dinner tea or coffee? We never got to it."

"What does she think she is, a riverboat captain?" Anna said, her voice trembling. "I've just been told how splendid you are, that I better appreciate you, or Stella and a mob will carry you off, rape me, or take you for themselves."

"Did she say all that? She's stoned, forget it."

"No, half of it I made up, but you get the point."

Hope put her hand under Anna's chin and leaned down and whispered in her ear. "Anna, come here. Anna-parsley, I feel appreciated, and, what's more, like licking your ear," she said, blowing warm air and whispering, "for a starter." Anna shivered and moved closer to Hope as the sound suddenly vibrated through the room and the lights all went out. In the blackness someone screamed "whoo-oo-pee" and a glass shattered. A flash bulb exploded to the left as the music began its pulsing beat and the strobe lights began to turn. The startling brilliance of white light in the darkness made Hope's face seem like a negative, pale with blackness around it, and into this stepped two beautiful women straight off the cover of Vogue dressed completely in white.

Holly hissed to Hope, "The Whites. Watch this."

They were thin as models, one wearing a white skirt slit up to mid-thigh, her blond hair twisted tight and bound up, the other in white skin-tight pants with a white band around her forehead. Their white satin made soft folds on their bodies as they moved with the skins of white snakes, rippling.

The other dancers stood back as The Whites were caught in flashes of the turning center light. Sudden illuminations showed them—arms out, fingers just touching, dancing as if beneath a glass globe. At first they danced in conventional patterns, turning away, turning toward each other. They began to circle about one another, first moving their hips, then slowly knocking hips as they watched one another, their arms raised. In that deafening sound with that glaring light flashing off their clothes they shimmered even in the mili-seconds of blackness. They glowed, light white-line drawings as all lights were shut down for an instant. Then one stayed front as the other swung her hips and she received the motion full on. As the music throbbed she thrust out her trousered leg and the other swung her leg over it, and, facing her partner, slid her pelvis down the extended leg as her partner's hips moved. The other dancers seemed to shudder and turn closer to the shelter of their partner's arms, as The Whites danced on beneath their soundless globe. In boneless art deco one arched her back toward the floor, the other turned her back on her and slipped and shimmeyed her back along her partner's body, moving along her partner's breasts down to a crouch, her neck and shoulders below her partner's pelvis. Then drawn up by her partner she was swung into a dip, her hair touching the ground when the light switch was thrown on full.

In all the applause Anna watched them. Their skins glistened. Their faces, made up for the strong lights, looked a faded pink. Unable to leave the dance floor in the pressing crowd, they began the ordinary dancing together of two tired married people, but for a few moments in that blackness they had been glimmering creatures out of fantasy, Titania and her glorious consort.

"How d'ja like them apples?" Stella called out as they pulled out their chairs to sit down.

"Beautiful, they were beautiful," said Anna.

"They were wicked," Brenda said, setting one hand on her hip. "Real wick-id."

"I've seen them before," Holly said. "Last Memorial Day."

"Oh, they turn out when they're sure there'll be those to see them," Stella said, as if she could say more.

"Do you know them?" Anna asked.

"Does she know them?" Dorothy said rolling her eyes. "You may regret the question."

"They sure do in public what I'd like to do in bed," said Joyce. "But I'd break my back."

Brenda laughed. "Please, don't aspire; my gymnastic days are over."

"Listen, they need the turn-on." Stella relit her cigar. "Perverse. After this they won't go home and have an orgy. They'll go home and sleep, gratified that they made you lust after them."

"Well," Joyce said with a sign, "they should damn well go home and sleep gratified."

"Come on, woman," Brenda said, pulling her up. "I can't take this competition sitting down."

"Must I?" With a look of anguish Joyce sailed off.

"You really get turned on watching what the simple folk do—don't you?" Stella said, putting her hand between her legs and humping her chair forward. "Don't you, Anna?"

Anna looked to Hope for help.

Holly said, "Take it easy, Stella, Anna's a visitor here."

"Just my point, baby. She's a visitor—like the visitors brought to view the mad people in Bedlam. 'My, my' and 'tsk tsk' aren't they strange and wonderful! Shall I take you on a tour. . . . "

"Shut up, Stella!" Hope was on her feet, looking as if she would smash Stella's face against the table top. "You've said enough."

"Going to protect the little lady?"

"Stella, you don't know when to stop and never did."

Stella stared at Hope a second. "Chris' sake, Hope." Stella's voice was a whine. "I like it here. I have a right to be here. I've earned it. She makes me feel like a goddamned voyeur—watchin' my own people. Chris' sake, Hope." Stella stamped out her cigar, looked as if she was going to burst into weeping, heaved herself up and stamped toward the bar, one pant leg caught up in her shining western boot.

Sheryl looked toward Hope, then Anna. "I'm sorry. She doesn't mean anything." She got up and started after Stella, saying, "I guess she's had too. . . . "

"Can we go, Hope?" Anna said. "Will the others?" Anna was biting her lip.

Dorothy stood up and spoke to Hope. "No problem. Holly and I can go home with Brenda and Joyce. We'll see you later."

As Anna and Hope made their way through the dancing couples Holly said, looking after them, "Stella always had a yen for Hope and she can't stand it."

"Is that it?"

"Part of it." Holly grinned. "Why do I feel like such an old married?" She patted Dorothy's hand. "And I can't even get you to marry me."

"Let's have another Scotch."

"You have one. I'm driving."

"Since when?"

"I feel like being mistressful—or something," Holly laughed as she signaled the table hop.

"Well, you two really missed it," Dorothy said when Dorcas and Gloria reached their table.

CHAPTER TWELVE

HOPE was driving slowly to Dorothy's, aware that she could throw her eyes from the road and wrench the steering wheel toward an oncoming car.

"You know I didn't mean anything, Hope. I am just interested. Why shouldn't I be, Hope? Is that so bad? It's all new to me, after all."

Suddenly Hope felt anger leap to her throat. "So it is new, but you forget, it's been a long time brewing."

"What do you mean? What are you saying?"

"I'm saying that you act as if you aren't a part of this, but you are. Stella is right, you can't go about like an interested tourist. You've made a commitment, some kind of one anyway, that says you can't go about the island looking at the interesting natives."

Anna was silent, her hands clenched together on her knees, a proper school girl again.

"I know that, Hope. At least, I think that is true. I didn't mean for you to think I was . . . I was. . . . " Anna began to sob and Hope pulled the car over beneath some trees. They sat side by side until Hope put her arm around her shoulders, "Let me get us back to Dorothy's, honey, we can't sit here." Anna gulped and nodded and Hope drove them home silently, her brain rushing.

When they were sitting on the big double bed in Dorothy's guest room Hope said very softly, "I don't know how much of this I can stand myself."

"What do you mean?" Anna's voice was shrill. "I'm doing my best. I can't know everything."

"But you play dumb, as if you don't understand. Are you hiding or what? If you tell yourself you know nothing of all this, does that make you less guilty? Or what?"

"I don't feel guilty. I just love you, Hope. Why are we fighting?"

"We aren't fighting—it's just that . . . I never had children . . . when you act so . . . curious, innocent and curious . . . I feel, I know how you feel, or felt in Canada, but it makes me feel . . . like a freak, like a . . . "

"What?" Anna leaned her head on her arms, "I never meant . . . "

She was shocked at Hope's running eyes and gasping voice, saying, "Never mind what you never meant. There are consequences of actions

119

whether you meant them or not. I am real. Not just the big protector . . . or . . . or the big corruptor, either. You can't play games and put your toe in the cold water. You've got to admit . . . grow up . . . "

"I have admitted, Hope; I'm saying how I feel about you."

"But that's something special, right? It's me. You're not one of us. That stigma doesn't apply to you. Christ, I don't mean decide whether to be straight or not. God knows whether that's a decision or what it is—just realize what you are and be it, but don't make me watch you as you hover and play coy. 'Do they really? Is that so?' As if we were all freaks at a side show."

As Hope's sobs quieted she barely heard Anna say, "I won't."

Early in the morning Anna left. She had waited until Hope was breathing deeply and then, when the others returned early in the morning, she got Holly to drive her to the station. Because she had no place to go, Holly gave her Dorothy's keys to her own place, saying, "I'll be back late tonight. You'll have to pick up food. You're sure you'll be all right?"

Anna nodded, picked up her bag, and walked into the train station to get her ticket, calculating how much money she had, conscious that she was clenching her mind like a fist, not to let something through. She would get a paper and look for places to live, for jobs she might apply for. She had a summer with the children set at Mother Johnson's and money for a while. Money meant time. Carl . . . she couldn't think of. If she could just think, but now she would get her ticket, one way, get her ticket, then a paper. She would sit over there away from the sunlight. No, she would go outside to wait for the train. She would get her ticket, then a paper.

She had to think about something but not now. Her eyes met those of the newspaper vender. "You want something else, Miss?" She shook her head and walked quickly outside. Holly lived in Greenwich Village, off Hudson, somewhere near Horatio. She barely knew the area except that it was near Pik-a-Treasure Kennels where they had looked at puppies once for the children. Anyway she wouldn't stay there. She couldn't stay with Holly. She needed to be away from all of them. She had to sit, just to sit, run no more, just sit where no one could see her and then maybe, maybe . . . She didn't know . . . something might happen. Had she gotten her ticket? Yes, and a paper.

As she stared out the window at the telephone poles and the ground passing her eyes, the swift telephone poles taking giant steps, her throat suddenly constricted. What was she doing going *away* from Hope? She should be running toward her. Something might happen. The train might be derailed, or Hope might crash her car not knowing that Anna loved her, wanted only to be with her. What if Hope thought she was angry or hated her or wanted to hurt her? By her foolishness she was running away from the only person she would ever want to hold in her lifetime. She might see hundreds of Carls, and Mother Johnsons, and Stellas, on and on forever. She got up suddenly, dropping her purse to the floor and started for the front of the train. But of course, the train was already moving. People were looking at her, moving their feet back so she could get by. The tram was swaying in its speed. She fished up her handbag as she struggled out and went to the water fountain.

The water was good. Where she had been with Carl and her children was crazy. There was nothing for her in those locked-in houses. How could she not shout at Jamie and Tim when she was trying to be Mother Johnson and hated Carl's very smell? How long had she hated him? She mustn't let too much through at once or she couldn't bear it, like a giant valve on a pressure cooker that begins to sputter, then to jiggle, then to tremble and make tiny leaps and shakings as it hisses and hisses warning her about the tumult within.

Beautiful Hope calling herself a freak. Anna had said things, but she hadn't meant them. "Mean well." The traitors who meant well led their lovers through centuries around the infernal regrets. The weak smile, "but I meant well." She was really a woman, not a freak, because she had borne children. Is that what she thought? The train's noise helped, granting a small mat of privacy because no one could hear through it. Having children proved her womanhood, hadn't it, so it didn't matter if she slummed a little with the gays. It didn't mean she was gay. Was that what she had thought? Hope was right to be doubtful. She'd never married or had children. Stella was right then. She did feel herself to be a real woman visiting the crazies, not the crazies, the cripples. She had been saying, "Oh and look, look see see. How they dance! How they sing!" It was their celebration, their joy. At what? They were together, maybe— not being stared at by the normals, just the way she and Hope had watched the beautiful giraffes. They were the people; the animals bore it patiently.

Was that what it had been, really? She, the earth mother with her loved children, could sympathize with the poor cripples—how well they managed to live. But she was womanly and rich with maternal hormones spilling through her body as she welcomed Hope against her ripe breasts. That was the way she had felt in their hot little tent in Canada. She turned to the Apartment section of the paper and started with 'Studios.' How would Hope take the note she had left? Had it been too curt? She couldn't remember what she had said, but she had begged Hope not to follow her or call her, she knew that. How could she have? No, she was right. That brilliant sexual thread ran through everything: loving children, loving mother, loving teacher, loving friends. Why did the golden twist make the cripple, or was it a cripple?

She stood in the center of Grand Central terminal and let her eyes float up like every tourist's before she remembered and followed the signs for the shuttle to Times Square. She had to save money and didn't want to reach Holly's too fast. The noise and the busy people moving by her, walking around looking, buying, talking, were hitting her like a wet towel, stunning her and energizing her at once. She wanted to walk, bustle, walk busily somewhere as if she had a purpose, and she wanted to drift, to ask the nearest woman where she was going. She walked down the stairs to the shuttle and passed that same nun with the tambourine held out for coins. The woman had been there for years, ten at least. The city had once been her friend and could be again.

"But I gave you a dollar for two tokens and you didn't give me any change."

"That's right. I didn't." He looked at her—refusing, forcing her.

"But I don't understand. If it's thirty five cents a token then . . . "

"Where ya been, lady? Tokens been fifty cents for a year and a half." He shook his head with pity and concealed delight. His win.

She swallowed hard against the foolish tears rushing to her eyes. SHUTTLE. She followed the sign. It would take another token to get down to Sheridan Square. Why didn't she just get out and take a taxi? She had the money. She didn't know why she wanted to make it this way. She kept telling herself she had to save money, but she wanted to walk there by herself, see it all, get through the shock of the city all at once.

In truth she wanted to be tired. She wanted to look grimy and tired and feel she was abused so she could pity herself. A sudden thought struck her belly like an opened palm. She stopped suddenly and leaned against the tunnel wall. It was grey, filthy. She had to bend down as if to touch her suitcase to let the dizziness pass. The thought had dissolved into vertigo. The ground seemed to be waving beneath her feet like . . . trying to dance under the whirling strobe lights. The wall was turning slowly. It was like being in the bottom of a grey bowl. She hadn't noticed the heat. The tunnel echoed with footsteps. She turned slowly, propping herself up by an elbow set against the wall. She saw a heavyset man looking at her suitcase, her bag, his eyes sliding toward her, then away. She picked up her suitcase, pulled her handbag further over on her shoulder and tried to walk firmly toward the shuttle to Times Square.

"Please do not follow me or call. When I can I will call you. Do not think I am 'playing coy.' " "I am sorry" was crossed out. The note was trembling in Hope's hand. She stared at it and around the room. She slashed her arm down the clothes bar in the closet. Anna's clothes were gone, even her bathing suit off the chair. She walked to the window and back to the bed, to the door, and turned back. She stood in the middle of the room. She sat down and stared at the floor.

Dorothy and Holly looked quickly at each other when Hope opened the door. She walked to the window and spoke to them with her back to them. "I just want to know the answer to a couple of questions. Do you know where she is, Holly?" She turned to see Holly's quiet nod. "Is she going to keep in touch with you?"

"I think so. She had made no plans."

"Did she say she was going back to Carl?"

"She didn't mention him. She just came to me as we came in this morning. She said she had to go away, asked if I could help, said that she had nowhere to go if I wouldn't, then spoke of YWCA's and such. . . . You promise you won't follow her?"

"Yes."

"She'll be at my place tonight—perhaps for a few nights—until she makes her mind up where to go."

"At your place?" Hope collapsed into an arm chair and sat still until Dorothy nodded to Holly, and she poured out the breakfast juice. To Dorothy it was all much too public. Fortunately, Brenda and Joyce were still sleeping. Obviously Anna was unsuited to Hope and it was just as well it happened fast, before either of them had invested too much. Holly would justify Hope no matter what, but Hope hadn't shown such good judgment in her last choices.

"Judgment—smudgment," Holly said later. "Are you crazy? Something clicks or it doesn't. Dorothy, let me tell you something," Holly said, perching on the arm of Dorothy's big chair. "I have loved you long, but it is very much against my better judgment."

Dorothy gave her a shove.

"No. Honestly. We don't agree much of the time. My metabolism and yours collide. It's mornings for me and evening for you. We meet with luck on occasional afternoons. But I tell you, chicken, pissy as you are, and dear as I am, I can stand your vices, you appreciate my strengths, sometimes, and I love, repeat lo-ve you, sometimes. So shut up about judgment."

Dorothy shook her head, "She should cut her losses and forget Anna. She's a dodger. You watch, she'll just hang around a little, try out some ladies in the big city, and then decide that since men can take better care of her, she'll just take her sweet parts back to them to be protected for the rest of her life."

"Maybe, but why did she leave Hope, then? Hope's trouble is that she endures all. She'd never have thrown her out. She'd have protected her forever."

Hope heard their murmurings through the door as she packed her things. She couldn't even remember what it had all been about. She had said something about Anna's being coy, and she didn't even know what

she meant by it. She surely hadn't meant that she wanted Anna to leave.
She wanted her closer if anything, closer. She bent her head into the V of
her clenched arm. How had the poison spread so fast?

Hope's past . . . the spiteful Eleanor who had stamped out saying that
Hope gave her no air, Stella's encounter with Anna at Belinda's, and
Anna's leaving provided the conversation for Dorothy and Holly as they
drove back to the city that July fourth weekend. Dorothy expressed herself as not particularly pleased that Anna was going to park herself at
Holly's. She wasn't so unattractive after all, and Dorothy knew Holly's
susceptibilities. They planned out the following week before they would
meet again to go out to Dorothy's.

"Shall we invite Anna to spend the weekend with us on the South
Shore?" Holly said. "She hasn't anyplace to go."

"Isn't it enough to offer her your apartment, Holly? She's got to find
her own way. It'll be soon enough if we invite her out over Labor Day."

The streets were dark when Dorothy pulled up outside Holly's brown-
stone. Holly patted her hand quickly. "See you Friday—maybe sooner?"

"I'll call tomorrow night as usual. Stay out of trouble, dearie,"
Dorothy said with a small smile.

"Fear not." Holly tugged at her overnight case, her raincoat and
purse, leaving the car with a thump and a slamming door. As she turned
the key in her own lock she regretted having given up her privacy to Anna.
As she opened the door slowly she saw Anna resting on her elbow watching the door open.

"It's just me." As the light from the street lamp sliced through the
slats of the blinds, Holly could see the sheets half falling off the sofa.

"I'm glad you're here. Was your drive all right?"

Holly bustled about the apartment after apologizing for turning on
the lights. At midnight, with a class to teach in the morning, she had no
time to chat, though she supposed that's what Anna wanted.

"I'll leave early in the morning," Holly said over her shoulder as she
checked the refrigerator and poured herself some milk. "You got some
breakfast stuff, good."

"I won't stay long. I'll start looking tomorrow, don't worry."

Anna's voice sounded so thin that Holly peered around the refrigerator to look at her. "No problem. But we can talk about it tomorrow over
breakfast if you're up, or over dinner if you're not. I'll write on the memo
board when I'll be back tomorrow." When Anna did not move, Holly
said, "OK?"

"OK," said Anna and slid down under the bed clothes.

When Holly came out of the shower to dress in the morning, Anna's
sofa was made up for the day and the table was laid for breakfast.

"Any job ideas?" Holly said, pouring out cereals for both, opening a window, pulling out an apple and putting it in a plastic bag as she turned the gas to boil water.

"First, I thought, the apartment, then the job. Maybe receptionist?"

"Tomorrow, after school, no meetings. I'll meet you at the printers."

"What printers?"

"Old friends, job for them to do for the Women's Center. You can come. Maybe they'll have something for you." Holly's shorthand speech was punctuated by bites and swallows as she stirred her coffee and reached over to write on the memo board, "back by five." Her briefcase was propped by the door to be picked up on the way out as she tucked in her shirt, and she waved at Anna, saying, "Take care now," and was gone, her feet tapping lightly on the stairs.

Anna saw the briefcase whisked up and the door shutting and felt the silence fall around her shoulders like a brown blanket. She sat with her head down and her hands in her lap as the refrigerator whirred, turning its motor on. She supposed it needed cleaning. Could she get an apartment without having a job or a credit rating, she wondered? Words were forming on her lips the way they did on the pale lips of old women who talked to themselves on the street. I want to go home. I want to go home. She stared at the coffee spoon. But there was no home. When the roar of the sanitation truck began outside and she heard garbage pails clanking as they were dropped empty to the sidewalk, she got up.

"Well, I'd better get busy," she heard herself say as she started to clean up the breakfast dishes.

The next day Holly led her briskly through the warehouse area, saying, "Dorothy won't come here. Can't stand them."

"Who?" Anna asked, avoiding a man with a dolly pushing cartons of paper goods.

"The jewels." Holly pulled Anna's arm just before she stepped in front of a backing truck. "The printers. They all left impossible lives and took new names: Crystal, Jannschild, Opal Sarahschild, and Pearl Pearls-child—screw the patriarchal surnames."

"Why does Dorothy object? Thanks."

"Herstory. Come on, this way, watch the stairway." A bell was ringing as an iron stairway cover opened up, perfect to fall into as one rushed by.

"What do you mean, her story?"

"They call themselves Herstory Printers, meaning to take the 'his' out of history, which never had it. Drives Dorothy up the wall. This way." Holly dodged between two trucks and led Anna down a wide sidewalk.

"Isn't it just symbolic? What's bad?"

"Here, this is better," Holly said, getting into her swinging stride.

"Dorothy's in Classics, language. She says you can't falsify language—that it may be man-derived, but there it is and we must accept it. She dies over the jokes taking the 'man' out of 'maneuver' and 'manage,' and 'men' out of 'menstruation'—where they never were. Says women make fools of themselves with such garbage."

"But it's symbolic. If we see it there, it operates on us."

Holly stopped and stared at her. "What are you gonna do then, re-write the language? You can't turn manage into womanage!"

"She must hate 'person'—like chairperson."

"Thinks 'one' would be better, like in 'someone.' 'Chairone.' "

"So she agrees to change the language in some places and not in others?" Anna said, glad to be talking with Holly for a change.

"I guess so. Point is, and she's right . . . " Holly said, jabbing her index finger into the air by her right ear. . . . Anna lost whatever truth Holly was expounding in the rush of sound as the traffic moved at the green light.

"Stop a minute and have some coffee?" In surprise Anna agreed. They walked into one of those fast food places where the counters surrounded the waitresses in their little white caps and yellow aprons.

"Dorothy's a real scholar. Working on Horace. An article now."

"You teach too, don't you?" Anna wished she could see Holly's face, but they were seated to stare at the customers opposite or the slow-moving waitress.

"Yeah, reading, though. I like it, really like it, but it isn't being a scholar."

"But you did graduate work, too, didn't you?"

"ABD."

"I beg your pardon.?"

"Got a B.A., then did doctoral work up to the dissertation and quit."

Holly said she had decided to quit when she realized she wasn't learning anything important, that she had quit in order to learn valuable things. Anna respected Holly for flouting the system so satisfactorily. She had been teaching remedial reading at a senior college now for three years.

"Fact is—want a doughnut? Fact is, I'm not the digger Dorothy is. I like teaching reading, think it's important, do it pretty well, very well, really, but I had planned to be a big deal scholar too—Milton, but I got cold feet. Woman's disease. No confidence. But Dorothy's a digger. She'll know more about Horace than he did before she's through."

As they went up in the elevator to the Herstory Printers, Holly chuckled. "Dorothy says when she heard they call themselves Crystal, Opal, and Pearl she wanted to call herself Brick. Come on through here."

They walked down a carpetless hall before they came to an arrow pointing to "Herstory Printers."

"Hi, Jewels," Holly said striding in and calling through a half-door. One woman came out with a big smile and embraced Holly. As Holly made arrangements for the Women's Center flier Anna walked about looking at their bulletin boards, the neat mail boxes for each worker. She could see the presses in the back room, and when one of the Jewels nodded, she walked back. There were two women in jeans and tee shirts, braless both, moving about the presses, adjusting gadgets and machinery, peaceful in all the noise of the machines. They called something to one another and one dark-haired woman came over to her. "You with Holly?"

"She brought her," called the other in the lavender shirt.

"OK, then, just don't touch anything."

Holly re-emerged from the front and introduced Anna to Opal, the dark-haired woman, Pearl, in the lavender tee shirt, and Crystal, the woman in the front.

"Crystal was saying that there were no jobs then, but she thought she had a line on the living thing. Wants a summer apartment, right?"

Anna was startled when Opal said to her, "A lot to try to do at once. Job and a place to stay. Where you staying now?"

"With Holly for a day or two."

"Where's Dorothy?" Opal looked surprised and busied herself straightening some stacks of posters.

"No, I mean. . . . " Anna knew she was blushing fiercely, but the other woman's low chuckle made her drop her explanation.

"So, do you know the firehouse? Why don't I show you one of our favorite gathering places." Anna liked the "our" and looked more closely at Opal. The plain face unadorned by the merest shrewd of cosmetics gave her confidence somehow.

"Where is the firehouse?"

"So, that's the story," Holly was saying to Dorothy as they drove out to the South Shore that Friday. "Anna went with Opal to the Firehouse for some dance or other on Tuesday night, went with her to some meeting of the gay women over thirty at some church on Thursday night, and god knows what is planned for the weekend. Since I haven't bugged the apartment, we'll never know."

"She's not grieving over Hope then."

"Maybe not, but she makes me think of *The Education of Henry Adams*."

"A crash course, you mean?"

When Opal picked Anna up Saturday morning at her apartment she sent her back inside to dress down. "Put on sneakers or sandals and an old shirt."

"Thought we were going to your place."

"We are. My kids are excited about meeting you. Come on, I told them lunch. You look fantastic, let's go." Opal put her arm under Anna's and turned her toward the door, stopped and looked at her a moment, then leaned over and kissed her lightly on the mouth, "Mmmm—you smell good, let's go."

Turning her key Anna realized that she had no idea where they were going, had left no note, but what difference did it make? Her kids were all right. Hope . . . well . . . it was a gorgeous day, going to be warm, and Opal was saying something about friends who wanted a cat sitter.

"They want to leave their apartment to tour around Europe. They don't want to leave their cats and dogs with a vet because the animals are miserable, so they're looking for an apartment sitter for the month of August. Crystal's idea. She made the connection and asked me to ask you."

"Where's their place? Apartment sitting! Never thought of it. Where do they live?"

"You dig it!" Opal laughed, "So do I. Riverside Drive somewhere. Real nice in summer. Wind sears you up there in winter."

"When do they go? When could I see them?" Anna caught Opal's arm and looked into that soft, smiling face, thinking, "How amazing!"

"We'll see them tomorrow, if you want. They said they're free Sunday afternoons."

Opal led Anna down into the subway and they went uptown to 42nd where they shuttled across town to the IRT. Opal contrived to pilot Anna into a front car before she had time to see the destination, and the train started with a jerk. Large Puerto Rican families hefted picnic hampers, black children and parents held fishing rods. Hundreds of sexy teenagers with bathing suits swung their hips against one another, stared into each others' eyes and snapped gum. Opal's soft breast was against Anna's arm before she turned her head sharply. "I wondered when you'd notice."

"Where are we?"

"Roaring up to the Bronx. So? You don't need a visa. Most of these people going to Orchard Beach." Opal shouted in her ear as the train started up again. They were disgorged with the others and ran down the long stone steps. Many families crossed directly by the pedestrian bridge into Pelham Bay Park, the kids streaking ahead, shouting and pushing one another.

A rickety bus took them across the highway through a park near a dump where hundreds of gulls wheeled, scavenging for food, to a small bridge where clanging bells and flashing lights stopped them as the bridge folded upward. Anna looked out the window and was annoyed with herself for putting herself into Opal's hands this way. She could spend her time better than traveling on subways for a whole beautiful Saturday morning. Hope was probably in her garden now, maybe working at Threshold. She knew she couldn't go there and mustn't think about it, her own failure. How she could so disgust and turn from her a woman who had turned warm and melting in her arms appalled her. She swallowed hard and tried to notice what Opal was saying, but she felt the hot resentment in her throat, her anger at Opal and at herself for permitting this non-sensical venture. A day among crowds of yelling picnickers she did not need.

The bus thumped to a stop and the Orchard Beachers lined up to push their way out of the bus. "Not yet, just a few more minutes." They banged and shook their way to a small bridge where some people were fishing, but did not stop. The small bridge led across to an island lined with boats—fishing boats, rowboats, barges, sailboats. Soon they were rattling down a small main street lined with marinas and seafood restaurants. At a traffic light Opal finally pulled the cord. She led Anna into a marina when Anna finally stopped her. "I thought we were going to your home."

"We are. Come on. The kids are waiting."

Anna shrugged, promising herself to avoid Opal and her outings after this. Opal stepped carefully over a paint can and nodded to a woman shellacking her tiller, waved to a man caulking something, and led the way briskly through the marina to a small boardwalk that jutted out into the water. The boats moored there were filled with people fixing their boats, rigging them, calling to one another. Opal stopped at the end of the broadwalk and put two fingers in her mouth. Her piercing whistle brought heads out of galleys and started two dogs barking. She whistled again, two shorts and a long. In a second Anna heard in the distance her whistle's near-twin, two shorts and two longs.

"In a few minutes."

"Opal, tell me about them—their ages."

"Lil is twelve and Ad is ten. Here she is. See the dinghy?" A blue dinghy that said "Lil's" was moving sturdily toward them from the center of the bay where a rugged barge rode at anchor. The youngster showed a bony back as she pulled on the oars, each stroke firm and steady.

Lil notched the painter around the piling, pulling the dinghy close to the boardwalk, and looked up at Anna. As Anna looked down into that skinny face she felt a jolt. As sure as a telegram the eyes set in the cavern of those bones said "I am myself. This is my world. Who are you?" Anna wanted to shake her hand suddenly, and did so.

Upon their formal meeting Lilith did not smile, or say something polite; she merely nodded gravely, and, when they were settled, pushed off. Anna felt embarrassed to be sitting back in the dinghy as a twelve-year-old child pulled at the oars, but Lilith did not even seem winded. "Ad and I figured since it was so warm we'd put up the awning on deck and have lunch outside."

"Good idea. The lines still in good shape?"

Lilith nodded. "And we made a couple trips for water. But nothing else happened. Just lunch."

In answer to Anna's questions Opal explained that they had lived on the houseboat for four years, that they imported all their water by dinghy, but were going to get a holding tank soon, that they had no electricity on the boat, but in winter when they used the marina's hook-up they had both water and electricity. Lil chipped in with explanations or additions occasionally but mainly she concentrated on her rowing. When Anna told her that she was a few years older than her "own little girl" Lil showed no interest. She negotiated their mooring with practiced ease after Opal and Anna climbed up the rope ladder. When Lil reached the deck Opal began to take Anna around the houseboat, showing her everything. Below decks her brother was whizzing around putting tomatoes, tuna fish, mayonnaise, and lettuce on a platter. Holding his mayonnaise-covered hands in the air and licking a thumb he gave Lil a questioning look. She shrugged. "OK, I guess."

"The bread and iced tea," Adam said, and Lil turned to take them up to the deck.

As they sat on cushions at a low table rapidly passing platters and making themselves sandwiches, Opal was explaining that she commuted from the house boat. The children made elaborate constructions with ketchup and tuna fish and salami, and Opal did not correct them. Anna could hardly believe that she was not a plane's flight from New York City. The air had the fresh quality it gets from breezing over water. Anna inhaled a tangy gust that she could almost taste. They had set small boxes of privet around the deck so that they had some protection from curious boats. There was even a small spice garden in one corner of the deck. Anna wanted to inquire about such things as laundry, reading at night, and rent in the winter, but instead she inhaled again, sipped her tea, and wondered about Opal. Obviously celibacy was not precisely her choice. Yet she and the children made a very strong community. Anyone would enter it at her, maybe his, peril. Her own children would adore such a life, but she wondered if she would dare leave them alone on a boat even if they were older.

After lunch Anna found herself stretching out on the deck under the children's awning and studying the way they had hooked it up. She heard them calling to Opal, "Going to the other side to see if anything's in our pot. Flounder otherwise, OK? We'll swim when we get back."

Opal settled down next to Anna after taking things below decks. "Maybe lobster tonight—if anything's in our pots. You'll stay, won't you?"

Anna sat up and propped the pillows behind her against the wall. "That's generous of you, but I hadn't intended to. This has been wonderful."

"It isn't over yet," Opal said, running a finger lightly along the hollow in Anna's cheek. "If we're going to see those people, your apartment people, Marge and Audrey, tomorrow afternoon, you might as well stay here on the boat for dinner and the night, and we can leave tomorrow after a leisurely Sunday morning on the water." She added the last phrase as if she knew how tempting it would sound to a city dweller. When Anna was silent gazing out into the bay, Opal said, "Well, at least you don't have to make up your mind yet, do you? Whatever you want to do. It's a gorgeous day, the sun is hot. We can loll in it, then swim, have a good dinner and I can take you home. . . . "

"I can take the bus."

"Or put you on the bus later tonight, OK?"

"OK."

"So, let's loll." Opal pulled her cushion out from under the awning, rolled out of her jeans, slipped off her shirt, and settled herself on her back in the sun and was soon asleep.

The water lapped the sides of the houseboat. Anna slid down and lay in the awning's shadow. The boat's movement was gentle. She closed her eyes and drifted in to a semi-doze listening to the sea bird sounds and the far-off voices from the shore. In a few minutes she sat up, her nerves jangling. She let herself look across at Opal, lying with loosened thighs and generous breasts slipping to the side. In irritation got up and began to roam around the boat. The central room looked like a living room with sofa and coffee table, small library, and sleeping alcove. The children's room looked like any child's room in Stevensville. Anna glanced at the tiny kitchen and went up on deck. Standing, she could see the sail boats littering the bay like small white handkerchiefs, but she could see out to the Whitestone Bridge and the long, low profile of the Throg's Neck Bridge beyond. The bridge on her right must be the one they crossed to get onto the island. Indeed she was a tourist . . . exploring the terrain . . . almost taking notes on the natives. Suddenly all countries seemed remote, fit for the anthropologist's index cards.

She kept hearing horns, little toots in groups of three. A launch responded and came to pick up a family on its way home—signs, the language they spoke on water. As she stood on the deck a small sailboat tacked across their bow and a man, woman, and child waved to her. The houseboat's flag was snapping in the rising breeze and she was glad to lie down in the warm sun out of the wind. She wanted to wake up Opal to warn her against getting too much sun on her breasts, but the thought was almost tactile and besides Opal wasn't a child.

"I wondered when you'd wake," Opal was saying as she stirred. She was leaning over her, her full breasts warm against her shoulder. Anna turned her head and caught the smooth nipple between her lips, her tongue exploring its delicate surface. Abruptly she tried to roll away, but Opal's weight held her down and her tongue, hard as a diver, flicked within her lips. When her arms gripped Opal's back, feeling their bodies pull together, her mind watched that hillside she had seen not long before. But she had been wrong—there were borders, fences, even neat stone walls on that wind-cleansed hillside. The old borders were gone, but there were borders. Clear ones.

"Anna, what is this?" Opal bent near her head. "Let me hold you. What is it, dear?" Opal whispered in her ear, "What is it, Anna?" When Anna remained silent Opal said, "Anna, you don't owe me anything. We're making no promises, darling. This is just comforting, just good feelings; you're not telling me anything forever. Do you understand?" Anna raised her head and looked into that open face. Deciphered its language. Then, slowly, propping herself up on an elbow she put her hand gently along Opal's cheek and drew her down to her.

"Pull more on the starboard, Lil." Adam's shrill voice shocked Opal and Anna into propriety and Opal into her shirt. "Two lobsters, Ma!" Adam was shouting as they moored. "How about that! Will Anna stay for dinner?" Blushing, Anna nodded her head in the affirmative.

CHAPTER THIRTEEN

WITH tongs Lil dropped the twitching lobster into the pot. "Looks like they've got something going between them." "Great, we get to sleep out on deck then," Adam grinned.

"I guess I've never tasted fresher, sweeter lobster in my life," Anna said, working hard at getting the meat out of a small claw.

"That's not the way to do it," Lil said.

"I sold fourteen last summer," Adam said, cracking a claw.

"You've got to suck real strong, like this," Lil said, demonstrating with gusto.

Opal looked across at Anna. "OK, Lil, I think she has the idea."

Anna smiled in glazed fashion at Lil, and setting her lobster claw down she asked Adam how and when he set his traps.

"Aren't you going to eat it?" Lil asked, reaching to borrow Adam's claw cracker.

Anna glanced at Opal, who put her head back and laughed.

"What's so funny, Ma?"

"That's what I'd like to know," Anna said, taking the bread from the center dish. "Does your mother laugh often unprovoked?"

"Oh yes, she laughs a lot."

"Who was unprovoked?" Opal said, looking arch.

"If we're speaking of provocation," Anna said, "you know more about that."

"Jerry Bilinski is the really funny guy. You should see his rubber spiders."

Lil turned and whispered to Adam, who nodded and said, "After dinner I want to show Anna my sand painting. I have this set, see and . . . " He looked at Lil. "Anyway it's neat." He resumed eating.

Opal put a platter of corn on the table. "Early, probably Mexican. Four minutes exactly."

"That *and* strawberries, fan-tas-tic," Lil said.

After dinner Ad and Opal did what Opal called organizing as Lil showed Anna her astronomy chart and told her how on clear nights she plotted "where things are."

"Do you grasp this?" Anna said as Opal re-emerged from the galley.

"Partly. Anyway, Lil explains it to me. Let's settle. Where's the wind, Lil?"

"Southwest, this's the best place." They followed Lil and set up their deck chairs in the place she showed them. "Out of the wind but in it enough," Lil said with satisfaction, propping herself up on her cushions. It was quite dark. Lights from the island made bright roads toward the boat.

They lay back listening to the water sounds and the dimmed music from the restaurants at seaside.

"I think I envy you people," Anna siad to Lil. "Do your friends at school envy you?"

"You bet." Lil sat up cross-legged. "I explain the jobs we have to do, but they wish they lived here anyway. In the summer we miss TV, but it's no good in the summer anyhow."

"And I go to Jerry's if there's something special I want to see," Adam said, pushing his sand painting toward Anna and holding a flashlight so that she could see it. Muted as the colors were, the design was startling, filled with the wings of birds, it seemed. Anna looked sharply at the wiry boy, thin and small for his age. His eyes glinted and his eyelids crinkled slightly at the edges as she said softly, "Nice."

Anna reached toward him feeling that shock of connection. "Very nice," she said, her voice low.

Anna wanted to ask questions, immense ones that even Opal probably could not answer. Instead she tipped back in her lounge chair and tried to let the world be, tried to let herself hear the water's lapping and chuckling against the hull. Everyone was quiet as the jukebox somewhere sang a song she remembered that sounded very different here. The lights shivered paths outward from the shoreline, and overhead the ancient stars wheeled.

Anna awoke in a tangle of legs and sheets, her moist hand holding Opal's breast. The sun was pouring in and the boat was rising and falling gently. Quickly she slipped out of bed, put on her damp swimsuit and in a few steps dived from the deck, seeing her own stomach yellow in the sun's light just before her head and shoulders struck the chilled waters. The cold was delicious.

"You can't do that. She's swimming with no one watching." Lil peered over the edge and then climbed down into her dinghy to act as lifeguard. In a moment Ad came sailing through the air in a cannon ball. When they heaved themselves dripping up to the deck, Opal appeared, grumbling. "Some leisurely Sunday morning."

"He's blue at the mouth," Anna said, wrapping her towel around Ad and embracing him in a rough hug as she rubbed his back and arms.

"Glorious day," she said, splashing into the kitchen to put on some water, tea for her, coffee for Opal.

The deep-throated barks began from a back room and proceeded up to the door until a smartly dressed woman opened it and the dogs rushed out. Anna was aware that she was observed carefully as she coped with the springer spaniels knocking against her legs, until Alfred placed his heavy paws on her shoulders and leered at her with sloppy jaws and one of the women rescued her. Anna surreptitiously wiped her face with a kleenex as Audrey and Marge led the beasts off. A 'little walk' with them would be something to see.

As Anna heard the dog-sitting plan rehearsed she reminded herself that she liked dogs and the plan was generous. She would live there rent-free and receive a small stipend for her duties and for dog and cat food for a month. As she told Marge about her experiences with animals, Audrey called from the linen closet, "My first husband always used to say, 'You can tell a person by his dog friends.' Don't you think people even look like their dogs, a little?" Audrey said, bringing in a tray beautifully laid with the coffee pot, cream, sugar, tiny tongs, napkins and petits fours. Anna looked narrowly at Opal who was sitting daintily in her high-backed chair, her hiking boots crossed at the ankle.

"Opie dear, how is Lil?" Audrey poured the dark liquid into fragile cups. "People laugh, " she said quickly, glancing at Marge, "but I keep thinking that my Ralph may someday love to meet Lil. He's in forestry now. Isn't he, Marge?"

Marge inclined her head. "So then that's settled. We'll leave you addresses and phone numbers of vets, electricians, landlord, etc. and where you can reach us . . . " A wired ball of fur struck Anna behind her right ear and she rose in the air, the cat's claws digging into her neck, sending cup, saucer, and cake into a splendid arch and cascade to the floor.

"Sissy! How could you?" Audrey said, getting up to get another cup as Marge picked up the shattered bone china and Anna wiped brown marks off the rug. As she was scrubbing at the carpeting Anna looked up suddenly into the yellow eyes of Sissy's friend, Missy, who was curled on a blue foot stool. Missy rose and walked away as two kittens strolled out of the kitchen, their tails straight up in the air. Anna whispered to Opal, "Four cats and two dogs?"

Opal called across to Marge, who was down the hall pulling out a map to show their itinerary, "Who does the needlepoint?"

"Audrey, of course," Marge said. "That and crossword puzzles, which she does with a pen. That one is my favorite," she said, gesturing toward the blue footstool cover.

"When she goes off judging in horse shows during the summer, I get plenty of needlework done." Audrey smiled.

"But Audrey doesn't care much for horses," Marge sighed.

"They're so big, for one thing." Audrey gave a small giggle like an audible ruffle and led Anna off by the hand to show her around the apartment. She showed her Marge's law books in ponderous splendor with their gold littering, from floor to ceiling, facing an immensely important walnut desk, She showed her sewing room with the greenhouse built out from a window, indicated "the master bedroom," and avoided the back room "where the boys are."

Anna was curious to learn how Audrey, a twice-married woman with grandchildren, met this swashbuckling lawyer, horsewoman, pilot, and sailor and how she got "the idea" after she did meet her.

"We met at a country club dance. Isn't that all-American, though?"

Anna heard the ruffle again.

"I was there visiting my grandchildren. Marge, as judge of horsemanship was invited with the other judges to the Country Club Ball held during the show. My son was the organizer of the dance, so of course I sat with him and his party. First Marge danced with my son, and I danced with the club's President, then she arranged for us to go to the ladies' room together, and then she led me down the garden path. As simple as that," she trilled. "I thought she was so handsome, as, of course, she is." Her small hand gently drew a straying lock into place. Anna and Audrey were in the kitchen leaning against the counters as wives do all over America, telling one of the sweet stories in the family mythology.

Opal gazed at the patriarch framed over their mantlepiece, his hand resting on a column evidently erected for the purpose. The room was crowded with heavy Victorian baroque highboys, lowboys, marble-topped tables, old tapestries, Queen Anne chairs.

"You aren't doing any women's cases then? Class action suits . . .?"

"Class actions are a separate field. I really haven't become interested in any of that . . . ."

"I made it—so pull up the ladder?"

"What's that?"

"Flo Kennedy."

"Who's she?" Marge asked, her cup in mid-air.

"Christ." Opal rolled her eyes upward. "Let me know when you decide to join the twentieth century, and I'll arrive with a load of newspapers and a rearview mirror."

"*And* a garbage pail?"

Audrey appeared in the door-way. "Marge, Anna knows your friend Miriam Green, did you know that?" As she spoke her eyes went from Marge to Opal. "Anna, tell Marge what you told me." As if she had not noticed their fixed expressions and the stillness between Opal and Marge, Audrey led them away from the fire like little children. By deflecting their interest and changing the conversation, she danced them around the roadmine until they were piping down another road, she seeming to follow.

"Marge, isn't that fun? Miriam is the wife of Anna's husband's boss. I love finding connections."

"My own Miss Marple," Marge smiled. " 'Marge, dear, that odd Lucinda Mayhew reminds me of an old friend I knew in Savannah who dropped her baby down a well.' "

"Marge may tease, but I was proven right in the end. Wasn't I, Marge?"

"Absolutely. Lucinda was found guilty of embezzlement—evidence quite clear."

Cupping the match within her hand Marge lit another Gauloise. "Did you say you aren't living with your children? How difficult." Marge and Audrey's glances connected.

"Carl—my husband—said no judge in the world would give me custody of my children if it was known that I was lesbian."

"Probably true," Marge said, tipping back her head blowing the harsh-smelling smoke toward the chandelier, "though I read of a judge in England who reluctantly turned the children over to a known lesbian mother because the father couldn't possibly afford to keep the children and the mother was a successful professional. But the judge's principles had opposed it; materialistic considerations prevailed."

Opal pushed her boots out ahead of her. "It figures."

"Anna." Marge brushed the rim of the ashtray softly with the cigarette, "What do you want to do?"

Anna was sitting forward, looking down at her palms set together as if they were a book she was reading. She answered slowly, "I want to find a way to live quietly with my children . . . independently . . . without Carl."

"That will probably involve heavy sacrifices for you, personally." Marge's tone was gentle, unintrusive.

"So be it."

In the brief silence that fell Anna did not see the inscrutable look that Marge and Audrey exchanged. In a flutter of activity that followed Audrey insisted that Anna have some of her newly-baked brownies, "the chewy kind," and both Anna and Opal were invited to dinner the following week. With easy assurance Opal accepted for them both.

"Whew. That was exhausting," Opal said as they stepped down onto the airless street. "But you got your job." Opal shrugged a sweaty shoulder. "Frankly, they bore the hell out of me. Marge and Audrey. With their christ-awful, bone-crushing boring, idiot-child's play role-playing. I cannot stand Audrey's simpering and her every other word, 'My first husband used to say,' and 'a boy I once went out with,' and 'my grandchild,' and 'Don't you think so, Marge?' She has to be a frilly mother earth to Margery Erhart." Opal looked for Anna's agreement, but Anna appeared to be thinking of something else.

"Opal, didn't you boast about a great Indonesian restaurant near here?"

Sitting in the litter of seven small dishes, all of them empty, Opal said, "So—where are you going to stay in the two weeks before Marge and Audrey leave?"

"I've been thinking about that."

"Good. You've been thinking about me, I hope." Opal's smile was broad and easy. "You'll come stay with me on the boat until you begin housekeeping? Think of a lovely night like this, dinners on the boat, sleeping under the stars if you'd like. The kids are keen to have you . . . . So am I, in every sense."

Anna pulled her hand from the top of the table where it was almost touching Opal's and said, "No, dear. You and the kids are generous, but I need to go and see my own kids, if I can. It's almost six weeks since I left."

To Opal, Anna's face looked too thin, too serious. "Why don't you bring them to the houseboat for the weekend? Wouldn't they love it?"

Anna looked at Opal's eager face, "Yes . . . ." She nodded slowly. "They would love it . . . but no . . . not yet."

"Why not? They would love it. They could have fun with Ad and Lil."

"Yes, Opal, they would love it, but I do not think this is the time for it," Anna said firmly as she signaled to the waiter to bring their bill.

"Will I see you, or what? How about Friday? There's a dance . . ."

"Opal." Anna put her hand on top of Opal's. "No promises, right?"

"Well, but the least you can do . . ."

"There were strings then?"

"Anything done implies . . ."

"All the more reason for me to do nothing, then," Anna said, putting her money down. "My treat."

CHAPTER FOURTEEN

ANNA left a grumbling Opal at street level and climbed the four darkened flights to Holly's apartment. To her surprise Holly was in when she arrived.

"It's a rotten set-up."

"What is, Holly?" Anna called as she unpacked, selecting things to wash.

"Not living with someone you want to live with. When you see one another on Friday you're spilling over with all the things you want to tell one another and with pure anticipation. But then, as the weekend goes on you can get lower and lower. If things go well, you brood because you have to separate in twenty-four or forty-eight hours. If things go badly you are down because you have the whole week to face without being really able to talk again until the next weedend. It's really rotten. Every Sunday I get the blues. I wish I were a drinker."

"Don't joke."

Holly stood in the doorway watching Anna's fingers squeezing out drops from her washing. "Have you lost weight?"

Anna shrugged.

"How are things going with you anyway?"

"I'm coping, I guess. Can we talk a minute?"

"That's what I'm trying to do."

As Anna told Holly about her plans for the next six weeks Holly's eyes were playing over her face, noticing the dark smudges under her eyes, what seemed to be new hollows in her cheeks. Her language was firm, slow but clear as she outlined her plan to leave Holly's apartment the next day if possible, go to Hillcrest Manor where Mother Johnson lived, in a town near Stevensville. She expected to be able to stay there for the full two weeks because she thought that Carl would be in New Jersey and Washington, D.C. following up sone contacts Bob Green had given him. Then she would move into Marge and Audrey's place for the month. Once there with a base of operations she would look for a job and then an apartment near the job.

To Holly it all sounded pretty desperate and quixotic. Why couldn't she just go back to Hope? What had the fuss been about anyway? Without training what could Anna hope to do—waitress, receptionist, cashier, maid, check-out, call girl? Holly realized that the more resolute Anna became as she sorted out her options and tried to take hold of her life, the more attractive she was finding her. She wanted to put her arm around her, just in support, but wasn't quite sure Anna would let her, so she tried to look attentive, but her thoughts were straying.

"Now, Holly, I need to talk to you about something in your field."

"Amour!"

"Reading."

"Reading? What a bore!"

"If I am going to bring up my children I need to have a good steady job. I can't let us be dependent on anyone else again. Anyone. From what I read in the paper the big thing needed now is reading teachers, but there aren't many places to get training."

Holly was glad to be put in the position of mentor-protector to this serious upturned face. She got them each a beer and settled down to consider with Anna the possibliities of taking courses toward a Masters in teaching in remedial reading. Anna took notes and resolved to go to Columbia to get a catalogue before she went to Hillcrest Manor in the morning.

As Holly watched Anna methodically taking notes in outline form she wondered why she had seemed such a waif, so hopelessly unable to deal with life. She wondered about Opal and that weekend she had heard no report of. Although Anna always appeared to be chatting openly, Holly began to understand how selective she was about the information she passed along. She had to admit she was somewhat flattered that Anna wanted to enter her field and had come to her with her questions.

That Monday morning Holly left her apartment without knowing if Anna would be there when she returned that night. It was going to be one of those murderouslv humid July days that New Yorkers ignore when they describe their climate as temperate. Although she was wearing the coolest things she owned, when she got off the subway in Brooklyn Holly felt as if she had worked eight hours. She hated skirts for many reasons, but on a day like this every reason melted. Thinking the cops should be wearing short pants and cork helmets and admit the truth of the evil climate, she walked up the cement steps, feeling their heat through her soles. Teaching reading on a day like this would be absurd. Half the class would be physically absent, gone off to Jones Beach or Orchard Beach, and the other half would be mentally absent. Still, she had their reading tests . . . and who was that? Someone looking like a mint julep sauntered by, blonde hair, short, curling, brushed up. Suzanne Delaporte was back? Holly took her mail from her department mail box, nodded at the new secretary just transferred from a recently closed senior college, dropped a note in the Women's Center mailbox and went down the hall to her office, wondering if Suzanne was here on leave from another college or back in town.

When Suzanne hit town, couples shuddered and kept looking at one another for reassurance up and down Manhattan island. Holly kept thinking that she knew better, that Suzanne's intimate attention span rarely survived ten minutes, just long enough to unsettle one's thinking before Lady Clairol drifted off in a gossamer shimmer.

"Hol---ly, dear one."

Holly was enveloped by someone tanned and sweet-smelling, dressed in something white and soft. "You are he--eh--ere. How absolutely von--dere--fool you loo--oo--ook. I aim hair for the summairrrr." Soon Holly lost track of the accent, or it disappeared, she never knew, but when she had her thoughts in orderly sequence again she realized that she had agreed to have lunch with Suzanne the next day. The flutter she felt put her on her guard, and she ran her mind over her feelings like a scholar riffling through notes before a lecture. She was too experienced not to watch her own libido; she was probably in for one of those weeks when she was responding to everyone, when her pulse zinged up and down like one of those balls in a fun house registering the pound of the mallet. The weather was too hot for this.

As she faced the class she put Dorothy's sudden phone call out of her mind to think about later. More of the class was there than she had expected. Dennis Graham looked half sick, probably that extra job he was carrying, and Maria Rafaello clearly had cramps. As she handed out the papers she said each student's name and looked at each one carefully. Most students thought they were invisible, unable to imagine that whether they were pale or listless or bored or angry might be of interest to anyone.

She had long passed the time of thinking about the fact of integration in her classrooms, though whenever a teacher said "I don't notice if my students are black or not" she knew he was lying. But she began to find, and she admitted it to Dorothy, that she enjoyed all the colors: the cinnamon, the chocolate, the coffee, and realized why blacks thought whites were grey, like ghosts. When your eye got used to the mellow, healthy colors of brown, you began to find white a little sickly-looking unless it was very pink and hearty. But she had worked in the city system for ten years.

In her early days she had been shocked when a black student had been outraged that in their workbooks the spelling of "Negroes" was set after "tomatoes." In these days she had called his angry reaction paranoia. But now she understood it was all much deeper than intention. He should have shrieked, "It's not what you intend. It's what you do unconsciously that kills us."

As they worked their way through a passage on the rainfall in Egypt, Holly did not question the annihilating boredom of the passage. South

American toadstools. Turtles of the Southern Bahamas. Someday she was going to write a series of racy readers. They needed delightful reading passages to reward them instantly for their new skill. As they plodded on through deserts of boredom, they could hardly realize the joys of their new power.

But the system was wedded to canned passages served up in paced booklets, with grading charts, answer sheets, discussion questions—all the petty artillery for evaluating, skimming, and scanning. Meanwhile, the big game—delight of the heart at reading something truly illuminating or exciting—quite eluded the booklet planners. Someday she must talk about this to Anna, ask her, when she studied at the knees of the great, if there were new plots in academe to solve this problem.

Holly was glad that the class didn't rush out at the bell. It encouraged her, and she stayed and talked to Dennis and Maria before they all left the room. The corridors were cool but tainted with the smell of cooking hamburger and felafel floating up from the street. Now that class was over she realized she was worried. Dorothy had been so low Sunday night that Holly suggested they meet for lunch the next day. Dorothy, predictably, had refused, but one hour before class, called and suggested they meet. It always seemed that Dorothy went through her measured pace at the library equally unruffled by PLO terrorist bombs and the Fall of Rome. A believer in the stoic virtues, she never acknowledged her moods, not to mention occasional depressions. That she would suggest to see Holly, breaking her routine and journeying from 42nd St. in Manhattan to Brooklyn, had to indicate need.

As Holly moved through Blimpie's revolving doors, she saw Dorothy, crisp as a leaf, perched on a counter stool waiting for her. Holly's broad smile expressed that flutter she still felt when she saw Dorothy in public places. "I meet scholars in such strange places," Holly said, leaning over Dorothy and helping her off the bar stool. "Let's go back to a booth back here."

As they went through the menu procedure, Holly considered strategies. To question directly or imply Dorothy needed support seemed equally unwise. "How's the research going?"

"Um, well, so-so. How was your class?"

"Not as bad as I expected on a humid Monday. You look great. Why aren't you picked up at the library? Don't tell me, I know. You have been."

"No new library stories today. Thing is, Holl, I'm really worried."

Holly watched Dorothy silently shredding her paper napkin.

"The thing is, I'm afraid I'm getting bored with Horace. Well, not bored exactly. I really do admire him still, of course."

She would probably get to the point in a moment. "Is this so bad? Why not take a rest for a day or two?"

"It's worse than that."

"You want to quit Classics or something?"

"Dear God, no. I'm afraid that I want to go into Ovid studies."

Holly wanted to shout with laughter, but Dorothy looked too troubled.

"But Ovid isn't in good standing in the department. He's considered frivolous by all right-minded Classics people. The only people who take him seriously are the feminists, whom the old guard ignores, and even the feminists hate him." Dorothy fiddled with her fork, sipped her water, and looked miserable.

"Why do you like him then?"

"His poetry, his imagination, his wit, his urbanity. I could take a book to show it. That's the trouble. I'm laboring over this Horace article and I want to write a book about Ovid."

"Will the department hold that against you?"

"Don't know. The vote for my tenure comes up in a couple of months. I'm supposed to be turning out an article now. You know that I have two others published, and to have tenure you're supposed to give evidence of growth, because, of course, they're banking on you to keep growing for the next thirty years. I am growing, that is changing; who knows if it's growth? But if I shift over to Ovid I'll lose the time I spent on the Horace article. But the life had gone out of it for me. I'm trying to decide whether to grind on and do the article hoping that it will get my tenure for me, or whether I should play, do what I want to do, and work on Ovid. Randolph is such a stickler he probably wouldn't approve the Ovidian interest. People in the Humanities Division who vote on me would approve, since the romance language people and the Medievalists think everything important started with Ovid and the Arabs, but my own department would probably think I'm getting brain softening." Dorothy's heavy eyebrows were drawn together.

"Honey, I can't advise you. You know *my* impulse is always to say do what you want, really *want* to do. Then you can work on happily, and the laboring that you must do anyway you can, at least, enjoy. But the world . . . I guess I am going to try to . . . The big romantic truths we tell ourselves usually conceal our own self-deceptions."

Dorothy looked up sharply, "What's that? Again."

Holly tipped her head as one of their favorite tunes came onto the juke box playing dimly in the background. "I found Anna suddenly very attractive last night and today guess who turns up? Suzanne Delaporte, Dream Girl of Sigma Chi, and Holly's little heart is all atremble. Why, you may ask, am I saying this now—to ruin our pleasant lunch? Because my libido is no compliment to my hostess, but a sure sign of my being low. And why should Holly, happy girl teacher, be low? Maybe because she followed the romantic truth 'Do what you truly want to do.' I did, and quit the Ph.D., thinking I was following my private star, but I wasn't; I was dodging the tough part—never mind why.

"I can't urge you to quit on Horace now if you are about to start writing your article. You've been doing research on him last summer, last winter and six weeks this summer. Does it make sense to stop now and turn to a new interest? They are all fascinating at first. Isn't there always a dry patch when the time one is spending isn't as exciting as it was at first? You can drop Horace any time if you want, but now, just before you begin your article and just before the tenure vote? Oh, Dot, I don't want you to compromise, but the big romantic truths. . . . I don't know." Holly's voice dropped and for the first time suggested her own depression.

Dorothy's eyes were sharp on Holly's. "You do *like* to teach reading, don't you?"

"Sure I like it. It's valuable. It's the best thing you can give a person, I think, a real gift, to read well. I believe all that. But the fun is in the teaching, in their learning, in their progress—whatever it is. There is very little intellectual fun in the subject itself. The rainfall in East Asia is not precisely Milton for the imagination. So, following the gleam, I bartered my heritage for a mess of pottage, or something. Ugh! I'm oozing in self pity."

Dorothy touched her arm lightly. "You're entitled."

Holly made a fuss about looking at her large wrist watch. "My five minutes are up. Hurry up, please, it's time. Dot, I've got to go. Reading lab. And I was going to cheer *you* up."

Dorothy tucked the tip by the side of her coffee cup. "Listen, friend, much as I hate to admit weakness, I think we both ought to break down and meet tonight for dinner. Why don't you come to my place, say about six. One way to get you out of Anna's clutches too."

In the clanging heat outside the restaurant they agreed, and Holly dashed off, taking the steps of the college building two at a time.

In the later afternoon Holly reached her apartment to shower and change and leave Anna a note in case she returned and thought of holding dinner for her. The trip to Dorothy's uptown east side apartment would be hot and damp unless she was lucky enough to hit an air-conditioned train, but with a good mystery to read she wouldn't care. She would pick up a single rose for a dollar from that tubercular man who sold flowers on 86th Street, some Mateus in the liquor store around the corner from Dorothy's, and reach her place about six. Dorothy would have been back from the library for about an hour, moving serenely about her apartment, arranging things for dinner. There would be some soft classical guitar record, Segovia or Bream or maybe Satie. Holly teased her about being Total Woman in disguise and so nice to come home to.

Holly's apartment looked like a transient's, as if she might sell everything and move to Arizona on a whim, but Dorothy's looked like a navy blue dress, matching bag and shoes—stolid, boring, square, but comfortable. There were bits of beauty here and there, not quite by chance, like the shining copper pitcher set near a cloth woven in Greece that glowed in an intense blue-violet. She had a silver letter opener set on a velvet cloth, sent her from Peru by a friend before Holly. Although the sheer weight of the books in Dorothy's apartment surely tilted the house a little to her side, she continued to build and fill up book shelves.

As Holly walked down from 86th Street through the crowds going home she thought as she had so often of the simplicity of this yearning to be home with one's person. The tanned, brown, pink faces concentrated on the fastest way to cross the street as the taxis and the trucks charged down it, the most rapid way to thread a path through people eagerly walking against one, all seeking home, to sit down, or be cool, or have a shower, or something to eat, or to hold a lover. So simple it all was.

They did not show unless they were disturbed, these bonds. Once when she had been in a fire in the subway and had walked the catwalk in the darkness with others, hearing their steps, their voices calling to one another, and they had all emerged up in the middle of the Bronx somewhere looking for buses, directions, restaurants, gas stations, places to use to make contact with their network of severed connections to home, she realized how they all reposed on a cat's cradle of beloved inter--connections, part routine, part affection, part need. Just the voice of the lover on the phone line helped. She had stood in line waiting to call Dorothy and heard people telling their families of their trouble, just to hear sympathy and the promise to keep the stew warm. When there were bomb scares or blackouts she would feel the panic rising—how to reach Dorothy? They didn't even share an address.

As she walked down the warm streets toward Dorothy, the light breeze carried bits of dust and fragments of paper. A restaurant had set up a boxwood hedge with tables set out on the sidewalk, pretending to be Paris. She clutched her wine bottle and the twist of paper from the florist's and ducked quickly behind a newspaper truck and crossed to Dorothy's street. The buzz, answering voice and bleep, and she was inside with the door clicking behind her. Because the elevator came from the basement she was careful and pushed her button fast, knowing someone below could bring her down to the basement merely by pushing the button before she did, but the elevator moved smoothly up to Dorothy's floor where she waited at the doorway.

When the door had closed behind them they embraced and just stood for a second holding one another. The apartment was cool and quiet.

"You look and smell like a glass of iced lemonade."

"Made in the shade."

"Don't be vulgar. I didn't know you had a new fruit and vegetable vendor on the corner," Holly said, walking into the apartment and looking about. 'Looked wonderful with purple eggplants, bright fat tomatoes, and green grapes. How I love the summer," and she caught Dorothy around the waist as she walked into her kitchen.

"Scandalous, your bringing a rose—but I love it." Dorothy filled a glass bud vase for the scarlet flower. "And wine? What is this?"

"Pure joy. I know a way I could save money, though."

"Stop spending it. That's how."

"And I know a very easy way to do that."

"OK, I give up—how," Dorothy said, setting the timer.

Holly put her lips by Dorothy's ear as she stood behind her and whispered, "by living together, that's how. I was thinking coming over here how much time we waste trying to get to one another. Why don't we just give up and live together?"

"Good thinking. Now, why don't you put something soothing on the phonograph while I set up a gorgeous salad."

Holly went off to the living room still calling back her conversation. "Really, Dorothy. Let's talk seriously. OK? Don't tell me it makes you nervous. Just, for once, talk to me about it. OK?" Holly appeared at the kitchen door holding a record. "OK?"

"OK, for heaven's sake, now clear out while I concentrate."

"For a big brain I cannot understand why mere conversation and a few pieces of lettuce are so difficult to orchestrate." Holly curled up on the floor with the records and was silent for a full five minutes.

Dorothy came in to snip some fresh basil that was growing under the lights with the sage and thyme. "I got "Moon Circles" in the blue jacket; you'll adore it. Put it on," and Dorothy went back into the kitchen.

They sat in the cool room listening to the ice clink in their glasses as Kay Gardner's beautiful flute song began, and in its subtle breathing dropped curves of silver about them. A note, sustained, would swell, almost ripen as they heard it, before it was set free to float along those moving waters.

They had to listen to both sides of the record before they could turn it down and let it become background to their conversation.

"And the summer is a grand time to move, particularly after my school ends," Holly said, as if they hadn't had dinner since she raised the topic. "Now, don't get up and get coffee, just sit a second and tell me why it isn't good to move this summer."

"You know the tenure vote will be in November."

"Why should that affect our moving?"

"If they don't give me tenure I will have to find a new job, and it's convenient to live near where one works, right?"

"Dorothy, are you afraid that if we move in together it's too much like coming out?"

"A little."

"Your mother?"

Dorothy nodded. "Still, the department, Randolph, nobody at college need know we're living together. People are fairly discreet. Miriam Green wouldn't comment if I ran naked through Grand Central. The gays I know would just be happy for us. If after five years we took the plunge. . . . " Dorothy said.

"It isn't as if you didn't know all my evil habits. Let me get you your coffee for a change." Then Holly called from the kitchen, "What would your mother know if we lived together? Anybody knows it's safer for women to live together in this evil city, cheaper too—as I said to start with."

"You're right. But, I just can't do it yet, Holl. Will you wait until after this tenure vote when I can put my mind on it?" Holly stood listening, staring down at the two mugs of coffee. The kitchen glared white, but "Moon Circles" spun on in the distance about a silver age of limpid clarity when tension served only beauty and desire.

"Alas, I must return to the iron age of servitude," Holly said, glancing at the clock as she returned to the living room with the coffee.

"Why not spend the night here? It's too late to go down to the village."

"The village, my dear, is not Mudville. The village comes awake at eleven o'clock."

Dorothy drew her to the sofa. "But I want to hold you, silly nut. You look like a crunchy, a crunchy . . . "

"Cactus?"

"Granola nut bar—that's it. Do you know granola?"

"No, thank God, I do not and never hope to. A granola nut bar indeed! It's enough to shake a person's dignity."

"Dear, do stay." Dorothy finally caught Holly's shoulders, tried to pull her close, but she resisted and tugged at Dorothy. Soon they had slipped to the floor in a bearish wrestle. Wherever one pulled, the other tugged back in an aimless struggle in which neither wanted to dominate enough to exert full strength, but neither wanted to be conquered either. Soon they were gigling and grunting like children. Holly wrestled Dorothy onto her back, put her head down into her neck and blew, making a wet trumpeting sound. Dorothy gave a mighty heave and slipped out from under her friend, and with a twist was pushing Holly back until they both gasped and collapsed, breathing deeply, lying back in one another's arms looking at the ceiling.

"You should stay. This is such a waste. We're stupid."

"Glad you said it, my dear," Holly said, getting up and brushing herself off. "But I have books at my apartment to take to school and hate to be discombobulated in the morning when I face the kiddies. I always feel I'm not the dedicated teacher if I come direct from a bed of sin."

"Good grief, how would you feel if we lived together, then?"

"Christ! You got me." Holly stared at her. "My Jewish-puritan ancestors still stalk me, don't they?"

"If you're going, you'd better go. I hate you out so late."

Keeping well within the circles of light on the darkened streets Holly walked rapidly to the subway. They hadn't talked about her plans, and once again she hardly knew why they weren't living together. She would wait until the tenure vote and then insist. Then if she didn't get tenure Dorothy would probably want to wait until she found a job. But how could she not get tenure? Her teaching evaluations were glowing; her students took every course they could with her. Old man Randolph didn't like her, Holly was pretty sure, although Dorothy didn't seem to know it. Dorothy had told her that once after she had been on the office phone to another teacher, Professor Randolph had said to her, "You weren't talking to a woman, were you?" He had acted surprised when she said she was. He seemed to have considered her too polite, too formal, or something. Dorothy had said, "What idea does he have of the way women speak together? I don't know." But Holly had always considered that the tip-off, that Randolph had figured something out. Dorothy was so proper that Holly could hardly see what Randolph sensed unless it was just obvious to him that she didn't consider him an available sex partner. He probably felt that. It made the big difference when most women were batting their eyes and suggest bed when they passed the salt.

Would the days go on this way? She wondered if she should just pull herself together and leave Dorothy, if what she wanted was to have a home with a person in it. She had known enough people to know another lover always did come along. The problem wasn't sex but what Camus called that mixture of desire, intelligence, and affection that he termed loving. Dorothy at her most difficult and prickly was still more interesting than the sultriest bombshell. That lunch with Suzanne tomorrow. Holly began to consider what she would wear to make herself look slim. That was impossible, she knew, but until she gave up eating she had to depend on disguise. As she walked on the subway platform she kept an eye on the two men who talked together, watching her. She decided to go to the front car at the last moment, just before the train took off. She settled her arm heavily over her bag just as the train pulled in, and, seeing them at her left elbow, she dodged and ran to her right, slipping through the doors of a forward car just as they closed.

CHAPTER FIFTEEN

MOTHER Johnson's breath had sounded short when she spoke to Anna on the phone, so glad to hear from her, so glad to have her come by on Monday, yes, she must come, although Carl was away for a few days. Should she call him? Well, if Anna insisted, she wouldn't. For Anna the experience of leaving Holly's small apartment in the village to go out to Hillcrest Manor was like having a cleft brain. One half was filled with the warmth of the hot streets, their summer odors, the grit underfoot and the ease of people lounging about on steps, in book shops, with their music spilling out into the streets, women shopping for long french loaves holding children by the hand, tee shirts and jeans, ponchos and Dashikis, Greek food and Mexican. The other half of her mind crisped with that sense of the old order, the blue-haired matrons visiting antique shops, blond children on the tennis courts, expensive houses and their bluestone drives lined with stones painted white.

She had dressed carefully for her visit to Mother Johnson, her blue seersucker suit and stockings despite the heat. As she walked up the hill from the bus stop she regretted the delicate shoes. She had forgotten how it felt to walk where everyone drove. She soon had her jacket off as the sun beat down and she watched the old slate sidewalk to avoid turning her ankle in its cracks.

Water was running between her shoulder blades when she stood at Mother Johnson's door and heard the cool tones chiming down the hall. "She's here, Mummy's here!" Sneakers thumped fast on the carpet and the screen door was thrown open by two bullets of energy that struck Anna at her mid-section. She sank to her knees forgetting all the words she had expected to need as she held her children close. She was holding their wiry bodies, rocking them, laughing and crying. Jamie was saying, "You came, you said you would, Timmy and I knew you would." Timmy's skinny arm pulled her down as he curled into her neck, just holding on.

She wanted to see their faces, sniffed, and looked at first one, then the other. Jamie's intense dark eyes, pupils like black needles with energy pouring out of them, Timothy, strained, a little pale, uncertain. She had preferred Jamie and he knew it, was that it? Carl's heavy maleness impossible for him to deal with? She pulled them both back for a last hug and saw two newly whitened shoes on the green carpet. "Mother Johnson, how dear of you!" With the children clinging she struggled up. In their embrace she sensed Mother Johnson's tentativeness. Was she expecting Anna to be half-mad, angry, half-sick?

That white, slightly blue hair piled in fluffy waves, her pink complexion and pale eyes, Mrs. Johnson carried her burdens long after she should be through with them.

"Come, dear, you're hot, have some iced tea on the porch. Children, take Mommy to the back porch while I get a tray for all of us."

Each child hung on to a hand and they tried to walk three abreast down the hall and manage the doorway at the back of the house. The porch was lined with stone and was wonderfully cool. All three climbed on the swinging couch with Anna in the middle, and each child appropriating an arm and a shoulder. Then Timothy climbed up on her lap sucking his first two fingers. Jamie babbled non-stop about swimming races, a birthday party, and Timmy's two wheeler which "he still can't ride." When Mother Johnson emerged with the tray of iced tea, milk and cookies, they shouted, "Cookies! We can't usually have cookies before lunch!"

"Now settle down, children. Mommy will be with us all day. I thought that we could have lunch directly, but we will want to chat first and you should rest. I wish I had a car to pick you up at the station, but Carl has it in Jersey."

Timothy had his mug of milk in two hands watching her over the rim. Mother Johnson reached over quickly and with a soft napkin wiped away his milky moustache. Jamie sat back with a cookie in her fist and began to listen to the grown-ups, just tugging at her mother's arms and moving her side closer at times. Anna wanted to say "Let him be," but she owed too much to Mother Johnson.

"Why is Carl in New Jersey, Mother? Is Bob Green spreading out?" Anna breathed deeply and stretched her arm along the back of the couch to stroke the back of Timmy's head. His hair was fine and curling at the soft nape of his neck. The older woman cleared her throat and looked down. Was she now seeing herself as stage mother?

"No, dear. It isn't that. A little sugar for your tea? Dear, you see, I think that Carl has been having a difficult time. It isn't just . . . it isn't your fault. This is, I begin to think that before you had . . . had your . . . spat he was having a diffidult time." She looked quickly at Anna as her slender silver spoon turned in the iced tea. "Shortly after you left he became very angry at work—perhaps drinking a little too much, too. I don't know the details. I'm sure no one told me, but he did say that he and Bob had words."

"Had words." Anna had forgotten when she had last heard the phrase. It described the generation that taught her. She had learned never to say "lie"; a person did not lie; he "told a story." One was not furious; one "had words." A wave of regret for misdirected civilities—for Mother Johnson's efforts, her own straining, Timothy's pinched look—passed over her, leaving her angered and tense. The scrim was up, indeed. "Had words" probably referred to Carl's brutal obscenities, Bob's fury, Carl's doubled-up fist, and Bob's shouted phrases that drove Carl out of Stevensville.

"Is Carl no longer working for Bob, then?"

"No . . . that didn't really work out," Mother Johnson said, and told Anna about a large company that seemed interested in Carl for its training program. "Not exactly a job he would prefer, I should think," Mother Johnson said.

One he'd probably hate, Anna thought.

"But Buddy will be there until the end of the week, I think." She sat back. "You look well, Anna. We were worried about you. Buddy behaved badly, I'm sure, but he had been very upset by his work and by Bob." She leaned forward, offering Anna cookies that were refused. "Men have these difficulties at times. All we can do is stick by them until they work them out." She sighed in the small silence.

"At any rate, after he and Bob had their altercation, Buddy drove the car to check out a customer's pool being built in Scarsdale and on the way over there a truck banged him on Hartsdale Avenue. Actually it was quite serious. The car's been laid up for new parts." She sighed again. "Children, Mother is going to help me put our lunch together. Why don't you play on the swings?"

"Swings?" Anna looked out to see behind the garage a new set of swings and a slide. Caring for her children was taking money, she saw with a groan.

"Mother Johnson, you've done too much. Children, look at that. Isn't that wonderful, a slide and swings—just what you always wanted!" The children went slowly out the door. Anna wondered how quickly she took on the manner again. How could she go back to talking like that to them again—calling them "children" in a lump, like batter, making them 'ooh' and 'ahh' on command like playful sea lions working for a fish. Obviously the swings were a bore to them now, and her requirement of gratitude could only make them feel ungrateful. She had put on Hillcrest Manor in an instant like a favorite blouse.

Ignoring Mother Johnson's voice Anna followed the children out into the back yard where they stood together at the bottom of the new slide. She touched the shining metal surface, "Ye gods, that's hot!"

Jamie nodded. "It's no good when the sun's out, if we've got on shorts."

"It's going to be even hotter this afternoon. I guess you'd like to swim."

"But we can't. Daddy's got the car."

Anna sat on the edge of the new sand box. When had they last cared about a sand box? "That slide might be fun if it could be cooled off. Mother Johnson must have a way to water her flowers."

"We play under the hose sometimes."

"We'll have to ask Mother Johnson's permission. I don't know the water regulations in Hillcrest these days, but maybe after lunch you could get into your suits and set the hose at the top of the slide."

"And slide down the running water!"

Timothy jumped and said, "Neato! We'll play in the hose!"

"Play in the hose"—a far cry from a waterfall. Was it the way she felt about Hillcrest Manor—as far from life as playing in the hose was from Watkins Glen?

"You're all right on the swings out here?"

"Sure—I watch Timmie," Jamie said, walking firmly toward the swing.

"Mother Johnson, I just had to go admire the swings. You must have spent five hundred dollars for that whole outfit."

"Not quite, dear, but it is well worth it. The children love them and, of course, it does keep them out of the TV room."

"Are they behaving well? I don't want you to have to keep them much longer."

"Oh? Tell me, dear, about your plans. I wish I could advise you, my dear. It is all so very difficult and, since your mother is . . . away . . . I feel responsible." In the silence Anna followed Mrs. Johnson's lead, set table, and took things out of the refrigerator. They chatted aimlessly, it seemed, until Mrs. Johnson began to talk in a way that suggested a planned speech to Anna.

"Once, when I was a young mother I had a somewhat difficult period with Charles."

Anna sat down. Mother Johnson was looking out the window, her fingers just touching her pearl necklace.

"He had had . . . financial reverses . . . and had begun to drink heavily. He became angry often, stayed away from home, gambling with some wealthy, attractive friends. I was home with three children and at my wits' end. Finally . . . perhaps I shouldn't say this . . . and Carl doesn't know this story himself . . . finally. . . . " Her gentle voice became even softer. "One night . . . one night I even locked my bedroom door. I moved the bureau against it and the matttress against that. It was a wild thing to do. I don't know how I did it really. He pounded and pounded, threw his shoulder against it . . . dislocated his shoulder, actually, we learned later . . . but he couldn't manage it.

"The next day when I came out to give the children their breakfast, he was greatly shamed. That, I am glad to say, was the turning point."

She signed. "Things got better after that." She turned from the window and went over to Anna seated by the table. She looked down at her for a moment and gently touched Anna's right temple, smoothing a lock to the side.

"Anna, I have always loved you dearly. I have known Buddy would be a difficult man to live with, but he is a good man, really . . . at heart. Dear Anna, I would be very happy and very very grateful if you would try to live with him again." Her eyes were swimming with tears as she leaned down and put her soft cheek against Anna's. Anna suddenly buried her head in Mother Johnson's loving shoulder and wept like a beaten child.

Mother Johnson smiled then. She patted Anna's back a moment. "We are having some of your cucumber soup for lunch, chilled."

"Mother Johnson!" Anna groaned, "You are incredible."

"My credibility is a good deal better than some people's I could mention."

"Whose do you mean?" Anna said quickly.

"I'm thinking of Mr. Nixon's and Mr. Goldwater's, actually," she said, setting out soup bowls and tiny sandwiches.

"Oh, I see." Anna relaxed. She began to think how she could explain her plan to Mother Johnson. After desultory talk about the lunch being prepared, Anna said, "Mother, how would you feel about my coming to visit you for two weeks?"

"Dear, you don't have to ask me that. You know I would love you to come and stay as long as you like." Her smooth brow was rumpled with her unspoken inquiry.

"I would contribute to our grocery requirements, of course, but . . . perhaps if I explained the larger. . . . I have made arrangements for the month of August. I'll be keeping an apartment in the city for some absent owners, taking care of their pets."

Mrs. Johnson did not ask but stood, hands folded, waiting out Anna's explanation.

"During that time I would like to look for a job and another place to live. In September I want Jamie and Timothy to come to live with me. This is all temporary, of course. Until I decide what exactly to do about Carl and. . . . At any rate, you shouldn't be doing this job. You've done yours. I should do mine . . . granted that Carl and I can't do it together."

Mrs. Johnson's eyebrows went up as Anna's explanation proceeded. "Dear heart, there is no need to think of me. I enjoy the children and am only too happy. . . . It does take energy, of course, but they are good. . . . "

"Mother, don't tell me. Children, no matter how "good," are . . . " The image of one of her favorite Donatellos appeared in her mind—a bas relief with fat children kicking and shouting, his amused, humane view of children depicting rowdy angels.

"But dear, about the other part of it, your moving to the city and taking the children later, that we'll have to see about, won't we? Let's see what Buddy says, when he comes. He'll be here at the end of the week and you'll be staying . . . "

"I won't stay if he's here."

"But this is his home as well as yours, my dear." Mother Johnson looked steadily at Anna. "And you are his wife."

"I can go to the Stevensville house or a motel. I mean it." Anna's voice was almost inaudible.

"Very well, Anna, if you think you need time." Mother Johnson said with a sign. "I'll tell Buddy that."

When the children came in to lunch, Jamie reacted as if she had walked into a vibrating electrical field and looked curiously from one grown-up to the other. "Do we have to take our naps today?"

"Of course," Mrs. Johnson said quickly, setting small sandwiches beside the children's soup bowls. Jamie looked at Anna, who said, "Suppose we all rest outside under the trees on deck chairs. Wouldn't that be lovely?"

Mother Johnson stopped and looked reproachful. "If you'd like that, we could. Of course, the children won't get their proper rest."

"But Mummy isn't here every day."

"I'll be back tomorrow for two weeks. Mother Johnson said I might." Anna couldn't see Mother Johnson's face as the children shouted. She had gone to the kitchen for more milk.

"Mother, you were right. No one's getting much of a rest out here. Even I can see that." Jamie was secretly patting a visiting cat underneath her deck chair. Timothy was rattling a little box, trying to tease a ball through a maze. The usual outdoor sounds of dogs, children, lawn mowers, cars passing were leading no one to sleep.

"But it is pleasant under the trees. It takes a visitor for me to enjoy it," Mother Johnson said with a yawn.

When Mother Johnson asked Anna about her job plans, Anna brought up the subject of Jamie's swimming and was able to avoid that conversation for a while until, with Mother Johnson's dubious approval, the hoses were linked together to reach from the garage out to the slide.

"C'n I put the hose up here?" Timothy called from the top of the slide.

Anna watched the water cascading down the slide to channel out a hole at the bottom. "Oh, lord, bad idea."

"No, Mummy, I'll get that big tub in the garage." And before Mrs. Johnson could protest Jamie was off to the garage. Anna looked inquiringly at Mother Johnson, who shrugged.

"We'll have to turn the hose off and on, won't we, Timmie, or it will soon run over the tub's rim," Anna said, walking over to the faucet, regretting her master plan.

Timmie squealed and zoomed down the slide splattering water and waving his arms. When Jamie set the tub in place, he shouted, "More water, Ma!" Anna turned on the faucet full blast, but finally moderated it to a small stream so the children could play and the tub could fill slowly.

"This is an idea we won't repeat."

"It does seem dreadful, when you think that the Western and Central states are in such a drought, for us to be letting the children play in it," Mrs. Johnson said, settling comfortably in her deck chair.

"If Carl is looking for work in New Jersey, will he be planning to sell the Stevensville house, then?" Anna asked, hearing in the background, "I'm gonna dump some of this water out."

"Why, Jamie, it's good? Get back."

"It shouldn't be running over."

"Mind your own business, drippy."

"I think that's his plan, although dear, although he hasn't called Magruder on it yet."

"Jamie, get on back. I'm coming down head first. Watch out!"

There were screams and a clatter as something struck the metal tub. Timothy wailed and Jamie cried. The women later deduced that Timmie had come charging down head first into the tub that was being tipped up, knocked himself and Jamie on the ground, engulfing them in water.

Each of them took a child to console, and Anna turned off the water, saying, "The slide is cool now. Enough of that. When it gets too hot, you can spray it or douse it with a bucket. I wonder how you kids would make out on a houseboat."

When Jamie quieted down Anna asked her, "Now, what have you been doing usually in the afternoons? Mother Johnson doesn't sit with you all afternoon, does she?"

"Pretty much. Or we go to the pool."

"Honey, we can't. So how about building yourselves a hut or something. Mother and I are going into the house to talk about things."

"C'n I bounce a ball against the garage?" Timmie asked.

"Against the wall, dear, not the door," Mother Johnson called, dragging the tub to the garage.

"Let Jamie help you, Mother." Anna gave a quick signal to Jamie who seemed to grasp the turn of events and went to help her grandmother. "But we can cool the slide with the water, can't we?"

As Mother Johnson folded and put away dry sheets and towels, Anna thought she might as well put away the dishes and flatware. Collecting the items Mother Johnson always called "silver" she reached over to open a drawer. It remained stuck. She pulled again. It moved out two inches. She could see the drawer was empty. She opened the drawer next to it to see knives and forks and spoons tumbled on top of one another. Clearly, one drawer doing double work.

She put down her towel and jiggled the drawer lightly until it came all the way out. The center runner had swiveled off to one side. One or two nails would do it. Anna went to the cabinet that housed Mother Johnson's little supply of equipment: hammers of different sizes, brads, tacks, washers, screws, from the days her husband repaired around the house.

The short taps drew Jamie. "Mom's fixing your drawer, Grandma."

Anna turned. "Jamie, if you'd just hold that center thing."

"Sure. Mom's fixing the . . . "

"I see she is." Mother Johnson stood looking down on Anna as she squatted before the cabinet, squinting along the runner.

"That's it, just here, Jamie."

"Jamie dear, watch your fingers," Mother Johnson said.

Neat taps, more peering, and the drawer was re-inserted.

"OK, now, you try it, Jamie. See if the drawer works."

Jamie gave a tentative push. "Hey, lookit, grandma." She slid the drawer back and forth with loud whacking sounds.

"That should do it," Anna said. "We can put the things back in it now."

Mother Johnson smoothed her dry hands on her apron, "Anna, that is just wonderful, dear. I was going to ask Carl to fix it, wasn't I, Jamie?"

"Yes, but Mom fixed it—and I helped her. Did you see me?"

"Yes, well Daddy would have, but isn't it nice that Mommy did?"

Sitting stiffly through the jerks and bounces of the small train on the way back to the city, Anna was blushing. How had Mother Johnson made her feel she had done something inappropriate in fixing that drawer? Was it in her voice, the way she drew herself up and said something about Anna's handling a hammer and nails so well, as if it was grossly unfeminine—but so helpful.

She tried to remember whether Jamie was three or two years younger than Lil. She supposed her children were "better brought up," meaning neater and more polite than Opal's children. Maybe she was being hard on herself, but she doubted it. Just as she slipped into being a child with Mother Johnson, if she didn't watch herself, they would stay children, polite, docile, courteous, and end by being fit servants for another Carl. Now *she* was sighing. She wondered if she could stand hearing Mother Johnson's sighs for two weeks. With a little thump of the heart she thought of Stevensville, just ten minutes away by car from Hillcrest

Manor. She might drive by Threshold some day and perhaps see Hope out on the grounds. No, that could not be part of her plan.

According to Opal's plan, Anna was to visit Marge and Audrey on the twenty-ninth, the day before they left for Rome, but, close to panic, Anna called ten days earlier to ask Audrey if she could come by. She had explained that it would be convenient for her since she had to be in town anyway and it might be harder later. In fact, Anna felt that if she didn't see someone who knew about her she was going to be suffocated. Now that the scrim was up, everything she saw and heard excluded her, or seemed to have a double meaning. Mother Johnson continued to sigh and suggested with every dropping tone in her tired voice that disappointment was all one could expect, after all. One did one's "level best," "sacrificed" for one's husband who "after all, poor man" was "scrimping and saving for his little family." It was little enough to offer a "listening heart" when he came home tired after a day of hard work.

One day while she was staying with Mother Johnson, Anna as she was ironing, began to hum an old tune. Soon, without attending to what she was saying, she began to sing the words, some song out of her years of dating Jim, long before college: "A fellow needs a girl to sit by the fire at the end of a long, long day, to sit by the fire and listen to him talk and agree with the things he'll say." She put down her iron with a clang on its stand. What? What were the rest of the words? "To sit by the fire and listen to him talk and agree with the things he'll say." Yes. "When things go wrong da dah dah da," more words she's lost, thank god, he wants to share the prize he's won. When no one cares and no one shares ... what's the good of the job well done, or the prize he's won?" The phrases were laden with infantile need, primitive seduction. They should have been called subversive and unAmerican by the Veterans of Foreign Wars. She remembered humming the song, walking home from school on a dark, snowy afternoon. There was another she was singing then, from one of her sister's favorite records: "What's the use of wondrin' if he's good or if he's bad. He's your fella and you love him, that's all there is to that." She resumed ironing, singing the next verse. She wanted to remember it all. She supposed Mother Johnson thought she was carolling away out of light-hearted delight in ironing. She felt like an iron-hearted private eye tracking down Moriarty: "Somethin' made him the way that he is, whether he's false or true"—determinism—and "Something gave him the things that are his, one of those things is you, so-oo-oo ... ." She gave the iron a flip. "When he wants your kisses, you will give them to the lad, and anywhere he leads you you will walk, and anytime he needs you,

you'll go runnin' there like mad. He's your fella and you love him and all the rest it talk!" She almost burned Timmie's best shirt with that one. How many years had she sung that venomous treacle? When Jim was rough, self-absorbed, which was always, she thought herself all sexy, and just like the womanly woman in that song—giving, loving—although the burly dear one didn't understand. "One of those *things* is you." Indeed, just so. What betrayal it was to pour this into young women's ears so they equated it with nurturing, loving, and then to turn on them when they became masochists or martyrs like Mother Johnson.

"You certainly did a lot of clanging with the iron, dear."

"She's singing, gramma." Timmy was fixing his mitt.

"She said she's brainwashing," Jamie said, looking up from the bird feeder she was making. "Does it go this way?" She held up the interlocking pieces of wood.

Anna guessed what she had said aloud, as she tried to read the directions for the bird feeder, "A simple job even a child can do." Even a child! Everything was getting to her. Except Hope. What did women do when the scrim was up and everything was this plain? One could rage, strike the walls . . . or the children. She had to talk to Holly or maybe Audrey. Then she had decided to try to arrange to see Audrey earlier than planned.

Anna supposed that Audrey was not taken in by her reasons. She may even have guessed that the visit was important to her. Still, when Anna arrived Audrey treated her matter-of-factly, showed her around the apartment more carefully, making sure Anna could work the dishwasher and the clothes dryer. Did she like music? She showed her the elaborate stereo and had Anna set up a record or two while she made tea, glad Anna drank tea, most young women didn't. Anna was wondering why Audrey thought of herself as so old when Audrey admitted to fifty-five, saying she could be Anna's mother. Watching her, Anna caught the trick of it and could see how Audrey must have looked with a flat, firm skin, a smooth neck and her delicate features. She had been a singer or had wished to be. She had won an award as a seventeen-year-old and had plans to "go on" with her music when she had to marry her first husband. When she became a widow she went back to her music, even sang in supper clubs to earn money for her voice lessons. She could have stayed independent with Frank's bequest, but "foolishly" married again. At any rate, she'd been lucky. "He died." She gave a soft laugh. "How hard-hearted I became. At his death I felt only relief. And then I met Marge."

She spoke in short phrases always, as if she stopped herself from saying much, much more. Yet what she said was tough enough, despite the softness of her voice. Anna wanted to ask her if she felt schizoid sometimes, living two lives at once, but it seemed so melodramatic she didn't know how to put it.

"Was it a big shock for you when you realized what you felt about Marge?"

"Not really. It seemed so right. . . . " She signed deliciously. "So completely right. Besides—and I guess I'm like you in this—I never worried about being gay much. I knew I was a woman, didn't want to be a man, just wanted Marge." She laughed, "Marge says I'm dodging, that I still don't want to admit to being gay. But then, why should I? I'm more than that. I think most of us are and we should just relax about it. Love whom we love. That's what I say. Have I shown you my pictures of the children?"

She reached behind her head for the pictures set within an accordion frame. "My children's children, I should say. Aren't they darling?" She reached down and patted Alfred who lay quietly at her feet now that the uproarious first five minutes were well in the past. George had taken a liking to Anna and was leaning against her legs.

"I would love to hear you sing, sometime."

She laughed her tinkling laugh of the pretty woman, flattered, self-assured. "I hope you will soon. When we come back from Europe I expect to be singing with a new operetta group that's forming. Imagine, it's taken us this long. Munich has a standing repertory that does operettas all year long; still, at last it's coming. I expect to be singing in *The Merry Widow*." She laughed. "Quite fitting for my debut.

"But a dear friend of mine, since we were children, just sang at Carnegie Hall—her first recital in twenty years. She was wonderful. Glorious. She gives me courage to go on with my singing. Of course, she's a younger woman, only forty-seven, but . . . " her voice drifted off. "She's been through a lot.

"One puts things off, you know. And time goes by. Now living with a woman like Marge. So well set up in her career. High-powered. One can be wiped out, you know." She looked questioningly at Anna. "Even living out roles, you know. Makes things easier. In a way. For us old folks anyway. But you 'need your own thing.' As the kids say. Or you feel wiped out . . . a bit."

Anna was seeing the two women, like alternative photographs, the young vivacious Audrey, chatty and delightful, the older woman, still pretty even, but resolute with a coiled, relentless energy, determined at last to live out her talent. The small mouth, speaking, seemed able to pout in the supposedly kissable old fashion. But at rest those controlling lines settled her lips into a determination that the young Audrey could never have understood. A small linen handkerchief that had the barest hint of lace touched her lips and forehead. "I wish I'd been brighter when I was your age. Still . . . how about a drink of something? Scotch? Bourbon?"

When Anna finally did leave Audrey that day, they had arranged for her to return on the twenty-ninth anyway. Audrey said she had some keys to give her and laughed. "I won't give them to you now, so you'll be sure to come back." But she was only being gracious, because all Anna wanted to do was to stay there forever, sheltered by the older woman's experience, protected from the sorts of follies she'd been going in for. Crazy nights with Opal. Dashing back and forth toward and away from her own children. Staying perilously close to Mother Johnson and so within Carl's reach. Avoiding Hope as if she hated her. When she said at the doorway that she "looked forward" to seeing Audrey on the twenty-ninth, she was using a formal phrase that hid her feelings. She meant that if she stayed sane until then, it would be partly because she had Audrey's words and image in her mind. But her polite handshake and smile could hardly have conveyed that to Audrey.

"But damn it, Dorothy." Hope sent the ball in a whistling cross-court that left Dorothy standing watching it. "I don't see how you could have known that Anna was staying two weeks at Hillcrest and not have told me." Hope was standing up at the net bringing her racket down hard on the tape. "I just don't get it."

Dorothy stared at her. "How should I know it would matter to you?"

"How should you know? Christ sake, you were a part of all that."

"That was weeks ago. Holly didn't say that you were still hot for Anna."

"Why are you so deliberately crude?" Hope kept bouncing one of the tennis balls, slamming it down and snatching at it. Without speaking further to Dorothy she walked back to the service line, threw the ball low and slammed a flat, hard first service as hard as she could. It struck the tape and fell back on her own side. Two weeks Anna had been living ten minutes away and no one had told her. She didn't want to ask herself why Anna had not come by herself. She knew she could have, if she had wanted to. Mrs. Johnson had a car. Again she threw the ball up badly. This time she spun a soft second serve in; Dorothy was waiting for it up mid-court and in a beautifully timed short shot put it away. Those soft serves were gravy to her.

"Well, where is she now?"

Dorothy supposed she should answer. Holly hadn't said that Hope wasn't to be told anything, but Dorothy did have the feeling that for some reason Anna wanted to keep clear of Hope.

"She's not still living with Holly, is she?"

"Lord, no. She only stayed with her a week after . . . after . . . "

"Yeah, I know. Where are we?"

"Hope, it's my ad." If Hope couldn't keep her mind on the game enough to keep score, she shouldn't play. Another rotten first serve. Hope's first serves were nowhere. She should know that puff-ball second service was an easy put-away. If she was so interested in Anna why didn't she do something about it? As far as Dorothy knew Anna was making out beautifully, perhaps in every sense for all she knew. Her game. Now to finish off this set.

"Well, do you know?"

Dorothy was lining up a strong serve to Hope's backhand. "What?"

"Where she is living!"

Dorothy bounced her service ball, anxious to serve. "Somewhere on Riverside Drive, I think, apartment-watching for Marge and Audrey."

"Who are they?"

"Hope, play the game, for God's sake." Dorothy socked a strong high bouncing service to Hope's back hand. Suddenly Hope was everywhere, hitting strong cross-courts, drop shots, over-heads, forcing Dorothy back against the back court fence with high bouncing shots and pulling her up to the net with slices, playing hard, angry tennis. Dorothy lost her own serve in ten minutes. But what was Hope mad at?

As they changed sides, Hope said, "You remember Eleanor Molina?"

Dorothy pressed a towel against her forehead. "Who could forget the mellifluous Eleanor?"

"She's going to be spending the week-end with me . . . with her friend . . . wants to play some tennis. Would you be free sometime Sunday, say maybe at three? I think I can reserve the courts ahead. Her friend is really a ringer, ranked nationally when she was under eighteen."

"Sounds intriguing. What's her name?"

"Rusty something. Can't remember. Eleanor always mumbles when she says her name; I think it's long."

"Sure. I'd love to, but my doubles is creaky. How'll we team up?"

Hope pushed a piece of the court clay back into place with her toe and carefully stepped on it. "I suppose they'd better play together first. After they mop us up we'll rearrange ourselves somehow."

"Hope, do you mind then if we skip the set and practice? I need work at net."

As Dorothy set herself at the net, Hope bounced a few balls and said, "Well, where are her kids going to be?"

"Whose?"

"Anna's."

"I really don't know her plans, Hope. Just that she's got a job somewhere."

"Does Holly know where?"

"Probably she does." Dorothy neatly blocked a hard forehand.

"Good shot. Look, find out from Holly, will you, where she is?" At net Dorothy nodded and tried to keep her mind on hitting the ball well in front of her with a stiff wrist.

Anna pulled the small pad out of her apron pocket and jotted down their order, glad she had checked on the vegetables. She recommended the veal piccata, because Fern was cooking tonight. The place was filling up, and Fern wasn't that fast, although she was good. She had to check on the wine. They had two kinds in carafes, rotgut red and rotgut white, but someone had to go down cellar to get it and with a new table coming in, she couldn't. She set out the bread sticks as the bell sounded and she went in for her order.

Mother Courage was in the west Village, one of the few women-run restaurants, a simple place with one room, brick walls, no music, no carpeting, a few plants in the window and announcements of women's exhibitions and concerts tacked to the walls and in the one bathroom. The owners used the dining room walls to display women's graphics and paintings. Now they were hung with sketches of women, large, unsmiling faces—no make-up, no jewelry, dark pencil sketches that began at the forehead and eliminated any adorment the hair might give.

Each face looked outward, thoughtfully, as if it looked into its own life. Anna saw little joy in those faces. They were faces of women who had learned they could dance like trained seals and still drown. They no longer cajoled and coaxed the world to love them. They were themselves: serious, unsurprised, undelighted, taxed, worried—woman herself, no figure from romance, no nubile creature designed for delights, each merely a person looking into her life.

Sometimes when Anna stood in the center of that room with all those serious faces surrounding her, regarding her, she wanted to giggle like a child in church. They were a frightening jury of her peers. When the earthy, hoarse-voiced woman came to hang her work, Anna was surprised by her rich laughter. Anna managed to arrange and set the tables so that she could hear the comments and the calling back and forth as friends hung the works. Everyone called her Bea, and there was much hugging. Anna felt as if she was looking through a glass window at the real people. She could hardly imagine how far that woman must have come to think as she did. The most radical part about those faces was their lack of prettiness. To a TV watcher they resembled no one visible on any channel. They were women from the subways and the streets, people from the supermarkets and the offices. Their very plainness suggested that no other image one saw of women was the truth. All others were painted dollies, versions of the Barbie Doll At School or In Business, Barbie Doll as Housewife and Filmstar.

After that first afternoon when Bea hung her work, the simplicity of the way feminists dress made sense to Anna, and she chuckled to think of her own mother's shock if she could see her little Anna at work wearing jeans and a denim apron over her bright green ERA shirt.

By now she balanced her tray handily as she moved between close-set tables. The rising voices and clatter almost drowned Fern's shout. "Here's your piccata and marinara. Was it two spinach salads?"

"One." In the kitchen Anna quickly laid out her tray. "Anyone have time to get more white wine?"

"When Ray comes back I'll ask her." Fern turned back to the stove to test an omelette.

Anna flipped back a damp lock, hefted her tray, and headed back to table four. As she gave them their veal and wine, checked that all was well, she turned to the two guys who had just settled at three and saw out of her peripheral vision a certain tilt of head and angle of jaw. As she set out the menus she turned her back to the gleaming figure. Her hands were shaking as she noted their order.

"This is the work I wanted you to see," Paul said, gesturing toward Bea's sketches. "If I could get her a showing at Jason's gallery, I'd like to."

"Those tough women may spoil my dinner, staring at me."

Anna left them planning who would go around the corner to pick up some liquor. She would go straight to the kitchen without looking to her left where they were all in the corner at table fifteen—Hope and two other women. If Terry was overwhelmed she'd have to help her, otherwise it was Terry's table.

When she reached the kitchen she knew Hope had called her name, but she pretended not to hear. She stood with her head against the doorframe inside the kitchen door, just breathing.

"You OK?" Fern asked.

"Fine, fine. Two more piccatas. Everybody knows you're on duty, Fern." Anna smiled suddenly with delight and relief. "My, you must do good work!"

Fern, who had never seen Anna smile before, decided she really liked her. "Remind them we have Jennifer's walnut cake tonight."

"Right." Anna flashed out of the kitchen as Terry pounded in, two hundred pounds of perspiration. "One chicken curry hot, one chicken Kiev, one beef stroganoff. Where's the white wine?"

Anna made it back to the men with their salads but heard Hope distinctly—this time right at her elbow. She knew she had to turn and did so slowly, putting off looking at Hope's face. Her eyes flickered over the walls, someone's back, then she had to face the blaze—and saw timidity, caution, reticence. Perhaps in her fantasy Hope would appear, merely stand looking at her as electricity traveled down her arms and sparked blue from her finger tips, and then, with her arm around her, Hope would lead her away. Crescendo. Fade out. But here was this woman with her glorious bones saying something like will you be kind enough, would you mind coming over to meet my friends if you ever get a moment, before she retreated to the far corner.

Another group came in and sat at Anna's tables.

"Now, mother, you must look at each one of them. Isn't she fantastic?"

Her father was looking around, his bifocals glinting, "It's a wonder this place hasn't been raided. Look at those people, Sherri."

The mother tipped her red lacquered head. "Fantastic, she is, maybe, but she sure has some ugly models."

"Mommy, that's not the point." The young girl looked from father to mother, and Anna went for the bread sticks.

As Anna shook hands with the woman she heard the name, Eleanor, and disliked her instantly. This was *the* Eleanor then, who walked out on Hope, now coming back to reclaim the lost goods probably. Roxanne Pulvirenti, a.k.a. "Rusty," a husky baby dyke who wasn't enough for Eleanor, or what? Anna couldn't remember half of what was said and had to leave "or I'll lose my job," said with forced laughter, but she tried not to watch their table as she served the Brooklyn family, the two men, and the next two groups that came in.

As Hope listened to Eleanor telling about the successful strike she had organized, she tried to remember if Eleanor used to tell stories in her own praise. Hadn't Ellie seemed rather self-effacing in those early days? She had just come out of a long relationship with a tough alcoholic—she couldn't remember her name, Mavis something—who had been a painter of the moving drip school. They had a fancy name for what Jackson Pollock used to do, and Mavis still did it. Eleanor had been skinny and scared, so appreciative of anything Hope said or did. She had loved her food, her caring, her loving, even the way Hope dressed her at first, when she had no idea that one color might be better than another for her.

"Rusty was really surprised when that group asked me to negotiate for them. Weren't you, Rusty?"

"I certainly was."

She certainly was. That had been the way Rusty was, everywhere but on the tennis court. There she was definite. She planned everything and apologized if she didn't win the point on the shot she should have. She was one hundred and twenty-five pounds set so perfectly in motion and balance that every shot was hit with all that weight behind it. Although Hope towered over her she almost had her racket knocked from her hand by Rusty's powerful returns. But out in the world with Eleanor, Rusty was super-shadow, yessing Eleanor and trotting at her heels.

Hope turned at the squeals of greeting to see Anna embracing Brenda and Joyce. She wondered if Anna had seen them often since Belinda's. They seemed to be very friendly. Brenda was introducing Anna to another woman and her friend. Anna had gotten thinner, and someone had cut her hair. She wondered who. She didn't have the money to go to a beauty salon probably, but a lot of women cut hair well . . . starting with Holly.

Rusty had picked up the carafe and was refilling glasses all around, saying quickly to Eleanor, "We don't see many racially mixed couples out our way, do we, Ellie?"

Eleanor turned to see Brenda and Joyce. "When did they get together, Hope? Didn't we seem them once somewhere?"

"In the dear, dead days beyond recall, you mean?" Rusty said, gulping her wine. "And how must it be after years, my friends? Hope, do you think how it is with people who stay together long? I wasn't with any woman before I met Eleanor, did you know that?" She tipped her head forward heavily as if something might spill out the top, "She brought me out. Right. Eleanor . . . as you know . . . was vastly experienced." She hiccuped. "Vastly."

Eleanor looked around at the family table. "Don't talk so loud, Rusty."

"A feminist restaurant, isn't it?" Rusty shouted.

"But that doesn't mean it's gay, you . . . shut up, Rusty."

Rusty's head bobbed forward, "Ah, it's a question. Should one endlessly shut up, so wise of course, but . . . it's a question."

"She doesn't usually drink at all. I don't understand this."

"There is much you do not understand. Or, if the truth be known, me either."

"Don't worry, Eleanor," Hope said. "The noise in this place has risen so high . . . "

"That no one will notice? How kind. Sure, and why should . . . she . . . he? 'They' I know is . . . ungram . . . grammatical." Weaving slightly to the side, Rusty raised her glass to Eleanor. "Why should anyone notice? Sweet wine and honey, you said—now just while no one notices." She held her glass at arm's length and stared at it as if she could see something happening in her glass, "turning to poison while the bee-mouth sips—how could he know that and be such a baby? Did Fanny teach him that? Who believes it?"

Just then Anna appeared at their table. "I just have a minute before Fern rings the bell." Rusty smiled a secretive smile. "So you genuflect at a bell too? I thought . . . "

"We'll have to go. . . . " Eleanor put her hand on Hope's arm.

Hope stood up. "Anna, you must let me call you."

"Why not?" Rusty sang. "The wires are free. But Anna, you watch out. She wants to call you."

"Rusty, shut up," Eleanor hissed.

"Your number, Anna. I don't know it." Hope said, trying to put a message through the static.

"Hope, this is . . . "

Rusty pointed an index finger. "I've got it! Hopeless. Hope, this is hopeless." Rusty clutched her stomach as her giggles slipped into shrieks of laughter. "Hopie this is . . . Hopieless." Tears were running down her face. "Hopelessly . . . hopelessly poisoned."

The soft bell rang as Eleanor half-lifted Rusty out of her chair. "I'll take her outside."

Anna looked toward the kitchen at the sound of the bell, turned back, and said briefly, "I'll call you," before she went to the kitchen.

In the clatter of the busy restaurant, in the banalities between chicken Kiev and spinach salad, the art works lived on the wall, and genuine communication occasionally took place. But with difficulty. Two young women sat in one corner looking into one another's eyes. The Brooklyn family grunted *seriatim*, noting the garlic in the salad, the harshness of the wine, the softness of the spaghetti, the blandness of the veal piccata. Their daughter kept her eyes on her plate.

Every time the door opened Anna hoped some people were leaving, but more arrived. She had thought that Hope and company would leave soon, but they did not. Eleanor returned from the stroll outside without Rusty. Anna knew Hope was watching her and tried to keep from dropping a tray.

In time Rusty returned to find Hope and Eleanor advanced in conversation. " . . . to some extent, unfinished business. So I thought I'd check. But you seem busy," Eleanor smiled, as if children did have their toys. "Have you known her long?"

"Who? Anna?" Hope shuffled her feet under the table. "Not too long."

Rusty quietly resumed her seat and began to drink the coffee now quite cold.

"She's a married neighbor, really. Or was."

"Married? Hope, you're crazy."

"I haven't, that is, I don't really . . . "

"I am now quite sober, or am angry enough to be when I eat something, but if you, Eleanor, don't stop this grilling, I'm going to make a scene. Really try to this time."

"Grilling? Who's grilling? You'd better have some more coffee, friend."

"Don't call me friend. I've never been closer to being your enemy. So this is the big dominant Hope you've come back to measure yourself against. God, why are we such fools! So she's chosen another waif. Let her be. So what? Let her be, for God's sake. You didn't do badly yourself . . . "

"Rusty! Where did all this come from?"

"Do badly in choosing waifs, I mean. You'll never let yourself under-stand the alphabet, baby."

Just then Anna stopped by to show them Jennifer's delicious walnut cake and to recommend it to them. Rusty raised her voice.

"Anna would be smart to keep well back from you, Hope. Even that is clear to the mouse in Eleanor's audience. Ever seen Eleanor surrounded by admirers? She walks among them, bending her head gracefully to the right and to the left as if she wore a train and diadem."

The door opened and someone called, "Bea, they're wonderful," as the artist came in with a group of smiling women who saw friends all about the room to approach and embrace.

"That's her, Mommy. Mrs. Kreloff, my teacher." Mommy looked at Bea Kreloff and began her most ingratiating smile.

Anna stood holding the plates of cake, staring at Hope, then at Rusty, before she turned to give table ten their cakes. Finally Fern turned on the overhead fans which added to the din but did move the smoke about and help to cool the perspiring waitresses.

CHAPTER SIXTEEN

HOPE tried to ignore the chill settling on her neck and shoulders as she drove Eleanor and Rusty home to her own house that night. She was trying to forget Rusty's warning to Anna, thinking she did not understand it and wondering why she let them stay another hour at her house. Of course, she had invited them. Their visit had been pleasant up to that mad dinner, hadn't it? The next morning when they finally left, Eleanor silent and Rusty defiant, each waiting to fight it out at home, Hope had time to sit down in her deep chair with Beth-Ellen on her lap and try to think of what had happened.

She remembered the shabby restaurant and its comfortable feel, but that was years ago and not the way it had been for her the night before. She tried to think of how Anna had looked when she reached up for her in love, but all she could see was a business-like Anna, clipping her pencil on her apron pocket and saying something about the menu. She tried to remember what Rusty had said about herself picking up a waif again, and "let her, so what?" Had Eleanor been a waif once? She couldn't work it out and went out to her workshed.

With her gloves on, and tough clothing to protect against the thorns, she set out for the worst spot of all, the one she had avoided all summer, where the bull briars grew in a sprawling thicket. Once she had intended to make it a little grotto, with slate steps and a quiet spot for a hammock near the chinese maple that was regularly engulfed by the sailing bull briars. They grew in long whips and sprawled far beyond their woodland base. She held the wooden rod and swung it easily like a golf club. The sharp blade swiped off the leafy green briars easily, leaving short spikes forking out of the ground. In their lavish cascade one or two ramblers could cover large amounts of ground. She swung rhythmically and the young briars went down with a swish leaving a large clearing.

With satisfaction Hope reached down to pull away three long sprays and was caught in the shoulder by others. As she pulled the spray from her shoulder, the thorns scraped her face and caught at her long hair. She tried to step to one side but her jeans were caught and a thorn jagged her thumb. She was surrounded by briars and could not swing her blade to make a clearing. Holding her arms carefully up around her face she crouched down and caught the bull briar below its thorns and pulled up.

As she tugged, the soil-covered skeleton came free, pulling along a powerful system of interconnected roots. Dragging the long thorn-covered sprays, she walked to the edge of the wood and hurled the twenty-five-foot train into the brush. When she came back she saw an open patch.

Now she was free to swing her grass scythe with all her strength, and rapidly she began to extend the clearing. She barely heard the black bird but kept striking her scythe into the brambles. She remembered that strange story about the prince who hacked through the thickets to try to reach the sleeping princess who had pierced her finger with a thorn and fallen asleep for a hundred years. The story *was* strange. Weeds stretched out slender fingers and intertwined their roots in a lethal network. They drank the earth's available moisture and finally consumed the light. She was swinging in long, forceful arcs that carried her forward deeper and deeper into the center of the green thicket where the brambles arched high over her head and closed around her.

They clutched at her, blocking her light, preventing her from stepping back out as they caught and snatched at her slightest movement out of the narrow corridor she had made. Like pushing the rock that merely rolled down again, she thrashed against the green wave that merely returned again each spring. They would spike their green heads and clench their primitive hands in their thorny network below and above this woody hillside again in the next year. I'm supposed to be Nature's friend, she thought, as she began to sense the depths of her hate . . . or was it fear? Those gentle moments of inter-connectedness with nature were also partly self-deception, although she would bless them when they came again, she knew. Now, caught in a *cul de sac*, the only thing she could do was to crouch down and heave up another web of clutching roots. They could not be permitted while she lived there to clench together, those old bonds.

She left off her violent thrashing and began quietly to feel below the thorns and pull up those long roots. The hillside behind her was desolate now as spiked remnants jutted out of the dark ground. Gritting her teeth, she bent down and pulled upon the jagged remnant of each dismembered briar, tugged out its roots, and then carried it or threw it into the woods. By the end of the afternoon she had not finished, but the scarred hillside had lost its graceful cover of bull briars. By the end of the day's labors she knew she could hardly offer Anna the clarity she thought she could. But she had understood Rusty's remark about "another waif." Rusty, however, was wrong; Anna was not just "another," nor was she "a waif." Nor did Hope need to keep her partner a child, as Eleanor did, anymore.

Eleanor must have been a waif that she never let grow, and now she was doing the same to Rusty; Rusty was starting the rebellion that Eleanor must have gone through. Did one go on and on duplicating one's mistakes on carbon paper, leaving one's lovers to work out the unresolved tangles with other lovers in a long destructive chain? The network of old custom becoming a poisonous root system that gave death finally to every love-growth? Anna had been right to forbid her to call. Anna had needed to back off to protect herself against her "protection." Hope shook her head grimly as she walked to the work-shed to hang up her rake and scythe. If Anna didn't watch it, Hope might protect her out of her own life. She knew she should't try to see Anna that night. But as she looked toward the old rhododendrons, she knew she could not wait any longer.

She could not wait for Anna to decide when she was ready to see her, and she could not trust that she would change her life merely by letting time pass. Within the pull and tug of things she had to try to work it out. She wasn't a sleeping beauty herself, who would awaken to find all the terrors of the darkened wood beaten away by a gallant prince who fought for her and suffered her wounds. Or was there another truth in the fairy tale, a secret one: that one must wrestle, struggle, like the prince, to free one's own psyche, the sleeping beauty in one's own life? The days of her countless hobbies were over, her staying blameless by doing nothing like some ice princess, bearing her life by living blamelessly. She had to leave the sacred ground where she hurt no one, except herself. She had to go to see Anna Tuesday night.

Feeling foolishly like Anna's date, waiting in a car outside the restaurant, Hope had parked where she told Anna she would and waited until after the doors closed. About midnight she heard the door slam as voices rose and fell and criss-crossed one another, exchanging good-nights. Anna did not look or gesture in her direction. In fact, after leaving her friends she started walking quickly away from Hope's car. Hope thought she had forgotten. Just when she had decided to turn the key in the ignition she saw Anna approaching the car from the front.

She opened the door. "Why did you go around the block?"

"No need for them to know everything, is there?" Anna's smile flashed under the street lights. She caught Hope's hand. "You look very different."

"You should talk. I hardly know who you are."

"Anna girl-housewife or Anna chief waitress, you mean?"

Hope shook her head. "Not quite. Can't we go somewhere quiet?"

"This is quiet." Anna sank back into the cushions.

"And be alone."

"We are alone."

"That's not what I mean. Don't play games with me, Anna."

"Here we go again. Maybe I'd better go." Anna reached for the door handle.

"No!" Hope shouted. "No, Anna. You can't do that again." Hope caught her shoulder too hard. "I'm sorry. I didn't mean to hurt you. Now or ever."

"What is this, Hope? Why should I stay and put up with this?"

"Anna, for God's sake, slow down."

"I barely get into the car before you are accusing me of playing games. I'm not playing coy—or willing to take this."

"Anna, Anna, please. Don't jump so!"

"Why shouldn't I jump?"

"Anna. Please wait, WAIT! Don't say another word. Let me explain. Honey, please. We are at the very beginning, the very beginning. At Dorothy's I said . . . things, but they did not mean 'leave me.' They meant, 'I love you and I'm hurting.' You took them to mean . . . " Anna stared at her in the filtered light and then lowered her head.

"Do you see, Anna? Do you see that was a preliminary bout, not even a fight? You jumped and left me, and, like a fool, I let you leave and wasted almost eight weeks because you told me not to follow. But then perhaps it was better. Anna, I can't say it all now. I want you to come live with me."

Anna looked at her and shook her head. "Where are you? I can't do that."

"But I love you and will give you a home."

"Will *give* me a home?"

"The children too, I've thought it all out. I'll build an extension for them. They'll love it. Today I worked out the plans. Do you want to see them?"

"No! No! No! Hope, I'm going to the subway." She opened the door. Hope reached behind her and held the door, her arm and a shoulder around Anna. Anna breathed in Hope's scent. "Don't play games yourself, Hope. I know what Rusty was saying. Let me go for a while. Perhaps I can turn up again." She tried to smile. "Give me time."

"No, I'm taking you home now. No, not to mine—to yours. Give me the directions."

Anna's look was guarded, "You cannot stay with me. Marge and Audrey just came home, two days early. Audrey was sick or something."

Hope couldn't tell if Anna was lying and didn't care. She would take her directions and drive uptown, rushing the lights.

"Now we've got to speak softly to keep from disturbing Marge and Audrey. They're just letting me stay through Labor Day." Anna turned the key in the lock, flicked on the light and walked directly to the windows to pull the drapes. She stood at the window a moment before she pulled the silver cord.

"You don't need to pull them," Hope said, standing stiffly by the door.

"The lights on the river are beautiful from here," Anna said, slowly pulling the drapes. She knew she should wait longer to be sure, but she had waited as long as she could bear to. She turned and faced Hope across the room and simply let her careful plan dissolve with the ache in her throat. With quick steps she walked through the tangle of plans, follies, charted moves to reach the warmth of that shy body. With a small cry Hope caught her and held her close.

They stood holding one another, swaying, speaking in soft gusts. "I thought you wanted me to go," Anna kept saying.

"Anna, Anna, I never wanted you to go."

"You were right about so much. The being coy, being a tourist. Hope, I know . . . "

In the alien room with its icy chandelier, Hope drew her down to the stiff sofa. "We have to go through the 'I said's' and 'you said's' but I admit it all, all of it. And I will admit much worse and much more than Rusty saw."

She began to tell Anna about Eleanor, finally, and in a mixture of courage and humiliation she drew out the long saga of her own supposed protectorship of the waif as she prevented Eleanor from breathing her own clear air. Now, she saw Eleanor's healthy need to be spiteful and finally her compulsion to run away and leave her flat, simply because she couldn't hold out against Hope's superior reasons. Hope's reasons had been irrelevant, no matter how right they were. It was poison and Eleanor had had to leave to survive. Her own noble protectiveness was all self-deceit and, in hopes that Anna would protect herself later, she told her.

And someday—not yet—she would have to admit to Anna what she now understood—that her invitation to Anna to go camping was just one more example of that self-deceit in a noble guise. Just as her being so open to Anna was probably a way to elicit Anna's admiration so that she would half-disbelieve what ever Hope said in self-criticism. Cynical Dorothy would have been right to crow about a seduction scene in the woods. She *had* rigged it all but so perfectly that she had not even been the seducer. Innocent Anna had been that. She wondered if Anna could bear always to be on her guard against her. The roots held on so.

Anna listened, her head tipped to one side, trying to sort out what was self-punishment and what was legitimate self-criticism. Hope might be going too far the other way now, she knew. And she had to tell her about that time in the subway when she had almost fainted as she ran from Hope. She had to tell her about the vertigo, the realizing like a blow in the stomach that with all her innocent questions she *had* believed that she was the real woman—never mind how glamorous the others were. She had had children, hadn't she? That way she could always feel a little superior among most gays. If Hope had felt like a freak, innocent Anna had been making her feel so.

This inter-connected thicket of self-protection had already grown too high, but perhaps there was some consolation in knowing how vigilant the psyche always was in its own defense. Still, Hope was not Astraea come

down to earth, as she admitted her failings to Anna. Nor in her sharp
questions was Anna the soft waif or the superior mother.

"You people kill me."

"What's this, 'you people'?"

"Experienced gays. Right. You are still 'the other' to me!" Anna
tossed her head. "You resent it that I came to you from a marriage. 'The
man' was mean to me so I turned gay. You want me to be politically pure
or something. Choose the lesbian life—by what? Some freer choice or
something, like yourself and Opal and Holly and Dorothy—most of them.
What am I supposed to be—some kind of suspected turncoat for the rest
of my life? So maybe if I tried one hundred and fifty men I would find
one that did suit me. So what? I don't intend to sleep around in a railroad
station for the next three years. I want you, and you'll just have to accept
the insufficiency of my reasons and experience. I'm going to stick with
you until you throw me out."

Hope was sputtering with eagerness to interrupt, but Anna roared on
in a torrent not to be stopped. Hope ended by gasping, something between
a laugh and a cry, and by holding her as they both talked at once. "It
isn't that . . . "

" . . . until you throw me out . . . "

" . . . which I won't . . . "

" . . . though maybe you should . . . "

"Why?"

"I have to ask you something!"

"What about?"

"This monogamy hang-up."

"Hang-up?"

"Opal thinks it's one. So does Fern, at the restaurant. Maybe it is.
Don't say I'm being little Miss Innocence again! I would ask this if you
were a man, which thank god you're not. Have a sex-change operation and
I'll leave you! Or have one myself. They're talking about the stupidity
of trying to make it with one relationship. I suppose I'm infantile, wanting
some super-security forever, like a crib."

"Anna, who knows? And so what? Some people want security most,
and some want variety most. Some want depth with one, and some want
ecstasy with many, and both may be for infantile reasons. What's the
difference? Let'm have what they want. I'm so tired of these people who
make every enterprise an exercise in self-improvement! If you like apples,
you should teach yourself to like peaches. If you like external sex, you
should like internal sex. If you like . . . shall I go on?"

"No, no. I get your point. But I can't live with you yet, Hope!"

Hope threw up her arms and got up. "That again! What kind of an
octupus am I . . . ?"

"I just can't. It isn't your problem . . . just . . . it's me, too, as well as . . . all the rest." She signed and gestured to legions of reasons waiting on the other side of the door.

Then Anna roused herself. "For the big experienced one, you certainly are conventional!"

"What do you mean?" Hope's voice sounded as if she had been accused of a public indecency.

"I thought I was the one brought up with the marry-and-live happy-ever-after bit. Here you are thinking everything will be settled by one bedroom. It won't. I need time before I'm up to you. Where most novels end—girl gets girl—is the beginning. And I'm not up to telling that story yet."

With Rusty and Eleanor thudding in her head in accusations and counter-accusations, Hope could hardly dispute Anna.

To Anna, it was all so absurd. At the very first the gates of their beginning had seemed glowing, intricate, wrought-iron, but she was finding in their first pull and tug-of-love as they led one another through those gates again, each confessing, each forgiving, that the gates of beginning were of steel and very plain.

CHAPTER SEVENTEEN

THE NEXT morning, despite her three hours of sleep, Anna was determined to keep the appointment with the lawyer and dosed herself with strong cups of coffee. Having resolved to be candid, Anna was nervous. A long-haired secretary in a tee shirt welcomed her into the office and offered her tea or coffee, nodding toward a corner table that had polystyrene cups, Nescafe, Sanka, Tetley and assorted plastic spoons, stirrers, sugar, saccharin and powdered milk in a messy pile. When her lawyer came out to greet her, Anna almost looked around her for the lawyer. Who could believe this brisk freshman with corduroy pants and a tennis shirt could cope with a law brief? She smiled, used her kleenex, apologized for her cold, poured them both some coffee, and nodded Anna into a bleak office. As Anna seated herself and looked around she was acutely conscious of having dressed in 1948 to meet someone from 1978. With lipstick and her Mother Johnson seersucker suit she hardly looked as if she was going to say what she must and surprise this plain-faced woman with the bright eyes. She suppressed her weak-minded wish that Hope could have been there with her.

After explaining to her lawyer that she wanted a divorce, that she had left her husband's house after a rape and a beating, and had gone to live with a woman friend, her neighbor, she asked if she would be able to gain custody of her children.

"On the face of it, I don't see why not. First, will your husband contest?"

"He sees no reason for the divorce. And why should he? He's comfortable. He gets all the services a male stud needs who eats and dirties his clothes—if I'm there."

"If he does not support you, how will you live?"

The conference went smoothly enough after Anna got used to the sharp questions that brushed aside the clutter of the social amenities, including privacy. But after Anna said that she wished to live with the woman, that her husband suspected the relationship was lesbian, and he was right, the young lawyer began to make loving references to her own husband and children. Her sub-text said clearly, I am happily heterosexual, although I will take your case.

The lawyer laid out the legal situation for a lesbian mother who wanted custody of her children. Unless she vowed to go straight or vowed never to see her lover again and *absolutely* never in the presence of her children, no court of law would permit her to retain custody of her children. No matter what she said or did, if she admitted that she was lesbian, any court of law would presume she was an unfit mother. If she were a child-beater she would have many times more chances of obtaining custody of her children than as an admitted lesbian. The lawyer's crisp voice added, "However, since heterosexuality is the prevailing sexual mode, it is quite acceptable for men or women to have numerous lovers of the opposite sex while they retain custody of their children."

"My choice then is give up the children or give up the only person I want?"

"Openly."

"What do you mean?"

"I mean that if you keep a low profile, if you do not proclaim from the housetops that you are gay, if your husband does not see you living with the woman in an obvious domestic arrangement, he may agree to an out-of-court settlement of some kind. Besides, time is on your side."

"How is that?"

"If you insist on not living with him, and he is the type you suggest he is, he will find some other chick to shack up with, and you'll be home free—provided she doesn't want your children, which she probably won't, particularly if she has or wants children of her own."

That had decided Anna on a course Opal had suggested. Opal had dropped in at the restauraurant one evening, in her continued pursuit of Anna.

"So--if you won't adjourn to the houseboat, why not the commune? I'll ask the other Jewels and let you know."

When Anna heard about the set-up she chuckled and decided almost on the spot that it would be ideal, provided she could get on with the women. In ways Opal was a wheeler-dealer like Holly and had connections that made the CIA look underdeveloped. She knew of a commune that had been going on for about six months and needed another woman. It had been started by a friend of Brenda's, Maureen, who had a four-year-old child and too large an apartment in the west Village when her lover had walked out. Two women, a lesbian mother, her two children, and her lover, a woman who worked in another printing establishment in the Village, had moved in with Maureen. They had four rooms, a living room, kitchen, and two baths for a very low rent in a Mitchell-Lama building paid for out of government subsidies, so the ongoing rent wasn't much.

When Anna met the women and walked around the rambling apartment, she asked about schools and playgrounds and watched Maureen with her little girl. The child was absorbed in some small piece of plastic in her hand and looked up at her mother with large eyes gently smiling. Her mother bent over her and said something softly, their connecting river running deep and warm no matter what din went on the world outside. Anna suddenly wanted to be with them and hoped they would accept her.

When she told Holly and Dorothy about the possibility, Dorothy began to consider Carl's reaction. She wondered whether Anna's move would influence his giving her custody of the children in an out-of-court arrangement. "It certainly looks like a straight group," she said to Holly. "Looks like what it is, a group of women getting together to pay the rent and supply each other with child care."

"And since Maureen is in law school, she and I can have a study period while the kids are taken care of by Belle or Constanza."

"Is Maureen the Black woman?" Dorothy asked.

"Right. Her lover walked out on her and left her with the apartment in the first place."

"Well, Carl would hardly presume you were pursuing the gay life with her, then."

"Knowing Carl, true." Anna said, "More fool he."

Holly laughed. "So you noticed?"

Anna grinned ruefully. "Holly, she's quite straight."

Although she could have gone to live with Hope and delayed moving into the commune until after school began, Anna used her job at the restaurant to keep her in the city. She arranged to move into the commune within days of learning about it. It was so easy for her to go limp, to abdicate and let Hope, in her resourcefulness, run everything. She thought Audrey would understand, but didn't get a chance to talk to her about it. One Sunday when she and Hope visited Marge and Audrey they discussed it. Anna felt it was her life and her problem, and she wasn't all that delighted when the subject was brought up by Hope. Marge agreed with Hope that it seemed unnecessarily strenuous, the life Anna was leading. Why work, go to school, keep the children and herself in an apartment when they could be in Stevensville with all its comforts? Why in fact go to school at all? There Audrey and Anna exchanged a look as firm in sodality as locked arms. Anna then asked how the lesbian mother case being tried in California was working out, and Marge left the track. Marge had become very interested in Anna's situation and was looking into the legal aspects. She agreed with Anna's lawyer that time was on her side.

Still, after leaving Anna at her new apartment, Hope walked through the corridors noting the mess at the incinerators, the trash fluttering in the halls, the paint flaking away. She loathed these Sunday-evening separations. It all seemed such unnecessary suffering . . . until she thought of Eleanor and then she kept silent. Anna was right.

The wind was growing chill as Anna returned from the market with some extras because her mother was coming. She hadn't been a bit pleased to read in her mother's letter: "Since Joshua is attending a banking convention in New York I thought I would come along and drop in on you. Josh will be terribly busy during the day, but in the evening we could all be together." As usual her mother assumed the unmitigated delight it would bring to share an evening with her. But that wasn't fair. Her mother had a very strong sense of family, and, naturally, if she flew in from Ann Arbor, she would expect her daughter to meet her and to set aside dinner-time for her and her father.

Later in the letter she had written in that flowing hand, "We were so sorry to hear that our little girl was suffering the slings and arrows that so many young people seem to suffer these days. Although we have never had a divorce in our family, we understand that these things do happen in the best of families. Mother Johnson spoke on the phone about a temporary separation. You must just go ahead and do what you feel will be right for you and your dear little children." Still holding the letter, Anna reminded herself of her mother's loyal support. When she and her sister were little her mother had encouraged and supported—true, it was always in conventional paths—to learn knitting or piano, but that had been precious and loving support. And when either one of them came wailing home from school with a private tale of bitterness or childish brutality, her mother never brushed it off as childish. She had known its importance.

"Still I am anxious to see you before anything is definite." By "anything is definite" Anna supposed she meant divorce. If she only could divorce him. When she reached the apartment she picked up a Fresca can banging around in the elevator and put it in the bag of groceries to drop into a garbage pail on her way. With forty-five minutes before her mother arrived she began dashing around the apartment picking up the bag of potato chips before the TV, checking that Belle and Constanza's beds had the table between them, taking the pantyhose off the shower rail. If she was going to try to be honest with her mother she had to have the apartment looking neat. She would be much more receptive if the apartment was neat.

"Somewhere, my dear, you have gone off on the wrong track." Her gentle voice, dropping with sad resignation that Anna and Jim wanted to be out still another night together that week when Anna was going to summer typing classes and needed her full eight hours of sleep.

She zinged the vacuum around the floors before she went out to the playground to bring the children back so Maureen could go to classes. Belle would be home for the late afternoon shift when Anna went off to school herself. Constanza would help out over the weekend and do the shopping. If her mother knew the half of it. Of course, Jamie and Timmie thought this was one great party with friends around all the time and four mothers available. The big issue for Anna was their current disagreement about diet, but they would work that out. Maureen agreed with her in her war on sugary between-meal snacks, but Constanza was foot-dragging, and Belle wasn't strong enough to deal with her.

She was just washing Timmie's face when the front door rang, and she opened it to that distinguished-looking woman in the mink stole. Instantly she slipped into her Hillcrest Manor mental dirndl: "Mother, how wonderful," she squealed, and drew her mother into the apartment with one hand while she carefully laid her sweaty cheek against that perfumed surface. "Come, children, here's Nana," she twittered, and the loyal yeomen came stomping to the door to be hugged while Maureen and Belle's children stood back and watched.

She introduced her mother to them, but they did not come forward to shake hands, smile, and, god forbid, to dip politely as she had done for years through the catholic school. They merely stood quietly, got a good look, and then ran back to their play. When they had gone, her mother said under her breath, "They have a colored child in to play with them?"

"Oh, yes, mother, we have a wonderfully interesting group of UN people in this apartment house. Want some tea? Too cold for iced—right?" When Anna turned from the kitchen, she saw her mother holding Jamie's hand and staring at the five beds and piles of children's toys in the living room.

"Oh, we won't sit there," Anna laughed gaily. Then hardly caring if she was making sense or not she explained at 78 rpm that they had decided to put the children all together in the living room and to turn one of the bedrooms into a sitting room.

Despite Anna's ease in picking up the old manner again, she knew she was far from being "little Anna," and had, in fact, a sense of fragmented vision, like a Picasso that gives you the front and the side vision at once. Partly she felt herself pulled once more to please this woman, the most powerful figure in her life for twenty years at least—and perhaps still. And partly, as the beautifully-groomed woman smoothed her skirt before she sat down, jangled her silver bracelets and tosed her head up to show her still firm chin to best advantage, she felt she saw her with a clearer lens.

"Your father is anxious to see you, dear. Will you be able to visit us at home soon?"

As Anna tried to explain that she had classes and child care duties, her mother interrupted, "You mean you help these other women care for *their* children?"

"Oh, it's very helpful to me, mother. I get to go to school this way." Then, of course, she had to explain why she wanted to go to school, a silly time-consuming plan since Carl made quite enough money.

"I take it that while Carl gets settled in New Jersey you are lodging here temporarily. Or that's what Mother Johnson said to me." The implication of her tone was that Mother Johnson might not have told the whole story because she might not have understood it. Anna's mother always separated herself from Carl's mother, implying that the other woman was a trifle slow or old-fashioned, sentimental or unaware somehow—perhaps because Carl's mother was not fashionable, and Anna's mother had grown more so as Anna's father had grown more prosperous. Her tone was "Tell me and I will understand what might escape dear Mrs. Johnson."

In fact, Anna had been turning over in her mind for weeks, even months, what she might say to her mother if ever she tried to be wholly honest with her. And just before she had opened the door to her she had resolved to say it all: Carl, Hope, the works, completely. Now the Picasso images kept popping up before her: the tiny spike heels with the slim ankle straps, the reddened pointed nails and shining lips. Like mirrors they reflected odd angles: a softly-relaxed arm along the couch against the rigid, boned girdle, the gently smiling face against the tense voice and savagely plucked eyebrows. One segment said relaxed, feminine, charm, and the other said strain, control, anxiety. The powerful woman, her mother, went disguised as a filigreed feminine creature and like any devoted Chinese mother of the past would bind Anna's feet in yards of linen strapping if she could. She saw her mother as she might see a fashionable woman across the room at a cocktail party, wondering how that woman kept her hair in a flip if she slept with anyone.

"Mother, how do you keep your hair so perfect? Mine is such a wreck."

"Do you like it, dear?" She actually pirouetted with one hand at the back of her head as if she were on the ramp at a fashion show. "I do my best. Your father likes it to look just so. This trip is such fun for us. It's the first trip we've had since our wedding, so it's almost a second honeymoon for us." She stopped, looked suddenly around the sitting room, and said, "Is this apartment very convenient for you, dear?"

"Mother, would you really prefer coffee to tea? Tell me, honestly. We have plenty of both."

"Coffee really would be a pleasure, if it's not too much trouble. And its price!"

"Tell me about Dan, then. Jamie and Timmie haven't seen their aunt for years—is it three?"

Her mother's face lost its wary look and began to relax into comfortable lines of pleasure as she told of Dan and her "lovely little family."

Anna wondered how her mother felt about being a grandmother five times over. Although she adored the grandchildren as babies and children, she did not mother them as Mother Johnson did, and she still delighted in compliments about her own trim figure. It was as if her first connection was always to her husband, and the rest was merely a part of her gratifying place in the great chain of being. She drew Jamie and Timmie closer to her. "You hardly know your first cousins, do you? Anna, you really must come out to Michigan so the children can meet one another and become friends when they're young. Jamie, your cousin David is just about your age . . . . And Timmie . . . "

With a jolt of anger Anna wanted to tell her mother the whole works, hard and fast. For a second she remembered standing in the darkness of the woods listening to the whispering and giggles from the neighboring campsite before the boy had begun to groan with fear. Just as Hope said, "They had inherited the world, hadn't they?" Let her know the stench of her smug world. But as Anna set out the coffee cups, she nodded at Timmie who wanted to go to join the squeals from the children's room.

From the sound of the thumps they were now jumping on the bunks, one of Timmie's favorite sports. "Ignore the racket, Mother, if you can, and tell me about Dad. He must love this traveling. How he used to reel off all the connections from Albuquerque to Memphis! Does he keep those old schedules?"

Her mother's face looked fond and gentle. "Can you imagine your father without his trains? I had expected him to shift off to airplanes because, after all, they go to more exotic places. But trains are his love. His only worry is that the government will give up on subsidizing them. He notes every station dropped from service. You should have seen your father the day we drove by Buckler Heights Station and he saw that it's now a fancy restaurant called "The Siding." He almost swears or spits every time we pass it." Her laughter was throaty, indulgent. "Jamie, you remember your Grandpa Joshua, don't you, dear?" As her mother stroked Jamie's hair, talking to her, Anna watched her, considering the moment.

Pouring a little more coffee into her mother's cup, she said in preparation, "Mother, I don't know . . ."

"Dear, you can't believe what a treat this trip is for your father and me!" Her mother turned suddenly from Jamie and gave that light, brittle smile that suggested their distance once more.

"Tonight we're going to an Indian restaurant—after he's finished with the men and their talk. And we both want you to join us with the children. Tomorrow afternoon we're going to take the Circle Line, which everybody says gives you the very best view of the island of Manhattan. The children should love that."

Anna sank back and sipped her coffee, calculating when she should start preparing lunch. The children would be hungry in about half an hour.

"Nothing is breaking in there, is it?" her mother asked. Anna could hear that blocks were now being dropped from the second level of the bunk bed as Maureen's child played waterfall, and Timmie or Belle's child caught the wooden missiles in a plastic bucket. They could be bonked on the head, of course, but until someone screamed Anna was fairly certain all was well, unless there was dead silence. They hadn't, as far as she knew, started playing doctor yet . . . but surely they must have.

"Mother, do go on. We won't worry yet."

She wondered if her mother had ever had multiple orgasms with her father. She hadn't known the word until college. That arty girl who used the word masturbation said it. She poured herself a half cup of coffee and smiled at her mother. Said them both in the same sentence, she thought. Now she would like to know what that sentence was. Jamie was starting to wiggle, so Anna agreed, and Jamie trotted off to join the furor in the next room.

"Anna, I am so very proud of you!" Inwardly Anna gasped and raked her mind back to find whatever syllables must have preceded this remark.

"You are handling all of this so easily! All these children, you manage them so well. And this . . . this difficulty with Carl. It makes my very happy to feel that my little girl can show such fortitude. Still, dear, you need not live in a place like this. Those *people* that I saw in the elevator . . ."

Anna wondered if she had run into Lily, the drag queen, in all his paraphernalia. Her mother's shudder when she said "those people" was so delicate that Anna did not see it; she almost smelled the piquant fragrance of her rejection.

"But you know, I have always found Carl . . . difficult. His drinking has taxed you, I am sure, to the utmost." Anna remembered Carl waving a beer bottle at her mother and telling her for Chrissake to clear out. She had been lucky.

"But you have not complained. Your father and I knew nothing whatever about this until I called Mother Johnson, because I thought your telephone must be out of order. The house has been empty for months then?"

It was time for Anna to give her mother details about who and when and what happened, and she began to do so.

"My dear, you may not," her mother interrupted with lowered voice, "prefer Jamie over Timmie, but when your children have children, I think you will find as I did how particularly precious your daughter and her little family are to you. Of course, you will always love Timmie and his wife—whoever she is—but your daughter is your daughter. She is, I suppose, yourself again or perhaps the proof of your good upbringing. I suppose some clever woman will say it some day, but Anna, I am very proud—about the way you have gone about living your life and trying to build a good life for yourself and your children.

"If you have to give up on Carl, so be it. But you are, I can see, setting about trying to fit yourself for a profession so that you can raise your little family. Of course, it really is not necessary. You will find a nice man. It wouldn't be too hard to find a nicer man than Carl, I should say." Suddenly her mother giggled, a tiny explosion, before she suppressed it and looked rather tentatively at Anna, who had to laugh.

But the laughter took Anna in a storm that led to her weeping and her mother came quickly to her side and embraced her softly, assuring her that she had no reason to weep, that she was well out of it. "You'll see, my dear, in a few months some fine man will come along and all of this will be behind you. It is very sensible to live with other women now. You all can help each other through your bad times, but it won't last forever; you'll see, my dear."

Anna shook her head in agreement, struggling to find a kleenex. She couldn't take from this gentle, blind woman the evidence of triumph she offered. Whatever her own doubts, shown in all the fussy grooming, the vanity and jewelry, the mink stole, her mother had to believe that she had done her work superlatively well. And now, at least, her mother would be shored up by her separation from Carl, whom she'd never liked. As Anna drew herself back from her mother's arms she wondered if she had wanted to be honest with her mother or if she had wanted just the luxuries of the confessional. But there could be no priest or mother to grant her absolution. Feelings were as factual as the rounded globe. Forgiveness had nothing to do with them.

And later, after a chaotic lunchtime, when her mother picked up her stole to leave, kissed the children, and they agreed to meet at the Raga restaurant that night, Anna turned from the door, her face aching from smiling. Was her drawing back from full disclosure truly a wish to protect her mother, or was it the sheerest cowardice? Hand still on the doorknob, she recalled her mother's psychic shudder at "those people." It was a bitter mixture she was planning to drink. She would simply live it out, and her mother would see what she could bear to see by herself, because Anna would not shame her.

CHAPTER EIGHTEEN

IN THE year that followed Anna was able to keep Jamie and Tim with her while she lived at the commune and used words like "temporarily" and "for the time being" to Carl and Mother Johnson. Even seen through Mother Johnson's account a picture was becoming clear. Carl was "seeing" a "little woman," "pretty they say, though, of course, I know nothing about it." But Anna supposed that to Carl it was more important that the woman had inherited her husband's impressive concrete business. At last Carl wouldn't have to work for anyone else. That would take the pressure off him. Anna just hoped it would "take."

In that year the two couples, Marge and Audrey, Hope and Anna, saw each other frequently for dinner at each other's houses or out at restaurants. Occasionally as she sat with the other women Anna remembered the terrible night when she, Carl, and the Greens went out for dinner and the play. She remembered conversations riddled with obscenity and the implied physical threats that were considered humor and good fun in most of the heterosexual world. Jack from MENSA had laughed the night at their house—so proud of his association with that elite group. He had waved his cigar in the general laughter as he told of Junie, who was so big her lover "could stuff an apple between her legs and still get in." Even the women had appeared to be amused. Anna wanted only to be invisible to them, to be permitted to withdraw completely from those grim lives and the primitive barter of services for privilege that their couplings implied to her.

They went dancing sometimes, but rarely in a foursome because Marge had to be careful about running into clients. Still Marge had begun to take an interest in women's class-action suits and Audrey's singing career was starting to take off. The fact was that Hope and Anna loved to be with the other couple. They found themselves able to talk fully and freely with them. Time vanished so with them, they had such difficulty separating at the end of their evening together that weren't they even a little in love with them? The idea was frightening at first and neither Hope nor Anna wanted to consider the implications of it, but, after admitting it to each other, they were relieved. With care they tried to see more of other friends.

Commune living worked with difficulty because nothing is more personal than eating and the way one treats one's children, but gradually an accomodation was reached. Maureen and Anna had become staunch friends so that each of them could conduct her private life knowing her children were being treated with consideration as people, not wayward poodles. Constanza and Belle were usually at the apartment all weekend, and Anna could have left her children with them, but usually she and her children were all together at Hope's house for weekends and sometimes Maureen and Delia were able to join them. Reluctantly Anna had come to realize that although her long talks with Maureen about children, men, women, Blacks, and whites brought them close, significant distances would always remain. Finally Anna saw what Hope had predicted, that friendships with straights were circumscribed as if someone had drawn a magic chalk circle and said "safe within—not beyond."

For Maureen her training in law was her visa to independence, so she understood Anna's obsession with her classes and her rising periods of anxiety before tests and papers, when any noise or postponement of her work drove her frantic. But Maureen's training in self-discipline had been so much more rigorous that even under heavy stress Maureen never raised her voice or complained. To Anna this was heroic, but Maureen would smile and say, "When I have time to learn to be angry and to shout a little, baby, I'm gonna learn it." She thought Anna's wild expressions of self-doubt were healthy, and Anna thought her self-control was exemplary. Maureen would shake her head and say, "It all depends on where you're coming from."

They agreed that if you started with too much control you could loosen up, but if you started with no discipline you had a struggle to gain method. Belle and Constanza would have thought punctiliousness was a joke or a punctuation mark. Belle's children were growing like happy weeds, but they *were* happy. Whatever was felt was out in the open, with no child covertly pulling the wings off flies or squeezing the cat's tail. You couldn't accuse them of being quiet children, but there wasn't hidden hostility and nastiness either. For a family of nine they were managing to support one another well, and each woman was grateful, both privately and publicly, that her life was her life, subject to no man's whim.

All the same Anna felt, at times, when her anxiety and frustration shot up the scale, that is was impossible. This weekend, for example, she and the children would have to visit Hope on Friday and Saturday and then, because of the party Hope was planning, she would have to leave Hope Saturday night, bring the children home, to return herself on Sunday alone, leaving the children with the other women. She called Hope Wednesday night to grumble about it. After a moment of silence Hope agreed. That *was* impossible and besides, she argued, when Anna and the children finally came to live with her and she had parties they would be there, built in, wouldn't they? She wasn't thinking to ship them off to the vet's whenever there was a party or something, was she? Anna chuckled, thanked Hope, and after a few more minutes of conversation she hung up, trying to keep her telephone bill down. She wished Hope would not keep talking as if she and the children were going to move in any minute. She had done well to keep Carl and his suspicions sleeping by living with the other mothers, but as soon as she moved in with Hope he might cry 'queer" and take the children away.

She didn't believe in forbodings, archaic storm clouds with hulking Heathcliff on the moors, but to be celebrating Marge and Audrey's twentieth anniversary next door to her old house was just too bizarre, she felt. Surely Carl's beery ghost would trundle over to visit them, pushing his power mower. The house had been sold for a good price six months ago and Carl was happily ensconced in a ranch house in Oradell around a circle with fifteen other houses in three alternating styles. If he did not turn up at Mother Johnson's on Thanksgiving weekend, he was not likely to turn up a weekend later. Yet if he did, if he did, he would find twelve women and five children banqueting like the old Romans. Well, not quite.

Anna turned to the phone again and called Mother Johnson, who was so glad to speak with her, and how were the children? No, she didn't expect to hear from Carl for a while. Out of town visiting friends in Buffalo. No, she didn't know the connection. She was fine, busy with the Mother's March of Dimes against Muscular Dystrophy. After suitable civilities Anna hung up, somewhat reassured.

Sometimes Anna felt that living this way would drive her to ulcers, a psychotic episode, or she'd "just flip out." Anna jumped up and began to pick up around the apartment, trying not to hear the commotion coming from the children's room. Holly and Dorothy had told her how endlessly difficult it was living apart as long as they'd been worried about Dorothy's tenure. Then, when Dorothy's tenure did not come through and Dorothy was told she had her job for only one more year, Holly had thought that once more there would be a reason for Dorothy to refuse to move in with her. Wouldn't Dorothy feel that until she knew where she would work they shouldn't find a place together?

But this time Holly was wrong. Dorothy had been on the rack for a year and a half worrying over tenure and when it did not come through, she did not tell Holly for a week. Then she invited Holly to have dinner with her at Mother Courage alone and told her, actually celebrated, Holly said. According to Holly's vivid account, Dorothy had decided that life was too difficult to spend it waiting, that most women spent all their lives waiting for something to happen *to* them. Hadn't she tried to choose a life in which she chose? Why should she keep on waiting to live miserably ever after with Holly? Why not begin at once, the sooner the better? Job hunting would have to follow and be worked out as it was for other married folk. Period. Holly practically danced around the snowy playground where Anna was watching the children.

"Of course, I know she's marrying me for my money, but I'll accept her on any terms."

All this had happened last December, just before Christmas, but by January 15 Holly and Dorothy were hammering and sawing in an old loft in Greenwich Village.

Salty old Dorothy had gotten a little sweeter in the months that followed, so Hope was saying, "See how pleasant I might become if you'd break down and move in with me."

They had so little time together that it became a craving like that for food. Still they had had two weeks in the time before summer school started when all four of them had gone camping. The children had adored their own private tent, a devastating lime green. This time they had gone directly to Algonquin Provincial Park, had found a woodsy campsite and had settled down for ten days. The children wanted to go to the nature movie almost every night. The anticipation of a movie was still wonderful to them no matter how much disappointing experience they had. Returning to Algonquin was precious to Anna, but soon they were caught up in the children's version of the experience, their sallying forth to find new friends and their learning to sail. Still, the evening hours were their own when the tent flap was zipped closed and they had all the freedom they cherished, barring trumpets and drums.

"Come on, Jamie and Tim, it's time to pack your things for Hope's." Maureen and Delia were going to go to the children's zoo, so Delia wouldn't be unhappy about Jamie and Tim leaving for the weekend.

"What'll we need?"

"You'll need sneakers, jeans, tee shirts, warm sweaters . . . "

"Oh yeah, that." Jamie went off. Anna would check their duffle bags later to be sure about tooth brushes and the rest, but she kept wanting them to be responsible for their own things. She never forgot Opal's remarkable children. Jamie would check Tim's bag first.

"Here's the gang with the teeny duffle bags. Pile in."

With shouts the children hugged Hope at the train station and clambered into her car. When it was Anna's turn to hug Hope, she held her suddenly, very tight, then drew back, pressed cheeks, and kissed vaguely in the proper public manner.

Hope said, "Been a rotten week? Me too. The hell with it. You're here!" She started the car with a rush and they were off, the children telling Hope an important list of minutiae in extravagant detail, as she nodded and said, no, yes, you're kidding, at judicious intervals.

Friday nights were always the best. They had the whole weekend before them and could just luxuriate in the hours. The children always ran to the cellar to play ping pong as soon as they had stashed their clothes out of sight, and Anna and Hope could go to Hope's bedroom and close the door. When the sneakers came thudding up the cellar stairs it was usually time to pull themselves apart, neaten up, and think about preparing dinner. This night Hope had had spaghetti sauce simmering before she went to the station, so there was little to get together.

"Timmie, help me with the salad," Jamie said, taking fresh spinach out of the refrigerator.

As Tim washed the spinach, none too carefully, Jamie handed him celery and cucumbers, while Anna cut the onions.

"She talks a lot, but what's she doing?" Tim said, looking at Jamie under his beetling brows.

"I'm setting the table!" Jamie answered.

"That's done now. My job takes a longer time."

"OK, Jamie. You can put out some grated cheese. And find your mother a good bread basket and a cloth napkin to put over the garlic bread."

Tim looked pleased as Jamie was given more work to do. Hope gave Anna a quick hug by reaching around her back to hand her the tin foil. "Quite a group we're having on Sunday."

"Hope, run over the final list for me. I've lost track."

"Well, in addition to Marge and Audrey—who won't be coming early by the way . . . Marge has taken Audrey to the exhibition at the Met today, first day she's skipped work during the week in ten years or something. Tomorrow they're going to dinner and a play. Big weekend. Anyway, Sunday they'll arrive about one, because Audrey sings in the choir. So there'll be Dorothy and Holly, of course, and Opal and her current flame Hazel Oppenheimer, a character Opal met in her karate class."

"Karate?"

"Not such a bad idea for Opal actually, considering the whole of New York City is her oyster—not to mention lobster."

"So, who is this Hazel?"

"I don't know, Anna, but Opal says she's 'really great,' so we'll have to wait with that for the time being. And then there's Brenda and Joyce who are bringing Claire and Sue. I didn't get all this straight, so I don't remember who was whose old lover. Either Claire was Brenda's or Joyce's old lover, or maybe it was Sue who was."

"You're a great help."

"Brenda will tell you. Get her off alone and ask her quickly. Anyway, Claire. . . . OK, gang, we are *ready*. Jamie, hand me the plates, please."

As Hope dished out spaghetti with great dollops of meat sauce poured over it, she continued. "Claire is, according to Brenda, a beautiful singer. Lord, I don't know if the beautiful described her or her singing."

"Hope—you're killing me!"

"Probably both. And Claire has a son—or daughter—college-aged. Did I say Sue, her friend, was a doctor? No, she's not the Sue who runs Belinda's. She's an Asian-American, plays drums in her own rock group, a lot younger than Claire."

"Leave the garlic bread in the oven for a few more minutes."

"Claire sings German *leider*. What do you suppose she does with Sue's music? She is, Claire is, by the way that old old friend of Audrey's. Audrey knows Sue, too, heard her give a terrific performance at a village coffee house one night and went up to speak to her later. Timmie, want more?"

"Hold it! The garlic bread."

"I'll get it!" Jamie scraped her chair from the table.

"Don't forget the pot holders!"

"Yee-ouch! It's OK, Mom. It's OK. I just forgot about the tin foil."

"And yeah, you've got to try our salad," Tim said, reaching for the wooden salad servers.

Jamie came back with the garlic bread in a woven basket. "Don't stir the salad, dopey, toss it!"

"Oh, yeah, right. Shall I put on salt and pepper?"

Anna nodded, "But go easy, not too much, OK?" Anna remembered her own family dinners commencing promptly at 6:22 to account for her father's 6:02 train. By her father's elbow at dinner he always had a large silver salad set which contained oil, vinegar, salt, pepper in graceful glass cruets with silver waists. He would turn the moveable central ring, select each ingredient judiciously and pour precisely the right amount into his large wooden spoon. Anna always thought his salads were too vinegary or too peppery, but he performed the salad rite with the seriousness of a priest. For Timothy to put together the salad was in one way to violate her father's victorian tradition, but in another to revere it.

"A delicious salad," she said.

Since Hope had Sunday's preparations well lined up, Saturday was spent outdoors doing what Timmie described as "putting the garden to bed." He seemed to take pleasure in wheeling Hope's noisy wheelbarrow back and forth from the compost, where Hope was turning over the leaves and setting out the decomposed material, to the flower beds where Jamie and Anna would lightly rake the mulch, arranging it around the plants, "to keep them warm in the winter, like sweaters."

"If we didn't have Timmie's running commentary, I don't know how we'd understand what we're doing."

"Never mind, he's got it right, but why does that wheelbarrow thump so?"

"Something's loose."

Hope turned to raking the lawn and to piling the newly-fallen leaves into plastic bags for Timmie to tote to the compost pile in order to start the winter's new batch for next winter's mulch. And the roses needed particular attention. She would teach Timmie how to grow roses if he showed interest in it.

"We should remember, Anna, to stack some wood in the living room next to the fire place for tomorrow evening."

"When did you say they would arrive?" Anna called back.

"About one." Hope was carrying a plastic bag of leaves to the compost pile when Timmie skidded up like a taxi thumping with a loose hub cap, "You want him to go to Grand Central, lady? I'll take'm, plop'm in." Timmie started off to the compost pile. Hope decided that he must be stronger than he looked. He stopped.

"Jamie, take an arm and help me with this." So the two of them coped with the barrow together, and tipped all the leaves out of the bag into the heap, before they ran and jumped in it.

When her flower beds were done Anna came to join Hope in her general raking. Pausing a moment to push her sweater up her arms, she looked across at the wild rhododendrons, those magnificent old plants that she would always consider with a grateful shudder. She remembered them as immense, ancient, and gnarled, granters of primeval maternal protection that terrible night when she shrank low to the ground within their shadows and fled like a beaten animal to Hope. She had been astonished the next year to see those dignified matrons looking positively lyrical in early July in their profusion of milky-white blooms with delicate pink centers.

Beyond them was Carl's house, newly painted avocado, "one of those new colonial colors," its new owner had told Hope. "How it could be 'new' and 'colonial' I didn't ask the lady," Hope said, telling Anna about the new family, their beagle hound that howled whenever it was put out, and their adolescent sons who were digging a saw dust pit for their high jumping practice in the backyard.

"They sound busy," Anna said.

"What'll happen to the high-jumping pit when their mother wants to build what she calls her 'potio'?"

"Hope, where are the children?"

Hope led Anna back of the rhododendrons and pointed. "Out of gas."

They were both sprawled on top of the pile of leaves, spread-eagled in the sun. Still, it was chilly and time for lunch.

CHAPTER NINETEEN

EARLY Sunday Morning Anna stretched slowly. tentatively, feeling yesterday's exercise in her arms and shoulders. She turned over on her side so that she could cup Hope's back and warm flanks in her own curled body. Hope liked to awaken gradually and she stroked her softly, feeling the long back and the slant to her waist and the sudden hip bone, thinking, "above, below, beneath, between." When Hope stirred and turned, she said to her, "Don't wake up. Just keep sleeping."

Hope's peach-colored mouth turned up a little at the corners, but her eye-lids remained closed, hiding the blue beam still.

"Not likely." Hope made a comfortable sound and pulled Anna down to her.

In the peace of the generous bed in that quiet room, flooded by the bleak late November sun, they could float adrift in pleasure. They played like fish flashing their silver backs down in their dark waters unseen by the fisherman. They could shiver a silver thigh and lead each other down through shadowed caverns, then swoop upwards to arch their gleaming backs and swing off alone on the long dive down to the caves of sleep.

"Timmie, they did! I've seen it!"

"You're kidding!" Thud, thud, slam. Clearly it was time to be up. Anna snatched at her clothing, leaned down to nuzzle in Hope's neck. "Morning again, sweetheart. I'm going downstairs."

Jamie strode in through the kitchen door, indignation writ large on her face.

"You know what, Mom! They did! I've seen it! They're digging a big enormous hole in our back yard. Can they do that?"

"Honey, it's not ours anymore. You know that."

Jamie looked at Timothy. "We know that. But it doesn't seem right."

"Doesn't it help having the house painted green?"

"We think it's a crummy shade of green."

Timmie put his hand over his mouth and rushed around the kitchen giggling and making grotesque visceral noises.

"Timmie says . . . " and Jamie's peals of laughter doubled her up. "Timmie says that it's vomit green!" The two pounded each other on the

195

back and ran crouched over out of the kitchen to fall on the sofa. "Vomit green! Maybe even," whisper whisper, "mmmmmmm green!" with bubbles and gulps of laughter they rolled about on the sofa as Anna shook her head and began to get breakfast together.

By one o'clock the ham had been in the oven for half an hour and two tables, one for the adults and one card table for the five children—Opal's two, Sue's child, Jamie and Timmie—had been set up. Jamie was managing their table, even writing out place cards because she wanted to sit Lil next to herself.

"You can hardly be very far away at a bridge table, Jamie."

"Still, anyway. I want to," she replied, bearing down hard on a felt-tip pen.

Holly and Dorothy arrived just after one. "We came as soon as we dared because we wanted to see you alone."

When delivered, their news surprised Anna, who had always felt Holly's commitment to teaching reading was absolute.

"Anyway, starting January I'm going to teach two classes of eleventh-grade literature at the Shadwell School in the city . . . as well as two reading classes at my old job. If this works out I may even try to switch to teaching lit. full time at Shadwell, if they like me. Of course, the money's less but . . . "

"We've been very up about this and wanted to tell you alone. Holly's not been . . . "

With the ringing of the door bell accompanied by deep-throated barks, Beth-Ellen, who had been curled near the fireplace, turned and bounded up the stairs to withdraw for the day. Opal was at the door with Lil, Adam, and Hazel, who was gripping a large German Shepherd on a stout chain.

"I hope it was all right for me to bring Brute. He'll be all right if we chain him outside."

Anna rolled her eyes at Hope, who sent Timmie down to the cellar for a rope hanging near the washing machine. Brute tugged at his chain.

"He's really a dear and so good with children, isn't he, Opal?"

Opal assured everyone how wonderful Brute was, and went the rounds embracing all the guests.

Lil smiled at Jamie. "You have almost woods in the back, don't you?" The children went off with Anna and Hazel to tie Brute up as close to the woods as possible. Anna wanted to be sure the knot was secure, and with Hazel she suspected loose knots.

When Anna returned, Brenda and Joyce and their friends were slipping out of coats for Hope to hang in the closet, chattering about the snow threatening and the chill winds moving down from Canada. When

Hope began to take the drink orders, Anna signaled Jamie to bring in cheese and crackers for her friends. Lil followed Jamie with the tray of ginger ale. Sue's child was standing slightly behind her mother near the piano, her head about level with the keyboard.

As Anna was introduced to Sue and her child she felt the woman's scrutiny. Although Sue smiled and nodded her head politely, her quick eyes appeared to notice everything. Claire, too, held herself erect, like a performer on stage, head slightly back, eyelids lowered as if she shielded the power of her intensity from this woman of little achievement. Claire asked for Audrey, saying she was thrilled to be included for their anniversary and what a lovely home Hope had.

Joyce was saying, "You should have heard Claire in Boston, Anna. She was simply wonderful." Claire inclined her head graciously, smiled, and passed on to speak to Brenda.

Her child keeping close at her side, Sue began to tell Anna and Joyce about her own engagement coming up at the Peppered Pumpkin. Anna got away to check on things in the kitchen. Of course a woman like Claire would think she knew nothing. Claire had gone through a lot to get where she was, and Anna looked as if she had had everything and she had done nothing with it. Still she was studying now and maybe by June would have that degree.

"I didn't know Holly was bored teaching reading." Anna checked the sweet potatoes.

Hope was putting the salad together. "I'll tell you more about that later. It's a longer story than . . . "

"Here they are—at last!" Holly said, opening the front door.

"Marge and Audrey!" Hope snatched a towel as she left the kitchen.

"Welcome, honored ones."

"Honored?"

"Twenty years! That's an achievement!" Brenda smiled at Joyce, who answered, "Never mind about the achievement. You aren't suffering." Brenda just laughed.

"Audrey had to sing in the choir. Sorry we're late."

"They understand, Marge. Don't fuss." Audrey entered smiling, followed by Marge in another gorgeous suit. "Here is dear little Anna; the boys send their love."

"The boys that Anna took care of."

"What?"

"Not boys, dogs!"

As the women were given their drinks they sorted themselves out in different patterns, chatting with one friend, then another. Anna passed among them with celery, radishes, and the dip.

"No, as a matter of fact I didn't get it," Dorothy said to Brenda.

"That's rough. I'm sorry."

"You don't have tenure yourself in your business, Brenda," Joyce said.

"I really don't see the point of tenure. The rest of us do without it. Why do teachers need it?" Sue said, selecting a stick of celery and crunching down on it.

"Historically there has been some point to it, Sue."

"Historically? This is now."

"Now, Sue." Brenda's voice was firm. "Compared to what I make or you make, teachers are still underpaid. Also there's the academic freedom argument. . . . "

Opal was feeding Hazel a celery stalk with a gob of dip wobbling on its tip. "Imagine, twenty years."

"Do you think they would both swear they were good?" Hazel laughed and ran the tips of her fingers along Opal's throat.

"Good who . . . them? Or the years?"

Audrey came up to Anna and put her arm gently around her. "You are such dears to give this party for us." Her voice was oversugared as it was sometimes when they felt strange with each other. "And how marvelous of you to include Claire," she whispered in Anna's ear. "You remembered my telling you about her, and you spoke to Marge."

"Marge sneaked her phone number from your address book."

"Anna, there's a special reason why it's even better that she's here. As a surprise anniversary present to Marge I want to sing two or three songs and one of them is one that Claire sang at her Carnegie recital. I loved it and told her, and she gave it to me to prepare for Marge. So it's wonderful that she can be here, for me a little scary, but . . . she will understand."

Hope must have forgotten to tell her, but that explained the piano tuner in yesterday. Hope had moved the piano so that it commanded a good view of the audience and received the afternoon light from the french windows.

The telephone was ringing insistently before Hope heard it and lifted it off its cradel. "Well, yes, she is, just a minute." Hope met Anna's look and nodded, her face set.

"This is too much. Mother Johnson said he was upstate. . . . " As Anna walked into Hope's study to take the call, she closed the door blotting out the disorganized sounds of a good party. In front of the hemlocks she could see Tim and Adam talking near Brute, who swung his tail heavily back and forth. She must answer the phone. Hope would be

waiting for her to pick it up. A deep breath . . . "Yes Carl, of course."
As she listened to his request, harsh through the wires, she shivered.

"He's coming here. In a few minutes. I couldn't stop him, Hope."

The room went quiet. Holly had been giving the group around her
background details about Anna. "I have a wonderful idea! Why don't I
take the group on a small tour of the house?" Holly said, finishing
preparing the martini she was making for Joyce.

Dorothy agreed, "Knowing Carl's views, he better not see twelve
women together at a party."

"We could be the DAR. What does he know?"

"Joyce, you don't know the story. Come on, ladies, let us pretend we
are visiting one of Westchester's fine old houses. Here you have the ornate
old bannister, bring your drinks with you, and don't lean too heavily on
the bannister."

To Anna's surprise Holly was followed like the Pied Piper up the stairs
by Brenda, Joyce, Claire, Sue, Opal, Hazel and Dorothy, while Marge and
Audrey followed Hope out into the kitchen.

"Take it easy, honey."

"Don't tell him anything."

Anna could hear Claire's melodious voice carrying from the top of
the stair. "But when my daughter said . . . "

"I hope to God this isn't a re-run of the last time," Dorothy muttered.

Anna looked at the litter of ash trays and drinks and canapes behind
her. There was no concealing the party, of course. And no need to. She
heard the car in the drive. There must be four cars parked there already.
He would have to park well back and walk up to the house.

At the bell she opened the door. Carl was standing there in an
obviously new blue suit, smiling, ducking his neck in an ingratiating
fashion, glad to come in, yes he would, and he smoothed his shoes at the
door mat. He glanced quickly around. "No people? Looked like quite a
party from the outside."

He sat down with care, his hands hanging in front of him as if they
were too heavy. He nipped his trouser legs up by a small crease to ease
them over his knees. "I happened to be up here for the day with mother
and a friend and thought you might be here."

"Yes." Anna could hear the steps moving about up stairs. Evidently
Holly had taken them up to the attic first—to start with the hobbies?

"Actually I have something to speak to you about. All right if I
go right into it?" He cleared his throat. "I have let you keep the children
during this last year while I got fixed in Jersey—got a good house and
all—job's good. Work in precast cesspools. A real field opening out with

all the developments and all. Anyway, I'm in good shape, real good shape now to keep the children."

With this prelude Anna went cold. Now he would take them. But she was trying to understand his good-boy manner. If what he wanted was his to take, his courtesy was uncharacteristic.

"Thing is. You may be wondering why I haven't come to get them. The children. The thing is that . . . um. Mind if I smoke?" He made great business of cutting off the tip of an expensive cigar before he lit it and blew the heavy smoke into the room. "Matters have changed for me. Not just the good job and the house, but, uh, since you have been . . . well, healthy man and all, I have plans for settling down again." He drew on his cigar, turning it in his moist lips.

"The woman I have in mind's a wonderful mother, really doesn't let her kids off the reservation a second. She'd be a great mother for Jamie and Timmie, I know, and she'd love to have 'em. but the thing is . . . " He nudged the heavy ash off the head of the cigar and held up the cigar sideways, admiring its length. "The thing is that what with her running her husband's cesspool business, since he died, and her own three kids, although she probably won't keep working after we marry and I manage the business, still it pays to avoid salesmen and commissions, and she will want to have kids with me, of course . . . so with one thing and another, I guess I am asking you if you would hold off . . . that is . . . not contest a divorce. . . . If I give you, say, what you're getting now, plus another hundred a month until you marry again, will you let the divorce go through without any trouble?" His palms rested on his knees as she stared at her, the proposition made.

His well-brushed look, his self-effacing manner, even his final flourishes with the bootleg cigar now made more sense. When power was in someone else's hands he knew how to be conciliatory. Did bullies know the uses of power better than anyone? She had always thought it was the other way around. Her face was completely bland as she replied, "I would want to talk to my lawyer about that, Carl, but I think I would agree to those terms."

"Well, yes, well, naturally you'd want to clear it with your lawyer. Give me his name and I'll tell my lawyer to contact him in the morning." He pulled out a small spiral note-book and a silver Cross pen to write for Anna's dictation.

When they shook hands at the door Anna felt her icy hand enveloped, and he quickly leaned over and kissed her cheek. "You're a good kid, Anna." He shook her hand again. "No hard feelings, eh? Well, let me know what your lawyer says. It's uh . . . negotiable. . . . Take care now," and he backed out the front door, his polished shoes skidding on the brick steps. Anna watched him stride to his car, loosening his tie and throwing his jacket on the front seat despite the chill wind. When he started the ignition, she closed the door.

She sank onto the window seat gripping her hands, staring at the floor—seeing the excitement in Carl's face just before his heavy hand struck her jaw, his approach with his tee shirt straining across his belly, his skinny legs spraddled, his swollen cock up . . . his clumsy courtesies today, "good kid, Anna," when he'd won, but she had won, too. She had won, too. "Hope!" She jumped up, but Hope was right there putting her arms out and all the others were standing around asking Hope what had happened.

It may have been an hour or only fifteen minutes later when they were all seated, and the ham, sweet potatoes, vegetables, and salad were being passed around family style, that someone suggested a toast.

"God, not that," Joyce called down the table.

Hope winced in fear that someone would try to be witty.

"Look, I want to say . . . " Holly was on her feet, waving her glass. "In ad . . . mir . . . a . . . tion of Marge and Audrey . . . Congratulations, friends, you made it." Holly sat down. "That's all I had to say."

"Well said." Brenda applauded and they all laughed and touched glasses.

To everyone's surprise Marge stood up and began to talk. "I think I want to give a toast, if that is what one does with a toast."

"Besides eat it."

"Never mind—this group will accept willingly anything you're giving, beautiful."

"Who said that?" Claire asked Sue.

"That person," Sue said, emphasizing 'person' as if she had said vermin, looking over toward Hazel, whose hair was in her eyes as she stared into her wine glass.

"The younger ones don't have to worry that I'm going to talk about twenty years and how it's done. I don't know how. You may laugh, thinking I'm being arch, or concealing something. All I know is that it's precarious, risky—it's day-by-day pleasure and worry, and worth it beyond measure in its depth, but that's all I'm going to say about it. It's mysterious and surprising, like reading a fascinating book written by Iris Murdoch, John Fowles, Carl Sagan, and Emily Dickinson in committee." In the laughter Marge said, "I've already said more than I intended."

Anna was sitting back, not quite relaxed, but enjoying the afternoon immensely. As she listened to Marge and watched her graceful figure, witty and at ease, in a circumstance she herself would dread, she felt such admiration and pride that she had to whisper something to Audrey, who just smiled back her own pride. Audrey would never have tried to speak to any group extemporaneously, but Marge, laconic as she was in daily life, could chat easily with any group after dinner or before.

To Anna, Audrey did not look very well. She was pale, extremely so. Anna had to ascribe it to her nervousness for Marge and for herself later, but Hope had said something about Audrey's going to the doctor for tests for something. Gyn, Hope had said. Marge had spoken to Hope in anxiety, about the ovaries being like a time bomb in a woman's body. Sooner or later. Still, Audrey was singing with a music repertory group now, before the light opera company that she sang with last year opened again in a musical version of *She Stoops to Conquer*.

The children at the small table were so engrossed with their own affairs that they weren't noticing Marge smiling and resting her eyes upon each woman, turning from one to the other saying something personal and amusing about each. Anna meant to listen, but it was all so unbelievable that Carl was backing off, that she and Hope would have their time, that she could only withdraw for a bit, rest and watch this graceful, civilized group of humankind through a glass, and think how fortunate she was.

" . . . so that Audrey and I often notice there comes a time in most couples' lives when they decide to breakup, to start swinging as a couple, or . . . "

"What's left?" Opal chuckled.

"They build something. I mean it. They build swimming pools. . . . "

"Too much! How about a fireplace? More like it," Hazel said.

"A sleeping porch? That's what I'd like," Joyce said.

Marge had turned to speak directly to Anna, her eyes observant and mischievous. Anna distinctly heard Marge saying, "May Anna and Hope see fit to build an extension on Hope's house, very soon."

Anna was flushing with embarrassment anyway, but in the general murmurs of approval she wished heartily that Marge would stay out of it. Sometimes Marge was so heavy-handed. Was Marge getting nervous about their closeness as couples now, feeling what she and Hope had experienced earlier? Timing was always so crazy. "Me on the ground, you in midair." Marge had nothing to worry about. She and Hope knew what they wanted and were willing to wait to get it.

Hope looked delighted at Marge's comment. Of course. But didn't Audrey look a little troubled as she grinned at Anna? "I wish I had a nickel for all the advice people have given me," Audrey said in a low voice to Anna and shurgged. "Now, Anna, keep your fingers crossed for me."

As Audrey rose and walked toward the piano, the others pushed back from the table and moved toward the sofas and chairs.

"How did she ever get the glaze on that ham?"

"I'll never eat again."

"Did you ever go to that phenomenal restaurant in. . . . This was easily . . . "

Holly and Joyce helped Anna whisk things out into the kitchen.

"Where's Beth-Ellen? I didn't even see her when we went upstairs," Joyce called out, balancing dishes as she rounded a turn. "I'm practicing, Anna. Have I got the knack?" Meanwhile Hope poured coffee in the other room and called to Anna to take over as she went to the piano.

Anna filled the small cups as the women chatted and served one another sugar and cream, arranging themselves facing the piano. Audrey faced away from them out toward the darkening woods as she breathed deeply for a moment or two, while Hope set the piano stool's distance properly and clicked on the small light above her music. Lil peeked in and gestured to Jamie and the others to come into the living room to see something interesting.

"While the men enjoy their cigars in the library. . . . " The women laughed and fell silent as Audrey went on. "As you rest . . . as a post-prandial digestive . . . Marge, are you ready for this? I want to set by your plate, darling, a couple of songs—lighthearted and not so. Hope, dear gorgeous friend and closet musician, will accompany me."

A ripple of interested comments followed as the women resettled themselves to see Audrey better. She stood slightly back from her music stand, a diminutive, perfectly-groomed figure, in shades of soft peach, her gown falling into soft folds at the neck and waist, her feet set in what seemed to be a modified ballet Position Two, to permit perfect balance. Anna did not look at Opal and Hazel because she knew what they would be thinking. The older generation. Anna wouldn't have cared if Audrey sang with a guitar and a snapdragon between her toes; for her it would have been equally important as Audrey's work, but Opal and Hazel would see Audrey as super-square.

As Audrey sang her first selection Anna's mind remained divided. Richard Strauss's "Freundliche Vision," a classic model of love in the old style, was not Opal's dish, she knew. Walking with one's lover in a field of flowers toward the beloved house where coolness and beauty await would hardly send Hazel and Opal into spasms. Except of laughter. But the voice had a lovely timbre and gradually it wooed the listeners away from the other concerns that rattled in their minds like unwelcome castanets.

Claire's handsome head was tipped back, her eyelids slightly down as she listened. At the end of Audrey's final lingering phrase she sat still a moment letting the note dwell on before it died; her lids slowly closed before she nodded to Sue, eyebrows up, expressing highest commendation, silently.

The second piece of music trembled in Audrey's hand. She spoke rather stiffly, as if she had written the words out beforehand. "The last song is not, I hasten to say, very appropriate for this occasion, but it was so exciting that I begged Claire to let me try it—to borrow it for today.

It was written for Claire who sang it at her Carnegie recitial, one of a cycle of Edna St. Vincent Millay sonnets now being written by a man who loves women's voices. You'll see that he does, even you, Holly."

People were amused and murmured, shifting in their chairs. Holly blushed, thinking her mind had been read. Brute barked somewhere near the woods, probably pulling on his rope. Lil went to the windows to see if he was all right.

The voice rang out suddenly against strong chords:
> What lips my lips have kissed, and where, and why,
> I have forgotten, and what arms have lain
> Under my head till morning.

Indeed for an anniversary not very appropriate, though perhaps it was. The voice compelled Anna to understand as the piano's dissonance described the pain in loss.

> For unremembered lads that not again
> Will turn to me at midnight with a cry.

The power of the voice communicated more richly than the sonnet could alone, or than the woman could in her own words.

> I cannot say what loves have come and gone.

Only the glint of Audrey's deepset eyes warned them. The fluttering Audrey was gone as the rich voice of this powerful woman of experience brooded and rose to fiery power.

> I only know that summer sang in me
> A little while, that in me sings no more.

The strong music and boldness of her attack contradicted the pallid self-pitying words of renunciation.

As that brilliant force poured its richness into the room, Anna cherished what it must mean to be close to that passion. The warmth of the full tone promised vitality of loving. That autumnal power should be dressed in russet and gold, not soft peach; it would be worth many summers, had even been won by them. And so much for summer's songs anyway, Anna would say to Audrey later. "Make no apologies for your loss of summer's songs, dearie."

But that would be to conceal what she felt as she watched the vein in Audrey's forehead pulsing under the light. The force required for the song was formidable. Her pretty face contorted to shape its perfect notes as the strong voice reached the height of the final notes and the deep red blood coursed under the fair skin. Her icy resolve had strained against whatever strength the years had taken from her, and now, almost by will alone, she had pulled back vitality to sing again and more brilliantly than in her youth. Her fair, lacquered head was tipped back as the cords in her neck tightened, singing of loss, and Anna heard, in the splendid courage of that voice, how wrong she had been about their adversary. Carl, society, the judge in his black robes, her own doubts—they were threatening, yes, and ignorant, but not as malevolent finally as the ultimate adversary that laughed in the darkness just beyond the city walls.

Anna thought of the hours she had turned from Hope, supposing she had time to develop the strengths she would need to live with her. Time was not on their side and would never be. She would have to cope as they lived. She had watched time pour down that splendid cliff and had said how beautiful it was, had looked through the mighty sluice and had not understood what it meant, that each particle ran away from them, and all they could do was hold a pinch of water in the hand. Hope must start to build soon, but they would not wait for the extension to be built. They would not wait for anything.

Anna's Country was typeset on an IBM ESC,
an electronic selectric composer,
in Press Roman 10-point Medium type.

The chapter headings are set in
11-point Univers Light.

Publications of
THE NAIAD PRESS, INC.
P.O. Box 10543 • Tallahassee, Florida 32302
Mail orders welcome. Please include 15% postage.

Toothpick House by Lee Lynch. A novel. 264 pp.
ISBN 0-930044-45-2 $7.95

Madame Aurora by Sarah Aldridge. A novel. 256 pp.
ISBN 0-930044-44-4 $7.95

Curious Wine by Katherine V. Forrest. A novel. 176 pp.
ISBN 0-930044-43-6 $7.50

Black Lesbian in White America. Short stories, essays,
autobiography. 144 pp. ISBN 0-930044-41-X $7.50

Contract with the World by Jane Rule. A novel. 340 pp.
ISBN 0-930044-28-2 $7.95

Yantras of Womanlove by Tee A. Corinne. Photographs. 64 pp.
ISBN 0-930044-30-4 $6.95

Mrs. Porter's Letter by Vicki P. McConnell. A mystery novel.
224 pp. ISBN 0-930044-29-0 $6.95

To the Cleveland Station by Carol Anne Douglas. A novel.
192 pp. ISBN 0-930044-27-4 $6.95

The Nesting Place by Sarah Aldridge. A novel. 224 pp.
ISBN 0-930044-26-6 $6.95

This Is Not for You by Jane Rule. A novel. 284 pp.
ISBN 0-930044-25-8 $7.95

Faultline by Sheila Ortiz Taylor. A novel. 140 pp.
ISBN 0-930044-24-X $6.95

The Lesbian in Literature by Barbara Grier. 3d ed.
Foreword by Maida Tilchen. A comprehensive bibliography.
240 pp. ISBN 0-930044-23-1   ind. $7.95
                                                                              inst. $10.00

Anna's Country by Elizabeth Lang. A novel. 208 pp.
ISBN 0-930044-19-3 $6.95

Lesbian Writer: Collected Work of Claudia Scott
edited by Frances Hanckel and Susan Windle. Poetry. 128 pp.
ISBN 0-930044-22-3 $4.50

Prism by Valerie Taylor. A novel. 158 pp.
ISBN 0-930044-18-5 $6.95

Black Lesbians: An Annotated Bibliography compiled by
JR Roberts. Foreword by Barbara Smith. 112 pp.
ISBN 0-930044-21-5   ind. $5.95
                                                                              inst. $8.00

The Marquise and the Novice by Victoria Ramstetter.
A novel. 108 pp. ISBN 0-930044-16-9 $4.95

Labiaflowers by Tee A. Corinne. 40 pp.
ISBN 0-930044-20-7 $3.95

Outlander by Jane Rule. Short stories, essays. 207 pp.
ISBN 0-930044-17-7 $6.95

Sapphistry: The Book of Lesbian Sexuality by Pat Califia.
2nd edition, revised. 195 pp. ISBN 0-930044-47-9 $7.95

The Black and White of It by Ann Allen Shockley.
Short stories. 112 pp. ISBN 0-930044-15-0 $5.95

All True Lovers by Sarah Aldridge. A novel. 292 pp.
ISBN 0-930044-10-X $6.95

The Muse of the Violets by Renee Vivien. Poetry. 84 pp.
ISBN 0-930044-07-X $4.00

A Woman Appeared to Me by Renee Vivien. Translated by
Jeannette H. Foster. A novel. xxxi, 65 pp.
ISBN 0-930044-06-1 $5.00

Cytherea's Breath by Sarah Aldridge. A novel. 240 pp.
ISBN 0-930044-02-9 $6.95

Tottie by Sarah Aldridge. A novel. 181 pp.
ISBN 0-930044-01-0 $5.95

The Latecomer by Sarah Aldridge. A novel. 107 pp.
ISBN 0-930044-00-2 $5.00

VOLUTE BOOKS

Journey to Fulfillment	by Valerie Taylor	$3.95
A World without Men	by Valerie Taylor	$3.95
Return to Lesbos	by Valerie Taylor	$3.95
Desert of the Heart	by Jane Rule	$3.95
Odd Girl Out	by Ann Bannon	$3.95
I Am a Woman	by Ann Bannon	$3.95
Women in the Shadows	by Ann Bannon	$3.95
Journey to a Woman	by Ann Bannon	$3.95
Beebo Brinker	by Ann Bannon	$3.95

Naiad Press, Inc. and its imprint Volute Books (inexpensive mass market
paperbacks appear in Volute Books) may always be purchased by mail as
well as in your local bookstores.